THE RACE FOR FLUGAL FARM

By

Edward Johns

Please Note: As this publication is based on certain incidents in the
life of the Author, some of the names and situations have been
changed in order to protect the identity of the individuals.

ISBN 978-1-907407-80-2

THE BLACK LEAF PUBLISHING GROUP
Eaglesen House
22 Bracebridge Street,
Nuneaton, CV11 5PA
Warwickshire
England
www.blackleafpublishing.com

Dedication:

Dedicated to my wife June and daughters Rachelle and Charlette; I hope one day you enjoy reading this as much as I enjoyed writing it.

1

Flugal Farm sits peacefully and serenely, deep among the lush verdant, rolling hills and sprawling meadows in the county of Burberry, deep in the heart of the English Midlands, which for centuries have helped form the spine of a country and county proudly steeped in a rich, profound heritage and tradition; this land of unfathomable tranquility and beauty was the birth place of one William Flugal, George Flugal's ancient ancestor.

William Flugal had been a soldier, not of fortune, but one of honour, loyalty and above all chivalry; he had fought with great gallantry and bravery beside his King in the defence of his monarch and country in the fifteen century. His reward for his unbending allegiance was, by royal decree, the estate that now sits in the centre of Burberry County; albeit now much reduced in size, it still remains the envy of those around and is known simply to all those for hundreds of miles as Flugal Farm.

Flugal Farm, within the last century, had once been a thriving cattle business, exporting beef across the length and breadth of the country and eventually abroad, gaining a reputation for the finest quality of lean meat. Times then had been good for the Flugals, but with the advent of the Second World War his farm had been put over to raising mostly crops, and so the beef side of the business invariably suffered, and sadly for the Flugals, never truly recovered when the war finally came to an end.

The present Mr Flugal tried desperately with his father to re-build the cattle business, but to no avail; an outbreak of foot and mouth in the seventies finally put paid to any ambitions along that front. It cost them a small fortune in lost revenues.

It had been decided, when Flugal's father passed on, that the farm should go to his son George, and that he should make a go at whatever he saw fit; his special talent lay in teaching or to be more specific teaching people to ride horses, and so it was only inevitable that he should eventually go down that road and after many business adventures, some good and some not so good, Flugal finally settled on his Horse Riding School.

Over time Flugal built up a solid and reliable reputation as a good and patient teacher and the Riding School flourished; at its peak Flugal had over thirty horses, but in recent years financial pressures had once again reared their ugly heads and he was sadly forced to slowly contract the business resulting in him having to sell a vast number of his livestock until the number of horses he owned had reduced to the unenviable number of four. He supplemented what meagre income he had by renting out stables to local horse owners; this welcome addition to his funds from liveries allowed him extra valuable time to try and rectify the family's dire financial situation, as he was always on the lookout for horses with the right temperament to join the stables.

This day started just like any other day; Mr Flugal checked on his four equine friends in their stalls and fed them their breakfast, scattering it neatly in and around the floor directly under their respective water basins, which was also checked for purity lest it had been contaminated with feed.

He had long wished that one of his kids would take over the family business, but he was now resigned to the fact that their fortunes lay elsewhere; the family consisted of Flugal, his wife Mary, a son and a daughter. Flugals parents had passed away years earlier, and both their kids had flown the nest in pursuit of their dreams; Tom was in the army and had attained to the rank of Major and June was still at medical school. This just left Flugal and his wife now to survive on what savings they had tucked away for a rainy day, and any monies that they could make from the school. That rainy day, tragically for them, had appeared on the horizon far earlier than anybody gave credit for.

Flugal, some years earlier, had needed an urgent injection of funds to see himself through the hard winters, and that outbreak of foot and mouth in the area, when the stables housed an abundance of horses. He borrowed further to help finance the children's further education; he was always keen to inform anybody who cared to listen that "Family comes first, and sacrifices needed to be made!"

He worked hard to repay the loan, working all the hours God gave, but he ended up on occasions being backed up into a corner which necessitated the selling of most of his horses; it was a necessary evil, the farm belonged to the Flugal family, and he was determined not to lose it while it was under his care and protection. The bank on the other hand was eager to have any monies owed to them repaid regardless.

Chance looked on; he was the oldest of the remaining four horses and had been a champion race horse in his day; a runner up in the Derby one year, but his career had been cut short by a serious injury to a tendon on his left foreleg.

On a wall in Flugal's office, hung proudly over his desk, was Chance surrounded by admirers and his previous owners being escorted to the winning enclosure after one of his many victories. Everybody reckoned he was twenty going on thirty, no one really knew and nobody really cared. Chance loved people, he loved riding and giving pleasure to all those kids and adults who climbed aboard his mighty back, for he was over seventeen hands, to learn to ride, and people loved Chance; for a mature horse his chestnut coat shone like a silk overcoat especially when the sun was out and beat down upon the horses and riders while out on a hack or in the yard. He was gentle, forgiving and rode with the patience of a saint, and Flugal loved him.

It was a routine he had seen many times before with previous owners, but this time it was different. Mr Flugal normally an affable, friendly man, always with a kind word or a funny story, was poker-faced as he carried out his morning chores. The clouds overhead were dark and foreboding, the forecast was not good and it matched his owner's mood perfectly.

Chance scanned the stable block for his companions, he knew it wouldn't be long before they showed themselves once they smelt the fresh feed, and sure enough he heard their eager hooves as they clamoured to their feet.

First to show was Pogo, a sturdy grey horse of over sixteen hands, who invariably skidded to a halt whenever he ran anywhere in the back field, which nearly always resulted in him taking out the trough and all its contents through the fence and down the path leading to the main stables; food was Pogo's first love, there wasn't much he wouldn't do for a tasty morsel, and quite frankly not much he did anyway.

A close second came the bay coloured Troy; although similar in stature to Pogo, he was just under a hand smaller, but he more than made up for it with his broad shoulders. It was Troy who always had the responsibility to cater for the heavier patrons to Flugal Riding Stables, and from this he derived his name, often reminding everybody of the wooden horse in Helen of Troy. For someone who ate like it was an Olympic sport it always surprised Chance why he was never first to appear, although he had long ago figured that Troy liked to give his comrades a healthy head start; he always caught up Pogo, thus making it more fun. Confrontation was definitely in Troy's make up.

And finally there was the black haired Biff; slightly smaller than his two friends, but what Biff lacked in size he more than made up for in brains; the one thing predictable about Biff was his unpredictability. He had to have a challenge, life was to boring without one, a horse of his IQ was wasted in Biff's opinion giving riding lesson, there must be other things far more important and interesting, he thought, and he spent endless days in pursuit of these goals.

Chance rested his head on the stable door listening to his comrades devour breakfast; he knew no matter how much they ate they would always be hungry for more. He was also the unofficial peacemaker; any arguments or disagreements were rare, but if in the off chance one should arise, old Chance would step in and calm the situation and rising tension down with a few well chosen words. Now fully awake himself he satisfied his hunger. Biff, Pogo and Troy never gave Chance a seconds thought.

'Morning gentlemen.' said Chance after a few mouthfuls

'What's eating him?' said Pogo.

'I dunno!' replied Troy taking time out between munching.

'Been like it for days!' continued Pogo.

'Money I reckon!' said Biff.

'Why do you say that? interjected Chance.

'Heard him talking with Mr Mullen, the greengrocer, he was trying to delay paying some bill or other. It's alright though, apparently he's coming into some money soon which will pay for everything.'

Chance followed Flugal across the yard with his eyes; his countenance betrayed him, he bore his burden like a man weighed down with the worries of the world on his shoulders. Chance suddenly lost his appetite.

'You not eating?' inquired Pogo. Chance offered no reply.

'Seen this all before!' Chance said to himself. 'It's not good!'

'It's fantastic!' chomped Pogo. 'Best scram we've had in a long time.' The other two grunted their approval.

'When times are hard, those closest and dearest are always the last to discover the truth.' Chance said philosophically.

The other three were not listening anymore or just simply ignoring him, he could not tell, feeding time had taken on far more importance, they didn't care much as long as their bellies were full, lessons were short and the lounging lazy days continued.

The clocked struck two o'clock; with the exception of Mondays and Fridays, these days being given to the general repairs, cleaning and stocking of provisions for the running of Flugal Farm, otherwise riding lessons were offered from three o'clock onwards, and all day Saturday. Today was a Sunday.

Biff opened one bleary eye then went back to sleep; he was in his usual somnolent state dreaming of exciting adventures far away from the dreary, drab backwater of Flugal Farm, as the first of the childrenstudents started to arrive for their afternoon lesson.

'I don't know why he sets that clock early. We never get there on time!' stated Pogo.

'Well I'm not moving. I hate giving riding lessons. And on a Sunday!' replied Troy. 'What about you Biff?' Biff let out an enormous snore.

'That's it settled then, no riding lessons today'.
Chance gently rounded on the three mutineers. 'Come along gentlemen, we've got work to do.' Biff snorted his disapproval.

'Now's not the time. We've got our keep to earn!'

'I'm lame.' shouted Troy. 'Look!' And he held up his left front hoof for inspection; this was now possible as the stable doors were fully open and any evacuation was prevented by a chain draped across the doors opening. 'It's serious!'

'I'm hungry!' Pogo started most conversations with this statement. 'Let's at least have lunch first.' Biff snorted again.

'Your three o'clock is here Troy.' Chance said desperately trying to inject some verve into his comrades, but in his eagerness to summon up that enthusiasm which he himself felt in abundance, and could not understand why these three loafers sadly lacked such an essential ingredient, he badly miscalculated. Troy's three o'clock was none other than a young lad named Picklelard, who it was whispered went nigh on twenty stone!

In the old farmhouse Mrs Flugal baked a cake while her husband watched nervously as the riders arrived.

'Don't worry my dear. Everything will be alright. You'll see.' said Mrs Flugal halting proceedings long enough to guarantee her words hit home. 'Those are good horses, temperamental at times I agree, but who isn't on any given day.'

'I know, I know. Old Chance will see them right, he's a good 'en!' replied old Man Flugal. 'Its just……' Mr Flugal paused. '……..the bank called me again this morning. Bennett wants me to go in and see him. He wouldn't discuss it over the phone. These banks are a changing my dear; call centres in another country, all correspondence by e-mail, banking over the Internet. I've never owned a computer in my life, nor ever will!' Flugal had taken the decision to keep previous letters from the bank quiet from his wife. He was starting to question his own sagacity on the matter.

'I don't like it when you worry. It frightens me!'

'Don't get me wrong, I'm all for modernisation and if that involves computers and all that they bring to the table then so be it, its just that it seems to me that the personal touch has some how evaporated along the way, and you now have to tow their line and play by their rules no matter what!'

Mrs Flugal walked around the table and put a protective arm around her husband. 'I've always paid back any money I've borrowed. I can't see what they should want to discuss.' It was a little white lie and he hated himself for it.

'Don't worry yourself. It's probably just a courtesy chat so he can introduce himself and he can put your face to the name.' soothed Mrs Flugal. 'You're placing far too much emphasis on this meeting with Mr Bennett. He's taken over a new branch and wants to make a fine impression on all the existing customers.' Neither moved for a few minutes; she always knew how to quieten her husband's distemper when it flared, which rare as it was caused her much chagrin; they had been married for nigh on thirty years, childhood sweat hearts, engaged straight of school and married a year later. Of their two children, the eldest son Tom had joined the army from school and through hard work and dedication had risen to that rank of Major, their youngest June had settled on a career in medicine and was in her final year; they had subsidised her years of study, unable to receive any grant due to their owning a farm, and it had bitten into them hard at various times, but like all loving parents they had promised themselves and their progeny every available opportunity to better themselves.

His pupils were now waiting expectantly beside their parents, their eager faces pointing out which horse they expected to be riding that day.

Like all stables, Flugal allowed a few of the older girls, normally those who rode at the school and sometimes owned a horse of their own, to help out and these willing workers now scurried across the yard, bridles in hand, prepping the four horses for their afternoon's exercise. The eldest of these was a local girl named Rachelle Perkins, the Flugals had known her family for years and knew she lived alone, a couple of miles down the road, with her grandmother.

Flugal witnessed the scene unfold 'So why can't I get those three horses to behave, to ride like I know they can! Is it me? They're so unruly, there was a time when they were the best training horses around, no one could hold a candle to them! They're all fit, of good stock and smart animals. So why can't I teach on them now?'

'Now don't start doubting yourself as a teacher. You're an excellent horseman.'

'Williams is now boasting his horses are superior!' Mr Flugal added.

'You don't believe that do you!'

Mr Flugal shook his head. 'I'll get Jenkins the vet to check them all over again. I didn't want to resort to this, it always looks so bad when the vet has to be called, and for all of them!' With that Mr Flugal kissed his wife on the cheek and went out to work.

Chance shook his head at his three companions attitude to work.

'Never in my day!' he muttered to himself.

Mr Flugal appeared at the entrance to the stable bock. Chance nodded his head to him, he was the only one left to be tacked up. Flugal walked up to his trusted companion.

'Chance my old friend. I can always count on you!' he said.

'What am I going to do with those three? They're costing me a fortune! I was promised they were good, hard working horses when I bought them all those years ago and now look at them! They lie around all day and do nothing but eat!'

Chance had to agree, but there was nothing he could do.

'Have I been too easy on them, old friend?' added Flugal, affectionately stroking Chance on the side of his neck.

The girls, after much cajoling, eventually managed to get the three layabouts tacked up. Chance, as always, when it came to his turn was the model professional,

All the riders were ready, helmets on, boots polished, jackets and back supports correctly fastened eagerly awaiting for their rides to arrive.

Chance was the first to leave the block, he took it upon himself to set an example, heading the mini procession as befitting his rank and seniority, but he could sense all was not well behind him and a cursory glance over his right shoulder reinforced his inner fears; his colleagues had ceased to advance one step, even with the help of the girls. He exhaled a loud neigh. The students all laughed; this light relief amused the parents initially, but Chance knew their humour was only a temporary rest bite, a substitute for any anger that had planted a seed to sprout at the least provocation.

Biff was the first to move, dragging his feet looking totally disinterested in the whole affair, Troy followed, gnawing incessantly at his bridle in a vain attempt to get free. Pogo was now nowhere to be seen.

'Can't get this thing off!' grunted Troy.

'Behave!' demanded Chance.

'You behave, you're not the one with one of these bridle things stuck in your mouth!'

'Oh really!'

'Anyway you're old and decrepit. The bridle suits you!' Troy was trying hard to gain the upper hand, but failing at every turn. 'And anyhow you haven't got Captain Doughnut to carry!' This was Troy's derisive, derogatory nickname he gave to any of the larger students he was forced to carry.

Their every step across the yard was interspersed with riotous laughter, and the occasional derogatory remark from all the livery horses witnessing the afternoon's spectacle.

Troy and Biff kept nothing back when retaliating to the "Toffs", as they called them.

'I'm bored!' claimed Biff.

'You're always bored!' answered Chance.

'Yeah, but this is extra specially boring!'

The three of them eventually made it over to the corner of the yard where the eagerly awaiting youngsters fidgeted with anticipation.

Mr Flugal appeared from within the stables pulling a wooden block which he used to enable them to mount their rides. All the smaller ponies and cobs had been the first to go. Bored stiff Biff shrugged his shoulders, stood motionless until Chance gave him as reminder from up the rear to keep moving.

'This is probably the most mind numbingly boring job I've ever had the misfortune to undertake!'

'It's the only job you've ever had undertake stupid!' said Troy in between chews on his bridle.

'Enjoy your leather lunch!'

'Will you two get with the program!' Chance's patience was wearing thin.

Biff did as he was told and sauntered over to the wooden block; a young lass of about twelve mounted. Biff let out a grimace; he wasn't hurting at all, he just did it to get sympathy. He looked over at Chance then Flugal. All ignored him. 'Typical!'

Next up was Troy, still chewing. 'Hmmmff, uurrgghhh, ooooommfff.'

'What is wrong now? You've already spent the last ten minutes getting nowhere with that bridle!' said Biff.

'I got gas!' And he let out the most enormous fart. It was a stinker! 'That's leather right there that is!'

Biff then got a lungful of Troy's produce. 'Did I eat what you ate?'

It was so bad even the livery horses shut up.

'Thanks for the sympathy. Anytime I can be of service..... I'm not available!....Oh, by the way I apologise for any future woofers in advance!' He then followed this up with a second stupendous woofer.

'Man you're one sick dude!' exclaimed Biff.

'Enough!' Chance was starting to lose it big time. 'Where's Pogo?'

Troy and Biff gave each other with that typical 'I don't know' blank look.

'Wonderful!'

For a while Pogo could not be found, and Flugal began to panic that one of his charges had abandoned ship and hightailed it out of his yard, but Pogo eventually appeared now rather the worst for wear; his legs could carry him no further than the end of a low wall that marked the beginning of the neighbouring block. He leant his weight against the stone structure and folded his front legs. The poor stable girl responsible for him could do nothing but shrug her shoulders when Flugal enquired, as to why one of his horses should disappear and now decide to prop up a wall.

Chance trotted over to confront him as to his less than perfect physical condition. 'An explanation please?'

'It was mighty sweet man!'

Chance took a whiff of Pogo's breath. 'Barley wine!' he exclaimed.

'Barley wine!' the other two said quite indignantly. 'The lucky.....' They were both cut short by Mr Flugal marching straight past them over to the inebriated Pogo.

'What's wrong with you my old friend?' he enquired of Pogo.

'How the hell did he get hold of Barley wine?' his two compatriots debated.

Pogo burped.

'You don't look too hot!' Pogo burped again.

'Hey Channshh you got a twin.' said Pogo.

'Poor Pogo must be a bout of flu.' Mr Flugal said sympathetically.

'You're drunk!' grunted an indignant Chance.

'Thank God for that! I thought your relatives had come to stay for the summer.' The barley wine had not wasted any time taking its effect on Pogo, whose valiant attempt to walk over to the kids was doomed to failure.

'Steady there big fella! It took all of Flugal's might to maintain Pogo upright. 'Back to the stables for you and rest.'

'The lucky.....'

'That's enough from you two!' exclaimed Chance.

'What....'

'We three have got work to do!'

'I got gas!' Troy reminded them.

The young lad fidgeted constantly; he studied the two remaining horses closely, and the third one, Pogo, now being led away by one of the stable hands. 'That one's got the hiccups mummy!'

After about ten minute delay, Mr Flugal appeared and approached the boy's mother. 'I'm dreadfully sorry Mrs Wilson, but Pogo, Jamie's horse has come down with something. He's unfit to be ridden today.'

'This is the third time this month Mr Flugal that my boy has been unable to ride.'

'Pogo's gone lame more than most I agree, and that has not helped!'

'Mr Bennett's horses ride all year round. My neighbour Mrs Clavell has never had a lesson cancelled on her. I'm afraid Mr Flugal that, although you are without doubt a wonderful teacher, and Jamie thinks very highly of you, I have my son's progression to think about. If you are incapable of teaching without the use of your horses, who seem to drop like flies at the most inopportune times, then I'm awfully sorry, but as Jamie needs to ride regularly, you force me to go to Mr Williams.' Mrs Wilson had no sooner finished that she collected her boy's hand, and without a further word turned and walked out of the yard.

Chance could feel the sense of doom slowly descend over Mr Flugal, especially as he knew the true state of Pogo's health and the attitude of the other two.

Mr Flugal, as if he sensing Chance's true feelings, patted him on the shoulder. 'Never mind old friend.'

'Mr Flugal?'

'Yes Mr Picklelard?'

'My son's horse there.' He pointed at Troy.

'What about him Mr Picklelard?'

'I don't think he's at all well!'

'No'

'No.' Then whispered so not to cause an offence. 'He's letting off the most awful smells.'

Troy hearing this winked at Biff. Biff chuckled to himself and Chance gave off a grunt of disapproval.

'They're real bad Mr Flugal!'

'I'll check him out.'

'Behave.' Chance whispered in Troy's ear.

'I got one coming. I can't control it it's coming out, it's coming out.'

Mr Flugal started to give Troy a check over; his forelegs were fine, his coat had a good shine, his nose was okay, a good sign, checked his gums for dehydration, he didn't act lethargic, his rear quarters looked good, then….Troy couldn't hold it any longer; the smelliest, nastiest, most odious, noxious vapour bellowed from Troy's rear end.

Mr Flugal froze to the spot; a no more foul aroma he had never smelt. The thought now occurred to him as to how he could maintain his composure in the face of such adversity. Unable to take a deep breath at this time he faked a cough, withdrew his handkerchief and breathed through the cloth.

'Are you okay Mr Flugal?' enquired Mr Roberts, whose son Jasper was due to ride Chance that afternoon, and after witnessing the earlier scene with Jamie's mother, was beginning to have grave doubts to the success of his own son's lesson.

'Just fine thank you…just fine.' Troy stood motionless.

'I'm changing your feed!' Flugal whispered to his charge.

'Hey Troy!' said Biff.

'Yeah Man.'

'It's a good job you don't smoke like 'Old Blue' used to.'

'I'm getting there.'

'You need a government health warning! And you with young Picklelard on your back today!'

'Enough!' said an angry Chance. 'Can you ride today?'

'Relax Man. Everything's cool.'

'Everything's cool eh! You smell like an out house.' continued Biff. 'Careful man you'll get Nigel excited!'

Nigel was the friendly neighbourhood pig, who while this scene was being played out wallowed contentedly in his mud bath.

'You and Nigel deserve each other.'

Mr Flugal led Troy over to where Picklelard was standing. 'He seems in fine fettle Mr Picklelard!'

Mr Picklelard looked on quizzically; he was not entirely convinced, but like all keen horsemen his main concern was for the well being and happiness of the horse.

'If you say so Mr Flugal, you're the expert.'

Her son was then helped aboard Troy by Mr Flugal, but the effect of the lad's prodigious weight on the horse's back only exasperated the problem in the trot over to the outdoor arena, where today's lesson was to be given. Troy's rhythmic flatulence was only matched by Chance's grinding teeth.

Biff while all this had taken place moaned, and groaned about the impending boredom that was about envelope his life. 'I'm bored!'

Mr Flugal had to physically drag poor old Biff over to the arena, once the young girl called Claire Wales was aboard. Chance was by the block by the time Mr Flugal had finished with Biff; he stood steady as a rock, never complained, did exactly as his owner ask and behaved in the most impeccable manner at all times; Mr Flugal could not have asked for a more obedient and trustworthy steed and before the lesson was out wished that all his horses could handle themselves with such distinction, as he had believed they would when he first purchased them.

Needless to say Troy farted his way throughout the whole unfortunate lesson; every step, trot and canter only added to the air his most miserable flatulence. Biff, bored stupid, behaved in exactly that manner, in some cases going out of his way to perform that exact opposite to whatever Mr Flugal or his rider requested, Chance on the other hand conducted himself perfectly; his breeding was for all to see and marvel and

Mr Flugal eventually lost count as to how many times he thanked himself for such a charge.

With each passing lesson that day the situation failed to improve, until every single student's parent had either threatened to cancel further tuition or resolved to move their children to another stables.

All that is except little Rachelle Perkins; she was the head girl among the volunteers. Quiet and unassuming, she went about her chores around the stables, mucking out, feeding the animals, including Nigel, and she loved Chance very much. The idea of leaving him and Mr and Mrs Flugal, who were like parents to her, was a thought to horrid to contemplate. Chance was the only horse she rode; he was fun, considerate and obeyed her every command without hesitation; it was the highlight of her week, her hourly Saturday afternoon ride where she could escape to the land of her dreams, riding her bold faithful stallion to glory in the Grand National or leading the Olympic Equestrian Team home to gold or what ever other equestrian dream she had that day, either way they all included her beautiful Chance.

Mr Flugal closed up the stables at the end of the day; Rachelle and the other girls had been away home, the horses had been fed and watered and settled down for the night, and with a heavy heart he retired back to the house for his tea. Mrs Flugal as always presented her husband with a perfectly displayed table, lacking nothing. Mr Flugal slumped into his chair.

'We'll be okay!' she asserted pouring him a cup of tea.

'I don't know my love, I was banking on today! We needed today!' He sipped his tea pensively. She knew not to disturb his thoughts. They'll be plenty of time to revive his spirits later.

Chance could no longer contain his anger and indignation towards his neighbours in the stable block. 'Have you three got anything to say for yourselves?'

'Give it a rest old man!' Pogo was the first to answer.

'Yeah, man I got gas. You it ain't easy riding with someone on your back with gas you know!'

'Troy.' started Chance. 'You internal machinations would work just dandy if you didn't make eating an Olympic sport; not every scrap of food belongs to you, you know! If you want to spend more time with Nigel I can arrange it!'.'

'Maybe we don't want to end up like you!' Biff retorted. Chance glared at him from over his stable door. 'What Biff you not bored! Not yet anyhow!'

'Give it a rest. I got a headache.' said Pogo

He now became the source for Chance to vent more anger. 'Where the hell did you get Barley wine?'

Pogo smiled.

'Yeah, we've been trying to figure that one out?' The impressiveness was clearly evident in Troy's voice.

'You do that again...'

'And you'll do what! Go on strike! I'm not going to end up like you; an old man with nothing left in his life other than to teach little kids how to ride so they can abuse us and take us for granted.' Pogo retaliated.

Chance remained silent; to carry on the conversation at this juncture was futile.

Mr Flugal sat playing with his food; a bad habit guaranteed to annoy his wife, but tonight she let it go. He had a lot on his mind.

Nugget was a sheepdog of Welsh descent, he was most particular about that fact, being a citizen, as he put it, of the greatest rugby playing nation on earth and was always at loggerheads with Nigel, being of Scottish ancestry, and the only resident of Flugal Farm who took issue with Nugget on such a point. The horses were all football fans and regarded "the egg throwers" with utter disdain whenever the subject of football entered the conversation, as they all supported a variety of teams from various leagues, and it always led to a heated debate during the regular season.

Nugget sat at his master's feet; he had been listening intently to the evenings proceedings, worrying for him was the tone, which using his canine sixth sense had alerted him to the gravity of the situation. He always provided comfort to them both through vexing times and today was no different. A dark, ominous storm cloud descended over his owners. Domesticated man, in his opinion, had long since lost the will or even inclination to sense when danger approached, not so the animal kingdom. Nugget shivered at the very thought of what all this could mean. There was only one person to talk to about this: Chance.

Nugget found the horses as we'd left them earlier on when they were being tended by Flugal: Mute. He ran over to Chance's stable. 'I think something's up!'

'I can guess.' he said eyeing the three offenders.

'You know?' The surprise in Nugget's voice was there for all to hear.

'He's been down for weeks. And these three have been as useful as a chocolate teapot!' Chance glared across the stables, but nobody dared challenge his stare.

'He's off to see the bank manager again tomorrow to extend a loan I think!'

'Today was the straw that broke the camel's back.' Chance replied. Nugget lost where Chance was going with this.

'We don't have any camels!'

'Never mind.' said Chance.

'What's a loan? continued Nugget in vain.

The remainder of the stables were cloaked in silence, whatever thoughts, guilty or not, our three mutineers held among the dark recesses, it was a secret they best kept to themselves.

2

The sun streamed through the patterned window of the former bank manager, Mr Miller's, office causing Mr Bennett, its new and recently appointed resident, to squint as he admired his predecessor's taste in paintings. Bennett was a tall man at nearly six foot four inches who didn't suffer fools gladly, and wasn't averse to using his prodigious size to that effect, as the few people in the surrounding area who had had dealings with him already could testify. Miller entered the room, braking off Bennett's study of a Picasso print.

'Sorry to disturb you Mr Bennett.'

'That's quite alright Mr Miller.'

'Now what was it again that I could do for you?' continued Miller, who was working his last few days before retirement in order to get Bennett up to speed on all the accounts.

'Flugal Farm.'

'What about it?'

'I'd like to see the all the accounts before old man Flugal gets here.'

'Certainly.' said Miller with an air of contempt; such a familiarity with an old client's name, with whom he had had no contact, rankled him. He was trying hard to hide his dislike for Bennett, but there were times when only a mute approach to the daily transactions was all he could manage. Now was such an occasion and Miller spun on his heels and vacated the office before the buffoon could request anything further. Miller had no sooner entered the main lobby of the bank than he ran smack bang into Mr Flugal.

'Hello Bob.' opened Flugal holding out his hand, offering a warm, sincere and affectionate hand shake.

'Morning George.' Miller replied accepting Flugal's hand gratefully.

'Not many days left then eh?'

'No, not many, just seeing out my time.'

'Going to buy that boat you've been threatening to acquire for the last twenty years?'

'No not yet, but the wife and I definitely want to see the world first while we're still able.'

'Excellent.'

'We're going to do the next best thing though,' Miller smiled, the very thought enrapturing him. 'and take a cruise, can't be done with airports anymore, to damn busy.'

'Wish I could get time!' Flugal replied.

Miller face took on a more serious aspect. 'Listen George-' at that precise moment Bennett appeared filling the doorway to Miller's old office.

'Good Morning Mr Flugal. Please come in.' Flugal smiled at Bennett's request.

'I'll come over later.' said Miller

'Do you have that account Mr Miller?'

'Just coming.' And with that he left. Flugal felt immediately ill at ease.

He entered the bright, airy room lit by the effulgent rays of the morning sun. Flugal was a man like any other from his generation; standards had to be maintained whatever the cost. His father often told him when they were young how the city kids from London came and stayed on the farm during the Second World War because of the blitz, the very farm he now came to inherit, and even though times were hard, and food was scarce, the family and all their guests maintained their dignity and self respect in the face of such dire circumstances. Flugal maintained his composure, though deep inside his stomach churned violently at the prospect of the next twenty minutes; he had been forced to take out the latest loan to cover the period immediately succeeding the latest foot and mouth outbreak some years previous; the farm had been part dairy then for a while, but it had still been badly hit by the mini epidemic. For some time before the outbreak Flugal had commenced transforming the majority of the farm into the riding stables, but the horses still needed to be quarantined and these quiet, non-productive months had necessitated a bridging loan. It was this loan that now bore Flugal his greatest discomfort, his 'Sword of Damocles', and he knew Bennett sensed this and had the advantage over him. Miller, whom Flugal regarded as a close and valued friend due to their close co-operation during this difficult time, had agreed the loan, knowing it would be repaid eventually, and protected Flugal when the bank queried the sagaciousness of lending him such a sum of money. Bennett sat behind his desk without giving Flugal any form of acknowledgment. 'Take a seat please Mr Flugal.' ordered Bennett in a military tone.

Flugal could feel the hairs on the back of his neck begin to rise; pre-empting the onset of his rarely seen but infamous temper. He began to think if all modern bank managers were sent to a training school to be instructed in dull, monotonous discourse and the swiftest way to get a rise out of their clients.

'Thank you.' he replied belying the tempest ascending within. Standards remained so far intact.

He no sooner had himself comfortable than Mr Miller knocked on the door, and entered on Bennett's command carrying the all important documents.

Bennett held out an all too eager hand, accepted the package without offering any of them eye contact and excused Miller. The whole scene was enacted in a cold, dispassionate, sang-froid kind of way that invoked nausea in Flugal.

Miller stood for a moment as if expecting an invitation to observe the proceedings; he still regarded this as his office, his space invaded by this alien of a man, but in truth he held no more sway over the business transacted here now than the window cleaner working furiously over the road at the hairdressers.

Bennett finally made eye contact with Miller. 'That'll be all thank you.' he said superciliously. Miller made no attempt at a reply, spun once again on his heels, his passionate, sorrowful gaze flashing for a second at Flugal and left.

Bennett browsed the documents like a detective searching for a missing clue in order to solve that career making case. Finally he raised his head.

'Mr Flugal.' The formal opening aroused doom in him. 'The bank has looked closely into your case. It is not the bank's policy to continue to increase its level of debt, especially in today's business world and when that debt has been poorly handled.' Here Bennett paused 'But that is a case for Mr Miller to answer and not you!'

'I see.' was all Flugal could muster.

'I am sure you are well aware of your financial position?'

'I am.'

'Good then you will fully understand the ramifications of not being able to meet your payments.'

'My credit has always been good at this bank, and those were exceptional circumstances.'

'That I don't doubt Mr Flugal, but these are exceptional times. The world's financial markets are in turmoil with the ripples of discontent spreading among the leading lenders, and it is felt no harder than at the very shores on which you now find yourself stranded!'

Flugal soaked up every word Bennett spewed forward. His wife would want a blow by blow account. 'I have tried to honour every loan, every penny of credit you have granted me, and will pay back any monies that I owe. What's the difference now?'

Bennett stared blankly back at Flugal, not wanting to give anything away; 'This gentleman is going to put up a fight', he thought, 'of which the outcome he surmised could only be his financial ruin.'

'The difference how I see it Mr Bennett is, where in the past you were more understanding of the needs of the small businesses, now it's just simply a case of "Where's my money"!'

Bennett's understanding of Flugal was accurate: The fight had began. 'Not so!'

'How?'

'This bank has a good record with small business-'

'-It did under Miller!' Ouch! That was sure to hurt Bennett, who was cut short. He didn't like it.

'Mr Miller has proved himself a poor judge of business!' he said finally.

'The bank has pressurised more small business's in the short time you have been here than Miller did in twenty years!'

It was time for Bennett to feel uncomfortable. 'Bad debt!' was all he said after what seemed an age.

'Bad debt!' replied Flugal, as if he hadn't quite heard Bennett the first time.

Bennett nodded.

'You are telling me I am bad debt!' he re-iterated.

Bennett stared imperturbably back at Flugal, then slowly and surely nodded. 'Mr Flugal you have fallen behind in your payments to the bank, as we spelled out in our correspondence to you. It has now reached that point where the bank has to act and try and redeem the monies owed!'

'I have paid all my debt to this bank in the past. It has made a small fortune out of me over the years, and I resent having to have this conversation, and being referred to as "bad debt!"'

'The bank,' Bennett drawled, 'must redeem all outstanding debts regardless of your length of service.'

'If you care to check your records Mr Bennett you will see that I have made all recent payments, and I rather hoped this meeting would be constructive enough to allow me to repay what is outstanding, but apparently not. I am "bad debt" as you put it!'

This last word sounded the death knell to the meeting, and Flugal knew it. He rose without breaking eye contact.

'You will have until the end of the month to make good all payments or to have guarantees to pay any outstanding monies to date on your loan.'

Flugal remained mute; the infamous temper was imminent and he thought it judicious to keep his own counsel.

* * * * *

Flugal slowly navigated his way through the large wooden gate that marked the entrance to the farm. Nugget ran over to him tail wagging, expressing his unbounded joy at the return of his master. Flugal parked up and met him half way across the yard and rubbed him behind his ears. Nugget loved that. The two companions strode up to the house, both rubbing their feet on the welcome mat as they entered.

'I'm home!' he called.

'Be right down.' Mrs Flugal answered.

Mr Flugal smelt the soup simmering on the stove. Nugget took to his basket by the back door so he could listen and covertly make notes on their conversation at the request of Chance.

'Well?' said Mrs Flugal as she appeared.

'Not good!'

'No!' Her face dropped, all signs of hope evaporating on hearing those two little words.

'No! We need to find money by the end of the month and clear all our outstanding debts!'

'Oh dear!'

'Mr Miller will try and delay the paperwork as much as possible.' continued Flugal.

'Surely he can do more!' said Mrs Flugal more in hope than expectation.

'He has no authority anymore. It's this man Bennett now.'

'Is he how you expected him?' she inquired.

'Worse!'

Mrs Flugal had started to stir the soup, but now paused for a second. 'How do you hope to get it?'

'We still have some farm stock to sell.'

'I can't believe that bank, a bank we've been with for over thirty years, and they treat us this way all for a few measly thousand when they can waste millions. They know surely the value of the farm and the collateral that provides?'

'Maybe that's the problem.'

'How long can we last?' Mr Flugal could see the panic rising in his wife.

'Long enough for us to find a solution. Look don't worry about it now, let's eat.'

The couple failed to notice Nugget slip out the back door; he had figured out how to open and close the door years ago, and so far neither his master or mistress had given it any thought.

Nugget scampered across the yard. The sun had begun to set, which reflected in Nugget's mind how long the discourse had carried on between Mr and Mrs Flugal, but like all long time inhabitants of Flugal Farm he knew the many pitfalls that catch the unwary stranger to the yard, as they wind their way through the many ruts and undulations leading inextricable towards the stables.

Chance had kept a vigil, waiting for the trustworthy Nugget to bring what he suspected, nay dreaded.

Nugget appeared panting and immediately started gibbering away whilst desperately sucking air into his lungs.

'Nugget!' Chance said finally after yet another failed attempt to understand what the hell he was saying. 'How bad is it?'

Nugget took a deep breath, composed himself then delivered the blow. 'Terrible!'

A solemn, sullen expression descended over Chance, intermingle with the faint hint of anger and contempt for his stable mates.

Biff on hearing the conversation appeared over his stable door to investigate. 'Evening Nugget!' he said joyously. Nugget offered no reply.

'What's up?' he continued.

Again Nugget remained mute; he was toying with the idea of breaking into discourse with Biff, who it has to be said he liked very much, but at the same time he didn't want to invoke the wrath of Chance, so he remained silent. Chance for his part gave no verbal or visual acknowledgement to his canine friend, not that he had any inkling that Nugget wanted any.

Biff now feeling decidedly ill at ease, as any right minded person would when you stumble on a conversation only to be met with a wall of silence, muttered something to himself and sauntered back to a corner of his stable.

'Why didn't you talk to him? enquired Nugget.

'Why should I?' replied Chance. 'They should understand what they are doing is wrong, they're not stupid, God gave them sense, so let them use it!' When he said this he tapped the side of his head with his hoof. 'It doesn't need me or you to tell them. I want them to have the opportunity to come to that conclusion without being led, wet-nosed all the way.'

'That's a bit harsh Chance!'

'Maybe, but that's how I feel.'

'I thought they were your friends.'

'They are! I don't wish them any hardship, although that seems the only outcome after today.'

Give them another chance, Chance.'

But Chance stood resolute; his mind was made up this time, these scoundrels had the same objective; "Of looking after number one", and "I'm alright jack!" Two philosophies Chance despised, almost as much as frequenting a muddy field during a downpour in the middle of winter, forcing him to endure that wet, sticky sensation despised by the very young when they're old enough to discern feelings and emotions, and borne begrudgingly by the elderly, and infirm when their complaints fall silently like the leaves of autumn.

'They don't see things as you do.' continued Nugget

It is worth noting at this juncture that Nugget was held in high regard by Chance; he had been born on the farm, so his tenure was longer than his. Nugget never knew his father. His mother, to the great surprise of the Flugals as no other dogs were ever seen frequenting the farm, gave birth to a litter of six, of which Nugget was the eldest. As a single parent she raised her brood as best she could, for after all she was still a working dog, but it naturally fell to Nugget to look after his five brothers and sisters; he often wondered what happened to them all, his last memory of them is seeing their sad faces, jammed hard against a car window, crying, pleading to stay, desperately trying to catch one last glimpse of the farm as they are whisked away. He heard one of them went and stayed with a vicar, who promptly chewed his way through a carpet and was instantly shipped off to a dogs home. His name was Buster due to his propensity to walk into things and look as though he had just fought a bruising twelve round eliminator.

Nugget had been chosen quite by chance, it was fate that's how he saw it. One summer's afternoon he was navigating his way across the yard, it had rained hard for several days and the sun was out so everybody was making hay. Old man Flugal was in the northerly field, and Nugget who's naturally nosey disposition took him off to see what was so important in the north field, came upon a most dreadful sight; Flugal, whilst attempting to manoeuvre the tractor around a tree stump, had tipped over and it was only the offending stump that had saved him from being crushed. On realising that his owner was in imminent danger Nugget ran like the wind, as fast as his little legs could carry him, across the sodden earth and into arms of his mother and Mrs Flugal. Nugget then made such a commotion that had never been seen in one so young, and before he could possibly be admonished ran back with equal speed to the field with them both in hot pursuit. The upshot was Mr and Mrs Flugal thought Nugget a worthy addition to the Flugal household and he was chosen to stay.

Nugget stood motionless for a few seconds, as if awaiting an order from his commander in chief to advance upon the enemy, then when realising Chance was not going to expound further, turned and made his way back to the farm house. He then finally got the answer he was looking for.

'Okay!'

Nugget stopped in his tracks and began to break into a smile that had only moments earlier held onto a forlorn expression signifying his disappointment at Chance's stance on the matter.

Chance could not possibly realise Nugget's reaction to his exclamation for he had resumed again his gloomy countenance when he did once again face him. Slowly, fighting all reasonable requests not to, Nuggets cheesy grin erupted in all is glory.

'I can see that meets with your approval.' Nugget nodded furiously. 'That's alright then.'

Nugget again nodded with much gusto and without so much as a peep, spun round and gaily danced his way back to the house, thinking to himself 'what a fine politician I would have made' and 'what a waste his life would have been working on the farm.' This last thought was immediately quashed and filed permanently under 'don't ever bring that up again'.

Still grinning from ear to ear Nugget slumped down into his basket, unseen by Mr and Mrs Flugal, rolled around on his back to smooth out a few wrinkles in the cushion, and then fell soundly asleep.

3

The next morning Nugget awoke, sprang out of his bed, much to the great surprise of Mr Flugal, who without muttering a single syllable let him out of the back door, and the two brothers-in-arms sauntered off into another beautiful, crisp clear morning.

'Aaaaahh!!!!' exclaimed Mr Flugal. 'The good Lord has once again provided us with a sumptuous visual feast to lighten up even the most dullest and morose of souls.'

Nugget didn't have a clue what he was talking about, but it sounded good by the tone of his voice and that's all he needed to know.

As they past the stables, Chance poked his head over the stable door. For a second Nugget thought his good friend had remained where he had left him the night before, but on reflection he knew Chance, being of that age, enjoyed his creature comforts. 'Morning Chance, sleep well?' A half asleep Chance nodded. 'We're off to inspect the southern field! See you later.' Again Chance simply nodded and retreated back in to the murky depths of the stables.

The southern field had been a cause of much anxiety and sleepless nights for Flugal; the drainage had not been up to the required standard; he had tried all the usual remedies, but all to no avail. Every time they had a period of persistent rain, the lower end flooded rendering it useless to man, beast or crop.

Flugal surveyed the miniature lake, to which he was now the less than proud owner.

'He spent thousands on drainage.' thought Nugget

'I spent thousands on that drainage.' said Mr Flugal

Nugget slung him a sideways glance. 'And now look at it!' he continued.

'And now look at it!' came Flugal's reply. Although it wasn't a reply at all, for how could he possibly know what his faithful hound could be thinking.

'Stuff Smithy!' Nugget was now in full swing. 'If this is the kind of handy work you can expect from him, he can take a running jump in our lake!'

'Stuff Smithy!' echoed Flugal; Smithy was the local contractor Flugal had paid to sort the problem. 'If this is the kind of handy work you can expect he can take a running jump in our lake. Can't he Nugget?' Nugget grunted his approval, and as if the proceeding conversation had laid the groundwork for the 'coup de grace', both chimed together.

'We need Uncle Dave!'

Uncle Dave wasn't really anybody's uncle; he had just been a friend of the family for many years. He was known around the town as "Old Turner the Hermit" and had in fact been named "Uncle Dave" by Flugal's kids and the name just stuck.

'Old Turner the Hermit' was famous for his refusal to have any contact, in any way shape or form with the outside world. He had shut his door to society. "The world's gone to the dogs" he would bark out whenever approached on the subject. There was though one rare exception: the public outcry over the unfair increase in the council tax and the re-banding of the rates on property; Turner in particular was hit hardest, his having a small farm that overlooked most of the town and its surrounding countryside, and the prospect of an increase in tax due to his diligence and foresight in buying such a valuable and desirable residence arose in him such an anger that was rarely seen in polite society, let alone a public march; he received for his efforts a sizeable fine and a criminal record. On hearing this would impact not very favourable on his credit rating, it was all Turner could do not to laugh out loud and be held in contempt, such was the disdain he felt for authority at the time.

But that was then. The very fact that he avoided all human contact was at loggerheads with Uncle David's greatest talent; he could turn his hand to anything, and no man made barrier ever held out against those in need, and so it was with the people of Burberry County, in particular Rumble Town. Prodger, the postman, needed a garden gate restored, Dave had a lathe ideal for the purpose; Jenkins, the headmaster, his petrol driven lawnmower had recently packed up and the dealers in the area refused to touch it on the grounds it was now obsolete. "But it's less than two years old!" he would say, but no, this undeniable truth could not lesson it being "obsolete", so he frequented Old Man Turner's Farm, who restored it to its former glory with all the skill of a renaissance sculpture. Jenkins from that day to this supplied Turner with a steady income.

Flugal had relied on Dave on many previous occasions; both men accepted the agreement with equal relish; Flugal because he knew that any farm equipment would not cost him an arm and a leg to restore and Uncle Dave could have his fill of Mrs Flugal's delicious cakes, for he had the wickedest of sweet tooth's. Dave to his credit was not averse to being bribed with any job around the farm, knowing full well what awaited the inevitable successful outcome, and Flugal always the business man felt no guilt in pampering to his friend's weakness as long as both parties were in complete agreement.

Back at the farm Flugal snatched the keys to his truck off a small circular table situated by the side of the front door, informed his wife as to his plans and hurried out of the house, but not without the obligatory pause to ascertain whether his trusty comrade had vacated behind him. All was well. He knew exactly where to find his friend at this time of day and they both set off without any further delay.

At the end of the road, that connected Flugal Farm to the public highway, there lay a most awkward unmarked junction that has seen the rise in many a driver's insurance premiums in Flugal's tenure. Flugal arrived at the junction, familiar with its pitfalls. He cautiously inched forward, poking the nose of the car into the 'B' road. Nugget sitting in his accustomed position of front passenger carried out the appropriate observations, mirroring his master. If it had been witnessed by an onlooker they would have sworn the two heads were connected by an invisible wire, so much were their heads in unison, rotating left and right. Flugal himself had bent his considerable frame, for he was no small man, onto the dashboard to get a clearer view of the road. Further and further forward they inched until the point of no return was reached, and the road being clear they entered it and proceeded on their way. Both parties now drew in a breath and calmly exhaled at the successful outcome.

The glorious beginning to the day perpetrated into the late morning, with the distinct possibility of an afternoon of blue skies and bright sunshine.

Our two comrades sat back and enjoyed the drive on the way to their rendezvous, relaxing not only in the face of nature's splendour, but the pleasure each derived from each other's company.

Flugal knew exactly where to find him on this particular day; this was yet another anomaly in Uncle Dave's character; everybody knew where he was at and what he was up to at this time of year. Today was fly fishing day on the banks of the River Stern; the fish would be navigating their way upstream just like their forefathers and mothers had done before them for a thousand years or more, driven onwards by some invisible force of nature. Many, if not all, will never make it or return, taking this final, desperate pilgrimage to prolong, populate and extend their species tenuous grip on life, but nature as always tries to maintain balance, never placing preference on one species over another in order to prevent the demise of one of God's creations, but it is man's untimely intervention, usually under the evil guise of remuneration, that exasperates the problem of their fragile existence.

This is not to be held against Uncle Dave; he is one of the few, those rare breed who fully understood 'the balance' that nature extends over its jurisdiction. If any fledgling or young adult should ever find its way on to his line he simply returned the creature back to its home. Any older fish, which he never numbered more than two, he religiously drew the line at two, made their way to his plate, and the 'balance' was maintained. One of the advantages of his trying to sever all contact with society in general, was his becoming aware of nature, its glory, its peace, its tranquillity and the damage man's passage of time was levelling on her.

Flugal and Nugget made good progress along the windy, twisty 'B' road, populated on either side by the plush verdant hedgerows, flashing past the open windows.

The cheerful chirping of the hedgerows inhabitants resounded around Flugal's truck, Nugget chuckled to himself; of the two he alone was aware of the trouble, strife and dangers, fun and sheer joy affecting their everyday life; to any outsider it was simply a magnificent symphony marking the beginning of spring.

Flugal, reacting to nature's choir, started to whistle to himself. Nuggets smile grew broader when he knew his master was happy, but as with all occasions of tranquillity, there must be a disturbance, to upset, distort the serene, and it came in the shape of Flugal's nemesis: Mr Williams!

Here was a most detestable man; short and stout in stature, he despised anybody remotely taller than him, and was driven by what most people saw as greed, but was in fact something far more dangerous, something which grew deep inside him and transformed itself into an emotion that swarmed over all and every personality trait he owned; an overwhelming desire not only to better his rival, but to crush them at every turn; in sporting circles it is often referred to as the 'killer instinct', but as we all know sporting life is not real life and even the most learned of practitioners in their respective fields will testify that sport only mirrors life, and is only a reflection on the true trials and tribulations that befall the common man. He was sadly oblivious to these finer points, every piece of him drove onwards and upward to gain the upper hand by fair means or foul and now he had Mr Flugal, who had always eluded him, firmly in his sights, and as any great hunter will corroborate, "one must strike whilst the iron is hot", "let loose your shot while your prey is in your line of sight and never, ever let them go!" Flugal Farm was now his number one priority.

History in its many guises over the centuries has taught us many lessons which we feel the need over time to forget, only to be reminded at our peril of it later. Every great leader, politician and warrior and a few sportsmen, good and bad, despotic to the righteous, has had a weakness, and so it was with Williams: His Achilles heel was his allergy to dogs! And Nugget again knew this better than anybody!

Williams flashing headlights, filled Flugal's rear windscreen half blinding him in the process; he swerved a number of times before Williams, either got the message and turned them off or more likely Flugal's eyesight adjusted itself to the brightness.

'Are you mad!' exclaimed Nugget.

'This driver's a menace Nugget!' exasperated Flugal.

The lights now dimmed meant Williams had accelerated alongside Flugal's truck and the two vehicles momentarily passed down the country lane side by side. Williams's passenger window was lowered on preparation for the forthcoming suicidal discourse.

'Flugal!' shouted Williams.

'Are you mad?' replied Flugal, re-iterating Nugget earlier.

'That's what I said!' Nugget reminded him.

'I need to talk to you. Pull over.' Flugal had no choice, he had decided on this course of action already.

With both cars now stationary with Williams in front, he vacated his vehicle and walked rearward to Flugal's truck, to his mild astonishment Flugal met him half way.

'That was a crazy stunt you pulled there!' The anger was all too apparent in Flugal's voice.

'This road's never busy.' countered Williams, shuffling nervously from side to side. 'You can drive as fast as you like, the only people who use this road are the locals, farmers like yourself. Oh, I'm sorry you're only a part time farmer.'

This last comment angered Flugal still more. 'You think!'

'But enough of that.' Williams remained silent for a while, mulling over how best to word his statement and allow Flugal valuable seconds to calm down.

'What do you want Williams? Flugal broke the silence. 'I'm a busy man.'

'I want your farm. I mean I want to buy your farm. There I said it, I'm sorry if that came out a bit blunt, but I couldn't for the life of me think of any other way to say it!'

'What!' Flugal was taken aback. 'It's not for sale!'

'Not now!'

'What do you mean, not now...........not ever!'

'Oh, come on Flugal. We both know your financial situation. You can't keep on hiding it.'

'What situation!' Flugal's infamous temper was about to erupt and even if he did have "a situation" he was not about to broadcast it.

'Do I have to spell it out?'

'I'm afraid you do!' Flugal had already pieced together the puzzle; Bennett had informed Williams of the outcome of their meeting, so much for client confidentiality and Williams thought he could muscle in on a piece of the action. Were these two in it together? Or was it just an offhand remark that Bennett let slip? He would have to find out.

'Oh, I can wait.' said Williams, so far he was enjoying every minute of this confrontation, he had originally only wanted to see the look on Flugal's face when he offered to buy the farm, but this was a bonus.

All the while this had been going on Nugget had grown more and more agitated by the cheekiness and affront of Williams, and as he had vacated the car with Flugal he now slowly backed off from the mounting argument to surreptitiously position himself by the passenger window of Williams's car, for in his eagerness to stop Flugal his enemy had left it wide open, and when neither man was looking sprung onto the passenger seat, clearly belying his advanced ten dog years, seventy in human, and hid himself behind the driver's seat.

Williams smiled that devilish smile exhibited by those rising to a position of authority, and who ultimately gain power over whoever is the recipient of their ostentatious and vulgar display.

'Forget Flugal Farm!' said Flugal

'I can't.' replied Williams 'I want it….I've always wanted it!'

'You can't have it!'

'That's too bad if we can't agree on a price! I would like to think we could come to some sort of agreement and I could have helped your family out of the dire financial ruin you have foolishly plunged them into, which undoubtedly would alleviate some of the inevitable pain and suffering that will surely follow.'

'Thank you for your concern for my family's welfare and my obvious financial incompetence!' Flugal's tone of sarcasm was obvious.

'You're for the knackers yard Flugal!' Williams did not appreciate Flugal's tone. 'You and those pathetic excuses for horses are finished!'

Flugal remained mute.

Nugget sat patiently in the back of Williams's car. Displeasure in a dog takes on many forms; stupid, senseless canines resort to biting and chomping on their victims and their possessions indiscriminately, no thought is placed before the act, only a desire to inflict pain; smarter animals wait for the precise moment to pounce. Nugget could wait all day, his resentment building. How dare he talk about his master and friends that way! Anyone who had but one true friend is rich beyond all their wildest dreams and Nugget was going to make him pay.

Williams sauntered back to the car. In his mind he had gained the upper hand and Flugal's momentary victory, which had clearly agitated him, only served to bolster his resolve to gain Flugal Farm by whatever means, fair or foul, were at his disposal. Flugal's fragile hold on the farm had been affirmed, his hesitant replies and indignation to his less than subtle probing again had only reinforced his comprehension that Flugal Farm was there for the taking.

Flugal himself had wasted not a second at the termination of the conversation with Williams, he turned on his heels and hurried back to his truck, fired up the V6 engine and then sat motionless, recounting the entire discourse with Williams, totally oblivious to the absence of his four legged friend.

Nugget watched for Williams to move off from the side of the road, this would leave him nowhere to go and at his mercy. He then sat bolt upright immediately behind Williams left shoulder, so he was just in view of his rear mirror.

Williams was so ensconced in his own thoughts on what had just passed, that he was totally oblivious to the dog's presence. His first inclination, and Nugget's first detection to the sly change in his demeanour, was the sharp tingling in his nasal passage. He rubbed his nose furiously.

The tingling rose to a peak, and no amount of rubbing or massaging could allay the unavoidable outcome; it exploded forth, a sneeze so violent it rocked the car, diverting it from its course. For a brief second Nugget feared for his life, but

Williams arrested the deviation and they resumed normal service, for the time being.

The sneeze was so loud it alerted to Flugal that all was not right and he turned to address Nugget, but Nugget was elsewhere! Without hesitation Flugal comprehended the portentous situation and followed in hot pursuit.

Flugal could make out Nugget's silhouetted form weaving from side to side with the meandering of William's car.

'Nugget!' he shouted to himself.

Nugget from inside the car was now having serious doubts as to the wisdom of this particular adventure; Williams was a now in the throes of a full on sneezing fit, and each expostulation only added to the oscillations.

During one of the brief rest bites, Williams spied Flugal's truck closing in on him.

'Flugal!'

On hearing his master's name Nugget, filled with sheer elation, could not help himself and called out for him.

'What!' exclaimed Williams.

Nugget had now alerted Williams as to the source of his sneezing, and that elation evaporated in an instant.

Williams adjusted his rear view mirror to get a better view of the unwanted passenger.

'It's you!' Nugget could sense the menace in his tone.' I'll teach you to be an unwelcome guest!' and with that Williams swung the wheel hard over, causing Nugget to slide the full length of the back seat and smack his head hard up against the side window, dazing him momentarily, then Williams repeated this trick again and again, but in his haste to teach old Nugget a lesson he omitted to realise that the poor animal would try anything to right himself and prevent kissing the two passenger windows in turn; Nugget dug his claws into the bright, shiny beige leather interior and furrowed eight symmetrical lines, ripping it to shreds.

'This'll teach you!' Williams guffawed between sneezes and swung the steering wheel hard over again left then right.

'And this'll teach you.' replied Nugget, digging his claws ever deeper. He was starting to enjoy this ride.

Now you have to understand that Flugal, who was following at a respectable distance due to the nature of the country lane down which both cars were passing, could not possibly know the full extent of Williams's reaction to the discovery of Nugget or his retaliation, he just witnessed Williams's car careering down the road and naturally worried for his faithful friend.

'Hang on Nugget!' Flugal shouted out of the driver's window, he knew what he was saying was hopeless; one Nugget could not possibly hear and secondly couldn't understand anything being said, but Flugal shouted it anyway, his own anxiety rising with every slide poor old Nugget made along the back seat.

For one brief moment Flugal had suspected Williams of being unwell and this affecting his driving, but as he never seemed to slow down let alone stop, he discarded that notion and this was cemented when he saw Williams's head spin around to confront Nugget during one of the straight sections of road.

'Stop!' shouted Flugal, but his request only made Williams speed up. 'Williams clearly hears me' thought Flugal and the first signs of anger tickled away at him.

Following another nasal explosion, Williams barked out 'Your Master is in on this too isn't he?'

Nugget all this while had for the most part kept his counsel, as he did not want to aggravate the situation any more than he already had, but he had kept mute long enough and now replied in full.

Nugget's canine articulation caught William off guard, but his vehicle maintained a steady path; Nugget thinking

Williams understood his pleadings for the car to brought to a halt, continued on.

The yelping, howling and snarling of Nugget panicked Williams, who now believing the dog to be mad, swung the car even more violently from side to side. 'Don't you come near me!' he cried desperately, and screamed for help from the top of his lungs out of his driver's side window, but it was all to no avail, as he had explained to Flugal, this was a quiet country lane only used by locals. 'Damn these quiet country lanes!'

Nugget pleaded with him yet again to stop.

'HELP!' he cried again followed by an enormous sneeze.

Nugget knew he had to take drastic action, and decided he was going to make a jump for it through the open front passenger window.

Flugal still at a respectable distance, viewed Nugget about to make his move. 'What are you doing Nugget?' but Nugget was determined to get out of the car.

'Get away from me!' Williams was petrified at now seeing the canine beside him and swung the wheel over hard right to squash the poor old dog against the passenger door.

This was all Nugget needed and he jumped straight out of the window as the car swung right; his flight, thankfully took him over a small hedge lining a cow pasture, but his delight was short lived and his landing was cushioned by freshly planted, noxious cow pats. He was thankful for small mercies!

Williams somewhat relieved at the exit of Nugget straightened the car and vented his anger at the pursuing Flugal.

'This is all you're doing Flugal!'

Flugal had by now stopped by the side of the road and was out of sight and sound when this exclamation was made, his eyes were already scanning the line of hedgerows and he vacated his vehicle to go in search of canine pal. The sight that met his eyes brought a smile to his face; he now surveyed poor Nugget prostrate, head first, in an enormous, aromatic cow pat.

'That was lucky!' It was all he could come up with at the time.

'Lucky.' said Nugget. 'You should be in my position!'

'Now, now Nugget' Flugal replied to the dog's grumblings, as he tried to placate his smelly friend. 'If you will try and jump out of moving cars, like some kind of super hero, then what do you expect!'

Nugget thought this over for a second. 'Super hero, eh!'

Williams was now way up the road, deciding for discretion over valour; that it was more prudent to continue on to his destination than to confront Flugal over his wayward dog.

Nugget stood up out of the cow pat and shook himself instinctively, as all canines invariably do in a vain attempt to clean themselves, his coat having attracted in vast sums and now thoroughly impregnated with all manner of sizes and shapes of cow dung, and these now peppered poor Flugal from head to toe like shotgun pellets, turning his multi-hued attire into something resembling polka dot.

'Thanks Nugget!'

Nugget now thankfully free of the greater percentage of manure, trotted sheepishly back to the truck. 'You're welcome.' he added, resisting further the desire to violently eject any cow droppings desperately clinging to his coat until out of the reach of his master.

He squeezed himself under the hedge, which minutes before he had cleared in one leap, shook his coat again and jumped through the passenger window and made himself comfortable in his usual position.

Flugal admired his new attire, how was he going to explain this one to the wife. He chuckled at the very thought, he could see the funny side of most things, although the pungent aroma for which he had not been up close to for a many a year took some getting used to.

Back in the car Flugal dumped his fragrant coat on the back seat, gunned the V6 engine into life and continued on their original journey without a further word from either.

Flugal and Nugget pulled up at a respectable distance from the river, the figure of Uncle Dave could clearly be seen through the verdant border of the footpath that ran parallel to it. He was an expert fly fisherman, swishing and flashing his rod as if some swashbuckler of old indulging in a duel with an ancient foe.

They exited the truck, Flugal donned his smelly coat, and they approached with great care. As they drew nearer he could be heard muttering to himself, coaxing the fish onto his line. Flugal saw by his net, half submerged and secured to the bank, that he was having a successful day. Uncle Dave's discourse with the local marine life was definitely paying dividends.

Williams finally reached his destination, his anger had not abated, and pulled the Jaguar car sharply into the driveway, bordered on either side by the sprawling grounds of Wellingham Park; this was another of the acquisitions that Flugal Farm was going to join in the not to distant future.

The crunch of gravel signalled the beginning of the arrival to the entrance of the manor house. Once alongside the impressive front door, he brought the car to a halt and took a deep breath and composed himself, the sneezing had ceased at least. He leaned into the back of the car to retrieve his briefcase, to be met with Nugget's eight tramline signatures the full length of the rear seat. He was speechless for a moment as the true extent of the damage to his beautiful leather upholstery sunk in, but there can be only one sane reaction to such a discovery and Williams let loose a volley of oaths that any soldier would have been proud of, slamming the car's inside with such force that any bystander would have thought a violent struggle was taking place, but not wanting any of the servants to witness his lack of self control, he calmed down and whispered menacingly.

'Nugget for that you can join your master!' Williams left the car where he parked it and stormed into the house. He was met just inside the porch by Humphries, his butler.

'We were not expecting you so soon, Mr Williams.' he said taking Williams's coat as he discarded it. 'You should have rung sir, I would have got the cook to prepare lunch early.

'I'm going for a ride, prepare everything.'

'Yes Sir.'

'I'll have lunch on my return.'

'Yes Sir.'

Williams ran up the long flight of stairs, ascending into the upper most reaches of Wellingham house, leaving Humphries to his task.

Flugal and Nugget stopped a few yards from the river's edge, behind a hedgerow. Uncle Dave could still be seen swishing his rod like a young Hussar flashing his blade in the heat of battle, so they approached with great care, paying Dave and the other fly fishermen the greatest respect lest they should startle them or the fish. Dave kept on muttering to himself, Flugal now got a better look at the size of Dave's catch, and it was mightily impressive, albeit he knew that Dave would return all bar two of the older fish.

Uncle Dave reeled in his woodcock yellow Scottish loch fly and proceeded to replace it with a Zulu that were arranged neatly in a sea of colours around his hat band. Flugal admired the dexterity at which he achieved this, bearing in mind the strength of the river current into which he was attempting to maintain a foothold, which was about a third of the way into the river itself. With the new fly attached Uncle Dave once more attempted to tempt a trout onto his line.

Nugget by this time had become fascinated with the river's populace, who seemed to be glaring at him, winking, as if to easy 'you foul smelling stinker', and being a natural swimmer and water lover, the two being good bed fellows, the third excuse his rather foul smelling coat, he advanced upon the river and jumped head first in after the fish that Uncle Dave was expertly trying to lure onto his line, and proceeded to splash violently in all directions; the fish by now were long gone, but he didn't care, what fun!

The commotion alerted Dave to the presence of Nugget and Flugal, 'Only Nugget would try body slamming a fish', he started, clearly showing he wasn't the slightest bit annoyed at the intrusion. 'How's tricks?'.

'So, so!' Flugal's replied. 'Sorry about Nugget, he's a law unto himself sometimes.' Flugal quickly scanned the banks of the river for other fishermen. The few who were out that day never paid him or Nugget any attention.

Dave could tell immediately all was not well with his friend's subdued persona, he was clearly out of sorts, and him being one of the cheeriest people he knew, which is why he enjoyed his company so much although he would never let on, and this being the opinion of a man that openly shunned all human contact, it disconcerted him.

'What's up?'

'Williams and some irrigation problems.'

'That man's name is popping up all too frequently these days. That same field again that Smithy was supposed to have fixed?'

'He wants my farm! And yes.'

'Oh dear' Flugal could sense Dave's growing concern. 'You're in a spot of trouble?'

'No......not yet.'

'How long do you have?' Dave said this as his sense of smell alerted him to a strange odour.

'Until the end of the month. The field I don't know.' replied Flugal.

'That's shaky at best' Dave sniffing aggressively as he spoke.

'Yes, yes it is.' Flugal's face drew longer. 'At best.' he concluded after a short pause.

'The bank can't help?'

'The bank are the problem; in the past they always gave me a little lee way. I fell behind on a few payments, which is due to the nature of the business and struggled to catch up for a while, and only now am I slowly working my way onto a slightly better footing, but this new manager...' he cut the sentence short, the despair finally caught up with him and it took all his self control to keep his emotions in check.

'But you've got a good reputation at the bank, surely that must count for something.' asked Dave.

'Apparently not!'

Uncle Dave suddenly came to realise that all the conversation so far had been conducted with him still over knee high in the river; his rod and line lying limp in his right hand like a Spartan surveying the trophies and spoils post battle.

Extracting himself from his watery battleground he checked on his catch, secured his reel and line and poured himself and Flugal a cup of hot coffee from a flask; it was not lost on Flugal, that he carried two cups with this coffee flask. Again that smell hit Dave's nostrils.

Sipping coffee their attention now turned momentarily to Nugget, who had now ceased his thrashing around in the river chasing lost causes and swam to the far river bank.

Shaking himself down just as violently as before, he was now struck with a sense of panic; how was he going to get back to the far side of the river without having to brave the water, this was no big deal you understand, Nugget was after all a fine swimmer, but when anybody has spent time and effort to make oneself presentable, after a coating of cow dung, the last thing one wants to do is to undo all that hard work and immerse oneself again in dirty river water.

Up and down the river bank he ran in a vain attempt to discover a bridge that would transport him safe and sound to the other side, but to everybody's surprise who witnessed him, he remained mute throughout, so intently was he trying to find a solution to his problem.

After about ten minutes, during which time Flugal and Dave had discussed the lower field and his unusual odour amongst other topics, Nugget came to rest in exactly the same spot from which he started his hysteria.

'Hey!' called Nugget to Uncle Dave 'Is there is a bridge near here?'

'What's he up to now?' said Flugal on hearing Nuggets growling.

Once again Nugget called from the far side. 'Where's the nearest bridge?' Flugal frowned as he tried to comprehend Nugget's outpourings.

'The nearest bridge?' repeated Nugget. From his side of the river his Master and Uncle Dave were in a deep discussion.

'They must be trying to figure out the quickest way.' thought Nugget.

Flugal now espied a vexed and agitated Nugget, growling, whimpering and barking incessantly.

'Is there a bridge near here Dave?'

'Yeah, about a mile upstream.'

'A mile upstream.' shouted Flugal regarding the futility of his actions, 'How can that dog possibly understand a single word I'm saying!'

'A mile upstream!' said Nugget to himself. All Flugal heard was another growl and eying the direction of the current, something Nugget had failed to do whilst thrashing around chasing the trout, now had his bearings and was off upstream in a flash.

Flugal, in unison with Nugget's first step in the direction from which the current was flowing, finished his coffee and walked at a steady pace towards the bridge, but only after informing Dave that he wouldn't be more than a couple of minutes. It had not gone unnoticed, that Nugget had sprinted off towards his salvation the split second after he shouted his futile instruction. Could he really understand him, Flugal had always had his doubts, and this just fuelled the debate raging inside his head. He banished the thought from his mind for now and concentrated on saving his faithful hound.

Uncle Dave, now having a few more precious minutes after he had decided abandoned the day's sport on the arrival of his two friends, readied his rod and line and fished some more before the realisation that the unwanted odour had dissipated with the exit of his friend.

'Farmers.' he said to himself.

Now that Nugget was in full flow towards securing his rescue, it would be prudent to explain the obvious discrepancy the reader has know doubt spotted; Nugget's ability to understand his Master's every word, but Flugal's inability to reciprocate; any dog handler will verify the intelligence of these animals to obey the simplest commands and the few exceptional animals who have the capabilities to understand more complex instructions, but we humans sadly can never testify to honestly understanding a word of the canine language; for this reason alone they can truly attest to be 'Man's Best Friend.'

Nugget followed the bend in the river for a mile or so until there finally appeared slowly and painstakingly, into his field of vision, the reward for all his efforts. He breathed a sigh of relief.

He slowed to a trot when he got within fifty yards of the entrance, when something caught his attention out of the corner of his eye. Paralleling the river bank was a road, only visible through the broken foliage bordering the bridge entrance, and cantering towards him were four magnificent black stallions, pulling an equally splendid black carriage; each horse was immaculately turned out, their shiny black coats glistening in the midday sun, but it was the lone figure, seated at the head of the carriage that disturbed Nugget. It was Williams!

Nugget stopped dead in his tracks, perplexed by what he perceived, he had not seen anything like this before and became an interested spectator, completely forgetting the bridge for which he had expelled so much energy to procure. He kept asking himself the same questions: How did he, William's, get here so quickly? And what was he doing riding on that contraption?

The carriage whistled past Nugget, gliding along the road, as if cushioned on an invisible blanket of air; the four horses in unison, trotting eagerly to the command of the driver, that despicable Mr Williams.

Unbeknown to Nugget, Flugal had reached the bridge and searched eagerly on the far side for him, but he was nowhere to be seen. Nugget had snuck through a gap in the hedge in order to gain a better advantage point with which to follow the progress of the carriage. For all its splendour, Nugget could not hide within himself the feeling of contempt.

Flugal concerned at not finding Nugget where he honestly expected to find him, crossed over the bridge and began examining the many openings of the hedgerow.

About this time Ralph, who was a particular gregarious rabbit, was on his way to join his fellow floppy eared friends in a game of cards; his luck had been in for quite a while and the new gambling den, which had just sprung up not far from his warren, was ideal. There had been much consternation about the den from most of the locals, but the elders decreed it essential to the well being of the community and any discontent quickly evaporated, or was plainly ignored, when it soon became aware that the mini casino would be both profitable and popular among the rabbit communities. And so it was that young Ralph was going to partake of the cards this fine day.

Tucking his winnings from previous successes into a little pouch, he set off hugging the hedgerow, mainly to keep out of sight of a couple of rascals, who had taken it upon themselves to lighten the load of any unsuspecting traveller making their way to this den of disrepute.

Ralph kept a good look out all around, especially ahead on the horizon, ignoring the carriage and four horses thundering down the road, when he suddenly came to an abrupt halt. A large dog had planted itself across his intended path. It was plainly obvious he was more interested in, nay fascinated with the horse drawn carriage than him. Ralph took particular care not to be spotted. He tiptoed around the canine, he wasn't going to take any chances; a dog after all is a dog, and he was a rabbit. Even so a couple of times Ralph instinctively froze solid, just as his mother had taught him to do when he was young, although it is questionable if this tactic actually works if they have spotted you already, but it all went according to plan and the canine threat was averted. But no sooner had Ralph, money jingling in his pouch accelerated his pace, than he ran headlong into a human. An even greater danger.

The human, much to Ralph's initial relief and then no small amount of indignation totally ignored him. This surprisingly angered our floppy eared friend no end; here was arguably his greatest foe, which to any other rabbit would be a godsend to be neglected by. But not our Ralph!

He stood hands on hips and glared at the behemoth standing before him, clearly preoccupied elsewhere. His indignation turned to anger and Ralph in a moment of complete madness, rushed forward and kicked the giant. Nothing happened.

So Ralph, undeterred, kicked him again and guess what? You got it. Nothing happened. Ralph, furious by now, at being ignored was bordering on apoplexy and this injected him with a severe dose of bravery. No poker face needed here, and he sprang forward and sank his teeth into the nearest standing leg; this finally got him the reaction he sought and the human let out an enormous wail and stumbled rearwards.

Nugget alerted to his master's presence by the vaguely familiar ear piercing scream, headed forth back to the bridge just in time to see Flugal fly backwards into the river. Nugget could only stand and stare in utter amazement at the sight of his master's aqua-aerobics.

'There's no trout this far upstream. I've looked!' he said totally misunderstanding the situation.

Flugal spat out any river water, and swam back to the bank that contained Nugget and the invisible Ralph.

Ralph had thought it prudent to use covert tactics from here on in and furtively slipped behind a bush and silently made his way to the gambling den. Flugal dragged his soaking wet person onto the bank.

'I told you there were no trout down here!' exclaimed Nugget

'Thank you Nugget for your concern.' replied Flugal, totally unaware to the meaning of Nugget's words.

'At least it's cleared all that cow mess off you!' continued Nugget.

Flugal eyed Nugget most carefully, the inflection in his tone once again raised doubts within him that he could fully understand what was going on around him.

'At least I'm clean of all that dung Nugget.' he said

That's what I said.' Nugget replied as he headed for the bridge and back to the truck.

Flugal shook himself off in a vain attempt to dispense himself of the worst of the water, and followed close behind.

Nugget stopped short of Uncle Dave, who by this time had finally decided enough was enough and had packed up most of his gear.

'Hello Nugget.' Nugget smiled. 'Where's your Master?' Just at this point a drenched Flugal came into view. 'You look as though you've had fun!'

'I've had better days.' replied Flugal; squelching his way past them both and into the truck on the other side of the hedgerow.

'You better take care of him, Nugget.'

And with that he scampered off to his master.

Flugal leaned out of the driver's window after the V6 engine had sprung once again into life, and Nugget had boarded. 'You'll call around later about the field.'

Uncle Dave hearing Flugal call to him appeared through a hole in the hedge. 'No problem.' he said cheerfully, as Flugal waved an acknowledgement and roared on up the road leading to the country lane.

4

Flugal, when the time allowed, cut a quizzical eye over Nugget, who could immediately sense Flugal's gaze interrogate him, so he kept his own line of sight straight ahead.

After what seemed like an hour, but was in fact no more than ten minutes or so as the farm being only thirty minutes away, Flugal opened discourse mainly with himself trying to catch old Nugget off guard, for he still wasn't entirely sure if he wasn't going a bit mad brought on by the worry of the farm, Mr Williams and Bennett.

'I wonder what's for tea Nugget?' Flugal opened with after much cogitation; after all that premeditation, this was sadly the sum of his efforts. 'Steak and kidney pie I reckon, my favourite, you know your mistress is a mighty fine cook.' he stopped there to gauge his canine companions reaction. Nothing was all he got in return.

'She always cooks a bit extra for you, you know.' Again silence, would Nugget ever answer?

Flugal sighed deeply, he was surely losing the plot; a talking dog, no not a talking dog, but a dog that can wholly understand man. He knew Nugget was smart, he had after all saved him all those years ago.

'Oh well Nugget old friend.' here he paused, the events of the last couple of days returned to haunt him; money and financial security are some of the many burdens shouldered during adulthood, that are protected from the very young; there's should be a sweet life, as delicious and comforting as a holiday ice cream on a hot summer's day or a room full of presents. This is the parental reward for many, long hours toiling away, Monday to Friday, nine to five, because we want our loved ones to be happy, secure, and want for nothing. The burdens that rise so sharply in latter life should be kept hidden, masked for the time being as a sweet, delicious holiday ice cream.

The profundity of his private conversation was not lost on him and he drove in silence for a few miles.

'So Nugget.' continued Flugal after the pause for contemplation and renewed determination to resolve his inner conflict. 'What do you think?'

Again Nugget kept his counsel; he dare not make the slightest exclamation or facial expression lest it should give way his secret and give support to the very idea, however incredulous to his Master, that he understood human speak; his last wish would not be to alter in any way his relationship with him. Would he be trusted again?Treated differently? Paraded in full public view? The last he knew would never happen as Flugal was not that sort of human, but it did not stop him worrying none the less. The status quo was all that was needed during these difficult times, if Flugal needed to know, he would let him in on his secret. This thought alone comforted Nugget.

'Yes I thought so too!'

'He answers himself' thought Nugget 'to the unanswerable question. He plays both sides of the conversation, as comedians sometimes do on that funny box they call television.'

The truck made its explicable way home under the guiding hand of Flugal, covering tracks, roads that it had been steered many times before and would navigate many times more. They finally pulled into the farm, the yard was empty save for young Rachelle, who as always was donating all her spare time to the animals; she sadly was soon to be the only girl left helping out around the farm, Williams would offer all the others jobs at his stables, but Rachelle, as always, remained loyal to the Flugals Nugget's tail immediately started to wag at the sight of the girl; she was one of his best friends and gave him treats, sometimes when he didn't deserve them.

There were riding lessons booked for that afternoon after four, and Flugal decided to take the optimistic approach, they could and would turn things around if they all mucked in together and he was content and confident that 'his team' as he referred to them would make him proud, but still when he least expected it the realisation of their predicament would leave him with a heavy heart and he would fight hard to relieve the onset of his depression.

Nugget sensed these melancholy mood swings more than most and barked fervently, furiously wagging his tail, desperately trying to extract a reaction out of Flugal, but it was getting harder by the day!

'There we are home again, and little Rachelle Perkins here to meet you!' Flugal said to Nugget.

As soon as the truck had come to a standstill, Nugget could not help in his display of impatience in exiting the truck to play with his friend and receive his treat. Flugal opened his door and Nugget jumped out, but only ran as far as the front of the truck; his idea was to surprise Flugal at the front of the truck, him thinking that he was off to help Rachelle, which he would later. Flugal closed up the truck and sauntered round the vehicle in the direction of the house, Nugget intercepted him from behind the bonnet and jumped up slobbering all over his face, with joy clear for all to see. Deep inside, Nugget knew responsibility lay solely with him to raise spirits. Flugal smiled as he always did, his aspect never altered.

'Oh, Nugget! I love you to!' said Flugal stroking Nugget behind the ears, completely forgetting he was covered in cow pat and essence of river; this sensation sent Nugget into raptures and his tail whisked itself up into a frenzy.

This mutual appreciation went on for some minutes until that inevitable time arrived when every righteous event in life approaches its natural end, and the two companions strode off to their new appointments.

Nugget and Rachelle went to muck out the horses, Chance as always was first, but the others never seemed to mind, if they had ever noticed at all. Whenever he wanted to gain her attention Nugget used that tried and trusted technique, the old favourite of the paw, but in his haste to covet whatever sweet, chocolate surprise Rachelle had in store for him, he had omitted to remind himself of the laws of etiquette and one's physical condition on reminding someone of one's presence.

'Nugget!' exclaimed Rachelle 'You stink!'

Nugget took a step back, shocked at his faux pas. Without a moments hesitation he spun on his paws and raced headlong towards the horse trough and foregoing a precautionary look splashed into his friend's drinking water.

Pogo stood in utter amazement at Nugget's acrobatics in the drinking pool, and on any other day would have cheered him every step of the way, but toda y he was thirsty.

'Oi!'

Nugget raised his sopping wet head to the level of the trough, Pogo's imposing frame bared down upon him.

'Hi Pogo.'

'You having a good time............. in our drinking water!'

'Yeah...... er, sorry about that.' Nugget looked around nervously trying to find an escape route; all were blocked and now Troy arrived on the scene. 'Wasn't the best decision I've ever made, I'll grant you that.'

'I'll grant you my size nine's up your...........' Pogo was cut short by Chance.

'Give him a break.' Chance always saw sense. 'Rachelle's got one her treats for him and Nugget you do smell real bad!'

'It's those cows!'

'But what are we going to drink now!' argued Pogo 'Definitely not bovine flavoured trough water with a hint of dog!'

'Looks like you'll have to use the lower field.' interposed Troy.

'Yep.' continued Chance 'those cows certainly know how to make it.'

To make up the quartet Biff trundled along to the water trough, sniffed, grunted 'Cows', then walked back to his stable. It was point of some considerable sore irritation to the livery horses that the four friends had the run of the yard when not working, when they had to stay in their respective stables until their owners let them out into either the indoor or outdoor arenas or whatever field had the best grass, and Biff was not averse to letting them know about it.

The pleasant aromas emanating from the kitchen elevated Flugal's spirits still further. 'Time for lunch old boy.' he muttered to himself. He tentatively eased open the back door to the farm house, not because he was afraid of his wife's reaction to being disturbed in the all important art of baking, but the slow widening of the door allowed his nostrils to explore the wonderful, intoxicating smells and fragrances manufactured within.

Nugget by now had extracted himself from his perilous situation, with the help of Chance and Rachelle, Pogo was appeased when Rachelle hearing the commotion lifted Nugget out of the trough and presented the horses with buckets of clean, fresh water, sadly Nugget failed in his attempt to satisfy his sweet tooth, Rachelle's chocolate surprise reposed itself in her overcoat, which hung in the kitchen, hence his now sudden arrival immediately behind Flugal.

He kept a respectful distance, allowing himself the added pleasure of surveying Mrs Flugal's reaction to their return; she enjoyed the homecomings immensely, not that she was the nervous type, she just took great pleasure in his being there, but Flugal's happiness at this rare pleasure, was in the present climate, tempered once again with sadness that maybe the end was not nigh, but pretty damn close and the loss of the farm would affect his wife beyond repair.

Nugget took a couple of strides to the side, to improve his view of the kitchen, the lower regions of the kitchen was his domain and the most advantageous vantage points he took without conscious thought; deep down inside he to wanted again to feel that warm, welcome feeling of a loved one.

Mrs Flugal was in the pantry, totally unaware to their presence, she sang to herself a popular tune of the day as she studiously searched for the vital ingredients necessary for her latest concoction, for they were famous around those parts and regularly won prizes at the local fetes.

Mrs Flugal came into view backing out of the pantry loaded with goodies, she never shopped like most women, food shopping was one of her favourite past times. Immediately after she spied them both that beautiful smile old man Flugal had fallen in love with all those years ago lit up the room.

'You back already.' she said 'What a lovely surprise.' But all was not as she would have expected; the full aroma of the country filled her nostrils and the broad grin soon evaporated.

Flugal was the first to take a step back as her aspect subtly changed at the realisation that he had dared to venture into her kitchen effusing less than sociable odours.

'What happened?'

Flugal took a further step rearwards. Nugget similarly retreated.

'It was an accident.' entreated Flugal 'It's nothing to worry yourself about my dear!'

'You return soaking wet, smelling to high heaven and still wearing your shoes in my kitchen!'

Nugget had by now furtively positioned himself by the backdoor, still regarding himself fortunate to be in the warmth. Flugal on hearing the accusation as to his body odour gave his person a cursory sniff. He could not argue.

'Get those shoes and clothes off this instant and have a shower, you have students this afternoon!'

'What about Nugget?' Everybody in times of chastisement needs an ally and Flugal knew his wife loved Nugget just as much as he did, but he miscalculated on this front as well.

'Don't tell me you led that poor animal astray into whatever caused that awful smell?'

Flugal thought it best not to answer this accusation; anything he said or did at this juncture could and would only incriminate him even more.

'That poor dog, Nugget where are you?' Nugget duly appeared. He had been reprieved.

'I'll run you a bath after that silly Master of yours irresponsibility.' Nugget looked sheepishly at Flugal; what could he say, a nice warm bath after the days excursions compared to spending the night in the yard was paradise, and a dog's sense of smell being far more advanced than a human's, made his present condition even more disturbing. He hadn't the heart to mention the trough bath, not that they would have understood him anyhow.

Mrs Flugal was preparing Nugget's bath when little Rachelle Perkins entered the farmhouse by the same door as our two smelly comrades, making her presence known by her giggly chatty manner which always had the effect lowering peoples guard and them embracing her warmly. Mrs Flugal was no exception.

'I'm off now, Mrs Flugal.' chattered Rachelle espying Nugget's warm, soapy bath and Nugget's pleading expression for her not to say a word. Rachelle understood instantly the delicacy of his position and kept quiet. 'I have to leave early today to see my grandmother. She has something planned for this afternoon.'

'Nugget's having a bath; he is filthy! Is she coming to collect you?'' said Mrs Flugal.

'I've renewed the horses drinking water, and no I'm going to take a walk and enjoy the day.' started Rachelle suddenly realising she had backed herself into a corner, for there could be only one reply to such a statement.

'Why the matter?' asked Mrs Flugal.

Rachelle was anybody's equal in these exchanges and thinking on her feet and believing that a little white lie, in defence of a friend was not too bad a crime went on 'Where have you been Nugget to allow yourself to get in such a state?'

Mrs Flugal nodded, the thought clearly had been bothering her.

'The Boys' Rachelle continued, as that was her pet name for the quartet, 'Were really thirsty today and I like to leave them with plenty to drink on riding days!'

Mrs Flugal could not have agreed more; she regularly had the notion that Rachelle reminded her of her when she was that age. 'You're a good girl Rachelle. Will we see you again later on?'

'Yes please. If's that okay.'

'Okay with you and Mr Flugal?' she replied eagerly.

'Would you like some cakes before you go? They've just been baked.'

Rachelle was also well aware of Mrs Flugal's prowess in the kitchen and her achievements at the local fetes, and any opportunity to partake of some freshly baked goodies was to good to pass up and sacrilege to refuse.

Soon handfuls of freshly baked scones and fairy cakes were devoured with much gusto, and Rachelle bade farewell, for the time being, happily satiated.

Nugget, now smelling like a rose garden in the middle of July, duly scampered headlong around the kitchen; for although he loved having a bath, it played havoc with his ears and the only way to alleviate the intense tickling sensation in his inner ear was to drag the offending lobe along the floor and dash around like a mad dog. Soon though he found himself back in reality and finally a good scratch sufficed.

Flugal now reappeared showered and changed and ready to face the world once more, and once outside he strode purposely across the yard over to the stables, furtively removing a couple of fairy cakes from his coat pocket which he had procured whilst his wife was otherwise disposed. He surveyed the scene ahead of him and suddenly those pangs of melancholy once again reared their ugly heads.

Chance stared back at him almost grinning, if a horse could carry out such a feat, clearly ready for the afternoon's work. The rest were not to be seen, but by the noises emanating from inside the pony barn, where Rachelle had now left them in readiness for their lessons, they were not far off.

After those few mouthfuls of his wife's fine home cooking though he could feel his spirit's resurgence and went about his business of readying 'the Boys' for their afternoon's excursions.

Chance eyed Flugal's every step from the farmhouse. 'Look lively lads!' he cried as Flugal reached the entrance to the stable block.

'What!' replied Biff, who had been nonchalantly kicking his stable door.

'Flugal's here!' answered Troy scratching himself. Pogo was asleep, having decided on an afternoon's nap.

'You better wake him up.' Chance said to Troy, as he was standing the closest to his somnolent colleague.

'You're having a laugh. You know what he's like when he's woken up!' pleaded Troy.

He glanced over at Pogo, snoring away, clearly enthralled in whatever dream he was experiencing, and him being naturally inclined to laziness and always opting for an easier path through life, lashed out with his right rear leg at a wooden board standing proudly upright by Pogo's head. The board was left with only one course of action, and splintered into three sizeable pieces. The upshot of this commotion, of Troy's vandalising, was Pogo's violent return from the land of nod; he reared up living the very moment in his dream that had signalled his reawakening, stepped backwards into a plastic bucket of water and begun to flail this way and that in a panic, figuring some awful fiend had hold of his leg and in a desperate attempt to stabilise himself and free himself from his captor, grabbed hold of the side of the bale holder, but that was all to no avail for he careered rearwards, kicked up his hind leg sending the contents of the poor bucket, which could no longer maintain the slender grip on its place of residence, and vacated the premises all over Flugal, catching him square in the face, spoiling the after effects of his sweet smelling deodorant and shower.

Chance for his sins found the necessity to duck as the now empty bucket spun past his head, Biff laughed himself stupid at the unexpected afternoons entertainment and Nugget, who appeared munching on his treat, left for him by Rachelle, gazed in utter amazement and awe at the aqua acrobatics performed by his less than dexterous friend, whilst Nigel, who was a rare visitor to the barn that day, in his highland drawl gave a running commentary to all and sundry.

5

Many miles down the road in the plush offices of the late Arthur Nostromos, former President of Nostromos Global Industries, a group of top level executives convened, seated high above the cities skyline; Global had fallen on hard times of late, mostly due to their founder, Arthur Nostromos, dying suddenly on a fishing trip and the eldest son Thomas being forced against his will to take on and help maintain the mantle of power within the Nostromos family. He had proved to be the dismal failure which he himself forecast to the surviving Nosrtomos matriarch. In hindsight and not through any fault of his own, other than his heart was never in such a business adventure, and being loyal to his family plus realising his inadequacies as a head of a multi-million dollar global corporation, he magnanimously resigned in favour of his younger sibling, who displayed a much greater tendency to rule. Added to this was undoubtedly peer pressure and angry shareholders on the brink of rebellion.

Charles Nostromos, who was that younger son, a man of only twenty five years of age, but already bearing the hallmarks of a great man of industry; he had visions for where this industrial behemoth, Global, should go: To mould better relations with their workforce, the very people who worked in its engine room and drove it forward, obeying commands from this very office, and to associate itself more personally with its customers. To this end the board meeting was scheduled to discuss and possibly implement programmes and procedures to attain those goals now that Global was placed under his direct command.

Charles, or 'Chuck' to his closest friends and confidantes, squirmed silently in anticipation on hearing the opening address which would be delivered from the dulcet tones of Mr Willoughby, the spokesperson for the troubled shareholders.

Their concerns were deep felt within their community at the extremely poor performance of late, resulting in the loss of several highly lucrative contracts to rival organisations, and the sliding of the share price on the stock markets as a result. Unless confidence was restored immediately the banks, to which they owed a substantial amount of money, would start to get anxious, plus they may find themselves the victim of a possible takeover. His brother had certainly dug him a mighty deep hole from which to extricate himself and the company, but Thomas being Thomas always emerged smelling of roses. The weight of expectation was now going to fall firmly on Charles's young shoulders.

He stared long and hard at the imposing portrait of his grandfather, hanging, lord-like over proceedings; he had built this company up with his own bare hands at an age similar to Charles, this thought alone filled him with pride and optimism, intermingled with the inevitable dread. The very name Nostromos conveyed unrivalled success to the city and potential investors; one of the main reasons they had managed to survive for as long as they had during these difficult times and kept the majority of the investors they had onside.

Charles was determined to succeed and constantly reminded himself of his late grandfathers achievements, who had always told him from a very young age, as if he had a premonition of this very moment, a talent friends and foes alike attributed to him, 'Of never being afraid to lose'.

Willoughby concluded his speech on behalf of the shareholders and took his seat. Charles would indeed be given the reins of power, for a short time at least, but he could sense the vultures circling above, waiting expectantly for one false move.

All eyes immediately fell upon 'Chuck'; some imploring him to announce solutions to the shareholders doleful, complaints; others leered at the young pretender, praying silently, begging for catastrophe to express itself on this secluded stage. Neither received what they expected or wished!

Charles raised himself to his full height, which was not inconsiderable, paused for breath to compose his thoughts. Having all pairs of eyes sharply focused on him made his position all the more daunting, far more than he had imagined, but he felt strangely invigorated at being placed under such a strain and rose to the challenge. His mind was in order and his decision made, rightly or wrongly; for in truth he had in fact entered into the meeting extremely well prepared, expecting not without a little foundation, that it was assumed he would fail.

He delivered his well rehearsed speech with much aplomb and not wishing to bore the reader with the finer points, we shall stick to the salient: Nostromos Global Industries had lost profitable contracts, which was not in its nature to do and the cause of their failure lay in costs and bad planning; the two villains bound to be the ruin of any business when allowed to run hand in hand. Relations between management and workforce had descended to an all time low, and unless Global wanted to find itself facing the possibility of industrial action, never heard of before within the company, these had to be improved upon and the onus was on them. As you can imagine this point did not go down well. Thirdly the general public had lost faith in Nostromos Global Industries; arguably the most serious of the accusations levelled at the corporation and this alone necessitated bridge building with immediate effect; to reflect this he was going to restructure sections of the management, which brought about gasps of horror, by appointing a Planning Manager, a serious Global oversight in his opinion..

One of the board members made a remark along the lines that this questioned his grandfather's management of the company, but Charles chose to ignore the slate. As holiday entitlement was a major stumbling block with the workforce, extra days would be added to this year's allowance, this immediately drew more grumblings of disapproval from the board, but Charles secretly hoped that these two minor points, in his mind's eye, would be the catalyst for some serious productive dialogue helping Global secure some of the more lucrative government contracts he knew were imminent, and also to decide on an event to sponsor, his next bombshell for the board, to help raise their profile locally or nationally. The after effects of which, if they were seen to be a keen sporting sponsor with a sizeable prize on offer, would quell any rumours that Global were on shaky financial ground.

So Charles placed firmly at the boards feet the responsibility of choosing such an event, but only after the long overdue plan of action had been agreed, with a sensible time scale to implement them, to help secure these contracts; this would hopefully alleviate any misgivings they might have if it was seen that they themselves picked a worthy beneficiary.

Again there was much discontent and consternation among their sacred community; several spoke in unison, each taking their turn to chastise and question such an investment, considering the overall condition the company unfortunately currently found itself in.

Charles counter argued that Global needed to speculate to accumulate, he also remarked to himself how they fell into two distinct groups, this fascinated him no end, and also gave him a valuable insight into the internal political machinations that run as an undercurrent to Nostromos Global Industries.

After a few minutes deliberations, during which time the grand total of suggestions reached the giddy heights of zero, a knock on the door signalled the arrival of refreshment in the shape of tea, cakes and an assortment of biscuits under the guidance of the capable hands of Lucy, a new member to the Global family.

Once the tray had been positioned in a way expeditious to supplying sustenance, she scrupulously and diligently conveyed to all the nourishment available.

Charles set to contemplating the sad lack of ideas laid before him.

Lucy slid a hot cup of tea conveniently in line with his right hand, and being a soul that used his right as a matter of preference, he dextrously lifted the cup and supped without a moment's hesitation.

'White with no sugar, sir!' Lucy said after Charles had taken the first sip, obviously to cover any possible neglect on her part.

'Please don't call me sir, Lucy.' replied Charles quietly, but still a little too sharply as way of a mild chastisement.

'Sorry sir... sorry!'

Her finer points, he found to his amazement, greatly humoured him, and then without giving it a seconds thought said instinctively.

'Do you know of any worthwhile local charities or events Lucy that could benefit from no small amount of sponsorship or a sizeable winning prize?'

She was struck dumb at the request, not expecting that her boss should inquire or think her capable of adding any weight or suggestions, to that topic currently under debate.

'That would depend on what interests you had sir?' she recoiled inwardly at pronouncing "sir" a third time, after he especially had made a point of expressing his displeasure on hearing it.

'That would indeed.' he retorted softening his tone, then added almost as an afterthought. 'What are your interests Lucy?'

'Horses!' came the immediate reply, but she remembered not to add the offending "sir"

'Horses! What charities and events are there in the forthcoming calendar, that we might consider worthwhile to sponsor Lucy?'

'I don't know of any off the top of my head Mr Nostromos.'

Listening very intently to this were several members of the board who instantly put forward a number of equestrian events. One of these struck a chord within Lucy, who belonged to the local pony club.

'There are a couple of local gymkhana's in the next few months, but they might not be as high profile as you would like.'

The return of the grumblings were testament to this last statement, but now the whole board were discussing possible equestrian possibilities in between attacking with much vigour the refreshments.

'Why don't you start a new event and name the trophy after the company, like the Grand National does.' Lucy added almost as an afterthought.

You could have heard the proverbial pin drop as a hush descended on the room; what a fantastic idea, so simple and what great potential for the publicity. Suddenly the whole room erupted into a hive of activity with each board member putting forward a worthy event to sponsor and a varied selection of suggestions for the name of the trophy.

Charles sat smiling; at least he had the board working now as a team. He tilted his head upwards to look at Lucy, she had remained rooted to the spot, struggling to comprehend the scene ahead of her, which must have reminded any onlooker of a chimpanzees tea party.

As the various concepts began to dwindle inevitable down, as nothing concrete could be decided, divisions had sprung open once again. Charles made the announcement that nobody was to leave this room until an event had been chosen. The complaints ceased and a few of the members took on a more serious tone and it quickly became apparent that the only course of action, to truly benefit from sponsorship, was to make it unique, and to that purpose horse racing was eliminated along with show jumping and three day eventing, all in quick succession.

The board now sat in complete silence, what was there left to sponsor. Some time earlier Lucy had taken her leave, but now returned with renewed sustenance, as this had had the desired effect of utilising, and invigorating their collective imaginations. Charles held out some hope.

'So what is there left?' said one board member. There was a collective shrugging of shoulders. Lucy laid out the refreshments.

'I'm all out of ideas!' said another. 'If we're not going to choose horse racing, show jumping or any other kind of equestrianism, what is there left? What is there left?'

'Carriage racing!' blurted out Lucy instinctively.

'What!' replied Willoughby, who had been noticeable by his silence!

'Sorry, I mean carriage driving Mr Willoughby!' she said again with a hint of apology.

'Carriage racing.' he replied incredulously.

'Yes, carriage racing.' Lucy reiterated, copying Mr Willoughby's reply, clearly uncomfortable at being the centre of attention, but angered that she should be questioned or even doubted on any topic equestrian.

'Never heard of it!' countered Willoughby.

'They perform it regularly around the country. It requires great skill and determination!' retorted the irritated Lucy.

'That may be so...' Willoughby started.

'...and I do believe the Duke of Edinburgh is a very accomplished carriage driver.' Lucy said cutting him short. 'And his royal highness used to compete at the highest level, although I'm not entirely sure where and when, and if at all he still does, sorry.' She secretly admonished herself for adding the sorry on to the end of her last statement.

After another moments silence Charles, who had been more than just an interested spectator to the discourse, added his weight to Lucy's suggestion. 'Why not carriage driving? But let's make it more interesting by adding a sizeable purse as prize money, that alone will guarantee the best carriage drivers will compete. We can get experts to set up the course, we can publicise the whole thing locally and nationally, and we can call it the Global Challenge. What do you think?'

'It's unique and if marketed right could be good, very good.' said one of the board excitedly after a moments contemplation.

'That's it then a carriage race it is! We'll agree on the size of the purse for the winner later, but let's get the ball rolling.'

It was obvious to all and sundry that Charles had made the decision and there would be no turning back; those who had prayed he would take a stand were temporarily placated, those who wished for his abject failure, and in all honesty had contributed noting to the debate, secretly rubbed their hands longing for the hour to come to turn this venture into the source of his downfall, humiliation and ridicule.

Once they had discussed all other business, which to be honest wasn't a lot as they were all very tired by this point, the meeting was brought a close and they all retired bar Charles, leaving poor Lucy to tidy up the mess they had all left behind.

* * * * *

Flugal eventually cleared up all the remaining remnants of Pogo's antics and readied all the horses to ride; this was now a necessity for him in light of present circumstances, as Williams had just offered all the girls a job at his yard for more pay, and as soon as one left they all did, except that is for little Rachelle Perkins, her love for Chance and the 'Boys' was too strong for her to leave. In return he gave her free riding lessons as a thank you, but it this had left little time for him to refresh himself and so reluctantly he accepted all the young riders, who arrived promptly, eager and "as keen as mustard", to advance their knowledge in riding, with as much of an open arm as he could without offending them to much as to his physical appearance.

Each of his young charges stood, twitching in eager anticipation, wondering what one of the four they would be riding this very day; Flugal had agreed with them and their parents that they would take it turns to ride each horse and so further their riding experience. The parents on the other hand had a different perspective on how the day was going to pan out and the rough shod appearance of Flugal did little to allay whatever fears and misgivings they perpetuated.

'Good afternoon everyone!' said a rather timid Flugal, well aware how the parents perceived him . 'I hope you're all well and raring to go?' He aimed this next question directly at the children, but it was the parents that answered, in particular Mrs Hogsbottom.

'I do hope we will not get a repeat of the last lesson, Mr Flugal?' bad news travels fast in any climate. 'I have been talking to Mrs Wilson.' She turned to the other parents and Flugal's worst nightmare came true.

'They all cancelled further lessons and now ride at William's farm.'

Flugal spent several minutes reassuring the now agitated parents that that was just a one off and it would never happen again and then went to fetch "the Boys".

Chance had studied the conversation with the parents very closely, he didn't need to be a lip reader to understand the severity of the discourse that has just taken place.

'Come on lads the Master's coming, let's put in a good display today eh!' he might as well have been talking to the bucket that Pogo had thrashed around the stables for all the good it did.

'You put in a good display!' retorted Pogo 'I've had a bucket rammed over my head and rudely awakened.' and he glared at Troy, but Troy being the stronger of the two, meant he didn't hold it for too long.

'It's been a nice old lazy day, why ruin it with a few pesky riding lessons.' added Biff to the debate.

'Because that's your job!' Chance relied sharply. 'That's your job! How else do you think your pampered lifestyle gets paid for?'

'He's got loads of money. I've heard people say so. This farm has been in his family for generations, so why does he feel the need to keep working, but for the love of it! Well let him have the love for it.' continued Biff.

By this time Flugal had reached the stable and begun to lead out the, yet unknown to him, obstinate "Boys", he remarked to himself the great difficulty he was having this time around gathering them collectively in the yard, all that is except Chance, who once again was temporarily allaying any fears he may have had about the forthcoming lessons.

'Well then who wants to ride who?' Flugal posed the question to the group of children.

A tall red headed boy raised his arm bolt upright, lest anybody else should beat him to the punch. 'It's my turn to ride Biff.' said Arthur Hogsbottom.

'Okay, Biff it is.' And he led the expectant Hogsbottom over to where h   e had left Biff beside the wooden set of steps, to aid the young Hogsbottom mount his trusty steed.

Biff glanced over his shoulder and let out an audible snort, Chance scowled at him; he had heard it all before from his friend and he knew it signalled a rise in Biff's obstinacy and reluctance to play ball. He whispered a timely reminder in his friend's ear as this being a necessity to maintaining his luxurious lifestyle, and being able to accept the rough with the smooth.

Arthur planted himself firmly astride Biff strong, stout back only to be greeted with a second longer drawn exclamation of Biff's disapproval at his present circumstances.

After successfully mounting Arthur, Flugal collected Pogo, now wide awake minus the barley wine this time around, and surprisingly chirpy, and positioned him beside the steps. Approaching the pupils once more Johnnie Braumfarten raised his arm and proclaimed Pogo was his ride for this week.

Johnnie Braumfarten was aged eleven, of average height, but above average build and more than capable of handling Pogo. Anybody who knew Johnnie weren't quite certain as to the origins of his unfortunate sounding name, but the potential for jocularity, enjoined with a fair measure of misery was unbounded. Contrary to him being the butt of any vulgar schoolboy jokes he was in fact regarded with great respect and warmth by his contemporaries, due to his infectious laugh and wonderful sense of humour and fun; he was a real "good egg" they would say.

He eyed young Pogo, being led sedately across the yard by Mr Flugal, with glee; it tickled his humour and brought to the surface a steely competitive edge that positively tingled within the young man; "you only become a true horseman", his grandfather once told him, "when you've been dismantled against your express wishes". It hadn't happened yet, but to ride a horse that could possibly be contrary at the best of times would satisfy his deep longing to be considered a "true horseman".

Johnnie stood resolutely by his mother's side, respectful of the horse, until Pogo stood statuesque by the side of the steps, bar occasionally rubbing his nose piece against them; he was afflicted with a most annoying itch at the point Braumfarten scampered across to the steps. Pogo gave the boy a cursory glance as if to say "not you again", as he hurdled them two at a time and only just halting himself a fraction short of the edge of the top platform, tottering, swaying like a tree in the wind or else he would have fallen headlong onto Pogo's back.

'Smart move kid!' said Pogo 'I hope you're not going to ride the way you run or you can run back to mummy!'

Chance again felt those pangs of doom; that today was no better than the last or maybe even worse and he was witnessing the closing chapter on this portion of his life. For once he did not admonish his younger colleague, partly because he may have been wrong and Pogo was cut from a different cloth to which he gave him credit, but mainly because he was tired of chasing all three and trying to instil into them some sense of pride in their work, which was proving a forlorn hope.

Johnnie laughed; it was plain for all to see the seed of his popularity; the loudest merriment as always was reserved for him laughing at himself.

Eventually after much tottering and indecision as to when to make that initial plunge to mount, Johnnie did, grinning like a Cheshire cat. He sought his mother, like all young boys do, for her approval, which he duly received in the shape of her happy countenance.

Now as there were only four horses at Flugal Farm, the number of pupils was reduced accordingly; sadly a large percentage of Flugal's pupils parents had followed the way of Mrs Wilson and transferred their allegiance and siblings over to William's stables. His equine and equipage consisted of over thirty horses, ranging vastly in quality it has to be said, but affording the parents regular, consistent riding.

By now little Rachelle Perkins had reappeared; after her trip out with her grandmother she had walked back to the farm and would now stay until after tea at which point Mr or Mrs Flugal would see her safely home. She was avidly looking forward to a summer of bliss; the school holidays would soon be upon them, and she could spend many more happy hours among her friends.

Her first duty was to lead over to the steps young Troy and her favourite Chance; Troy was as contumacious as ever and ended up being dragged to the steps, now vacated by Pogo and the ecstatic Johnnie, and poor Rachelle expended every ounce of strength she could muster just to get him to within any sort of mounting distance from the platform; she would probably have failed miserably if Chance had not intervened with a few choice words and a nudge from the rear. Troy, as was his want, always considering himself a kind of noble among horses, this being the result of his name, not his birth name it must be pointed out, that being Lucky, but as his birth name proved to be a burden, the proverbial milestone around his neck so it was judiciously altered to Troy. The seeds to the name change were planted, among those who knew him, just passed his first birthday when he accidentally kicked over a sign post, due to a then unknown spasm in his rear legs and used to great effect to awaken Pogo. The post left the ground, sailed through the air with the greatest of ease and firmly planted itself through the rear windscreen of a brand new Mercedes, whose owner it needn't be remarked upon chose a few well learnt phrases from past associations and billed the stables owner.

Six months or so had passed and Troy or Lucky, take your pick, was now keeping a low profile, sauntering casually through a field when he very aware he was not alone. He tried desperately hard to ignore the intruder on his private time, so he walked on, but immediately it became quite apparent that the said intruder was having none of it. Troy or Lucky spun round with full intentions to venting his spleen and laying on the stalker a firm piece of his mind only to be met with the cold dark, menacing, countenance of Geoffrey, a prize Bull, who had just taken top spot at the local fair.

Now it must be mentioned at this juncture that Geoffrey, like all prize bulls, knew his worth and was not afraid to let anybody know or see who he was and what he stood for and to that extent had the honour and pleasure of residing in his own field; if an Englishman's house is his castle then a field to a bull ranks no less highly.

Lucky froze; he had never seen anything so big and brutal as Geoffrey before and could only stammer out that small insignificant piece of his mind. Geoffrey to give him credit looked upon the whole scene with a kind of bewildered amusement.

'What your doing kid?' he said

'Taking a walk!' Lucky replied, then added indignantly. 'Is there a law against that?'

Geoffrey studied Lucky intently; did he really mean that to come out as it did or was it a slip of the tongue, an accident of youthful exuberance.

'After all this is a free country and a horse, being arguably the noblest of creatures that history can easily testify to, should be able to roam along green pastures free from interruptions and inquisitions!'

'Is that so?' The reply had been instinctive, but Geoffrey knew he had left himself open to a repost and he wasn't to be kept waiting long,.

'Does history ever recite the occasion!' Troy started. 'Where the mighty hero rode into battle mounted on a bull! I don't think so!'

Now Geoffrey was by nature a mild mannered kind of bull, apart from a slight tendency to arrogance and self importance, but all in all a pleasant kind of guy all things considered.

'Did Saint George confront the mighty dragon astride his trusty bull? No!' Troy continued. 'It was his ever faithful equine companion the horse!'

Geoffrey furtively slid a step closer, his mild mannered aspect slowly transforming into one of resentment for this arrogant, young, naïve trespasser.

Troy continued to expound the finer virtues of horses over bulls with the direct result that Geoffrey was now totally vexed beyond the point of no return, let out a snort that stopped the young horse in full flow, and made him aware of the precarious nature of his position. Troy the diplomat could still have extracted himself from his horse made hole, but no rather than offer any kind of apology, he stuck out his tongue to its fullest extent, turned on his heels and ran for all his might.

Geoffrey, as anybody with any self respect, followed suit and charged full pelt after the trespasser. Not happy with winding up the owners prize bull and sending him half out of his mind with rage, Troy proceeded to run rings round him at the same time reminding Geoffrey, by example, that this was the reason horses would always be far superior to your prize bull, let alone your average garden variety.

Whilst all the previous events were unfolding the farms owner, William Bodgit, was positioning his tractor into a lower field to aid with the following days ploughing. The site of his prize bull charging "hell for leather", which is how he described the scene later on to his wife, after one of their own horses relegated his jovial nature into that of severe apoplexy, sent his head into a spin. He was in such a hurry to vacate the tractor to go the aid of Geoffrey that he forgot to set the handbrake correctly which resulted in the poor machine wondering aimlessly down the field, he only reached the gate when the potential catastrophe dawned on him! To add insult to injury, who should he espy driving up the road for a visit but Florence Jambon, one of his wife's closest friends and William's fiercest critics! As in all such circumstances personal welfare always resumes priority and Bodgit ran after the tractor, only just boarding it in time to swerve it through the open gate, into a neighbouring field and lodge the vehicle in a sea of mud. The look Florence gave him at the appearance of the tractor semi-submerged lit up many an after dinner conversation for years to come.

Troy meanwhile was tiring of this game of mock the bull and realising the gate, through which he had passed to enter the field, was still unlocked and open ran for it. Geoffrey, as can be imagined, was not at all amenable to the idea of his antagonist getting off scot free, followed suit, but unfortunately for him Troy, with the blessing of youth, bounded towards the gate adding a few more valuable seconds on his pursuer and kicked the gate shut with his now infamous hind legs. Geoffrey, carrying far more weight than his adversary, and therefore more inertia failed to negotiate the closed gate. The result was he jammed his head between the cross bars and there he remained for six hours. Troy found the whole episode highly amusing and four days later he was sold to Flugal and renamed.

Back at the present Troy reluctantly reached the steps and resigned himself to yet another humiliation at the hands of today's youth, and was mounted by one Timothy Wellington, a lanky kid with a tendency to jab his heels fiercely into the sides of whatever poor beast he happened to be aboard. Troy received three of four sharp kicks for his pleasure.

Chance needed no cajoling and when Rachelle turned to fetch him there he stood raring to go. Rachelle greeted his arrival with a sweet, firm kiss on the forehead and told him how much she loved him and he would always be her favourite.

'I think I'm going to be sick!' Troy remarked at Rachelle's open show of affection. Rachelle, as if she knew perfectly well what Troy was saying, chastised him for being jealous.

With Troy now free of the steps, Chance assumed the position and Glenda Forthwright sat astride him; she was a nervous child and Chance was the perfect ride to help her allay any fears she might have. Rachelle, who happened to be in her class at school, had recommended Chance to Glenda.

Flugal led the way into the indoor riding arena, which had been a sizeable cow shed in its day and, after a small investment, now housed the training area furnished with jumps, cones and lettered marker boards at each corner and half station along each leg; the purpose of these was to turn the riders clockwise and counter clockwise in order they may practice turning the horse left then right, using either leg, whilst either walking, trotting or cantering. It was a recent addition to the stables and Flugal prayed that it would lead to more steady work, as they were now not reliant so much on the weather, which would in turn lead to reduced cancellations and the opportunity to rebuild his stock of fine riding horses.

Flugal for all the faults with his charges, for which he was blissfully ignorant, preferred instead to turn a blind eye to those he saw in a hope they might change, was an expert horseman; he had the ability to spot a fault in a horse in a matter of minutes, coupled with discovering potential where others found fault; Troy, "the trouble maker", as he was informed on his purchase of the horse, "was a good for nothing beast", this coming from the owner of the unfortunate impaled Mercedes, who was none other than Mr Williams. He clearly failed to see the passion and pride Troy felt in being a horse.

Chance, as befits one of age and respect, took the lead round the arena; with the exception of Glenda, a new student to Flugal Riding School and one Flugal himself had high hopes for, all the rest had been riding there some time and enjoyed immensely his style of teaching.

They started off with a sedate walk, so the horses could warm themselves up before the excursions really began, this increased into a slow trot down the longer sides of the arena followed by a walk along the shorter sections. Flugal kept a keen eye on Glenda lest she felt uncomfortable with the pace of the lesson. After about ten minutes of this warming and familiarisation exercise for the pupils Biff could not help himself and piped up.

'How long are we going to have to keep this up? I had a nice warm stable going and now I'm relegated to this!'

Chance had secretly prayed the proceeding ten minutes silence would bode well for the lesson and on hearing Biff's lamentation nearly fell into a rage, but managed to control his temper.

'It's what pays for your nice warm stable!'

It was not what Biff wanted to hear and he grunted his disapproval so violently that poor Arthur popped out of his seat by a good foot and landed back in the saddle with a bump, the other kids thought it all highly amusing and laughed, all this just added to Biff's frustration.

'You're not drunk are you? asked Pogo, who had kept the precise whereabouts of the barley wine a secret.

Biff, Pogo and Troy now laughed amongst themselves, the result of which was their riders bobbled up and down to their great delight, while all the time trotting and walking around the arena.

'Behave will you!' cried out Chance, he could see the ramifications of allowing this jocularity to continue; the horses would lose concentration and disaster could ensue.

Flugal brought the horses to a halt and inspected the three one by one. The riders giggled and interrogated one another of the experience of riding a real hobby horse.

'Hobby horse!' Pogo was less than chuffed to be regarded in such a degrading manner. 'Hobby horse!' he said again.

Chance could and should have said it served him right, but he didn't and it was a decision he was to regret. Pogo strutted forward with an extreme air of indignation.

'Hey hobby horse!' chided Biff who then broke in a violent fit of laughter, resulting in the inevitable bouncing up and down of the lucky Johnnie; this only served to broaden the grin on the boys face and cause his infectious laughter to peel around the arena and set the whole lot off again. Even young Glenda chuckled at the sight of Johnnie bobbing along on Pogo's back. Flugal called to Pogo to rein himself in and gather some self control. This initial mild chastisement exercised by trainers the world over was a vain attempt to maintain discipline, before more heavier restraints are brought to bear; Flugal refused point blank to use force to control "the Boys" and so spoke in soft tones to the misbehaving Pogo.

'Better do as your told old boy.' Troy called out to Pogo.

'Or the old man will lose his temper and you'll only get half-rations for supper!'

'Show some respect.' fumed Chance.

Glenda's smile evaporated as soon as she could sense the change in mood of Chance and instinctively tightened her grip on the reins. Chance to his eternal credit and being an extremely experienced trainer ceased, cooled his anger on Troy and Pogo at the first signs of Glenda's apprehension, but the others weren't to know this and Chance's silence was now taken as a sign that he had either agreed with them or was not going to interfere any further with their fun. It was now Biff's turn to wind up the already taught Pogo.

'It's better than being a rocking horse Pogo, and your name does rather suggest that the occupation of a hobby horse is more suited to you!'

'Yeah!' agreed Troy

'I am not a hobby or a rocking horse.' answered Pogo, his indignation rising by the second. 'I am a professional!'

Chance saw his chance to put an end this infantile debate and he took it. 'Then act like one!'

If Chance thought for one second that his was the final repost in this childish debate he was soon to be sadly mistaken for Pogo, now erroneously believing the whole world was against him, wasted no time in showing his displeasure. Flugal tried a second time to control his charges, for it must be added that the lesson had continued on regardless while this incident unfolded and it was not lost on the viewing parents that Flugal did not seem to have his usual authority today.

The two antagonists continued on unabated to rile young Pogo, who had shown to Chance at least a semblance of self respect after his "I am a professional" comment, something he had come to believe recently he lacked.

'Gentleman!' Chance said mildly and in a monotone of great austerity. 'We all no doubt agree that it was a worthwhile joke for its time and Pogo you would have laughed the loudest had it been any of us, especially me, but that time has passed and the lesson must take priority, so if you would all be so kind as to have a professional regard for your pupils, let us continue and save any joviality for later.'

There was moments silence at Chance's mini speech; he had never talked so long and it such revered tones for many a day, but it didn't last long; fun is fun to the young and responsibility be damned, that's the domain of the old and aged.

Pogo was by no means going to take such slurs lying down or trotting around an arena for that matter and went on the offensive.

'Listen fat boy!' his opening gambit was aimed squarely at Troy.

'I've got more brains in my left hoof than you'd ever get in a lifetime!'

Tory snorted at the attack and Biff drew a long deep breath through his teeth, signifying the utter abandon and danger Pogo had placed himself in; Troy was no slouch when it came to a foot race; he failed to match Pogo over a sprint, but more than made up for it in stamina and this coupled with his prodigious strength made him a formidable foe indeed.

'As for you..... ' Pogo's retaliation on Biff was cut short by Chance.

'What has got into you three, I thought you were friends?'

'Were friends!' said Troy, his icy stare never leaving Pogo.

'Yeah, were friends' repeated the recipient of the icy glare.

'Have you no professional pride? Do you want to be out on the street? Have you any idea of the precarious position we are all in?' Chance may have been talking to the brick wall for all the good it now did him.

Flugal frowned; it was so unlike his horses to neigh and grunt and have such a disapproving attitude towards one another. He spoke to them softly, his commands forceful in a very informal manner, but still they continued. He could tell from the body language of the parents that a storm was brewing in that quarter,w and he felt the first symptoms of that cold clammy sweat that greets the initial realisation that doom and despair have come a knocking at your door.

Biff didn't wait for Pogo to make an advance on 'As for you.' and went on the attack cracking hobby and rocking horse jokes one after another, as if he was the walking oracle on the subject. And it all came to a head two laps of the arena later; Troy hissed out a comment regarding Pogo's tack resembling a horse he'd once seen on a Punch and Judy show; it was the straw that broke the camel's back for Pogo and he spun round and confronted the formidable Troy. This caught Troy momentarily off guard and he retreated one step to the astonishment of Biff, Chance tried to step in and act as peacemaker, but even he realised in his heart of hearts that this moment was inevitable and backed off with a deep mournful sigh, resigned to what was to follow.

Flugal was flabbergasted at the sight that met his eyes; Troy, Pogo and Biff now all faced off against one another, each with a fearful look of malice and malignancy, the children who had laughed all the way through this debacle had not lightened up and each cheered on their charger with great gusto.

One of the parents called over to Flugal to ask what the hell was going on with his horses, and if he couldn't control them to bring the lesson to a speedy conclusion. Flugal reassured them that the horses were just being playful rather than contrary, but he was fast running out of ideas and could feel the beads of sweat now running down his back as he tried desperately to get the boys moving again.

He looked pleadingly at Chance, whose Master's utter despair and breaking heart only incensed him further and increased his rage at the youngsters.

But the three friends, now turned enemies, refused to budge to any kind of pleading, coaxing or petition from either

Flugal or Chance. The kids were still chatting away, furiously trying to gain an upper hand on their horses, willing him on in whatever venture the three of them had chosen, because the whole episode could not but strike any bystander with anything other than utter bemusement and amazement. This bemusement ultimately caused Arthur's mother to open the gate to the arena, confront a now panic stricken Flugal, as this was one situation he had never before heard of let alone faced, and demanded that Arthur start riding or have his lesson finished as she was not going to pay for him sitting, stationary cracking jokes with the other three. As is the way in all walks of life, whenever a group of individuals stand on common ground and pause to see who will take the upper hand and make the first move, so it was here; no sooner had Arthur's mother aired her displeasure at the outcome of the lesson than the other three took it upon themselves to adopt the same line and demanded equal rights for their child.

Flugal could feel and sense his head starting to spin, what was there left to do. Once again he looked to Chance for inspiration and guidance as he felt he may have a solution. Chance approached the three friends still maintaining a form of Mexican standoff.

'What do you think you three are doing?' he said studying each in turn. 'You have all displayed an utter lack of respect for each other and Mr Flugal. Any hope he had of resurrecting the fortunes of Flugal Riding Stables has just evaporated with your completely irresponsible display. I hope you are all very happy!'

Neither horse offered Chance a reply, but displayed nothing but unstinting resolution to stand firm on their obstinacy and arrogance, which beggared all belief. It left the parents no alternative.

'Arthur!' cried out his Mother. 'Let's go!'

'Oh Mum, do I have to! This is the best lesson ever!' replied a dejected Arthur.

Johnnie's mother didn't need to say a word; the austere look she gave the poor boy was all he needed to know, that it was wise to obey without objection.

One by one the parents removed their children and poor old Flugal was finally left desolate and alone in the arena with nothing but the sound of the departing vehicles breaking the silence of the late afternoon, but still he refused to chastise "the Boys".

Chance felt he had to say something. Flugal stood motionless, his head hung low, as if he was examining some insect crawling about his feet. Slowly and painfully he raised his head and the sight swelled up unparalleled anger and resentment in Chance, even Rachelle sucked in a deep breath which caught all by surprise: Flugal was crying.

He hung his head down again and slowly trudged out of the arena into the yard, it had started to rain and the weather clearly mirrored the pain and inner turmoil this proud man was suffering. Little Rachelle walked after him a ways then told him she would see to the horses; Flugal nodded an assent, but kept walking not making a sound, even his tears were silent.

Back in the arena Rachelle arrived and begun to lead out Chance. 'I'll come back for you three later, come Chance.' her stinging tone was not lost on any of them.

Once in the yard she felt the need to express her fears and anger and who better than her beloved friend.

'I fear this could be the end of our friendship.' And she wept a little as she spoke. 'It's not looking good Chance. I heard them talking earlier; they're in deep financial trouble and could lose the farm, and now potentially without any students. I will surely have to leave now. They will have no choice, but to sell up!'

Chance nodded.

'They will take you all away and I'll never be able to ride you again.' With this she broke down and cried uncontrollable. Chance rubbed his head up against her shoulder, she responded by kissing him tenderly on the forehead, her tears wetting his nose. Chance had to bite his lip to prevent any exclamation of anger at his stable mates. Even the livery horses stood quietly reflecting the sombre mood.

Now in the stables Rachelle removed his saddle and tack and prepared him for the evening, she had guessed right although she wasn't to know that there would be no more riding tonight. She took her time; the more the others stood there the more they might begin to understand their folly.

Rachelle arrived back into the arena hoping to find three contrite horses, but she was to be sorely disappointed, they had just continued the argument once all had vacated and it was once again in full flow.

'Don't you ever stop!' she shouted.

This did the trick, for they all ceased there and then and looked on little Rachelle with much incredulity; she was supposed to be a tame, timid little girl and here she was venting her anger with a force to be reckoned with.

Troy was the first to speak. 'Don't look at me Rachelle! It's not my fault that somebody can't take a joke!'

'Yeah!' reiterated Biff

'Joke eh!' replied Pogo, and off they went again, before being interrupted a second time by Rachelle.

'Enough!' she shouted at the resumption of their neighing, grunting, scraping of hooves on the floor and swaying of heads, dangerously close to one another that it was no small wonder that neither of them was not knocked unconscious. Once again the three combatants ceased their verbal sparring.

'Enough! I don't think any of you realise the position you have placed yourselves in. There are only four of you left now and Mr Flugal was relying on you today and you've seriously let him and everybody down.' Rachelle continued on in much the same vein for many minutes until she had exhausted herself of things to say; it made her feel good to vent her anger. She had no idea that Pogo, Biff and Troy understood every word, how could she.

One by one she led the horse back to the stables. The last to leave was Pogo; the other two had still left with a parting smirk or sneer in his direction just to make it plainly clear they both blamed him for his lack of humour on the whole scenario. Rachelle returned and Pogo solemnly trotted by her side.

'Just didn't like being called a rocking horse.' he uttered. 'They used to tease me about my walk when I was young Rachelle.' Rachelle remained quiet.

'I think I was born with a twisted back or something and it has affected my walk. Their jokes and name calling, brought back all those bad memories.' and then after a moment's hesitation when everything the young girl had said had hit home. 'You're right Rachelle I over reacted. I should have been more professional like Chance said.' Approaching the stables Pogo stopped, it gave Rachelle a start.

'What's wrong Pogo?' the tenderness in Rachelle's voice, bearing in mind the scene she played out only moments before, added extra weight to her concern and increased Pogo's resolve to lay the blame firmly at his own feet.

'Nothing, nothing you can't fix. More professional, I should have been more professional.' And he entered the stables.

6

Flugal sat with his head in his hands while his wife hurried herself around the kitchen making a broth; she had not seen him this worried or sickly in many a year, not since coming back from an exotic holiday to celebrate their wedding anniversary when he had contracted a virus. That was a worrying time, he was laid up for nearly a month. She felt his forehead, he was running a fever.

'I'll call Doctor Little!'

'I'm okay, please don't fuss!'

'You're not okay Mr Flugal. You will drink this broth when it's ready and in the meantime it's straight to bed.'

Flugal knew it was best not to argue and to be honest the thought had already occurred to him.

'I will cancel any lessons left today, and inform them off your ill health.'

'That's if they still want to turn up!' Flugal replied dejectedly.

'You should have more faith in people.'

'I wouldn't blame them if they didn't.'

Flugal hauled his tired body off the chair and trudged out of the kitchen and upstairs to bed.

Chance said nothing when Pogo arrived; he hadn't said much to other two either, he just couldn't bring himself to look at them let alone open any discourse.

Rachelle, now totally out of sorts, went solemnly about her duties, her cheerless expression mirroring Chance's heavy heart. Through the clanking, clinking and creaking of the old leather saddles and the respective tack could clearly be discerned little sobs and sniffles, which could not help but add to the air of despair.

Rachelle finally presented the first of the horses, Troy, with his evening meal, but for once he abstained; instead he looked dejectedly at the net holding his hay and said nothing. He too had had a moments reflection.

'What's the matter?' Rachelle said affectionately, blowing her nose with her handkerchief. 'Lost your appetite? Don't worry about it, everything will be okay.' She didn't believe a word of what she was saying, but she was the sweetest of creatures and no matter how vexed and angry she grew with anybody it could never last; she hadn't a hateful bone in her body, she loved them all.

Once the three sheepish companions had been catered for she came to Chance; he had kept his silence, eying his stable mates from over his stable door for any sign of remorse and guilt and had satisfied himself that they had begun to understand the gravity of the situation that they had perpetuated, if not caused.

'I do hope you've got an appetite Chance.' The concern was etched across the young girl's face and Chance eying the feed immediately tucked in with much vigour, the others followed suit and soon Rachelle beamed a smile of satisfaction.

'They were all waiting for you Chance. That just goes to show what well bred horses they are and that today was a one off.' Again Rachelle secretly could not bring herself to believe a word, just a nagging hope that all would be as before.

The crunching of tyres over gravel captured her attention and she turned to view Doctor Little arrive and enter the farmhouse.

'What's up? Who's that?' said Chance.

'Mr Flugal's not well.' she answered instinctively.

'Is it serious?' asked Biff

'Find Nugget!' injected Pogo.

'I'm here.' And Nugget's head appeared to them from behind an old bedroom cupboard that used to hold tack for one of the livery horses

'What are you doing in there?' Troy said in an interrogative tone.

'Grabbing some 'zeds' I'm knackered'

'We need you for a mission.' commanded Chance.

'I'm your dog.' And with that Nugget sprang, belying his age, out into the stable block and as quick as a flash had passed Rachelle, Chance and the "Boys" and was bounding across the yard.

'Hang on!' Chance shouted. The command halted Nugget in his tracks. 'You don't know what it is yet!' Nugget took a smart about face, returned and gave Chance his full attention.

'Master Flugal is unwell. Find out everything you can and then report back here.'

'Aye, aye.' replied Nugget, and if he could have saluted he would have, turned on his paws once again and disappeared into the evening.

'I pray it's not serious.' Chance said in a soft tone after his friend had vanished from sight into the house. Rachelle caressed his forehead and this gave him a brief respite which enabled him to forsake his worry for the briefest of moments.

It was now that the four friends became aware of the grumblings of discontent from the other stable blocks, as their residents aired their less than favourable views on the turn of events.

Nugget crept into the house unobserved; it was a custom of Mrs Flugal to leave the rear door slightly ajar for the purpose of Nugget's freedom, she had no qualms on this point, where others might question the lack of security, she would simply add that "Nugget saw to all of that and if they dared to enter, then he wouldn't allow them to leave".

The house was quiet bar some distant voices that Nugget immediately sourced from upstairs, and he moved expeditiously towards them.

'He has a fever and needs complete rest!' Nugget immediately recognised the dulcet tones of Doctor Little coming from the Flugal's bedroom. 'If there's no improvement in the next twenty-four hours then give him these; he must take one, twice a day with food and then you can let me know how he fares.' Nugget was struck with the good Doctor's tone; it was stern with a hint of concern and worry. Flugal and Doctor Little had been lifelong friends.

'Thank you Doctor. I'll make sure he stays in bed.' was Mrs Flugal's reply.

'Is there anybody who can help run the farm? Can the kids help?' added the Doctor.

'We'll be okay, don't you worry about us. Anyway Tom's abroad with his regiment, and June is in her last year of college; I don't really want to worry them at this stage, he certainly wouldn't!'

Nugget pressed his ear hard against the door straining to catch every word, nuance and if possible snatch a fleeting glimpse of the scene unfolding through a crack between the door and the frame. He held his breath. There now wasn't a sound emanating from Flugal's bedroom. He feared the worst when Mrs Flugal broke the silence.

'Doctor Little said you must stay in bed dear.' Nugget mouthed the exact words back to himself to reinforce his memory of events, for when it came to relay them to Chance and the "Boys".

The Doctor and Mrs Flugal approached the door. Nugget had only a few minutes to extricate himself from his position and finding his options seriously limited opted for the old faithful; he lay down flat on the floor, tail wagging and looked up at the two of them as they exited the bedroom with a pair of sad, doleful eyed that cried out with sorrow and pain.

'Ah, look Doctor, Nugget knows something's wrong and he's come to stand guard and protect his master.' Nugget smiled.

'He's a fine dog Mrs Flugal, the envy of many a farmer in these parts.'

'I've always liked you Doctor Little.' Nugget replied still smiling, and sitting up.

They had only proceeded but a few steps along landing away from the bedroom, towards the top of the stairs when the good Doctor's voice dropped to a whisper. Nugget's fur stood on end, this did not sound good.

'Has he been unduly worried or stressed of late?'

'What do you mean?' Like all people, Mrs Flugal did not like others knowing their business, even to an old friend like the Doctor, and so kept mute regarding their precarious financial position.

'Has there been anything out of the ordinary that might have caused him extra uninvited stress?'

'Nothing Doctor.' She suspected their old friend knew exactly what was going on behind the scenes at Flugal Farm; there were plenty of gossips in the local community, theirs was no different from all the many thousands of residential and non-residential areas around the country harbouring their fare share of rumour mongers.

'His blood pressure was a touch on the high side.' the Doctor started seemingly lost in contemplation, then quickly added, so not to cause Mrs Flugal any extra discomfort. 'Well, like I said he needs plenty of rest, and make him take that medication if you don't see any improvement in a day or so, but I'm sure he'll be fine and on the mend by the end of the week.' Here he paused to gauge her reaction and then once happy that he hadn't upset her, descended the stairs followed in close proximity by Mrs Flugal. Nugget spied them carefully, not wanting to give away the true meaning of his visit, for even without Chance's request he would have surely been found in no different a circumstance.

The Doctor and Mrs Flugal continued to talk about many things as they navigated their way to the kitchen; she offered him a cup of tea, which he politely declined and then bidding his farewell, departed to another eager patient.

Nugget crept surreptitiously down the stairs, halted in the hallway to gauge the movements of his mistress. Once he was content she was otherwise absorbed, he slid quietly out of the backdoor.

Now in the freedom of the yard he sprinted over to the stables to his waiting friends.

'Well?' surprisingly it was Biff that answered first, probably because he was the first to realise his presence.

'How is he? said Chance, as he approached Nugget.

'Doctor said he had to take medication if he doesn't improve!' replied a panting Nugget. 'He's in a bad way; we must be in serious trouble for the Master to be bed ridden. I've seen him ride out some difficult times, but this sends shivers down my spine!' Then realising they were all alone. 'Where's Rachelle?'

'She had to go home, it was getting late. Her grandmother came and collected her.' Chance said this with a touch of melancholy; he had now sadly and regrettably come to accept the end was nigh and he wasn't to have many more days with his friend. Each second with her was going to be precious to him.

'Is there nothing we can do?' Pogo by now was displaying a keen interest in the welfare of his Master.

'You've done enough!' Chance was still seething. 'You've all done enough!'

'All is not lost.' carped up Troy. 'All is never lost!'

'And what d'yee propose?' the voice butting in on the conversation hadn't been heard of for such a long time that many thought he might have upped and gone back to Scotland. It was Nigel.

'And what d' yee propose laddee?'

All stood in silence; there was nothing to propose, it was animal folly to even begin to comprehend any thoughts of rectifying Flugal's dire financial situation.

'Nigel, you're a worldly wise kind of pig.'

'Don't look at me, I haven't a clue!' Nigel replied losing the accent.

'Will you at least ask around? Enquire among all your contacts to see what they know, they might just be able to shed some extra light on our plight. ' pleaded Chance.

'That I'll do.'

'And you to Nugget. Let's hope Troy is right, that all is not lost!'

For the next couple of days all was quiet at Flugal Farm; the mistress busied herself with cooking and housekeeping and entertaining all those persons who came to visit the invalid, made arrangements for any remaining students to re-book lessons; she was happily surprised to find out that they all still wanted to ride there, even those whose mother's had threatened to cancel. Rachelle appeared at her usual time, never late, and made sure all the "Boys" were properly catered for and the private owners came and went, attending to the livery horses, at all times of the day as Flugal Farm didn't officially close until after nine most evenings. It remained unseen at this time, but the Flugals were deeply grateful to young Rachelle for her hard work, loyalty, never asking for anything, just happy to be working around horses and amongst the ones she loved.

As promised Nigel, aided greatly by Nugget, and a pair of odder looking spies you could not have been placed anywhere in the world, asked around. There wasn't a stone they didn't leave unturned, but they came up a blank every time; from the local and surroundings houses and farms nobody could add anything, other than what they already knew about a loan extension, and governing by Flugal's recent illness the answer was undoubtedly no. About their financial position they could only surmise that Misters Williams and Bennett were more than likely involved.

Then one day who should show up at the house than that very same odious Mr Bennett. Chance and the "Boys",

Nugget and Nigel knew nothing at this juncture of this gentleman by sight, but as animals always seem to sense danger, a trait bred out of humans through domesticity, they all agreed he was a most detestable looking man!

They were all about to wax lyrical on their objections to his visiting Mr Flugal when Rachelle appeared carrying a newly polished saddle.

'Who's that that's just turned up Rachelle?' said Biff immediately realising what an utter stupid question it was.

'Let me try.' said Nugget 'Who's car's that?' he barked.

'Are you talking to me?' replied a smiling Rachelle.

Nugget barked out his question a second and then a third time. Each time Rachelle answered she followed it with a giggle, as Nugget's animations grew more comical the harder he tried to get his question across.

'You're doing it all wrong.' Interjected Nigel, and then he to asked away. By now Rachelle was nearing the point of hysterics, not through fear, but the amusement of hearing all those grunts, snorts, whimpers and barks.

After a few more minutes of this carry on, all parties concerned had reached a dead end.

'This is getting us nowhere.' Pogo said stated the obvious.

'Nugget you go and jump on the car and see what Rachelle says, she's bound to mention the owners name.' Troy had had a moment of inspiration.

'You do it!' said Nugget indignantly. 'I'm no vandal!'

'Like I'm going to jump on a car!' neighed Troy in return. 'And anyway I've had the pleasure, if you can call it that, of watching you pee on many a car tyre in the past.'

'That's different.'

'How?' said Biff joining the debate.

'I'm marking my territory!'

'Well go and mark it on that car then!' continued Troy.

'No!' By now Nugget was feeling most grieved and embarrassed at the task being presented before him and stood his ground as a consequence.

Rachelle all during this conversation was giving each enquirer the double take, so much so that her neck was getting mighty sore.

'What are you all talking about?' she finally said.

'NOTHING!' they all shouted in unison.

Rachelle eyed each one suspiciously, she knew something was afoot, but unable as she was to decipher their lingo she was at a serious disadvantage.

'Look!' she blurted out with much frustration. 'You're all up to something and you better tell me or none of you is going to be fed for a week!'

'No way!' shouted Pogo; Olympic champions always being the first to complain whenever their favourite training aid is removed. 'Tell her nugget.' he pleaded.

'I can't.' he pleaded in return. 'She doesn't understand a word I say!'

'Well neither do we half the time, but it doesn't stop your talking!' Biff interjected not wishing to be left out.

'Steady!' Nugget was greatly perplexed at Biff's input into the conversation, but Chance soon reassured him.

'They don't mean a word of it Nugget! Rachelle's got them spooked. "I'm not going to feed you for a week" I can't believe you fell for that old chestnut!'

'Alright!' Nugget finally acceded 'What can I do?'

'You better tell me now what's going on?' Rachelle's patience was finally wearing thin.

'Show her the car, then run back here. All we need to know is the name of the owner.' Troy's clarity shocked even him, he then sheepishly retreated back into the stables, although he needn't really; his sagacity was much envied amongst those present.

'Okay, okay I'll pretend... pretend mind to pee over the car and if Rachelle says the name of the owner you all owe me big time!'

Never could a deal have been ratified so quickly or succinctly as Nugget's that very day. He knew that he had been backed into a corner and the only possible outcome was for him to carry out the dirty deed, even if it was only in simulation.

Now Nugget's aim, as he himself saw it, was to pretend to urinate over the driver's side front wheel, and it needs some minor explanation as to why the front wheel and on that side; that act of marking one's territory with boundaries in the canine world has been discussed and aired in many books, radio and television programmes, and it would be pointless if the very act itself was not known to the recipient, so dogs naturally aim any scent over the driver's side front heel as this would be the spot where it would be impossible not to observe any urinating having taken place.

Nugget therefore weighed down with a mixture of reluctance, duty and embarrassment sloped out of the stables and ventured into the yard, taking a line "as the crow flies" towards the vehicle. He was watched every step of the way by a wary Rachelle and his own comrades, their eyes burning into the back of his head. At about half way he stopped, took a cursory glance over his left shoulder secretly hoping that they would have honoured him with a little privacy, but he was to be bitterly disappointed; every pair of eyes stared back unblinking, even those from the livery horses, watching intently his every move! He could still make out Rachelle pleading with all and sundry to tell her what the hell was going on!

Finally Nugget reached the car of the unknown owner and cocked his leg, but to his extreme displeasure, Rachelle said nothing, she just stared straight back at him until such time that the penny ultimately dropped and she figured it all out, not that Nugget's finishing position left it in any doubt.

'Go on say something.' he pleaded, his leg tiring by the minute. 'Please say something, anything!'

Rachelle failed to avert her gaze from Nugget's raised leg. Instead her gormless expression perfectly suited her inner most vexations at that time.

'I'm standing here looking a complete prat!' shouted Nugget to his friends in the stables, who were watching proceedings with an ever increased interest

'You're going to have to pee!' shouted Pogo now approaching a state of uncontrollable laughter.

'Don't start me off!' Troy stated, seeing Pogo's shoulders let loose the tell tale signs of the giggles.

'If he starts laughing he'll never go.' joined in Biff.

'He's going to have to do it!' Chance like all in the stables had not relaxed his attention from Nugget, and he himself could feel a smile creeping slowly across his face. 'Go on pee!' he shouted

'Chance! I can't!' said poor old Nugget, in his later years, he thought, he should not have been subjected to such indignation.

'Pee!' shouted Nigel and burst out laughing.

It was the cue to let the flood gates open and great roars of laughter emanated from all corners of the yard, livery horses included, and filled the early evening air. Even Nugget started to see the funny side and gigged away.

'Nugget!' roared Rachelle 'Stop that!' This was more fire on the flames of joviality and the decibels increased.

'That's, that's' she nearly said it. 'That's.....that's whatshisnames car!'

'Oh great.' thought Nugget lowering his leg.

But as is normal in us all, the very fact about discussing the need to "break water" often brings about the act itself, and so it as with Nugget. He now had an incredible urge to urinate, and as he was near the ideal spot to mark his territory and satisfy all demands plus gain a few favours in the long run, he thought "happy days", and urinated all over the front side driver's wheel.

'Nugget!' Rachelle screamed again. 'Mr Bennett, the Bank Manager, will be furious!'

'Ah, it is Bennett's!' two or three said in unison. 'Excellent!'

'Not that Bennett?' quizzed Nigel

The two or three exclaimers remained mute; theirs had been a collective assumption that nobody would query them and they would be enlightened themselves without feeling in any way inadequate. Now they were the centre of attention.

Rachelle could still not remove her gaze from Nugget, who skipped joyously and contentedly back to the stables, along with a few choice words from the livery horses which concerned him not a jot, satisfied that his was a job well done.

'Well?' said Nugget on reaching the stable door. 'This Mister Bennett is now the proud owner of a car with one very wet front wheel?'

'We need to find out what he's really like.' said Chance, and all eyes once again fell on the couple of "know it all's" Biff and Pogo; Troy by this time had distanced and disowned himself from ever knowing anything about the mysterious owner of the vehicle.

'We're all waiting with bated breath.' said Nigel, shuffling closer.

After the obligatory silence that precedes great admissions of falseness, it was Pogo who first gave the game away averting his line of sight to the floor and started muttering to himself something inaudible. Biff's reaction to Pogo's submissive body language and admission of guilt was to bluff it out as far as possible in the vain hope that salvation might be nearby; this as it turned out was the best policy, for young Rachelle saved them both.

'How could you Nugget!'

A perplexed Nugget, who moments before was anticipating seeing his friends extricate themselves from their self made mire, now stood once again the centre of attention.

'I....I....' stammered Nugget 'I...only did what came naturally.'

'What?' continued Rachelle. 'What are you trying to say?'

'I said.' piqued Nugget suddenly altering his tone, he did not want to show any anger towards Rachelle. 'I was only doing what comes naturally to a dog.'

'You do know that is Mr Bennett's, the Bank Managers car!'

'Aaaah. No I didn't before, but now thanks to you I have been enlightened.' he replied. 'Way hey guys, I peed over a Bank Managers car.' and then just as quickly added. 'How about I give him some added interest?'

'And Mr Flugal,' continued Rachelle, 'not being very well at present is probably the result of his visit. Things are not going particularly well for him right now Nugget; he faces the very real probability of losing the farm.' Rachelle began to choke up with emotion at the thought and paused for a moment to collect herself. 'And you and I and all your friends.' And she waved her hand across all the animals in the stables to signify to Nugget whom she meant. 'You may never ever be able to see each other again! If that happens....' She had purposely intended the melodramatic finale, but its end result brought about her tears and she looked over to Chance, who had taken a step forward and was nuzzling her softly.

'I didn't know. You can't blame me for that!' Nugget was clearly very upset ay the very notion that his mini adventure with the car should bring about such a catastrophe.

'It's not your fault old friend.' Nigel gave him a friendly bump with his shoulder. 'We've known that this has been coming for a very long time!'

'Yep!' agreed Chance.

'You knew surely before now' Nigel quizzed Chance.

'I've had my suspicions!'

'How come you never told us!' asked Troy

'I tried to tell all of you, but you wouldn't listen, you only wanted to argue!'

The three protagonists stood silently musing Chance's accusation; he was right and they knew it. They had no come back.

'We can't turn back the clock, so let's get on with it! We've gotta find a solution!' Nigel's pragmatic approach to any form of problem solving was much in need and the stable mates all agreed and collectively put their heads together in a conference.

Rachelle dried her eyes and watched all the animals with utter amazement; as any human could not help but do when confronted with a group of animals clearly involved in earnest discourse and they are on the outside looking in.

'What's going on now?' she said quietly to Nugget as he brushed by her.

'Meeting!'

'What?'

'Meeting.' he repeated.

To poor, young, naïve Rachelle it was a series of whimpers and she was left none the wiser. 'You can't be serious! It must be serious.' She finally muttered to herself. she had not followed Nugget into the group, paying them and their moment the utmost respect.

Once the group had formed, each horse had earlier let themselves out of their respective stable, with Nugget and Nigel holding court on the floor, and formal discussions broke out. It was surprisingly Pogo who noticed that Rachelle had not joined in. Chance took this opportunity to take a small step back into his stable, nodded his head and called her forward.

Rachelle realised instantly the significance and wasted no time in filling the empty space beside him. Now in the group she lowered her head in anticipation of the resumption of the meeting; not that she was in any position to understand any of the discourse, as has been pointed out on previous occasions, but it made her feel as if she was part of the gang, which she had become; it was her unwitting disclosure of the owner of the car that had enlightened them all to yet another turn in the troubled circumstances of their master Mr Flugal.

* * * * *

We should now turn our attention to the arrival of Mr Bennett at the Flugal household, and the events that led to a bank manager scheduling such an unusual visit at such an unusual time, to one of his less than favourable clients.

Bennett had received a phone call from none other than that odious Mr Williiams following his adventure in the car with Nugget and it had not gone unnoticed by him, when he had been out exercising his prize horses, of the small, straggle haired hound eyeing, curiously his progress along his private road that bordered the river; he needed the thrill of the run, the fresh air to clear his thoughts, as to his next plan of action to gain control of Fugal Farm and fulfil his desire to own and manipulate the lands and ultimately the people around his part of the county; Williams saw himself as a landowner of the old feudal system that dominated counties and countries during the eighteenth and nineteenth centuries and before; he believed this was the only way to truly, efficiently run the land and to personally prosper from its ownership. The more he could own the stronger and more powerful he would become.

Williams was of a new breed of despots who believed that true power must be cultivated at source to achieve tangible gains. He had a grand plan to buy up as much of the available land as was permissible, whether that be farmland like Flugal's or residential, his portfolio must be impressive, and then charge exorbitant rates of rent to the tenants as well as reaping in any cash profits or grants in the case of the farms.

In order to execute his devilish plans he needed the help of all and any unscrupulous profligates that he could find and recruited them freely on a strictly commission only bases; his thinking, not without merit, was that he would pamper to their greed, their love of money and that they would be more hungry and willing to succeed knowing it was their only chance of remuneration.

He always sought to get the upper hand in business; not that in itself is a bad thing, but the way it can either be executed or manipulated can be construed as clever or evil depending entirely on your point of view: Williams without doubt tended to lean more towards the evil. He hid his actions well and covered his steps obsessively, stepping aside when the time was ripe to allow unsuspecting fall guys to carry the can. As long as the ends satisfied the means his conscience was clear-"all's fair in love and war" he told himself, as a way of suppressing any negative thoughts that dare raise their heads above the parapet. Never had a doctrine been carried out so effectively or diligently!Bennett was going to be one of those unsuspecting fall guys fished out by Williams, he knew his weakness and his desires and they suited his purpose.

Bennett's obvious weakness, which made him essential to Williams master plan, was that he only saw Flugal as one of the bank's customers who owed money, and who needed to borrow more, and as that was a prime candidate for repossession and removal from the bank's black list, as he called it, of those who dragged down the bank's rating in terms money owed and collected.

Here, presented to him by Williams, was the ideal situation to force Flugal to either pay the bank all debts owed or be faced with the spectre of receivership, he could then recoup the money, prove his worth in front of the bank's seniors and plant his foot firmly on the next rung of the ladder to senior management.

Due to his illness Flugal had cancelled a few of the many appointments Bennett had arranged to call time on the loans, but when Bennett had personally heard through the grape vine that Flugal as unwell he hurriedly arranged this meeting. Miller had instructed the staff before his departure, not to discuss any clients around him or Bennett, especially Flugal; if he found out by his own recognisance then so be it, but don't under any circumstances tell him. The bank staff had heeded Miller's warning as much as Bennett knew Miller would give it and he took every opportunity to eaves drop on conversations about the staff and its customers, and so found out about Flugal's illness and made the necessary arrangements to visit.

Flugal was powerless to refuse; he himself had only received notification of the appointment the day before and in his delirious state forgot all about it, so when Bennett turned up on his doorstep, seemingly wholly unannounced, he thought it prudent to allow his entry into his house and to see him in the front room, no matter how abhorrent the thought was to him.

Bennett now stood over the stricken Flugal, seated in his favourite chair. Mrs Flugal had followed him very closely, making sure he only went into that room, figuring that he would case the house to gauge its true worth.

'I wish I could have arranged to see you under better circumstances!' said Bennett with all the insincerity he could muster.

'I got your letter.' replied Flugal.

'Good!' Bennett got his answer in quickly so as not to give Flugal any chance to make an excuse to cut the meeting short. This would all be done at his pace.

'Then we don't need to waste any of your recuperating time on explanations. May I sit?'

'Of course. Tell me-'

'-the bank has been more than fair to you Mr Flugal!' Bennett again cut him short, while seating himself across from the man. A tactic he used often to keep people off guard; he had replayed the conversation over and over in his head many times and was ready to head off any and all avenues of escape.

'The bank' he continued 'is now in a position that it requires any loans owned by you and outstanding to be repaid in full. Yours Mr Flugal is outstanding to the tune of ten thousand pounds and I might add, on top of that, you have requested a bridging loan of another five thousand, which with simple mathematics would have made a total of fifteen thousand pounds!'

Flugal laid perfectly still, his eyes never left Bennett's odious, insidious expression, he was talking to him like a child and loving every minute, his malevolence and sheer enjoyment of being in possession of the upper hand reflected itself in his icy stare.

'We are in a very awkward situation here Mr Flugal.'

'Is that so?'

'Yes, that is so!' The first hints of resentment towards Flugal tinged his reply.

Flugal felt the first signs of contentment; he had found a way to get a rise out of Bennett and decided to continue with blasé answers to his questions and statements.

'How are you going to pay your loan Mr Flugal?'

'Money's the usual way Mr Bennett!'

'And you don't have any!'

'I'll get it!'

'How?' Bennett began to panic at the first hint at losing the control he so desperately wanted to maintain, but he immediately suppressed it.

'I'll get it, that's all you need to know!'

'May I remind you Mr Flugal that our bank is a respected financial institution and that any transactions must be over and above board, and if I require to know how and where you are to come by these funds, I shall require you to inform me!'

'No!'

'Sorry!'

'No!'

'You are making this very difficult Mr Flugal!'

'Good! You will get your money. That's all you need to know!'

'Mr Flugal-'

It was Flugal's turn to cut short Bennett. '-how and where I get the money is of no concern to you, Mr Bennett.'

Mrs Flugal during these opening exchanges had remained quiet, although there were more than a few occasions that she nearly aired her views and opinions.

Bennett's fire was well and truly stoked and the flames of passion shone forth through the obnoxious veil that passed for his countenance.

'I will draw up the appropriate papers for you to sign Mr Flugal. I will make you accountable!'

Now Mrs Flugal could no more hold her tongue than a sieve holds water and let rip her first volley.

'We have been loyal customers at that bank for over thirty years! We have paid all our bills on time and legitimately, and the bank has profited immensely from our custom. You have made many a fine penny out of us!'

'That maybe so.' but he had no time to finish before the Lady of the house tried gainfully to force home her point.

'We are in need of some help Mr Bennett, and as far I can see the bank has just slammed its door in our face.'

'The bank has been more than patient with you!'

'When?'

Bennett paused, but his silence only gave more ground to Mrs Flugal.

'And now we get this attitude towards us, which I might say borders on the vindictive!'

Mrs Flugal, not because she had been standing behind Bennett, but primarily because he had not anticipated through all his minute planning and contingencies for any verbal onslaught by her, put him immediately off guard. Panic again rose within him, so he reverted to the tried and trusted routine that he himself had perfected when dealing with awkward customers and situations; looking them straight in the eye, unblinking and deny, deny, deny. It was an occupational hazard he accepted.

Bennett looked Mrs Flugal straight in the eye and categorically denied any personal vendetta against them or anybody, even though doubts had periodically surfaced; these were dismissed as quickly as they arose, he convinced himself this was just banking policy and an unequivocal lie. Bennett did have a short list of customers he personally wanted rid of at his bank, Flugal was the first and probably the most high profile of them, he had been a good friend of the old manager Mr Miller and that in itself made him public enemy number one.

'I don't believe you Mr Bennett!'

'Deny, deny, deny.' he thought, this was the game plan while this little act was being played out. After a while Mrs Flugal frustrated at not getting anywhere near a straight answer from this pernicious man, broke off her attack. Bennett in his own little mind had won and once again turned all his efforts on to the seated Flugal.

'What I need to know Mr Flugal is when and how you are going to clear this debt of yours with the bank?'

'Like I said before, you will get your money. That's all you're going to get right now!'

Bennett adjusted his coat, straightened his collar, took a deep breath, giving all the outward signs of about to deliver an enormous verbal onslaught on the sickly patient, but in reality he had no more to give and simply reiterated that he would draw up the necessary paperwork and then retreated in a most fearful temper. Mrs Flugal followed him out of the house and to his car at a respectable distance.

'That went well!' Mr Flugal said sarcastically as his wife re-entered the bedroom.

'What an awful, awful man! Have you been having to deal with him all this time?'

'No only lately!'

'There's nothing else for it, I'll have to sell the family jewels or heir looms or anything that I can lay my hands on!'

'No!'

'Yes!'

'No!'

'Yes! Are we going to carry on like this all day?'

'I couldn't stand to see you part with them!'

'They are only material things and I shouldn't covet them and they do have value; the important thing here is that we need money, we are in bad shape!' She could sense gloom starting to descend over her husband. She leaned forward and planted an affectionate kiss on his forehead. 'We've just had bad luck that's all. It's nobody's fault, just bad luck.'

'Every man wants to provide for his family. I feel such a failure!'

'You're not a failure. We've just had bad luck that's all.' she reiterated. 'I'll sell them for a good price. Selling any livestock doesn't bear thinking about. It should be a last resort.'

'I'm not selling "the Boys". I can't!'

'If it comes to that then we'll have to.' said Mrs Flugal seriously. 'They are not performing, with the exception of Chance, but he's older and wiser, and knows better.'

'I can't sell any of them! We'll give them one more chance eh! If we are to get out of this then we are going to need all the help we can get recouping revenue.'

Flugal was unhappy and deeply troubled that his wife should be reduced to selling family heir looms, but she clearly had made up her mind and would not reconsider reversing her decision to sell these family treasures, some of which had been in her family for nearly a century, so he forced out a smile to raise her spirits.

'Something will break for us. You see.' She was much cheered by the return of his optimism and enthusiasm; it is strange that people when faced with the most frightful dilemma find unheard of courage and determination when this alone can sometimes be all that is needed.

7

Bennett drove at a break neck pace down the country lane that led from Flugal farm to the main road and back into town. He swore oath after oath under his breath against Flugal; round one to him, that's how he saw it and all that preparation had been wasted by that damn woman, why had he not made any contingency plans to counteract anything she would have to offer, because he hadn't thought her capable that's why, and that was his folly: Never again!

As the gold Mercedes approached the junction with the main road something caught his eye; it was a young man erecting a poster on a nearby bus stop, Bennett paid him no more attention and continued on his way. If he had bothered to enquire as to the nature of the poster he might have saved himself a lot of future trouble and gained a valuable head start on his quarry. As it was he didn't.

The young man finally had the poster just the way he liked and took three or four steps back to admire his handy work; 'yes it was straight' he thought 'better than the last one and you could read the heading without any difficulty'. It was of impressive design for a poster featuring a magnificent horse drawn carriage headed by four majestic animals, and with a style of font made for easy reading.

HORSE CARRIAGE DRIVE
PROUDLY SPONSORED
BY NOSTROMOS GLOBAL INDUSTRIES
FIRST PRIZE £25,000
ALL COMERS WELCOME

And then in smaller letters further down the page came the dates, a description of the three separate disciplines involved, and at the bottom a contact name and number from which to gain an entry form.

Satisfied with his work he quickly returned to his van, before anybody might spot him and start asking questions, and drove off to the next location that required a poster.

* * * * *

The group of friends had stood quietly outside the empty pony barn, anticipating they didn't know what; Pogo, Troy and Biff, being younger than Chance and therefore more inexperienced, expected some kind of firework display to erupt from the house between Bennett and Flugal, even though he was a sickly man, and be heard all the way down in the yard. They were left in no doubt by Bennett's fierce countenance on exiting that they had been fighting violently tooth and nail.

Chance stood motionless with an occasional glance over to Rachelle, who nervously mucked out the stables for although she was aware something was transpiring, busied herself in an attempt not to think about it to much. Chance was deeply anxious to the outcome of this inauspicious meeting, which he realised immediately could only have been planned by Bennett. Chance was by nature a very placid horse, the main reason Flugal always put the novices on him, but now a strange sensation returned to haunt him; he had not felt this way since his racing days; it was an almost hate like feeling bubbling away beneath his calm exterior; here was a man who potentially could and would destroy his livelihood with no regard for any of the farms occupants let alone the dire straits he would place the owners in, and at their age there would be no second chance.

During his successful racing career, which culminated in his second place in the Derby, it had made him the toast of the country where he lived and trained. The never ending competition ultimately left a sour taste in his mouth; he developed a severe dislike for all the other entrants and competitors in his race, it was the only way he could handle the hard, competitive world of horse racing and it manifested itself in several very dislikable personality traits. This hate had eaten away at him and along with his injury prematurely ended his racing career; too tired to carry on, he was sold on as a washed out has been, no good to anybody! Then Flugal discovered him languishing away in a field, fat overweight, seeing out his days quietly with no hope or ambition. Flugal gave him a lifeline: Teaching, and he loved it. He discovered to his astonishment that he enjoyed immensely the pleasure riding gave the humans who rode on his back, and this in return ignited once again his own love and desire to be ridden. He was proud to be a horse.

He saw Bennett exit the house, with the mistress not to far behind keeping a close watch on his movements; he stopped short of the car and investigated his driver's side front wheel and car body, a few words were exchanged with Mrs Flugal which they could not hear, and then he darted a steely glare over at the stables. Nugget instinctively jumped back out of sight. Chance held Bennett's glare, unblinking he wished this bank manager could read his mind and get a taste of the revenge he wished to execute on behalf of the Flugals.

Nugget felt a strong sense of guilt engulf him during the silence as they awaited for Mr Bennett to leave; he was an old dog with an extremely high sense of fun; he liked nothing better than to crack a joke, pull a practical joke and generally muck about, but coupled with this was a strong feeling of loyalty to the Flugals and his friends, and if he thought for one second that anything that he had precipitated could lead to any kind of hurt for them then he could not forgive himself. So Nugget stood quietly musing with his thoughts.

Next to him stood Nigel, who had originated from a pig farm from the east coast of Scotland. He came to Flugal farm a couple of years ago quite by accident, literally; he ended up in a lorry carrying him and his friends to market that just happened to blow a tyre directly outside the Farm and Nigel took the opportunity to make a run for it.

Nigel now viewed himself as the rebel of the outfit; if anybody dared to say go right, he went left, he was definitely not one to follow the crowd or convention, and he took every available opportunity to inform anyone in ear shot, often displaying open resentment to having orders and others beliefs forced upon him. He had lived close to the edge and survived, all his comrades had perished on that truck and they and that guilt, for having lived, never left him.

Flugal didn't need a degree in animal psychology to recognise the symptoms in Nigel and left him well alone to potter about the farm; he was good company to the horses, regularly paying them visits on the days when the weather kept them inside or lessons were scarce that day, and he and Nugget got along famously, regularly enjoying fun and games and generally fooling around the yard. Nigel for his part developed a deep rooted affection for Flugal; he had openly lied to the driver of the truck when he was examined as to the whereabouts of the stray pig, knowing full well he was holed up in his stables.

As far as the other animals were concerned, Nigel like all pigs showed great sagacity towards all problems and challenges that arose from time to time. They all trusted his judgement. So when it came to finding out any information it was naturally to Nigel that they should turned to. He had ventured after a while around the side of the house where he knew he could possibly get a better view of proceedings and hear any of the conversation between Bennett and Flugal from the front room.

On returning to the stables, just minutes before Bennett exited the house and left, he was grilled by his friends.

'Couldn't hear much, but what I did hear is not at all good guys!'

'Oh!' was all Pogo could muster.

'What exactly was said?' enquired Chance, and Nigel had the all the ears of the stable; he related everything that was said and done to the best of his ability, adding the caveat at the end that he may have misheard or misinterpreted some things.

When he had finished you could have heard the proverbial pin drop.

'Damn, we're really in trouble!' Biff summed up what all were thinking.

'This is the best job I've had!' exclaimed Troy

'It's the only job you've had stupid!' said Biff. For once Troy didn't take offence, the situation was dire.

'It's up to us!' Chance said trying to display some semblance of resilience to his younger compatriots who were waning in the face of such bad news.

'You're damn right!' Nigel took a step forward. 'Where there's a will there's a way! The solution is out there somewhere guys and we've got to find it!' he had no sooner said his piece and he was out of the stable and off on his quest.

Rachelle had positioned herself by Chance's side, she felt safe there, and earlier had had the first inkling of what the animals were discussing; the realisation had just sprung upon her on hearing the inflection in Nigel's grunting. 'It sounded almost human.' she thought and as Nigel continued and then the others joined in, clearly replying to him, it dawned on her exactly what they could be discussing. It was like that final piece of the jigsaw fitting into place; she decided wisely to keep her thoughts to herself. For the moment at least.

* * * * *

Bennett continued to speed along the winding, twisty country road that depicted most journeys along this part of the land; the drive started to calm him and he even whistled and sung along to a popular tune on the radio. His melody was broken up by the ring tone on his mobile phone. He examined the number on the lighted screen, and seeing it was Mr Williams very nearly refused to answer and let it be taken by the voice messaging system, but right at the last, approaching the ring that would automatically send the caller to leave that message, he answered using his handsfree mike. 'Mr Bennett.' he said knowing full well who it was; he didn't want anybody to know he logged clients phone numbers on his phone; it was mild show of vanity, but he forgave himself for it.

'Ah it's you Mr Williams!' he felt grotesquely obsequious and shook his head slowly.

'You will need to give me minute to pull over!' he carefully parked the car by the side of the lane after previously checking his mirrors.

'Yes Mr Williams, what can I do for you today?' Mr Williams digital voice pierced the silent pause left by Bennett.

'Flugal Farm!'

'What about it?' Bennett's curiosity was aroused.

'Is it for sale yet?'

'Not yet!'

'When then?'

'There are procedures that we have to adhere to first Mr Williams.'

'I understand, but what will be the asking price if you don't mind me asking?'

'I don't rightly know!'

'Whatever anybody's offering I'll match it and more!'

'That's a very serious offer indeed Mr Williams, considering nobody knows its true value yet and I have absolutely no idea when or if the farm will be sold or not.'

'Oh!' Bennett could immediately detect the menace and annoyance in Williams tone. 'I was led to believe a sale was imminent!'

It was now Bennett's turn to feel anger and resentment; somebody in his office must have spoken, he vowed to find who out it was and have them fired immediately; another good reason he surmised to spy on your work colleagues and subordinates, how dare they discuss bank business outside of work and especially against and without his express permission.

'Who may I ask informed you of the imminent sale of Flugal Farm?'

'I must have been mistaken Mr Bennett, but while I'm on the subject, I would very much like to talk to you about Flugal Farm and of what benefit I can possible be to you and the bank in these undoubtedly difficult times.'

'Difficult times maybe Mr Williams, but not for you!' he thought. Bennett frowned at hearing Williams laugh after his last comment; difficult times indeed, who did he think he was talking to!

'No Mr Williams, not for me.' he finally said, trying hard to hide the rising contempt he held for this man.

There was a moments silence. Bennett immediately recognised he had stung Williams with his curt reply, and there would have to be repercussions, Williams was that kind of human being.

'My secretary will call to make an appointment Mr Bennett, now I really must go goodbye.' And he hung up.

A perplexed Mr Bennett mulled over Williams comments trying to discover any hidden meaning and to how he came to know that Flugal Farm was indeed to be considered for sale in the due course of time, if Flugal could not meet the overdue payments, which he clearly could not.

He fired up his company car and once again made his way back to the bank; his first mission was to ascertain the source of the leak from his office, he could or would not be put in that situation again where he was at a disadvantage by any clientele, then he must organise the meeting with Williams; he was a powerful and influential man in the community and one who most definitely must be kept reluctantly onside. He chastised himself for his own stupid pride.

'He may well buy Flugal Farm' he thought 'and make himself the most powerful man in the county. What an idiot, of course he'll buy it. You could tell from his tone that he was eager, almost desperate to accumulate the farm, why did he have to aggravate the situation.' This last thought troubled him, but he didn't know why, just the mere thought that there was an outlet for the farm, and the bank recouping some of its losses should have more than calmed any misgivings he might have had.

* * * * *

Rachelle had finished her chores, said her goodbyes and had gained a lift from Mrs Flugal back to her grandmother's, but before she departed she entered the stables and said one last farewell, almost as if she too knew the final outcome and wanted to enjoy every available opportunity of their company.

'Goodnight all.' she said

'Goodnight.' they all replied simultaneously.

She knew that she did not have to express in words the true relationship between her and the animals, so she simply smiled and departed for the car.

Half way across the yard she had the uncontrollable urge to turn to face the stable, and there to her delight was Chance his head resting on the door then he nodded swiftly in that way she knew so well that signified, to her, he was wishing her a safe journey home, goodnight and see you tomorrow all in one movement.

'Goodnight Chance.' she called across the yard and continued her way to the car.

'Chance really loves you, you know.' Mrs Flugal said as she fastened her seat belt.

'I hope so!'

'Oh, he does. He cares for you very much.'

'You think he does?'

'Mr Flugal says so, and he's a fine judge of horses. None better.'

'I love Chance too.' and then just as a slimmer of guilt was about to rear its ugly head. 'I love them all really, I really do, but I love Chance the best!'

'We know.'

Rachelle smiled at the thought of Mr and Mrs Flugal talking about her and Chance over the kitchen table discussing who would be the best person to ride and take care of him if anything should happen to them. This final thought evaporated any signs of a smile and she was quick to hide the worry from Mrs Flugal. The car drive was over in a flash; funny how journeys vanish as soon as they are started when there is plenty to occupy the mind. Rachelle got the distinct impression that Mrs Flugal was in a similar state.

She said her goodbyes to Mrs Fugal, with a promise to see her tomorrow around eleven, then entered the house to make sure her grandmother was okay and in need of anything.

8

The sun rose bright and cheerful over the eastern sky; it was an auspicious start, the birds sung high in the tree tops, their melodies ringing in the birth of the new day.

Nigel was the first to show, trudging across the yard to where his breakfast usually awaited him. Only today was different; where once stood a bowl full of delicious leftovers from Mistress Flugal's experiments, intermingled with his everyday feed, even her disasters were remarkable indeed, there was nothing.

Nigel stared at the incredulous sight that befell his eyes, that of the empty bowl. Over at the house nothing stirred, so he had no idea or reference by which to govern how long it might possibly be before any delicious leftovers would or not would present themselves before him.

Back at the stables, the others were only just starting to show signs of life.

Chance was the only one still asleep; the side effects of old age, Pogo was stamping his feet in an attempt to accelerate his already poor circulation, Troy shook himself violently for the same reason and Biff just stood staring bleary eyed out at the yard at the blue, grey, morning light tinged with gold, as the early morning sunlight filtered in through the side of the stable block door.

Nugget was curled up behind a pile of straw; out of sight and out of mind is how he thought and saw after last night's excitement and debate; he had decided then to sleep in the barn with his mates. He was tired of talking and wanted only peace and quiet to collect his thoughts; time was short, and sooner rather than later an anecdote to their predicament would have to be found.

'Things are going from bad to worse.' Nigel muttered on entering the stables.

This exclamation woke Nugget from the light sleep he had drifted into as the morning broke. 'Not a scrap to eat anywhere! Not like them to miss me feed!'

'We need to investigate.' said Troy, taking a giant step forward, clearly volunteering himself for the task.

'I'll go.' yawned Nugget appearing from behind the bale of straw. 'It's best if I go, you'll scare the living daylights out of them if they find a horse staring at them through the window!'

'I suppose.' replied a reluctant Troy.

Nugget stretched himself, damn arthritis he thought, just creeps up on you all of a sudden; one minute your bounding across the yard, fields, jumping turn stiles, chasing rabbits and the next minute, wallop! Your struggling even to see a rabbit let alone chase one; at least with cars they stop at traffic lights giving you time to catch up. He chuckled at his little joke, the others just frowned thinking the poor fellow was slowly going mad.

'Poor Nugget!' said Biff once he was out of ear shot. 'All this is taking a toll on the old man!'

'It's starting to take its toll on all of us.' Nigel stated indignantly.

Chance was still asleep and they envied him his peace; no one was going to wake him only to be presented with the proposition of no food today.

Just then the sound of crunching over the gravel entrance to the farm broke off all conversation and captured their attentions.

Nugget who by this time had managed to negotiate half the distance of the yard, froze in his tracks, as he was now faced with the glaring headlights and grill of Uncle Dave's land rover. Fear had gripped him, and he made like a rabbit caught in a similar situation, and stayed rooted to the spot, either that or his arthritis had returned with a vengeance, and he found he was unable to physically carry out any actions or instructions issued to him by his over active sense of self preservation, baying frantically for him to jump out of the way.

The land rover bared down hard on our poor canine friend, coming to a halt just inches from Nugget's glistening, moist nose.

Nugget's eyes bulged at the enormity of the land rover front section; he could smell the strong aromas of burning rubber, oil and hot metal on metal. Then promptly fainted!

Uncle Dave blew his horn, to alert the Flugals to his presence, whilst still seated in the vehicle, espying the windows at the front of the house for any sign of life. There was nothing. After a short pause he vacated the vehicle and walked around the rear of his car to the front door and wrapped loudly three times with the knocker. Still there was nothing.

Dave frowned; 'Unlike old Flugal not to be about at this time of the morning, especially with a handful of hungry animals to feed and a passed out dog in his yard.'

'Damn funny business!' he added a few seconds later.

'Damn right this is a damn funny business!'

Uncle Dave was startled to find himself being addressed by a rather large pig with a series of short, sharp grunts, and as all humans do he only interpreted it as just that.

'You look as though you've had a mighty good breakfast this morning? Feels like we're on emergency rations around here!'

Uncle Dave ignored Nigel's comment as more incomprehensible pig talk and made his way around the back of the house.

'Tried that!' Nigel called after him, but Dave was gone. 'Deaf...' Nigel would have finished the sentence, but he was struck by the sight of Nugget groggily getting to his feet.

'That was cool Nugget!'

'Sorry?'

'That was cool!' he repeated. 'Remind me to try that technique when trying to flag down a car....not!'

'Who is it?' asked Nugget still trying to get his head back in order.

'It's that Dave guy! You know the one that appears from time to time. He's deaf a as a post though!'

Nugget saw Uncle Dave appear round the front of the house scratching the top of his head in bewilderment.

'What seems to be the problem? Nugget asked Nigel.

'Nobody home!' the reply had surprised Nugget just as much as it had baffled Dave on his arrival.

'Nobody home.' Nugget repeated Nigel's reply instinctively.

'Yeah nobody home!' Nigel looked at Nugget with more than a hint of concern; it must be the shock, or did the car hit him, he could not tell.

'Nobody home eh?'

'Yeah Nugget nobody home!' Nigel gesticulated over to Chance, who was now awake, and the "Boys" that Nugget wasn't at all well in the head.

'Hello Nugget old fella!' Dave knelt down and stroked him behind the ear; this seemed to bring the old boy round a little. 'Did I scare you with the car?'

'Scare him you damn nearly killed him!'

The grunts and snorts once again grabbed his attention. 'You again. Do you know why it's so quiet?'

'If I did I wouldn't be standing here having this conversation with you now would I!'

'I'll take that as a "no" then!' replied Dave, who in truth thought it best not to aggravate the pig; from previous experience he knew the dangers of annoying such animals, so he just ignored him.

Dave rose and studied the yard for any tell tale signs that might point to the absence of his friend and neighbour; he had asked him to look at the drainage of that field and he could always carry on inspecting it until they turned up, they must have gone out, shopping or such like. 'No' he thought he must investigate some more, this was highly unlike old Flugal, he loved the early part of the day, he always said he got most of the days chores out of the way or under way in the quiet dawning of the day.

'Try the windows and if that doesn't work then there's nothing for it but to call the police!' this last part of the sentence was said with a certain resignation, for to call the police meant admitting something other was up and it was invariably not good. Nigel grunted his approval.

Slowly, but surely he tried all the windows, 'Good job he's not got any close neighbours or the police would have been here by now and then she'd have some explaining to do.' he thought of Mrs Flugal's embarrassment at being the talk of the town if he found himself unable to solve this mystery, but it was to no avail, all the windows were securely locked. Then an idea occurred to him.

'Drive down the road a ways to the first public phone and call the house number.' he said quietly to himself.

'Use your mobile!' butted in Nigel. Again Dave ignored him.

'If only I had a mobile or better still somebody else's.' Dave was one of the last surviving band of the old school, who whole heartedly refused to own a mobile phone even if it is to their own detriment.

'If I had one you could use mine or Nugget's!' chimed Nigel sarcastically.

Nugget's punch drunk smile failed to ameliorate the growing concern building steadily within his friend.

Dave climbed back into the land rover and fired her up. Nugget had taken a step to the side to let Dave pass, Nigel stood beside him placing a protective hoof around him.

After Dave had vacated the yard Nigel trotted over to the stables, poor old Nugget laid down where he previously stood and let out a deep sigh.

'Need to take a look at Nugget!' Nigel's concern was mirrored in the faces of his friends.

'Did the land rover hit him?'

'I don't know Pogo, it was hard to tell. If it didn't it sure gave him a fright!'

'Let's us have a look.' Chance now said unbolting his stable door and stepping out into the yard. He remarked to himself what a wonderful day they had in store as he approached the prostrate Nugget, who failed to open an eye. He examined his friend for any external signs of injury.

'Are you okay old timer?'

'Never felt better!'

'You don't look to hot, if I may say so. Did that car give you a fright?'

'Just a little.'

'You've brought out the fatherly side in Nigel.'

'Didn't know he had it in him.'

'Neither did we!'

Nugget still had not looked at Chance and spent the whole conversation in the same state.

'Well you're okay then.'

'I'm fine.'

'Anything I can get you?'

'No, no you're okay.'

Chance for once found himself running out of things to say to his old buddy; this was definitely not like Nugget; he always had such a lot to say, cracking jokes, telling ripping yarns, most of which the farm knew he made up as he went along, but they didn't care they were good stories. He once again took the opportunity to examine Nugget for injury, but there were no signs of impact with the car.

The sounds of hoofs over the yard signalled the arrival of the other three and Nigel, Troy, Biff and Pogo had paid particular attention to the subtle way Chance had extricated himself from his stable, and now they encircled poor Nugget, each in turn making a visual inspection. All the concern over the dog had completely taken away the worry of nothing to eat.

'He looks fine to me!' said a cheerful Troy. 'You had me worried.'

'I'm fine I tell you. I just need a moment.'

Now that they were satisfied their good buddy was going to live, Troy made his way round to the house to investigate, Biff meandered over towards the fields and Pogo stayed beside Chance.

'That car came mighty close.' said Pogo.

'Too close!' Nugget now opened an eye, which was met with three cheesy grins. 'My whole life flashed before me!'

'Excellent.' replied Pogo, 'Not excellent that you had a fright, but I do look forward to hearing your biography.'

Nugget now sat up on his haunches. 'You know something?'

'What?' they all said together.

Nugget's vacuous expression highlighted the personal meaningless of the experience he had just undergone.

Biff returned from the fields will a slightly forlorn look. 'How was it? Your life?' he remarked before Nugget could speak, clearly signifying that he had heard his exclamation whilst inspecting the fields.

The remaining spectators looked on him with an air of incredulity at the level of his question.

'How was your life?' Biff said again while searching around the yard for something else to investigate.

'Well how's yours?' replied Nugget.

'Mine sucks at the moment!'

'Mine too!' piped up Troy back from the house. 'Although I'd be the first to admit that a large percentage of the ill fortune currently befitting the situation is wholly self inflicted!'

Chance tried hard to hide the feeling of self satisfaction and pride at hearing Troy say so; an admission of guilt was the first step in rectifying their problem, now if he could get them all pulling in the same direction, if only he could find some solution. In his heart he knew it would reveal itself when the time was right, and he felt pride in Troy for being horse enough to voice his personal responsibility in this drama.

'But who's got the rough end of the stick. Tell me that?' said Nigel

'Well it's not yours!' injected Troy.

Nigel had a valiant point, but the meaning was clearly misunderstood by the others, so he felt the need to expound. 'It's old Nugget; nearly half killed so he could see his own life in a home movie. That's who!'

'How was your life Nugget?' repeated Biff, confident that his question this time round would have some weight behind it.

'Not quite what I imagined.' lamented Nugget.

Just then their attention was diverted and drawn once again to the crunching of the gravel by the returning Uncle Dave; whatever had been the main reason for his mini adventure it clearly had not come to fruition; his dark, gloomy countenance mirrored the inner turmoil at having failed to ascertain any reason for the locked house.

Seeing the animals now grouped around a distraught and shaken Nugget aroused intrigue, suspicion and only deepened his concern for his friends. The intrigue was born out of his hearing the animals, mainly Nigel's dulcet tones, chatting away to themselves, and the mixed and varied resonances of the listeners and debaters. Suspicion rose dramatically within him and his unease increased tenfold when all those pair of eyes began interrogating his every move, because similar to Flugal with Nugget, he had a growing suspicion that this dog, as well as the rest of the farmyard, had the secret ability to understand every word he was saying. He decided to test his theory.

'Any of you know where your Master and Mistress are?' he said from inside the car.

The animal's conversation ceased immediately and they muttered amongst themselves.

'Nobody say a word!' said Nigel.

Uncle Dave felt the hairs on the back of his neck start to raise; was that a coincidence or did they truly understand. He was loathe to try again, but try again he must.

'So do you?

Again they all looked at him, and he swore there was an air of mockery in their faces.

'That's Uncle Dave you know, Flugal's pal that helps out around the farm.' whispered Nugget.

'Can't say I've paid him any mind.' added Biff.

'Is he for real?' said Pogo. 'Does he honestly think I'm standing out here unfed for my health?

'Yeah!' agreed Biff

'Yeah me too!' joined in Troy. 'I'm starvin'!'

'Now, now gentlemen you're letting the game away!' Chance quietened down his friends. 'He's looking at us mighty strange. Quick act dumb, which you lot shouldn't find too difficult.'

'Yeah let's act dumb.' laughed Nigel, and off they all went.

'Acting dumb Pogo, is your specialty.' Troy baited Pogo and he rose to it.

'I'll follow your lead Troy, you've got as much sense as that wooden horse!'

Nigel and Chance both laughed; it was good banter.

Uncle Dave stood now by the side of his car incredulous at the spectacle before him; two of the horses were squaring up to each other, one horse and a pig were clearly laughing, while the fourth horse was itching to get his four pennies worth in!

'I ain't no blockhead!' Troy retaliated.

'Just saw dust in them there ears of yours!'

'At least saw dust is useful!'

'To soak up all the muck around the yard, perfect description for your job around here!' Pogo continued unabated.

'But it's a job!' Troy squared himself closer to Pogo, who squared himself straight back. 'There's no room for loafers on this farm!'

'Flugal's got a nice pair of loafers.' Biff finally chucked in four pennies worth.

Nigel keeled over in a fit of laughter; he could hardly breathe he was laughing so loudly. Chance took to leaning against the garden fence that protected Mrs Flugal's prize flowers to aid himself, he was laughing so uncontrollably. Pogo was playing the unamused card to perfection.

'Well she does.' continued Biff.

It was only fuel to fan the flames of friendship and the laughter increased in decibels.

Uncle Dave found the animal's mirth infectious, and it enveloped him until he too started to laugh, but he didn't know why!

'My you animals is crazy!'

'Crazy is as crazy does!' chimed back Nigel.

'That I can believe.' Dave found himself answering back the animals and he secretly chastised himself for his unbelievable stupidity.   'Chatting to a pig, come on Dave wise up!'

'I'll have you know some of the wisest animals in all of Christendom have been pigs!' Nigel was not letting that comment go.

'Like who?' said Biff in an attempt to divert any poking of fun away from him.

'There's been many a fine, upstanding, law abiding pig that has graced this world, only to be taken before his time!'

'Like who?' Troy now joined in.

'Well let me see; Arthur the Anglo Saxon pot bellied pig, he rode by the side of his name sake and comforted him during times of great personal stress and anguish; Henry the lesser spotted pig, he lived throughout the reign of King Henry...'

'....which one?' barked Troy.

'The Eighth of course....'

'.....you're making these up as you go along!'

'I am not!'

'Yes you are; Henry the lesser spotted pig! You're having a laugh!'

'Henry was a famous pig among us pigs.' Nigel had got to the point of no return and was now starting to believe his own whopping great stories. 'He lived miraculously all through the reign of that great King narrowly escaping beheading at every turn.'

'Narrowly escaping being made into a pork chops you mean!' said Biff

'I resent that!'

'We all resent pork chops.' Chance said again trying to diffuse the situation, but secretly loving every minute of the banter.

'Give us one more and then we'll decide whether you is telling the truth, or a pack of whoppers!'

'Well said Pogo.' said Chance giving his comrade an ally.

'There are hundreds of famous pigs, where do you want me to start.'

How about with the truth?' Biff winked at Troy, who smiled back; it wasn't often that you got to take the rise out of Nigel. He was normally to smart for that.

'Well..........' Nigel paused trying to buy time to think of a famous pig that his friends could easily believe, and extricate himself from his pig made mess.

'Well!' said Troy.

'Well.' Said Biff.

'Well.' said Nigel 'Humphrey!'

'Humphrey!' Troy, Biff and now Nugget said in unison 'Humphrey; who the hell is Humphrey!'

That was it for Chance and Pogo, they were off, this time rolling about the yard laughing their heads off.

Uncle Dave's vexed expression was in complete contrast to the merriment displayed by the group of friends; even Nigel started to giggle at the stupidity of his stories, but felt compelled to continue.

'It's not common knowledge that Dick Turpin, the famous highway robber of the seventeenth century, had in fact a pet pig by the name of Humphrey.'

'Humphrey Turpin!' they all said through the raucous laughter.

'Exactly. Humphrey Turpin.' Nigel knew the game was up, but couldn't resist stringing it along for all it was worth. 'Well as history tells us Richard 'Dick' Turpin, the most famous of all the English highwaymen was originally a member of the infamous Gregory Gang that robbed and pillaged the area around Epping Forest.'

'Where's Epping Forest?' asked Nugget.

'Around Essex and London, but that's not important right now!' replied Nigel patiently.

'Where's Essex?' asked Nugget again.

'It's a big county in the south of England!' Nigel was relishing telling his story; they all knew that it was utter rubbish, but they didn't care, it was a great yarn. Even Uncle Dave was taking a closer interest in the proceedings.

'The Gregory gang one night broke into a farm not far from London in order to hold the occupants hostage, and find out where they hid all their gold.'

'Why was it called the Gregory Gang when the story is about Dick Turpin?'

'Good question Nugget. I forgot to mention that. Dick Turpin fell in with the Gregory Gang before he became famous as the highway robber. It was named after three brothers, Samuel, Jasper and Jeremy Gregory.'

'How come you know all this Nigel?' enquired Chance.

'It just comes my way!' nobody really cared how Nigel got the information, but it was nice to know in case they were asked at a later date.

'Back at the farmhouse Turpin and the Gregory Gang ransacked the house and found nothing; the owners wouldn't tell them anything, especially where they keep all their money. So Turpin decided to steal all the live stock, he used to be a butcher you know!'

'No!' they all said; that was as bad as being a highwayman to them.

'Yes, a butcher. So he decides that they should steal all the live stock they can within reason, and sell them on to make a profit. Well this old couple had been around for many years and had built up quite a substantial holding in the local community; they had cows, horses, sheep and a few pigs, one of these pigs was our Humphrey, who also doubled as a close family pet. He became famous to us pigs because the family put out a reward for the safe return of Humphrey. Turpin then rounded up all the live stock that the men could reasonable handle and fled the house with them and Humphrey. Sometime along the way Turpin got to liking that pig and decided to keep him as a pet, pigs being naturally intelligent you know.'

'Naturally.' Pogo said with a hint of sarcasm.

'Naturally yes! Well the live stock was sold to the local butchers.' All the animals now crossed themselves whenever they heard the word "butcher". 'Turpin kept on old Humphrey, and he would prove to be a very valuable asset to him, while he kept up his life of crime.'

Uncle Dave surreptitiously crept up on the group, who were now totally engrossed in Nigel's tale of Humphrey's 'derring do'.

'Carry on, carry on.' they said eagerly. Uncle Dave did his best imitation of a statue.

'Well.' continued Nigel, eager to fulfil his friends wish. 'The very next raid the gang took along Humphrey at Turpin's request, he trotted eagerly behind the band of horses, their thinking being "who is going to suspect a man with a pig!"

'Do you mean to say this famous pig of yours was an outlaw?' Nugget had just put an enormous spanner in the works.

'He was forced into it Nugget.' pleaded Nigel.

'But he's willing to trot behind the gang on their next raid. That doesn't strike me as being someone forced into a life of crime.'

The others all nodded in agreement; although they wanted to hear this great story they had to agree with Nugget's line of thought.

'He was forced into it!'

'I can run with that Nigel.'

'Good, just let your imagination go.'

'I'm trying Nigel. But he can get away anytime he wants to?'

'Maybe, just maybe.' started Pogo. 'he thought it wise to run with them, do as they said in case they felt that he was expendable and would end up joining his brothers and sisters at the butchers! All the animals crossed themselves again.

'A very valid point.' said Chance.

'See Nugget, that's how you should be enjoying a good story.' quipped Nigel.

'I'm running with it!'

'Right then, if that is all I'll continue. Humphrey was running along behind the gang, as I've pointed out, when a band of constables jumped out ahead and behind and had them surrounded. Turpin immediately drew out his pistols and started to shoot at the constables directly in front of him. Some of the other members of the gang did the same to the constables at the rear, and all of a sudden an almighty gunfight erupted.'

'So how did any of this affect Humphrey? He doesn't have a gun?' First Nigel had to contend with Nugget questioning the authenticity of his tale, now he had Biff on his back.

'Well Biff, if you could exercise just a little patience you will here.'

'Yeah Biff!' said Troy

'Humphrey could see he was now on a sticky wicket.'

'What's a sticky wicket?' asked Nugget. From the look on Nigel's face he knew it best not to pursue it.

'As the gunfight continued Humphrey figured that the constables were going to win due to a greater mass of numbers; the main members of the gang figuring out the same and made a run for it leaving old Turpin to fight alone. Now I must point out that loyalty is very strong within the pig community and although Turpin had in fact pig-napped him, for want of a better expression, he had also saved him from the "butcher"'. The obligatory crossing preceded the next instalment.

'Humphrey turned to where Turpin was fighting the constables now single handed.' Nigel continued. 'They closed on him like a net on a fish.' All the animals took in a sharp intake of breath; any mention of capture within the animal kingdom was treated with an air of fear and consternation. 'Turpin called out to Humphrey, why I do not know; what good could a pig do against such insurmountable odds, but old Humphrey rallied to his new master and charged the line of constables just as they were about to give off shot. The upshot was, pardon the pun, utter confusion in their ranks, shots disappearing into the wild blue yonder, each fellow looking to his comrade for orders and some semblance of direction and this allowed Turpin valuable time to make off on 'old Bessie' to freedom and to fight another day!'

'So Humphrey's a criminal!' said Nugget

'Not quite!' replied Nigel

'Yes he is!' reiterated Nugget 'he helped a known fugitive escape!'

'Yes, but you have to look at the glamour of the thing.'

'The glamour of the thing!'

'Yes.' Nigel's eyes were pleading with Nugget not to take the argument to its logical conclusion which was surely his humiliation. Nugget realised he was ruining an otherwise terrific tale and kept his counsel.

'What happened to Humphrey!' said Chance

All the other horses leaned a little closer to here the outcome of Humphrey's adventure; Nigel knew he could not disappoint.

'He ran away to freedom; a known fugitive himself for evermore!'

'Excellent!' they all said; each one dreaming secretly that they too could run off and be a famous highway horse or dog and live such a glamorous life beholden to nobody, but reality soon came back to bite and remind them of their ever so slightly perilous position.

'I'm hungry!' said Biff

Uncle Dave utterly transfixed by the passage he had just witnessed wondered back to the farm house in a hope that there would be some kind of sign, somebody stirring within. He did not have to wait long. Little Rachelle Perkins came bounding around the corner into the yard, singing to herself. She stopped short of the car when she espied Uncle Dave and the animals fixing their stares upon her.

'What's wrong?' she said instinctively.

'Nobody home.' came the reply

'Nobody home.' she repeated and drew a key from her trouser pocket. 'I have a key.'

'Excellent!' Uncle Dave stepped forward and Rachelle gratefully presented him with it. 'I was getting really worried.'

'I bet.'

'She had a key.' said Pogo, and he was the first to approach Rachelle.

'How did the animals get out?' she enquired.

'You know.' started Dave 'I couldn't figure that one out, and that just added to my worry!'

'I better feed them!' she said and joyfully went about her duties, even though she was equally concerned as to whereabouts of Mr and Mrs Flugal, but Dave reassured her he would get to the bottom of it.

'She's going to feed us!' shouted Troy. 'I love you Rachelle.' And they all agreed unanimously that she was the best mucker out any of them had ever seen.

Rachelle dug deep into her pockets as she entered the stables followed by Nugget, Nigel, the younger horses and finally Chance and produced a packet of mints, which she shared amongst her equine friends. For Nugget and Nigel two chocolate bars appeared and were devoured with much gusto.

'We all love you Rachelle!' Nigel's displays of affection were rare, this was always put down to his Scottish upbringing, but today it was well placed and deserving.

Rachelle made sure all were fed and watered and comfortable before she returned her attention once more back to the house, but not before she contemplated bolting the stable doors, but this she quickly decided against as it was clearly futile.

'What can the matter be?' she muttered to herself. She was startled by the soft spoken voice of Chance, who had stealthily positioned himself immediately behind her.

'It's fishy, that's for sure!'

Rachelle, reassured that it was Chance whinnying softly behind her, continued talking to herself in peace.

'It's not like the Flugals to leave without letting anybody know! I would be lying if I was not scared that something had come of them both.'

'I'm sure there is a perfectly logical explanation as to their whereabouts.' Chance said, laying his head delicately on her shoulder and Rachelle took the opportunity to stroke her friend lovingly and affectionately.

'I better take a look with that man, who I believe is Uncle Dave.' Until that point it had never occurred to her to ask his name or to enquire anything about his identity.

Chance lifted his head, relieving her of her duties for the time being, and she set off towards the house without any outward signs of fear or trepidation; deep inside she sensed the first feelings of doubt that the person she perceived as Uncle Dave was not in fact Uncle Dave at all and maybe some deviant criminal hell bent on harming the Flugals; maybe he was responsible for their disappearance and had returned to the scene of the crime even though all the programmes she had witnessed on television told her that to do so meant certain capture.

'Stop it! You're imagining things.' She chastised herself for being so foolish and condemning an innocent man to such accusations.

Her steps shortened as the front door approached; the man was nowhere to be found; 'He was covering his tracks' she thought   'Stop it! You're talking like a child, but I am a child.'

The door was now within reach, she paused to gather her herself before the fateful moment would be upon her to try the handle; slowly and purposefully she filled her lungs and begun the controlled exhale, that she had seen demonstrated on the television. Now she was ready. She stretched out her hand, tickling the door handle, still lacking courage to turn it and attempt to open he door. She pulled back chastising herself for her weakness as she did so; she must do this, the very well being of those she cared for was at stake. Again she tickled the door knob and then finally thrust her hand upon the handle and twisted firmly. To her surprise the door flew open, she could not comprehend her own strength; 'It must have been adrenaline or something' she instantly surmised.

'Hello Rachelle!' She let out a scream and fell backwards onto the garden path. It was Mr Flugal!

'Mr Flugal!'

'Sorry Rachelle did I frighten you?'

'Just a little.' her relief clearly tangible. 'Where have you been? We've been worried sick. Where's that strange man? Are you okay?'

'No, are you okay?'

Rachelle nodded.

'All these questions; yes I'm fine and that strange man is Uncle Dave, an old family friend.'

'I had the most frightful thought that he was a burglar or someone worse come to do harm and rob you!' Rachelle got to her feet and brushed herself down.

Flugal immediately felt severe pangs of guilt that this wonderful, lovely young girl who helped him around the farm; running chores, feeding the animals, mucking out and so much more, for which he had been mute in his admiration and gratitude for her, should be brave enough to enter the house unknowing who this strange man might be to see to the welfare of himself and his wife. He made a decision there and then that he would never again charge this angel for anything; it was the least he could do, although he regarded it as a little on the late side, and this only vexed him further. He enquired again as to her well being, and then once he was satisfied invited her in for a drink and some breakfast come lunch.

'All the animals are okay Mr Flugal; I have fed and watered them all!'

'I know, I watched you from the window.'

'Oh!'

'I should have called you sooner I'm sorry, but Uncle Dave's sorting some drainage for me in one of the lower fields and I was side tracked for a while.'

'Oh, that's okay.' Poor Rachelle didn't really know what to say; she was still after all a child and held Mr Flugal in awe to a certain degree; he was such a great teacher and she had her own secret dream of being a competitive horse rider in either equestrianism or show jumping, she didn't care as long as it involved riding horses, and in her dreams it always involved her riding Chance to victory. She entered the house hot on the heels of Mr Flugal and there, not to her amazement sat Uncle Dave.

'This young lady thought you might be a burglar Dave!'

Rachelle could feel her face flush crimson, and she was unable to make any eye contact with the seated man.

'Really.' was all Dave could muster, whether through shock or mockery she could not quite comprehend.

'Sorry.' came her reply, still with no eye contact.

'Don't worry Rachelle I find the whole episode quite amusing. Fancy a man who spends his whole life starting the day at the crack of dawn-'

'-Stop it!' Flugal interjected.

'Starts his whole day at the crack of dawn regardless.' Dave continued 'and then sleeps in because his wife orders him to.'

'I was ill!' Flugal said laughing.

'She didn't mean indefinitely.'

'No, no she didn't, but I must have been more ill than I imagined! And thankfully I have you two fine, loyal friends to come to my rescue, and I assure you both it will not happen again.'

Both could tell from the stern tone of his last statement that he was sincere.

'By the way.' started Dave 'Where is she?'

'I don't rightly know! She just up and left without saying a word.'

'Strange, very strange.' mused Dave.

'I'm sure she hasn't gone far and I know she would hate it if I made a fuss, so I'll give her a little while yet. Have you had any breakfast Rachelle?' asked Flugal.

'Oh, yes thanks. I made my grandmother hers and mine.' This was in fact a lie; Rachelle to be precise in these matters had invested so much time in the making of her grandmothers breakfast that she had completely lost all track of time and ended the affair running out of the house to the omission of her own sustenance. One of the many delights of an early start for her was to be allowed the morning walk to the farm on her own.

'Would you like some anyway? I'm making us both scrambled eggs and bacon?'

She could feel herself starting to salivate, but her self control was very able and she hid it with ease, but she was hungry!

'Yes please. If it's not to much trouble!'

'Not at all' Flugal turned to his old friend. 'All the animals are fed and watered thanks to my little helper!'

'You are a very lucky to have such an able assistant!' Uncle Dave's sincerity was not false, but Rachelle flushed crimson again all the same.

Flugal entered into his breakfast making regime with much gusto and in no time at all presented his guests with an ample size portion of scrambled ages and bacon.

9

While all this sustenance was being consumed, unseen by the other yard inhabitants, Pogo wondered out to the further field; why he felt the need to seek solace in his own company in that field nobody rightly knows, but the time spent in deep contemplation helped ease his troubled mind. To be honest with himself and to those around him, he felt personally responsible for the mire the farm now found itself immersed in; Biff and Troy were floundering in a similar sea; they were just as much to blame as poor Pogo, but he took this matter closer to his heart than the other two. Why? Not even he could tell you the answer to that one.

Just as he chastised himself for the umpteenth time a nondescript van drove past at break neck speed; Pogo remarked to himself as to the foolishness of the driver's actions, but nothing more.

The van veered around the end bend that marked the final quarter of Flugal Lane on which the farm sat, when an object caught his eye and distracted him from his inner melancholy; it was a piece of paper floating, fluttering in the wind, partly generated by the passing van. He watched the offending piece of litter waft on the morning breeze; its hypnotic air dance absorbing his every thought. As it approached his portion of the field, he could just about make out the large print: it was an advertisement of some sort. He would have to investigate. Finally the poster came to rest on one of the few grassy hewn pieces of field. Pogo could see from his vantage point that it advertised a forth coming carriage race, of some sort, sponsored by a Global Enterprises or something. As he tentatively approached the poster it was caught up in a gust of wind and it smacked him right between the eyes.

'What the.....' Pogo took a giant step back in a vain hope the poster would slide of his head. It didn't.

Eyeing the feint outline of a carriage through the white veil, he attempted to remove the offending article with his hoof, which only resulted in him poking himself in the eye; if you have ever poked yourself in the eye with a horse shoe you would begin to understand the discomfort Pogo now found himself in!

Pogo staggered and tottered his way back towards the centre of the field, and the farm. From some distance away one would have mistaken him for a drunk, but his friends, who were now alerted to his predicament by his calling out, knew better and quickly realised that he was in a spot of bother. Troy was the first to move, hurdling the fence that surrounded most of the field, Biff, acting in a composed manner belying his tender years, walked through the open gate.

'Hang on in there Pogo!' shouted a galloping Troy 'you're old buddy's coming to the rescue.'

Biff, having entered the field, summed up the situation in an instant and cantered over to the exact position he figured Pogo was more than likely to end up, at all times keeping half an eye on events in case a major re-evaluation should be required.

'I'm coming!' Troy's voice had gained another decibel.

Pogo came to a standstill, gathered his thoughts, composed himself and ever so slowly raised his hoof and gingerly wiped away the offending article, being as careful as a mouse with a large piece of cheese recently lifted of the master's table. Suddenly he became aware of a strange sensation; a dark shadow had begun to loom heavy over his restricted vision. The poster slid vertically down his forehead to reveal the dark menacing shape of Troy at full tilt, bearing down on him. He scarcely had time to let out a cry for help when Troy at full charge hammered into his side sending both of them toppling further down the field, dangerously close to the section that was on the verge of becoming water logged. The two friends hit the grass skidding at a rate of knots crashing head first into the mud patch, stopping just inches from where Biff had calculated they would.

As is the case when one's vision had been impaired the eyes take a moment or two readjust to the light conditions; Pogo blinked several times in quick succession trying to make head or tail of his predicament. As the mist cleared, there all in all his glory stood the mud splattered, cheesy grinning shape of Troy.

'Glad you're okay!'

'You came to help me?'

'You bet!'

'We're in a mud patch!'

'And your point is?'

'We're in a mud patch and you came to help me!'

'Mud patch, quagmire, grassy field, in a paddock, who cares dude, we came to your rescue man!'

Pogo sat up and looked vertically up at Biff sporting an equally large cheesy grin.

'You came to help too?'

'You bet!'

'But you're standing next to the mud patch!'

'Yes....yes I am and like our learned friend there, I am here to offer you any assistance I can.'

Troy slowly, ungracefully and with no small amount of effort raised himself to his feet. 'That was fun.'

Pogo wished he could share in his friend enthusiasm, but wallowing in a pit of mud and grime was not his idea of a good day out.

'Well, what can we do to be of assistance?' said Troy eying the offending article lying, delicately balanced in one of the dryer sections of the field.

'What have we here? It's your attacker!' and with that Troy with much dexterity plucked the poster of the mud and waved it triumphantly to his two colleagues.

'Struck down in your prime Pogo, by a dirty poster!' Biff's words stunned Pogo with indignation 'struck down' was he, the very thought, this needed had to be rectified; the last thing on his mind was now to be the butt of any more stable jokes and banter.

'Now look here.' said Pogo, and started to lay the foundation of a witty repost when a shout as loud as any train whistle cut him off.

'Wow!! Look at this!' It was Troy, his eyes as wide as saucers, his countenance flushed with excitement.

'What is it? enquired Biff

'A race!'

'A race?'

'A race!' Troy waved the poster at Biff who struggled mightily to read the mobile text.

'Hold it still, I can't read it.'

'It says here.' Troy held the poster up to his right eye 'that they are going to hold a race, and it says here it's going to be over a designated course or something, and there is going to be a big prize to the winner.'

'How much?' the excitement now clearly evident in Biff's voice.

Troy scoured the page, but the mud had obscured the bottom quarter which held the all important and relevant pieces of information.　　'I can't see it for the dirt!'

'We got to clean it up. Quick, to the trough!' shouted Biff, and the two of them scampered off to the water trough leaving the stricken prostrate Pogo to his mud bath.

'Hey..........hey! What about me? Your old pal Pogo.' But they were out of earshot and probably deaf to anything, but the thrill of the thoughts of a race and a prize to boot. 'Charming.' Pogo slipped and slid his way upright, inspected his coat tutted to himself, took one step to the side to avoid the worst of the mud and fell flat on his face. 'Marvellous!'

In the distance, two tiny four legged figures reached the water trough at the high end of the field that bordered the yard. He could make out Nugget, Nigel and Chance approaching and could only imagine the impetuosity of his two friends as they relayed the news.

'Don't you worry about your old pal, your old muddy friend Pogo! I found the poster, I suffered to find that poster, yes it was me and me alone who was responsible for such a momentous find and our possible salvation.' Pogo truly believed his own words and they provided him with just a small crumb of comfort.

Back in the house Flugal, Rachelle and Uncle Dave were totally oblivious to everything that was unfolding outside.

'I wouldn't get to upset young Rachelle.' Uncle Dave did not want the youngster to feel uncomfortable now that her secret was out regarding his less then favourable character. 'You wouldn't be the first one to bring my motives and character into question!'

'No!' Flugal was intrigued.

'No!'

'What happened?' Rachelle's curiosity had been aroused, dangerous in a girl so young.

'I don't mind relating to you both the story. It's quite amusing now, but at the time.' Uncle Dave's face took on a grave countenance. Then he laughed out loud as he saw he had extracted the reaction he sought.

'It took place about ten or so years ago while I was doing some work at old Mrs Dougherty's place.'

'Mrs Dougherty!' queried Flugal.

'The very same!'

'Who is Mrs Dougherty? quizzed Rachelle.

'Who was Mrs Dougherty!' said Flugal.

'A woman of questionable character Rachelle.' answered Dave

'But very rich!' interjected Flugal 'It was said she buried her fortune so her family could not get their hands on it!'

'Oh!'

'Indeed Rachelle. Many people spent many years and a small fortune trying to decipher the cryptic clues she left behind.' started Uncle Dave.

'But why leave clues if you don't want anybody to find it?' butted in Rachelle again.

'A good question.' Uncle Dave leant forward to add weight and emphasis to his next instalment, both Rachelle and Flugal instinctively did the same. 'Why would you leave clues! Everybody suspected the nephew Wilbur, but Wilbur wasn't bright enough to have thought up such a plan and the relatives quickly discounted him. No, she was just a spiteful old woman who didn't care a damn about anybody or anything; she even tried to buy Flugal Farm once. Didn't she?'

'From under my very nose, and offered my father top price too! He believed that she buried the treasure on Flugal Farm, regretted it, but was not in a position to retrieve it, so tried to buy the property!'

'I never knew that!' It was now Uncle Dave's turn to display a keen interest in another's story.

'He refused to allow anybody to attempt a search for it, but I know he had searched himself over the years and always confessed, when pressed on the subject, that he knew exactly where she buried it.'

'And you've never looked for it! said Rachelle incredulously.

'I have not given old Mrs Dougherty and her fortune a minutes thought until this very moment.'

'Well maybe we should!' shouted Dave. 'And to add further fuel to the fire I have the very cryptic clues she left behind and believe I may have an answer!'

'Yes!' Rachelle could not contain herself. 'A treasure hunt!'

'My father got to a point where he was thoroughly fed up with all these treasure hunters invading our land, that he put up boards around the place warning off any prospective hunters. He did though keep documents as to where he surmised she buried it!'

'And Mrs Dougherty was still alive at this time?' Rachelle found the idea quite incredible.

'Oh yes. In fact she positively revelled in it when she realised nobody was going to touch her fortune.' Flugal continued.

'Except your father?'

'No Rachelle, he wasn't interested. He always held the view point that there was no treasure, never was going to be any treasure and the whole story was a ruse to throw her avaricious relatives off the scent off the true story, which was that she was broke and was to proud to let anybody know!'

'I can vouch for that.' said Uncle Dave. 'Never have I met a woman who worried, panicked, fretted so much as to what other people thought of her. If only the poor woman knew the truth, but I still have them clues Flugal.'

'Which was?' Rachelle couldn't get enough of this kind of gossip.

'Everybody disliked her. They just put up with her for the sake of peace and quiet!' Flugal dished up his own portion of scrambled eggs and bacon before adding 'Sausages any one? My wife made them herself.'

'She now makes sausages?' said Uncle David salivating.

'Sure thing and they're delicious.' Flugal enjoyed emphasising "delicious" for the effect he knew it would induce in his friend. 'I'll have a hunt around in the attic later, once all the jobs are done, for those documents pertaining to old Mrs Dougherty.'

'Can we do it after breakfast?' Rachelle's enthusiasm for the hunt was reaching boiling point. 'I've done most of them this morning.'

'Maybe.' then Flugal remembered the original thread to this conversation. 'Sorry Dave you were going to tell us about your experience with Mrs Dougherty.'

'Well not really Mrs Dougherty, but her dog Henry. It can wait until another day. I'm with Rachelle we should investigate your father's papers sooner rather than later.' The smile on Rachelle's face mirrored the excitement growing within the kitchen.

'Understood, but what about the field?'

'Seen it. We can't do anything for a couple of days; the weather supposed to be brutal, we'll start next Monday, it won't take more than a few days.'

'Okay I'll bow to your superior knowledge.'

'Does that mean we can go treasure hunting?' Rachelle added again.

Flugal was mildly vexed at the delay, but hid his disappointment and anyway under the circumstances it may just work out to everybody's advantage.

'Yes Rachelle I suppose it does.' Flugal said placing six sausages into a frying pan and removing the rest of the scrambled eggs from the hob, so as not to burn them and then poured himself another mug of tea.

'Was Henry a large dog?' said Rachelle returning to the original conversation, now happy they were going treasure hunting. Rachelle aimed the question at Uncle Dave; she was still unsure as to how to refer to him, as she didn't really know him that well.

'Just call me Dave, everybody else does, it's only this man Flugal and his family who calls me "Uncle".' Flugal was astonished at Dave's openness towards a stranger; shattering in one fail swoop all his years of cultivating his reputation as a misanthrope.

Whether he sensed her ill ease she could not tell, but Dave wasn't half as scary as she thought, and then the two men laughed to dispel her assertion; this clearly was an ongoing joke.

'Yes Rachelle,' Dave replied once their mirth had subsided 'he was a huge Mastiff who guarded that old lady with a jealousy that was unrivalled in the animal kingdom.'

'And therein lies the problem.' Flugal was just about to expound on the said problem when a very flustered Mrs Flugal entered the kitchen; she tried valiantly to hide her discomfort at not finding Mr Flugal alone and that she was in great distress, but it was to no avail, they all noticed and out of due respect for her kept their counsel and proceeded instead to welcome her home with smiles and cheery dispositions; she in turn did cheer a little and bravely matched their mirth.

After a few minutes she made her excuses, wished them all well and to enjoy breakfast and vacated to the sanctuary of the first floor.

Flugal poured out a mug of tea, so typical of men when the delicacy of a cup and saucer is called for, and cries out to be injected into proceedings, man opts for that which he knows best; the good old fashioned mug.

Having now served up breakfast, he ascended the stairs, mug in hand, tiptoed up to the bedroom door, and knocked gently two or three times, he slipped the latch, opened the door and poked his head slowly into the room.

Mrs Flugal lay prostrate on the bed, sobbing her heart out. His heart sank at the sight of her so distraught and he broke out in a cold, uncomfortable sweat. Quietly and respectfully he approached the bed, and placed the mug on the table beside the bed and sat gently down beside her quivering, sobbing form. He was, it is true to say, utterly bewildered as to the cause of her vexation and suffering, and there ran through his head the entire gamut of causes and emotions he was likely to feel depending on the root of his wife's misery. He listed all the reactions he was more than capable of and placed them in order of significance and severity, and once all this was done ran through appropriate answers to all her future questions and inquisitions.

'Anything I can do?' he finally asked, immediately chastising himself for such a feeble question; it was a pathetic opening statement and he knew it, but at this precise moment in time he knew his powers to be worthless. It was the best he could do under the circumstances.

Slowly and painfully Mrs Flugal raised her head off the sodden pillow, removed a tissue from a box on the bedside table and blew her nose. She locked her most sorrowful gaze onto her husband.

He dared not ask fear the pain to be too great to bear, but ask he must and he summoned up the courage and posed the inevitable.

'What is it?'

'The family heir looms!' came the reply.

He immediately felt relieved, like a huge burden had been lifted, but his wife prized these possessions and the very fact that she'd probably been out attempting to sell them without letting him know disturbed him.

'What about them, are they lost?' he asked, desperately trying to gauge the true meaning to her statement, but secretly wishing his surmising to be false.

'Might as well be!'

Flugal prided himself that he understood his wife's every mood and wish perfectly and enjoyed immensely surprising her with gifts and acts of love and devotion, especially when such behaviour had fallen out of favour in today's society, but this had put his head in a spin for which he had no model to fall back on and to execute any kind of recovery.

'They're worthless!'

The mist started to rise ahead of Flugal; she had had them valued, any incompetent detective could now surmise that. Now a darker cloud brewed on the horizon; she should not feel the need to value such items of inexpressible sentimental value. A feeling of sudden inadequacy enveloped him.

'What did they quote you?'

This only brought back the pain and she broke down once again, but after a few minutes that seemed like hours to Flugal, because he was helpless to intervene, she managed to check her feelings and compose herself in order to relate the morning's events.

Slowly and succinctly she explained all; how she'd left the house very early, leaving him in bed sound asleep, not wanting to disturb him and worry him untoward, she could see he was through the worst of it. Flugal inwardly grew angry even though he understood her motives.

And anyway, as she continued, she had planned to return before he awoke and carry out all the morning chores, before the day could truly begin. Flugal saw through her well laid plans immediately.

Her well laid plans, she went on, had been far too optimistic, she had an appointment to see an expert in antiquities, who she hoped would pleasantly surprise her with a healthy estimate of her family heirlooms. Firstly, the expert antique dealer never materialised at the appointed time until nearly an hour after, and then stinking of stale beer, for which he never apologised for, and seeing Mrs Flugal's anxiety and agitation at arriving at this late hour, although it was still very early in the day, mistakenly read this as desperation on her part to sell. This caused him to deliberately undervalued all the items displayed before him accordingly; the offered price was only a fraction of their true worth. Much to his chagrin, a clearly disturbed Mrs Flugal fled the shop in tears carefully carrying her bundle of "worthless memorabilia", to quote the expert, adding insult to injury in the process; secondly, now running hopelessly late, she drove home faster than usual in a forlorn hope of making up lost time and being back at the farm in time for him awakening, in order he remain oblivious to her venture into town, but unbeknown to her this was the day that Mr Flugal had arranged for Uncle Dave to start the drainage in the fields. Mrs Flugal, who was a very safe driver according to all who knew her, got herself clocked for speeding by a roadside camera. If it couldn't get any worse, as she approached the turning into Flugal farm she was overtaken on the rise of the hill by a Mercedes. The shock at seeing the car on her right hand side attempting such a dangerous and utterly irresponsible manoeuvre, at the split second she herself initiated her turn in, caused her to violently yank the steering wheel to the left away from Flugal Lane, career off the road and only avoided burying the car in a hedge by a matter of inches by an aggressive application of the brakes.

Flugal kept a respectable silence throughout, and when she had finished he leaned over and kissed her gently on the forehead with much affection.

'Did you not wonder where I was?' she enquired.

'You would only go on such an errand without letting me know unless it was of the utmost importance, so I figured I'd better trust your judgement.'

Satisfied with this answer, which Flugal himself, it has to be said, was extremely proud, albeit true, she laid her head on the pillow, closed her eyes and fell asleep. Flugal then slid a blanket over her to keep her warm and crept downstairs as quietly as he could.

He found Rachelle and Dave were in the process of clearing away the breakfast things.

'You didn't need to do that!' said Flugal picking up the nearest piece of crockery and cutlery and placing it by the sink.

In truth he was secretly grateful they had taken the initiative and took this opportunity to gulp down the last remnants of his own breakfast, including the sausages, before it too was cleared away.

The commotion that had been building outside, to their blissful ignorance, finally reached their ears.

'What was that?' Dave beat the other two to the punch.

Flugal and Rachelle had already moved expeditiously towards the door and into the yard, to be met by Nugget spinning like a top, chasing his tail like a demented fool; a favourite pass time of his always whenever he felt exuberant.

Nigel was burying his nose into a piece of paper, shuffling the offending article through the grit and the grime.

'I can't get a good look at it! It won't stay still long enough!' Nigel had always had an affliction for which he kept mum; he suffered from hypermetropia, he couldn't see close up.

'Then stop sliding your nose into it, take a step back, focus and read.' Chance's calm tones could clearly be discerned over the mayhem, as all the animals were in a great state of excitement and expectation, chatting incessantly about the poster and the possibility of seeing the race.

Nigel failed to heed any of Chance's advice and finished jamming his head and the poster under the water trough.

'Damn it!'

'Oh, well done.' said Biff sarcastically. 'I haven't had chance to read that yet!'

Nigel's vanity tried to rescue the situation and he ignored any criticism or advice presented before him from either his friends or the few livery horses who had a ring side seat witnessing his mud dance.

'Try licking at it! You're good at that! said a tittering Troy.

'Imagine it's an ice cream.' Pogo had caught them up and now joined in the mirth.

Nigel's desire and desperation to read the poster in its entirety expressed itself fully through his nuzzle, squeezing, squashing and distorting its muddy way under the trough; the upshot was the only possible conclusion to this farcical scenario, the poster ended up embedded in a totally inaccessible position.

'Well done, well done indeed, a fine effort.' repeated Biff, only this time he got the reaction his comment was searching for and justly deserved; a rankled Nigel marched right up to the grinning Biff.

Biff lowered his head to Nigel's level.

'Can I be of assistance?'

Nigel in turn raised his head the short distance to be level with Biff's nostrils.

'You can remove your presence from my line of sight!'

'I may decide to remain in my present situation and fill my proportion of your line of sight!'

'I may not wish you to hold that proportion of my line of sight.'

'I may....'

Biff was not given the privilege to finish his "I may...." reply when a now impatient Pogo interrupted them. 'I don't "may". I desire you two to shut up! Hey Nugget, can you reach that poster Nigel so deftly jammed under our trough?'

Nugget immediately stopped spinning and in an instant had his paw under the said trough up to the elbow, but he found to his dismay that his ungulate friend had executed losing the poster to the utmost degree; it could have been a million miles away let alone a matter of inches for all the good it did the unfortunate Nugget and his prospects of retrieving it.

'No can do!' said a resigned Nugget extricating himself and turning into the imposing figure of Flugal with Uncle Dave and Rachelle in close attendance.

All the animals were immediately struck dumb, which disconcerted the trio immensely. Rachelle scanned the group as a sergeant major would do his troops before an inspection.

'They're up to something, again!'

Flugal let off a wry smile followed by a monotone grunt; a sign that he utterly agreed with Rachelle's surmising or that he hadn't a clue what was going on.

Uncle Dave seeing Nugget skulk behind the horses went to investigate the trough, got down on all fours and peered underneath, this had the effect of soaking his hands and knees with mud, but he didn't seem to care, it was old hat to him.

'I see it!'

'He sees it!' said a nervous Nugget. 'It's all your fault' he said in turn to Nigel. Nigel kept quiet.

Nugget caught Dave's suspicious gaze, and as their two eyes met Nugget, now keeping mum, slid further behind the horses rear hoofs.

Dave with each passing second was becoming increasingly round to the realisation he had had earlier, but he concentrated on the job at hand.

'It's a poster of some sort.' Dave said examining the dirty specimen he had just extricated from its muddy grave, and handed it to Flugal.

'I can't read it, come in the house and we'll give it a clean. The wife's got just the job for this.'

'You did a good job hiding the poster Nigel, now we can't even read it!'

'Take a hike Biff!' Nigel as not in the mood, he felt guilty at being responsible for losing the poster; now they would never get to see the race.

'It wasn't me.' protested Biff. 'I didn't lose it!'

Nigel turned to face his four equine friends, all of whom kept a straight poker face bar Pogo, he held onto his cheesy grin.

'It was your master plan along wasn't it Nigel?' he started 'Cause mayhem, lose the poster under the trough so the only person who could extricate it was Flugal, Dave or Rachelle, then they'd come to investigate, find the poster and we'd all go to the race.............brilliant!'
'It was a good plan.' agreed Chance.

Nigel could not bring himself to tell the truth, one minute he was facing being the laughing stock and now he could feel his stock rising amongst his friends, although there was a part of him believing the joke was still firmly on him, either way he was going to play it for all it was worth.

'I couldn't share it with you at the time, as it only came to me in a flash of inspiration.'

'All the best flashes come that way!' Troy took a step towards Flugal, who was still examining the poster whilst he entered the house, Dave and Rachelle it was noted by the group, regularly looked over their shoulder at the latest discourse amongst the friends.

Once inside the house Flugal went into the hallway off the kitchen and listened for any sound that might be emanating from his wife's bedroom; happy in the knowledge that she was okay and sleeping soundly he returned to the kitchen.

One of the few surprises and delights these turn of events had brought to his attention, and nulled any pain, was the realisation that Dave was not the hardened misanthrope he always led on to be; he found him in a deep, sometimes meaningful, conversation with Rachelle regarding, of all things, the ability of the animal kingdom to understand everything we humans said, yet the humans lacked this essential gift, and in most cases failed even the most basic understanding of animal needs. It would be very interesting indeed, they went on, to see if the boot, hoof, paw or shoe was on the other foot.

Flugal harkened back to the car journey with Nugget, yes secretly, subconsciously he honestly believed Nugget understood and comprehended his every word; it did not, as he thought it might, fill him with fear or worry, but enlightenment and joy that one of his best friends truly had insight into his human world.

Flugal with one ear on their continuing conversation took out a cloth, wet it with a liquid he retrieved from a bottle kept safely in a cupboard opposite the kitchen stove, and meticulously cleaned the piece of paper.

Unbeknown to the trio, the group of friends had surreptitiously positioned themselves around the large kitchen window that looked out onto the fields, but was easily accessible from the yard. Chance had taken upon himself the responsibility of acting as scout "it would not look as suspicious if he happened to get noticed," that was his thinking and everybody was in agreement.

'What's he doing?' Nigel ventured after a short pause whilst Chance scanned events unfolding in the kitchen.

'Cleaning the poster'

'He'll wipe all the ink off. I told you that would happen!'

They all eyed Nigel incredulously, each in turn trying to remember when he ever did say such a thing. Pogo, standing directly behind Nigel, motioned to the side of his head by tapping his hoof and mouthing the words that he thought poor Nigel was a little confused today in all the excitement.

'What now?' Nigel continued.

'Flugal's finished the cleaning and now he's trying to read it.'

Flugal held the poster up to the light. Rachelle and Dave had cut their discourse short now that he was attempting to decipher it. He stared intently at the brown stained leaflet, with faded ink barely discernible. He was unable at first to make head or tail of anything bar a feint picture of horses and carriages.

'Well?' said Dave impatiently.

Flugal cleaned the poster a second time and held it back up to the light.

'Aaah. I see!'

'What?'

'What?' Dave and Rachelle each said in turn.

'It's advertising a race!'

'A race! Fantastic!' Rachelle's enthusiasm bubbled over. 'Where? Can we go? Does in involve horses?'

'That's a lot of questions that need a lot of answers.' Flugal handed the poster to Dave. 'You have a look, see what you think.' Turning to Rachelle he began to answer her queries. 'Firstly, I don't know where it is, Dave can hopefully shed some light on that one. Secondly, yes and thirdly most definitely yes, but doing what I'm not sure although there's a picture of a horse and carriage which would suggest possibly a carriage drive.'

'They've worked out it's a carriage race.' Chance was now keeping a running commentary, if nothing much was happening he would fill in the gaps, by not so much as making things up, but by presumptions and educated guesses on future events governed by whatever facial expressions and gestures were being displayed.

'Anybody could see it advertised a carriage race!' Nigel remarked with an air of authority; he was though still infuriated with himself, his pride dented at having lost the poster due directly to his short sightedness.

'Maybe' started Pogo 'if we had had the opportunity to read the poster!'

'Like I lost it on purpose!'

'You did decide to take it upon yourself to inform everybody as to its exact details!' Pogo went on.

'I thought you pigs were the intellectuals of the farm yard?' Biff chipped in. His comment didn't so much as touch Nigel's nerve as slice it open.

'My intellect is not open to discussion!'

'Uncle Dave is inspecting the poster. Young Rachelle is very excited. That's a good sign, a very good sign.' Chance's final comment about Rachelle filled his heavy heart with warmth; when they had first discovered the poster he instantly thought of Rachelle and the enjoyment of her seeing her first race of any kind involving her beloved horses, and how he secretly longed to able to share his own experiences with her.

Dave agreed with Flugal as to the content of the leaflet, but was able to shed some light on the information that was lacking; the race was to be held in about a month or two over a new course, which he surmised was the one being assembled just down the road in White Valley, a small town only twenty miles from the farm. He had seen it for himself, there was some construction in process and he had thought at the time what it might be, but would never have guessed this in a million years. Eying the poster again he pleasantly informed them, to the great surprise and interest of all parties present, especially young Rachelle, there was to be substantial purse for the winner.

'How much?' Rachelle leaned over the back of Dave's right elbow to get a better view of the wording on the poster.

'Yes how much?' asked an intrigued Flugal.

'I don't know, that bit's missing, and I can't read the number you have to ring on the bottom. There's only on thing for it, we'll have to hit the road and find another poster and get all the details. There's bound to be more around somewhere.'

'What about the treasure hunt?' asked Rachelle feeling a little disappointed the hunt wasn't going to start imminently.

'I haven't forgotten, don't worry.' replied Flugal, seeing her demeanour change.

Rachelle, now placated for the time being, picked her coat off the back of her chair, which she had carefully draped there on entering the house, and made her way to the door. 'I'll go and see what they're all up to.'

'Thank you and I'll look up those documents this afternoon, I promise.' he called after her as she disappeared out the back door.

Chance had relayed to the gang Rachelle's intentions, so that when she emerged from the house they had all resumed positions and actions that any passerby, let alone someone who worked on the farm, might regard as nothing out of the ordinary.

Rachelle gave Nugget an affectionate stroke and a tickle behind his ear as he approached her; his job was to detain Rachelle sufficiently to gain them all time; to him it was a win, win situation, he loved being tickled.

Once in the stables Rachelle stroked, patted, displaying sincere open signs of affection and talked incessantly to all those present; she mentioned the treasure hunt, which as you can imagine stirred up no small amount of interest and chatter. Rachelle was so wound up in what she was doing and saying that she missed all the tell tale signs, including the fact that the four horses had walked back into their stables, which was quite astonishing really considering the circumstances of the conversation she had recently had with Dave, and spoke at length about all they had discovered about the race. By now this had easily overtaken the treasure hunt in her list of priorities, being in no small amount to it being her first real horse race of any kind, albeit with carriages, but she secretly hoped that the hunt would go ahead anytime soon, and wasn't it amazing how circumstances could change so rapidly. One moment they downhearted, and the next they had a race to look forward to and some treasure to find, which could save them all and the farm.

Chance could feel the giant shadow of melancholy overtake and shroud him once again in despair; if only he could be able to hold a conversation with Rachelle, just one, to let her understand everything he had seen, share his experiences and pass on to her even a tiny grain of knowledge so that she may further her own undoubted talent for riding horses, if only she could comprehend him just as they all understood her, but sadly the world doesn't always work that way and he had to content himself with his covert style of training; whenever Rachelle rode him, subtly and without fuss, Chance corrected Rachelle's mistakes, passing on the correct sequence of events and techniques, when they were required, in such a way that she could not but learn and improve whilst at the same time letting her believe that it was she who was in control. Chance knew, like all good teachers, that confidence is everything and he stimulated Rachelle's keenness to learn and bolstered her confidence at every available turn. Her riding skills for someone so young were exceptional; she would become an outstanding horse woman, of that he did no doubt, given the opportunities and right circumstances, but like everything in this world money talks and this lack of funding, he could envisage would only add to the hopelessness of her future position and ultimately drive her away from the horses she loved. It was a situation he had witnesses many times before, but now it involved somebody he cared for very deeply. Rachelle finally entered Chance's stall. Today he was last. She made a point of not putting anybody ahead of anybody else when it came to feeding time and cleaning out the stalls or showing affection, even though it was common knowledge Chance was her favourite; it just added to the high regard the farm yard held young Rachelle Perkins in.

'And so Chance my faithful steed.' she opened with. 'Where do you think all that lovely treasure could be buried?'

'Never heard of any treasure until today, and I'm afraid on this occasion Rachelle your guess is as good as mine.'

'Don't you find it quite extraordinary that Mr Flugal had forgotten all about the treasure and it took his old friend Dave mentioning an incident with a large Mastiff belonging to a Mrs Dougherty to bring it all back?'

'Maybe he doesn't believe.'

'And to top it all a race as well! I do hope we go and see it Chance.' she rested her head on the side of his, he loved that. 'What I wouldn't give to see that race and carriages as well, I bet it's exciting and terribly skilful.'

'The teams have to work in tandem Rachelle.' Chance decided to hell with it; he was going to try and impart something, he might, just might be successful. 'Each horse knows it job, responsibilities and position in the team; if any one fails in their duty it will undoubtedly lead to that team's ruin!'

'You seem to know a lot about carriage racing Chance?' shouted Biff from the rear of his stable. This was not a flippant remark, as could be testified by his tone, but an honest and sincere question.

'One of my old trainers,' Chance went on, 'was a keen carriage racer and trainer, he would regularly involve all the stable hands in a discussion as to what were the best methods of discerning positions and formations, that were best suited for his horses.'

'And this is also the trainer that trained you in flat racing?' said Biff.

'Yes!'

'A Jack of all trades!'

'And a master of none!' finished Nugget, then apologised to Chance lest he had insulted him. Chance assured him he had not.

'He was very good; his horses put a lot of faith in his methods and they invariably worked. He prolonged my career for a few more years after I injured my tendons, but I was never the same horse after that!'

Chance went quiet for the briefest of moments, as he contemplated and reminisced on his past life.

Snapping back into the moment he instantly checked that nobody had noticed his silence and fleeting meditation. To be honest even if they had they wouldn't have said anything to embarrass him, they respected him to much; he may be the old man of the stable and got under their skin from time to time, but everyone knew that Chance had all their best interests at heart; there wasn't a bad bone in his body, and it is one respect that they duly be extended to the elderly, as not to make their existence any more awkward than it will immutably become.

Rachelle carried out her chores with great diligence; cleaning and preparing the block and stables for the great comfort and splendour of her equine friends.

'How do you think they drove four horses at once Chance?' she asked totally oblivious, as all humans are, to animal talk.

'Tell her Chance.' Troy was keen to hear more and know himself.

'There has to be a lead horse, who is not necessarily the fastest, but he has to be smart, pick the fastest line through the course, and guide and navigate the team.'

'But there are two lead horses right?' Pogo chipped in.

'True, but one is designated the lead horse, the other may be the steadiest at cornering; he might have a shorter stride pattern and will aid the lead horse in attempting to bring the team into the corner at the right speed and tempo. There are three disciplines to carriage driving: dressage, marathon and an obstacle course, and each poses its own challenges for the team.'

The group all nodded respectively.

'The two rear horses, or 'Wheelers', are the power house of the team; their job is to take the weight of the carriage and driver, especially during braking, as the lead horses, called 'Leaders' by the way, cannot supply any braking; it is also their job to initially take the strain and get it all moving and generate enough momentum until the whole team can bring the carriage up to operating speed.'

Rachelle had stopped doing her chores and listened with great interest to Chance's grunting, whining, neighing and the subtle nuances of his voice; she didn't totally understand what was being said, it didn't need words, she had figured out it had to do with her question.

'A good team has to have a good driver; many a great team has seen their potential wasted under the guidance of an inexperienced and incompetent one.'

The conversation continued on a similar vein for several minutes, and all present had failed to notice Dave and Flugal exit the house and board Dave's car. Flugal had previously checked on his wife; she assured him she was okay and told him not to fuss, so he reluctantly agreed to accompany Dave on his search.

Dave drove at an almost break neck speed down the country lane. He kept up his forward speed into the main 'A' road leading into town, all the while chatting constantly about discovering more posters and information pertaining to the race and how big the prize must be, especially as they were advertising locally, not to say nationally. Flugal wondered how his great friend managed to concentrate on the road ahead, when clearly transfixed with discovering more posters and pertinent information regarding the race.

Dave, he accepted, had a weakness; one among many and that was gambling. He was the kind of gambler who would think nothing of placing a wager on how many times rain interrupted Wimbledon, which football team would score the quickest goals the most times, and so on; he prized these odd ball bets and the idea of a carriage race filled him with renewed vigour, exciting his gamblers intuition for making that elusive 'killing'.

'Steady! There's one on that telegraph pole.' said Flugal leaning forward to get a better look at the flier on the pole; sadly he was mistaken, it advertised a local rock band, and Dave, who had slowed, accelerated down the road.

A few more miles down the 'A' road the two companions has still failed to find that all elusive poster, but part of this was due in fact to the style and speed of Dave's driving; if they had bothered or had any inclination to stop at any of the bus stops or lay-by's their search would not have been in vain, but their eagerness to cover as much ground as possible in the shortest possible time only added to the length of their search, for they were not the only ones eager to find out more information and possibly participate in the race, and discarded posters littered the ground immediately surrounding the bus stops and lay-by's, stripped bare of those vital pieces of information.

'Stop!' shouted Flugal.

'Brake check.' Dave replied sarcastically as he duly obliged, his car skidding to a halt nearly rendering Flugal unconscious on the windscreen.

'I see it!' Dave stated enthusiastically.

'I see only stars.' Flugal still managed to raise a limp hand and point in the general direction to which Dave, having already vacated, and was scampering over the road to.

Dave retrieved the worn and weather beaten poster off the advertising board, paying particular attention not to be seen by any passers-by.

Back at the car Flugal gently caressed the lump that protruded just off his forehead. Dave jumped back in.

'Ouch....' Flugal complained as his friend entered the vehicle.

'I got it! I got it!' Dave's excitement was almost tangible. 'Have you got your mobile phone on you?'

'No.'

'Why not?'

'I always forget to pick it up when I go out. I just can't get used to carrying it.'

'How long have you owned one?' said Dave with a hint of friendly mockery.

'About ten years.'

'And still you forget!'

'Only if remember to turn it on.'

'Only if you remember to turn it on!' repeated Dave. 'Well I don't have one so I can't complain, on account that I refuse to surrender my right to any public amenity, and this one in the shape of a telephone.'

'My head hurts.'

'We'll just have to call from the house phone.' Dave continued, oblivious to Flugal's lamentation.

'Can I drive?' asked Flugal.

'I thought your head hurts!'

'I thought you didn't hear me. Driving relaxes me.' It was a blatant lie; Dave's driving just scared him out of his wits and one lump on his head was enough for one day.

'I'll drive and you read.' Flugal secretly praised himself on his prudence for such a remark, he read the situation immediately; Dave could not resist the temptation of reading the poster and being the first to glean all the relevant information and proudly explain the details to all who took an avid interest in its outcome.

'Sure.' came the reply, and the two men vacated the car and changed seats.

The drive back to the farm was pleasantly sedate, serene and delightfully uneventful for both men; Flugal because he could control their forward progress at a pace that did not vex him and eased his troubled soul, at the same time not irritating the throbbing, swelling lump on his forehead and Dave for he had plenty of time to study and memorise the information at his fingertips.

Flugal meandered down the country lane leading to Flugal Farm, enjoying the clear, crisp air, the harmonious lullaby's of birdsong and commented to himself yet again how much he genuinely loved this place, how much he loved his wife, who felt the same way about Flugal Farm as he did, and he was eternally grateful for that, and the joy his family, job and friends brought him every day, but such love, joy and happiness can only truly be appreciated and quantified when set against angst, stress and ill being, then and only then do we come to fully accept our luck and divine blessing on being honoured with such gifts. That dreaded expectation of failure and the loss of all they held dear, plus the relief of the withdrawal of such a burden weighed heavily on him day by day.

He turned into Flugal lane, the depressing thoughts only managing to evaporate only half the smile that once covered his whole face, and he slowed to an acceptable speed to enjoy the final moments of the drive.

The sharp pain returning to his head only highlighted further the fact he had not taken any notice of his discomfort during the drive home, and this added to his internal misery at the hopelessness of his situation.

The crunching of the gravel signalled the beginning of the entrance to Flugal Farm, when suddenly he was struck with a feeling of intense terror and agitation; he had failed to inform young Rachelle Perkins of their departure and his wife was fast asleep in bed. He brought the car to a halt and in a second jumped out of the driver's door leaving the gear in neutral and engine running. Dave called after him before shutting down the engine, but it fell on deaf ears. Flugal was half way across the yard by now.

In the stables he found nothing untoward, but its residents staring blankly back at him, he then scampered over to the fields; why he did not know, Rachelle rarely played in the fields, maybe it was to eradicate all the external possibilities before he ventured in doors. The fields were empty save Nigel wallowing in mud bath.

'Hey Mr Flugal! Come on in it's great; just what you need to relieve all that stress!' and he rolled belly up in the mud.

Flugal remarked to himself how crazy his pig had become and scampered across the yard to the house his heart beating nine to the dozen. All this witnessed by his "Boys".

'Is Flugal practising for the marathon?' said Biff

'Not the way I'd do it!' replied Troy

'We need a bigger yard.' chipped in Pogo. Chance said nothing.

What with his head, the vexation at not finding Rachelle, his sheer exhaustion, due to his appalling level of fitness, Flugal fell into the house.

Pushing open the door that connected the yard to the kitchen he was met by a wall of luscious aromas and fragrances that would knock a man off his feet and send his head into a spin. It brought home, with a grumble, his growing hunger.

At the table sat Rachelle smiling and tucking into a plate of his wife's delicious stew. His despair gave way to a beaming smile.

'Stew! Fantastic!' came Dave's reply from over his shoulder and he brushed past Flugal, eagerly displaying unabashed relish.

Mrs Flugal presented Dave with a steaming hot bowl of stew and he wasted no time grabbing a seat and tucking into his victuals, whilst explaining the root cause for their disappearance. Flugal followed suit. She had pre-empted their arrival by conveniently placing in the centre of the table a large plate of bread, within easy reach of all, to soak up the juices. Both famished recipients devoured the homemade bread. The two poster hunter's time away had been longer than either had realised; this was borne out by Flugal's wife presenting them with such a feast.

Just then the letter box flapper signalled the arrival of the days post. Dave suspended his enjoyment in Mrs Flugal's stew to vent his anger over the arrival of the post, and his resentment at yet another reduction to a public amenity.

'Only one postal delivery a day now! And even that one is normally late!.......Disgraceful!' he took another large mouthful of stew. 'One can still remember the days when you knew your postman on first name terms and there were two guaranteed deliveries a day; you could sort out the mornings post, complete any necessary chores that morning happy in the knowledge that an afternoon delivery would probably bring any remaining, anticipated correspondence.'

Mr and Mrs Flugal nodded in agreement, Rachelle remained mute; this meant nothing to someone so young.

Flugal left the table to collect the post, leaving his streaming bowl of stew to cool a few more degrees.

Mrs Flugal was very astute at gauging her husband's moods; she noticed any subtle shift in balance, and change in his demeanour. In his right hand he carried the bulk of the days post, about two to three letters and a magazine that his wife subscribed to, in his left a single letter in a white envelope which he furtively placed between the bread bin and a cupboard; he was saved from any embarrassment, not that any would have been forthcoming in the present company by the arrival of Nugget, who signalled his arrival by scratching vigorously against the back door. Rachelle did the honours and let him in.

Nugget sprang into the kitchen as Rachelle informed everyone she had work to do and departed. The aromas had penetrated the walls of the kitchen and wafted teasingly into the yard until he could bear it no longer, and instantly took to drooling incessantly. His mistress always saved a little something for him and today she did not disappoint. Nugget's appetite too was quenched by a huge bowl of warm stew.

Dave now finished, left the poster on the table for the Flugals to read, said his thank you's and bade farewell with the promise that he would find out all the relevant information and be back in touch. Secretly he was going down the bookies.

10

Rachelle was about to start her afternoon chores. This left Mr and Mrs Flugal alone at last with only Nugget for company.

'What's in the letter?' Mrs Flugal asked after her husband had studied it for a few minutes.

Nugget's ears pricked up, but he remained in a position of slumber.

'It's from the bank.'

'We knew it was coming.'

'I know, but it doesn't make it any easier when it finally arrives.'

'What are we going to do?'

'We can stall them for a little while, maybe a month or so, until we can sell some of the stock or something.'

'Hopefully not the horses!' Mrs Flugal said, the fear clearly evident in her voice. 'You really can't sell the "Boys", you do love them and need them.'

'We may not have any choice. It pains me no end to say this, but I know Williams would take them.'

'He'd work them into the ground you know that. It would be the end of them. Poor old Chance is too old, he wouldn't last five minutes, and Rachelle would be devastated!'

'I know, I know. I don't want too.' Flugal pleaded. 'That.....that would be a last resort, a very, very last resort, but we need money, we desperately need money.'

Mrs Flugal placed a protective arm around her husband and fought back the tears as she remembered her own experience with the antiques dealer.

'I will find us all someway out.' Flugal said after a few minutes contemplation.

'It's a shame you don't have any horses capable of racing carriages. If Dave is correct it could be an option we didn't have before.'

'It has crossed my mind.'

Nugget was all ears now; Chance and the "Boys" urgently needed to hear this. He slowly, deliberately made his way towards the back door, scratching the bottom left side lightly to alert either his master or mistress to his imminent departure. Mr Flugal obliged only after stroking Nugget affectionately and remarking what a good and faithful boy he was.

Once clear of the house Nugget darted straight for the stables, to where he found Rachelle about to start work.

'We're in big trouble boys! It's far worse than any of us ever realised.'

'What!' said Pogo 'How bad is your perception of "big trouble"?'

'We're in really big trouble. Flugal really is broke; the bank's written to him and they are going to foreclose! Lest I think that's the proper expression.'

'Bad, bad, bad.' reflected Nigel.

'And it gets worse; he may have to sell up and Williams has put a bid in for you guys!'

'That's really big trouble.' Pogo replied.

'What does he want with a pig?' He's not starting a pig farm is he?'

'I don't know, but I think you're okay. He wants the "Boys".' said Nugget putting Nigel's mind at rest.

'I'm not working for that lunatic. We won't last five minutes' Biff kicked out at the back of his stall to vent his anger.

'Not Chance anyhow.' Troy may have been more than capable of handling and enduring Williams demanding regime, but his instinctive statement regarding the senior citizen of their group reduced everybody to a brief moment of silence.

'Anybody got any suggestions?' Nugget broke the silence. 'At least you lot have got somewhere to go, albeit more like a work house, but what about Nigel and me!' Nugget continued in extreme agitation.

'I'm not filling anybodies plate!' exclaimed a clearly disturbed Nigel.

'And who wants a ten year old clapped out dog.'

'I'll take you Nugget.' Rachelle interjected.

Everybody was stunned to silence once again; in all the excitement and consternation they had all completely forgot about her. Could she understand what they were saying, had they underestimated her powers, they all waited for her next comment to receive confirmation. Nothing was forthcoming so they put it down to a coincidence.

'I don't know.' Chance broke his silence. 'We're not exactly in a position to offer any advice, even if we had any to give.'

'There's prize money for that race Nugget. You tell them.' once again Rachelle stunned them and caught them off guard. 'I saw Mr Flugal's friend Dave leave, he's bound to be going to find out some more, it could be a lot of money.' She approached Chance and stroked his forehead 'Wouldn't it be great Chance if we could enter that race. You and the three youngsters could show them, show everybody exactly what you're all made of, by winning the race, the prize money and saving the farm, but you're riding horses so I suppose not, and anyhow where are we going to get hold of a racing carriage, I bet there really expensive.'

Rachelle, sadly, had no way of communicating two way with any of the animals, but this mattered not a jot, her words rang through the stables as a church bell peels throughout the surrounding countryside beckoning its worshippers on a Sunday morning.

Nigel was the first to speak 'How to convince Flugal to enter the race. That is if you lot reckon you are up for it, you being riding horses and all!'

The three youngsters jokingly aired their displeasure at Nigel's remark although they all knew he was really only pulling their tails, and they all vowed they could beat, outrace any four horse carriage anywhere and anytime.

'And then to make him think it was all his idea.' Nigel continued.

Rachelle finished her chores, wished them all well, and said farewell promising to see them all again before the day was out and to make them comfortable for the night.

'How are we going to mange that?' said Nugget.

'Hang on just a minute,' interrupted Chance, 'who said we were going to enter a carriage race! Do you guys seriously reckon you are up to it?'

'Why not.' added Troy.

'Yeah, why not.' agreed Pogo.

'Because we know nothing about it.' Chance went on.

'You do.' chimed in Biff.

'Only from word of mouth; I have no practical experience whatsoever!'

'What do you remember?' Pogo posed the question everybody wanted to ask.

'Not much.'

'Well then, we'll help jog your memory.' Nugget's enthusiasm was fuelled now by an extreme bout of self-preservation 'I'll pull a wheelbarrow with Nigel and you tell us what we're doing wrong.'

'Yeah.' agreed Nigel.

'Are you nuts?' Chance was struggling to accept the situation unravelling in front of him.

'It's worth a go.' implored Nigel

Nugget pulled over a wheelbarrow that Rachelle had left leaning against an opposite wall, collected some tack that was hanging up and tied them very dextrously to the barrow to make their own make shift carriage, so he and Nigel could each pull it with their teeth.

Anyone looking on at the friends could not have helped but stare in utter amazement and disbelief at such a spectacle; Nugget and Nigel lifted the barrow of its legs and pulled it, with no small amount of effort, around the stables in a mini circuit.

Chance was exasperated, he was lost for words; this handmade carriage had about as much an effect on jogging his aged memory than watching Chloe the cat, who lived in the neighbouring farm and frequented Flugal Farm on a regular basis to be pampered by Mrs Flugal, drink a bucket full of creamy milk. He did admire his friends determination though.

This did not deter our two faithful friends from enthusiastically sprinting around the make shift circuit shouting and hollering for all their worth, strumming up as much of an atmosphere as possible. In their naivety, as innocent as it can ever be, they deduced it could only aid Chance's fading memory and help recollect all that was lost.

Pogo, Biff and Troy joined in the mirth, roaring on the two 'carriage horses' from the top of their lungs.

From within the house the Flugals and Rachelle were alerted to the commotion erupting now from inside the barn, and went to investigate.

Due to the excitement generated, Nigel now was taking joke bets on who would win, bearing in mind the number of participants, that they all failed to notice the arrival of the Flugals and Rachelle.

'Come on Chance what are we doing wrong?' shouted Nugget.

'I don't know.'

'Give us a clue will you, I'm knackered already!' pleaded Nigel.

'I think you're cornering to quickly... in my humble opinion.' Pogo tried to offer some encouragement.

'Cornering to quickly!' Biff said mildly incredulous.

'You can corner to quickly you know.' replied Pogo, trying hard to hide his displeasure at having his advice questioned.

'Rubbish!'

'And you've never seen a car or a horse box turn over from to much speed in the turn.' he quickly added, now happy in the knowledge that he had won his case.

'Nigel?'

'Yes Chance' panted Nigel in reply.

'As you're on the inside you need to turn slower. You always put a slower steadier horse on the inside.'

'Right.' And Nigel visibly slowed; almost immediately the 'carriage' steadied and they actually got faster around the turns.

'That means then....,' started Troy, '.....that the faster horse must have to slow himself on the flat so the team can keep pace with each other.'

'Exactly!'

'Who's the fastest out of us?' Biff had to asked the inevitable question that was sure to open up a huge can worms.

'Me.' said Pogo

'Why you.' replied Troy, his back now up.

'Because you're too big!'

'Too big!'

'Yeah, too big. Being the most muscular doesn't always make you the best at everything you know!,'

Troy squared up to Pogo, but any further disagreements were snuffed out by Mrs Flugal.

'What are you doing Nugget?'

Nugget and Nigel ground to a halt, but they had failed to take into account the laws of inertia and the wheel barrow continued on its forward motion and collected both 'horses' and deposited them both, head first, in a pile of hay situated in the corner of the stable block.

'Is that a recognised stopping procedure Nugget?' Biff could not help himself even in the presence of his owners.

Seeing Nugget and Nigel prostrate in a pile of hay, and neither had faired any better than the other, made Rachelle laugh out loud, and she pleasantly chided them both for their style and content.

'Strange.' queried Mrs Flugal.

'In what way?' Mr Flugal inquired.

'It's almost as if they could read our minds.'

'You mean about the carriage race.'

'Exactly! Nugget's told them about the poster.'

'They've been practicing.' laughed Rachelle.

'With a dog and a pig!' said Flugal gleefully, momentarily suspending his disbelief at the scene being played out before him; it did indeed resemble a practice ring with a dog and a pig as contestants.   'Okay if they are practicing...why?

Chance cleared his throat and looked at the ceiling, deliberately avoiding Flugal's eye line.

By now Nugget had managed to extricate himself from the hay, and he approached Flugal very sheepishly. Nigel was not so lucky.

'Did he see the crash?' he quizzed Chance.

'No.' came the reply. In fact he had, Chance was saving Nugget's blushes.

'Then has he figured out what we're up to?'

'Yes.'

'Excellent.'

'Excellent, yes!' the "Boys" all said in unison.

'Now we don't have to waste time in trying to convince him.' Nugget added.

'There's no guarantee he will enter, he just knows what you're up to. But it does appear they have been discussing such an enterprise.' Chance said, making eye contact with Flugal, who was staring straight back at him with the same expression he had when he questioned Nugget in the car.

'What's happening?' Nigel was now free of the hay. 'And thanks for all your help and assistance.......' He was about to say more until he realised the present circumstances and remained quiet, trying not to bring any unwanted attention onto himself.

'So Chance.' started Flugal 'Learn anything?'

'No, not really!' Flugal was again struck dumb; not only by the speed of the reply, but also the Chance's tone and inflection.

'What did you learn?'

'How not to corner!' They all laughed.

'I'm so sorry Chance, I wish I knew what you were saying, but it sounded good anyhow.' said Flugal.

'See they can talk.' shouted Rachelle.

'Of course they can talk' said Mrs Fugal 'They understand everything we say; it is only us humans who are ignorant of the animal kingdom, we are far too domesticated.' Flugal now looked at his wife with a mixture of astonishment, pride and respect; they may have been married for over twenty-five years, but she still on rare occasions, surprised him beyond all measure with her sagacity, wit and good old fashioned common sense.

'That's what I've always said too....they can talk!' and with that Rachelle paid particular attention to Chance, stroking him affectionately on the nose.

'Well if you're right then they can understand everything I'm about to say!' Flugal made eye contact with all the occupants of the stables one by one to gauge their reaction, but still ended up none the wiser; the one area where animals dominate humans is in the arena of safety and self preservation; animals always instinctively know when to remain quiet, keep perfectly still and can sense the imminent arrival of danger. Domesticated man has lost this innate ability.

Chance, Pogo, Biff, Troy, Nigel and Nugget stared back blankly at Mr Flugal.

This stale mate lasted a few seconds before Flugal decided it was such a futile gesture to even attempt to suss out his animals hidden abilities, but he was finding it harder by the day to convince himself that it was all a load of rubbish and utterly insane, and so in the end gave it one last shot.

'If we enter the race......if we enter the race,' he reiterated, 'how and where are we going to get horses who are more than capable of coping with demands associated with carriage racing, because I know nothing about it.'

'We could get some from somewhere.' said Mrs Flugal realising where her husband was going with this. 'Even though I presume they must be very difficult to source.'

'Extremely.' was his only reply.

Nugget turned out to be the guilty party and broke the silence 'We are more than capable of challenging anybody to a carriage race!'

'What do you mean "we" ' Biff was heard from the rear.

'That's the royal "we".' Nugget turned to look over his shoulder holding his nose haughtily in the air.

'How are "we" going to manage that?' Biff went on.

'You'll need back up.'

'Back up!' It was Troy's turn to question Nugget. 'Back up!'

'Ever successful team needs a smooth, efficient support team.'

'And not forgetting scouting.' Nigel faced the boys, nodding in agreement to his own suggestion. 'And we haven't even touched on diet yet!'

'Don't even go there!' Pogo turned his nose up at that.

'Well what do you think now?' Flugal said to his wife.

'I told you they could speak and understand everything you say!'

'We say!'

'Whatever my dear, whatever.' she said smiling.

Flugal's mind was now in a flat spin; he still resolutely refused to believe these, his animals, could possibly comprehend the English language, let alone discuss it, yet here they were answering his query and discussing possible solutions amongst themselves; horses to pigs, pigs to dogs, dogs to horses, the more he thought about it the worst it seemed and the faster his head spun.

'Use your own horses Mr Flugal.' Flugal looked Rachelle firmly in the eye; she did not flinch. 'Chance will lead them all to victory!' she uttered this with such conviction that Flugal, or anybody within ear shot, would have believed it possible.

'She's right.' said Mrs Flugal 'You do say yourself that Chance is the most intelligent horse you've ever known!'

'You here that old man? said Troy with a touch of friendly reverie. 'You're the Einstein of the equine world!'

'I am!' there's was no one more shocked at that piece of news than old Chance.

'You are!' said Rachelle beaming a big, bright, beautiful smile. Chance could not help himself and smiled back with equal measure.

'That's it then, it's settled, we'll enter the carriage race with the "Boys".' Mrs Flugal's mind was set and with that she marched back to the house leaving Flugal, Rachelle and the newly formed team to make preparations and plans.

'She is serious!' muttered Nigel to nobody in particular.

'I guess so.' said Chance.

'This is fantastic!' exclaimed Rachelle, giving Chance and then the rest of the group, including Nigel, the biggest hug she could muster. 'All of us together in a race, and I know we can win.'

'Your optimism is commendable.' replied Mr Flugal, striding now fully into the stables, scratching his chin in that time honoured way to denote deep thought, contemplation and resignation. 'We're going to have our work cut out, as we have no experience between any of us in any form carriage racing. I'll need to go to the library.' he then added as an afterthought.

'I'll get all we need to know off the 'net' Mr Flugal.' injected Rachelle.

'That'll be excellent Rachelle. Now all we need to do now is find a carriage, they don't grow on trees unfortunately. Where are we ever going to find one? And all this has got to be completed in less than eight weeks, as there will be three disciplines with much technical expertise to train for, over the two days of competition!'

'You're pointing out all the negatives, Mr Flugal.' Rachelle replied.

The "Boys" nodded in agreement.

'I'm sorry, but we've got to accept the job at hand. It's all well and good deciding to enter these things, but the logistics behind it all are a different matter.' he added without any thought. 'This is scary.' But the realisation that there may be a solution to their predicament, albeit long shot, lifted his spirits for a short while, only for them to be tempered by these new found obstacles in his path that he knew would trouble him greatly.

'None the less Chance and the "Boys" will win! Won't you Chance?' Rachelle resumed her stroking of his forehead.

'We can win Rachelle, don't you worry.' Troy for one was in a right bullish mood. All the talk, now that it had been decided to enter the race, was about winning and the odds against. It had summoned his blood and he was well up for it. 'We better not waste anymore time, we need to know as much as possible about these disciplines; where the course is, the layout, the terrain, how many turns there are, whether they be predominantly left or right and more importantly who is going where?'

At this all the animals looked to Chance to make some sort of decision, but how could he; these were his friends, and although he was well aware of all their strengths and weaknesses, he was no expert on deciding who would run where and why. This needed work, and a lot of hard graft.

'Well, Chance' started Flugal, 'everybody seems to be looking to you for guidance and leadership, so what do you suggest old friend?'

'See you do believe.' smiled Rachelle.

'Got to believe in something. If you can understand me Chance give me a sign; where do we start?'

'You can't Chance.' cried Nugget.

'Why not.' Pogo barked out.

'Because then he will know for sure that I....we can understand him. At the moment he still is not one hundred percent certain.'

'There are more important issues here Nugget,' started Chance looking respectfully at his canine friend. 'we've got to save the farm, Mr and Mrs Flugal, our livelihoods, and if in doing so we have to sacrifice something we hold dear in order to protect something far more precious, then so be it!'

Just at that precise moment, as if providence had ordained it, Dave arrived back at the farm.

Now would be a prudent a time as any, if not tailor made, to describe in full his adventure, for there is much to tell.

11

Dave did as he promised and rang the telephone number printed on the bottom of the poster then promptly gathered all the information his curiosity sought; the drive was indeed to be run, not in eight weeks time as Flugal had surmised, but six over a weekend starting with a dressage section followed by a nine kilometre marathon run on day one, with the obstacle section on day two; the difficulty of the courses expressed the gravity in which the event was beheld by its sponsors. They wanted it regarded as a premier event, especially as horse carriage driving was not publicised as much as other equine pursuits.

Once having ordered the application form, for they point blankly refused to accept Dave's entry over the phone, he took a brief reconnaissance over to where they intended to hold part of the marathon course. He had not expected anybody else to have been that smart to reconnoitre its layout, but he was to be bitterly disappointed. Who should be there, but none other than the insidious Mr Williams, who had himself entered the race the day before.

A third of the distance into the prospected course Mr Williams presented himself to Dave.

Taken aback by the surprise encounter with Mr Williams; Dave knew of him and had seen him driving around town, his reputation had indeed proceeded him, and he grew an immediate contempt for the man and chose to answer any questions falsely and incomplete. Williams opening gambit involved the race.

'What are you doing here? You're not seriously considering entering the race?'

'No!'

'So why are you here?'

'I'm out for a walk.'

'But this is private ground.'

'And why are you here?'

'I'm going to enter the race!'

'Good for you.'

'You're Flugal's friend aren't you?'

'I know the man.'

'I know you know the man. I'm told you're related to him!'

'That's a vicious and malicious rumour which has no concrete evidence.' Dave said jokingly, his tongue firmly in his cheek; his contempt for Williams knew no bounds, so he held the answer as a justifiable response, but it did kind of give away his true position to the cunning, contemptible Williams.

'He's going to enter the race...........excellent! You tell that relation of yours that I long for the day when we may do battle!'

Dave on any normal day would have retreated back to his misanthropic tendencies and delivered, at Williams doorstep, such a volley that the man could have used it himself on many similar circumstances.

Williams brushed past Dave in that way that disdainful human beings do when they want to make a statement short of any words, and once clear of the man it enabled him to gain a second or two breathings space, and openly laugh at the thought of doing battle with Flugal.

This was red rag to the bull; Dave's back was up and his blood boiling, but he had the good sense not to prolong the conversation or make any form of eye contact with his adversary. Instead he kept on walking in his original direction.

'Damn that man!' he finally uttered to himself 'Damn him. I would not put it past Williams, that he is behind Bennett and the bank's attempt to wrestle the farm away from Flugal!'

He strode on, running over and over the brief, but annoying conversation with Williams.

'He obviously thinks he's going to win this race; it's that kind of arrogant, conceited assumption someone like him would say.' he stopped a few hundred yards from where he set off the second time 'We'll beat him, that would stick in his throat forever; beaten by Flugal and his team.' and then as if a revelation had suddenly been revealed to him 'Yes!' he turned on his heels and marched back to his car.

For someone so excited, Dave drove back to the farm at a sensible sedate pace; maybe it was to do with the ramifications that went with the decision to enter the race. He could not have known that at almost the exact time he was bent on beating Williams, that Flugal had settled on entering.

At almost half distance to the farm Dave took a detour, which delayed his arrival back to the farm by nearly an hour. On his arrival he found Flugal where we left him.

'What's up?' he said approaching Flugal and Rachelle.

'Guess what?'

'No idea, but you not going to believe this. Guess who I met?'

'Williams.'

'How did you know.' answered a shocked Dave.

'It was an educated guess.' laughed a nervous Flugal, not knowing as yet what had transpired between the two.

'Oh, well as you've guessed right I did meet the odious Mr Williams. I met him on the site where part of the marathon section is allegedly going to be held, and what's more he's entered.'

'Williams has entered?'

'Yep! You're going to race aren't you?' Dave read the situation perfectly.

'It was the wife's idea. That was my surprise.'

'Fantastic!'

'I'm coming to realise this little venture is not at all what I originally thought.'

'I got us a carriage!' Dave beamed.

'What!.......Fantastic! Where?'

'Fantastic!' cried out Rachelle. 'That was giving us as major headache.' All the "Boys" nodded.

'Us a major headache?' Dave said jokingly.

'This will be a team effort.' injected Rachelle.

'That it will, that it will!' Flugal felt a little more at ease after this brief exchange now that Dave was firmly on board; for once Williams had done him a great service, he thought, he may have had a little bother trying to convince him of the merits of such a venture, but meeting Williams was a major bonus and with little Rachelle, wise beyond her tender years, this was indeed going to be team effort. Her deft touch with the horses was going to be invaluable. How right that was last statement was would only become clear when their backs were firmly against the wall.

'Where's this carriage?' Rachelle asked Dave.

'Yes, this carriage. How did you come by that? Flugal was as intrigued as Rachelle.

'You're not going to believe this, but I got a phone call a couple of days ago from a lad I did a bit of work for a couple of months back. It transpired his uncle, who had sadly passed away quite suddenly, had a carriage and did I know anybody who would want to buy it; he actually had you in mind Flugal, knowing your expertise with horses. I told him carriages weren't really your thing, but I'd ask. Well it completely slipped my mind until today and seeing that poster. I was going to run it by you first, but then I thought what if someone beat us to it and then what? So I rang him back, asked if it was still for sale. It was. And so I bought it and with everything else that's happened, you'll agree, it's been a hell of a day.' Flugal nodded.

'On my way back from the so called track I went by this lad's place and paid a deposit on it,' Dave reached into his pocket and produced a crumpled up piece of paper 'and I have a receipt. I really needed to get it before anybody else found out about the race!'

'How much did it cost?'

'A couple of hundred.'

'Is that good or bad?'

'I don't know. All I know was we needed a carriage.'

'True. Did he know about the race? Is that why he wanted to sell at this time?' Before Dave could answer, Flugal finished his sentence. 'Anyway it doesn't matter the main thing is we have one.' Flugal patted Dave on the shoulder. 'Thank you.'

'Hey, what are friends for.'

'What condition is it in?' inquired Rachelle.

'Couldn't tell you. All I thought was what a stroke of luck, almost like it was meant to be or something. His uncle did used it a lot, so it must be in some kind of working order, and anyway whatever needs to be fixed I'll fix it.'

'Our immediate problem now is to decide what order to place the horses in and find a place to train!' Flugal scratched his chin as he pondered the dilemma.

'Why not let the horses decide.' said Rachelle.

'Sounds like a plan to me.' agreed Dave.

'Or better still let Chance decide.' Rachelle backed up her argument with a suggestion she knew Flugal would not disagree with. 'You know that makes sense Mr Flugal.'

'Yes, yes you're right!.' he said striding forward to Chance's stable.

The animals had kept a respectful silence throughout the conversation, enabling them to gauge the mood of the moment.

Chance wondered for a second or two should he admit to and express his opinion on any formation the four friends could make, but on this occasion he chose to keep his own counsel on the whole debate. It is worth noting at this juncture the importance Chance held in keeping mum on the topic; that in order to gain the utmost advantage, it is an essential requirement to gamble the information at your fingertips, when to use that information is just as important as when not to and one should gauge the mood of the moment to use those circumstances to their fullest advantage. In short Chance waited to see Flugal's or Dave's or anybody else's ideas first, just in case his was the inferior plan of action.

Flugal pondered many different plans and stratagems that he had, many were just him voicing his mind, mostly they were worthless and he knew it, but it did not restrain him from airing them; they were flawed from the outset by lack of foundation and forward planning. Finally he shook his head, turned to Dave, followed this with a shrug of the shoulders and decided to check on his wife. Most of the day was now behind them and it was vastly approaching teatime in the Flugal household, and nothing could have been decided on an empty stomach. And with a passing remark that he would think about it over tea, made for the house.

'Good idea.' Dave gestured to Rachelle to follow; he was relishing the thought of another super Flugal feast.

Now alone Chance broke his silence by asking that peremptory question guaranteed to open the floor to debate and discussion and ultimately allow him to air whatever judgement he had passed without causing offence.

'Well what do you think?'

'I think we're in big trouble, that's what I think!' Nugget let out a deep sigh.

'Any suggestions?' Chance asked again.

'We could run away and join a circus!' Pogo smiled then seeing scowls emerging on some of the faces quickly added. 'Only joking.'

'If we're going to go down guys we've got to go down fighting, that's my motto.' Nigel puffed out his chest to emphasise his point.

'I'll go number one.'

'Where's one Troy?' enquired Biff.

'I take it it's at the front, I mean by that that it's the closest to the carriage......you know a Wheeler.'

Chance nodded, truth is he had no idea, but it sounded feasible.

'I'll go number one then.' Troy added a second time.

'Chance you've got the most experience at this kind of thing; racing I mean, you should lead from the second row.'

'Only if we all decide before hand, we'll put it all to a vote and stick to whatever we decide, we can't have any infighting or squabbles. If you want me leading I'll do it.'

'You should choose the formation.' said Nugget.

'That's not democratic Nugget.'

'I don't really care, this is our survival we're talking about here, you choose.'

'No, we all choose, we all share the responsibility.' Chance looked about him for any signs of decent; it would have bitterly disappointed him if any of them had argued over a joint responsibility, this was also their fight not just his, he would stand and fight with the rest of them, regardless of his advanced years, but to shoulder the burden of responsibility alone was inherently irresponsible.

'Pogo you're faster than all of us. You should ride up front with Chance.' Biff dropped his head after this recommendation, he was clearly upset.

'Biff you're just as fast as me!'

'No. I know my place, you are faster, you should lead with Chance's instruction until you feel comfortable, you beat us all to dinner; we all joke that you need to give us at least a two minute head start to reach the haylage and you still beat us. That is your rightful position.' Biff once again dropped his head on completion, but this time he turned in his stall to face the wall.

Pogo shrugged his shoulders, nobody could come up with any idea to relieve Biff's melancholy; this time they did look to Chance to lead and he did not hesitate.

'What's the matter Biff?'

'Nothing!'

'Liar!' shouted Troy

'What's the matter?' Chance asked again.

'There is nothing wrong with me, I am quite alright, in fact I have never been in so much total control of my faculties.' Pogo stepped forward to the opening of Biff's stable 'Then why the face?'

'Biff turned to confront them all face on. 'I can only bring weakness and vulnerability to your chances of success and salvation; I do not have the strength of Troy, to pull and carry the weight of the carriage; I do not have the speed of Pogo, so as to aid the swiftness of the carriage over the course and supply worthy support to Chance; of Chance I do not have your sagacity or knowledge of professional sport. What can I bring to the team? Nothing! Nugget and Nigel will add invaluable support and intelligence so you will not be competing blind.'

'Rubbish!' Nugget was the first to reply.

'What can I bring Nugget?'

'Brains!' Nigel uttered these words without a hint of anger and despair. 'Biff you're the smartest one among us, and that's coming from a pig.'

'Here, here.' said Chance, then quickly followed that up with 'No offence Nigel.'

'None taken.'

'This fight, race, drive, call it what you will, will need brains as well as brawn.' Chance looked directly at Biff than all of them slowly; they were all in this together and he needed to them to feel it. 'Gentlemen. The race is not always won by the fleet of foot or the strong, but sometimes, sometimes by those who simply believe they can. And we can if we pull together and believe, and nobody should think that their contribution is too small or insignificant, because it is also the small things as well as the large that matter in the long run, then we can overcome all obstacles in our path!'

'See Biff? said Nugget. 'Everybody has a part to play in this.'

'Chance is right, we must all share responsibility, for failure will be felt by all!' added Troy.

'Right then let's form a plan of action!' Biff was now back fully to his old self. 'Chance you're the only one among us that has any idea how to formulate anything remotely resembling a training program; if we are going to race three disciplines over a couple of days then we are going to have to get fit, learn to work as a team, learn each other's strengths and weaknesses inside out and above all eat properly.'

'I like the sound of the last one!' said Troy.

'Agreed!' added Pogo.

Now that they were all in agreement, no more so than old Chance, the joy and gladness he felt seeing and hearing one of the young ones taking on responsibility, filled him with pride, similar to any father would feel seeing their only son achieving success in the face of overwhelming odds, they further discussed tactics.

'Nigel you've got to be in charge of intelligence,' Biff continued, 'we need to know the exact layout of the course or courses, and how many left or right hand turns there are on each.'

'Consider it done.' replied Nigel.

'Nugget.' Biff went on. 'Security!'

'You bet.' Nugget was the ideal candidate for this sensitive undertaking.

'Williams has entered, he wants Flugal Farm, he will not want Flugal to win; his only chance to succeed is by achieving our downfall, and he can only guarantee that and assure Flugal's and our destruction is to prevent us from winning. Williams will do anything to gain the upper hand; if he cannot win himself then the next best thing for him is to stop us winning. We'll have to set up signal posts to warn us of his imminent arrival.'

All were again in agreement after Biff's speech.

Back in the house a similar conversation was running on a parallel track between the Flugals and Dave.

'William's is not to be trusted.' Dave's grave countenance supported the gravity of his statement.

'Neither is Bennett!' added Mrs Flugal.

'He's just a bank manager.' stated Dave in a matter of fact way. 'Nobody trusts them anyway!'

'You don't know that.' argued Flugal. 'He is after all only doing his job.'

This annoyed his wife immensely. 'You are so soft and far too trustworthy sometimes, and that infuriates me. He may be a bank manager, but look at the way he's treated us and Mr Miller! He wants to foreclose on us; we are a bad debt according to him.'

This news shocked Dave to his core; he knew things were tight and that trouble lay in wait for them on the horizon, but it still did little to prepare him or help null the pain and shock hearing it first hand from the Flugals. 'How long have you got?'

'We reckon a month or two, maybe less unless if we can stump up some capital in the short term.' said Mrs Flugal.

'Is that possible?'

'We would need to sell assets.' Flugal said after his wife looked to him for support.

Dave studied his long time pal; melancholic and dejected his old friend seemed to stare blankly at the table.

'The horses.' he finally and reluctantly muttered.

'Sell the horses!' Dave exclaimed incredulously. 'But you love those horses.'

'No!' shouted Rachelle in despair, she could and would not entertain again the thought of losing her beloved Chance.

'We don't want to, we really don't want to!'

'I've got some money stashed away for a rainy day and it's just sitting there doing nothing, far better it did some good.' Dave added.

'No Dave.' Flugal now sat back in his chair and confronted his friend over his very generous offer. 'This is our problem not yours, things just didn't pan out the way I thought they would and before we knew it the debts kept on piling up and we got backed into a corner.'

'You could lose the farm.' It was Dave's turn to look concerned.

'It would break our hearts to lose this farm, the "Boys", Nugget, Nigel, everything really, but we cannot drag everybody down with us. Yours is a very kind and generous offer Dave, but this is our problem.' Once Mrs Flugal had finished she stood beside her husband in a sign of solidarity and laid her hand on his shoulder and gave him an affectionate kiss on the top of his head. He in turn nodded in acquiescence.

'It's my money and I'll do what I want with it!' replied Dave. 'And if I can help out my friends, especially those I'm really close to, then that's my prerogative.'

'I have some pocket money saved up, it's not much, but it's yours if you want it?' Rachelle interjected.

Flugal felt a lump swell up in his throat and his voice dried up. It was left to Mrs Flugal to answer.

'Thank you Rachelle. We would like you to keep that money, which we know you've worked extremely hard to earn. You need those savings more than we do. We would feel very sad if we felt we had deprived you of whatever gift you had saved the money up for.'

'It's for my riding!'

In one fail swoop she had silenced any arguments and objections against her wishes to spend her money how she saw fit.

'You keep that money my dear.' Mrs Flugal went on with great affection. 'It's lovely to know that if we ever need your help we can rely on you.'

They both knew the Flugals would never have taken Rachelle or Dave up on their offers no matter how bad the circumstances.

Mrs Flugal laid out a sumptuous feast for the four of them; all talk of debts and selling assets would be suspended over tea. They all waited respectfully for Mrs Flugal to sit down before tucking into the delicious offerings, then they attacked the sustenance with great gusto and relish.

Back in the stables, similarly not a word was spoken; it had all been agreed upon, as much as could have been settled in that short space of time.

12

The sun rose high and bright over the beautiful, picturesque countryside that surrounded Flugal farm and bathed everything it touched in crisp golden sunlight, evaporating the pale blue of the morning twilight to reveal the sunrise in all its glory.

In the stables the comrades-in-arms had all slept soundly; eager to venture forth on their new adventure; for the gains now outweighed the expenditure, and personal motives were all suspended for the good of the team and ascended all others. They were keen to be underway and satisfy those two sub-desires of achievement and satisfaction. Each companion had lulled themselves to sleep dreaming of glory, hero worship from the many bystanders and spectators as well as gaining the respect and acceptance of their fellow team mates, friends and competitors; to stand on an equal footing and prove oneself worthy of the challenge.

In the house Flugal arose at his customary time; now being back to his former self he felt invigorated in a strange kind of way; the race had awakened a passion in him that he was totally unaware of. Listening to young Rachelle last night in the car, as he drove her home to her granny's, the school holidays nearly being upon them and she would be able to spend all her time at the farm and help out as much as her grandmother would allow, which was everyday really. She loved her grandmother very much and that love was mirrored in her allowing Rachelle to indulge in her passion for horses, and now they had a race to enter and the sheer excitement and enthusiasm she injected was infectious. She would spend the entire summer holiday or as long as was permissible on the farm, she expostulated about the race, her excitement of seeing the "Boys" take on other teams and winning the race and prize money, proving to everyone they were the best around.

Rachelle had no doubt as to the outcome; it would be the salvation they were all looking for. She spoke all the way home as if it was her farm and her horses in danger, and she was competing herself. Flugal never entertained the thought of correcting her or felt anything remotely resembling resentment or any other kind of emotion, other than eternal thanks that someone other than himself should show such love and dedication to them all. She was so persuasive that by the time he returned home he too believed whole heartily they would win and salvage the farm.

Flugal sauntered out to the stables, sucking up the morning air in large deep breaths. but he had an ulterior motive to the early start on this most handsome of mornings; a letter from Bennett had arrived the previous day to summon him to the bank that very afternoon. Whether he needed inspiration before the confrontation even he was unsure; he played his cards close to his chest, mainly out of care for his wife; she did not take stress to well and anyway if he could protect her from anything unsavoury he did so, the main reason for him hiding the banks letters and trying to resolve this predicament before it got out of hand. Any melancholy that might have been lingering dissipated little by little in sight of God's omnipotent beauty.

He felt like he meandered rudderless around the yard; there were many jobs to do, the horses required feeding, the tack was in need of a clean, the drainage in the fields was overdue a start and should be prepped, but he always found excuses not to begin that particular chore and continued on his way not quite sure what to inspect yet, if he was inspecting at all. Rachelle had set aside a hearty breakfast for all the farms four legged occupants, she also helped out with the livery horses whenever their owners were unable to make out to the farm. Regarding food they were mercifully okay, he had enough provisions for them to last the duration. Rachelle also enjoined the cleaning, organising and laying out of the tack and he loathed the idea of denying her that pleasure, and finally the drainage was undoubtedly the domain of his good friend Dave and it would be deemed after all bad manners to start without him, and so he convinced himself that his responsibility lay in a purely advisory and monitoring role.

There were many other minor chores alas that found themselves usurped by reasons to admire this beautiful morning and to enjoy his glorious surroundings; on many recent occasions such emotions had pre-empted the foreboding of the 'doom and gloom' mentality, but not on this day; the race and to a lesser extent Mrs Dougherty's buried treasure, although he still believed it was a load of old hooey, but even this wouldn't stop him finding his father's letters and correspondence on the matter, had lifted his lagging spirits; what if they could actually win the race, his mind switched violently back and forth fighting vigorously for the high ground, yes they could win, no it was folly to even begin to believe that such amateurs as they could triumph against more established professionals, but he had never heard of professional carriage racers, surely they are just keen amateurs just like them, they had a better than average chance, he was a horseman, albeit riding and teaching, but he would learn, he had to learn, there was nothing he could not learn about horses and there is no greater incentive than the protection and salvation of ones loved ones. Optimism ultimately triumphed and gained the high ground, it steeled his determination and he once again sucked in the crisp, clear morning air, fed the livery horses their breakfast, checked on their well being for all the owners, and vowed never to lose the farm or its occupants no matter what, no matter how great, dreadful and heavy the burden, he would succeed, enduring any circumstance or personal hardship to secure the lasting preservation of all that he held dear.

Flugal navigated his way finally over to the "Boys" stables. He stopped one full stride short of the entrance, not wanting to disturb the inmates for reasons totally unrelated to anything remotely resembling a guilty conscience. It was just early.

He checked the coast was clear, then slowly but surely inched his head around the side of the stable block door, respecting the comfort and tranquillity of his fellow racers and friends. He was met by six pairs of beady little eyes underlined by six huge cheesy grins. Flugal realised immediately he had been rumbled in his furtive approach to the stables and abandoned his futile effort, standing hands on hips facing the six.

'I take it you're all raring to go?' he still felt a complete fool opening any form of discussions with animals, even his four legged mates.

His team mate's cheesy, cheerful countenance never wavered and his question appeared to fall on deaf ears.

'Okay.' Flugal went on 'I can clearly take a hint and see by your reception this morning that we're all in for a lot of fun and games, and we are in agreement as to our participation in the race. I am very glad to see you're eager to get going!'

Again no reply was forthcoming; Flugal at least thought his latest statement would have extracted some signal to him that they understood him, but no.

To fully understand their continued silence, which to the uninitiated would appear as extremely bad manners, we will hark back to a brief, but important discussion, after their evening meal the night before. It was to continue in their original vein; to maintain an ignorance of the human ways and language. The reason for this was simple; if it got out that they were able to fully understand everything the humans said in discourse with them, or each other, even though Chance had mentioned earlier about making sacrifices for their collective good, then their competitors would be on guard around them at all times, this would only weaken their position and render them unable to source any valuable information that could help their cause. So it was unanimously decided to fool them all and that included, tragically, the Flugals, Dave and Rachelle.

Flugal waited in vain a further few seconds, eagerly anticipating some form of communication either verbal or physical, but he was to be sadly, bitterly disappointed and was forced to settle for six pairs of beady eyes coupled with six cheesy grins.

'How long are we going to stand here like a bunch of lemons grinning like cheshire cats.' whispered Nigel.

This stalemate may well have continued on indefinitely had it not been for those morning chores that were niggling away at Flugal's conscience, and an injection of circumstance from one of the stable inmates.

'My mouth hurts.' complained Biff.

'That's because you're such a misery, you never smile, just think of it as you pampering against your naturally morose tendencies.' Pogo elbowed Biff in the side of the ribs as he spoke, flashing his pearly white teeth straight in his face.

'Ouch!' Biff over exaggerated his reaction to Pogo's mock assault.

'If he doesn't move soon.............' Troy didn't have time to finish his sentence before Pogo let rip with an enormous fart.

'That'll move him!' exclaimed Pogo on completion.

This set about an uncontrollable bout of the giggles, as each one tried desperately to hold on to their smile.

'I thought the flatulence department was Troy's domain.' said Chance desperately trying not to breath.

'Not anymore.' replied a relieved Troy.

Finally a mixture of Flugal's conscience and the extremity of Pogo's flatulence forced him to vacate the doorway for a fresher climate, but their joy was short lived as Pogo's noxious deposit began to take its full effect.

'You sick puppy.' cried Nugget making a dart for the doorway.

Flugal, now having been partly forced through an act of self preservation to begin his morning chores, was alerted to the mass exodus by the before mentioned Nugget's exit, which momentarily suspended his chores opening act. He now found himself an interested spectator on first Nugget, then Nigel bouncing off Troy, who had himself muscled past Chance, and last but not least Biff. In times of necessity it's the same in whatever theatre of the animal kingdom you reside; it's everyone for themselves! Pogo trotted out behind, as you would expect being the perpetrator of the heinous crime, holding his head high clutching onto any remaining resemblance of dignity that was left available to him. He then found himself crowded out as his comrades huddled together in deep discussion.

Flugal looked on in joyous bewilderment. Pogo comprehended the true meaning of the huddle and waited patiently for the conclusion with a chuckle interspersed with an array of witty comments.

Flugal was now totally and utterly enraptured in this turn of events and leant against the side of the stables trying to gauge the mood.

The huddle stayed a huddle and Pogo started to shift his weight from one foot to the other as his impatience increased exponentially with every glance espied emanating from the group, even the livery horses joined in on the act reminding Pogo that his true talents lay with joining the cattle and eroding what was left of the ozone layer.

Finally Nugget exited the huddle and confidently approached the ever twitching Pogo.

'Pogo' Nugget opened with, 'we the team have decided, and I have myself volunteered to pass on the team's judgement.'

'Judgement!' said a startled Pogo, this was not at all what he envisaged.

'Yes, judgement!' Nugget went on, 'That any future flatulence, eruptions or infringements of any kind, for it has also been decided that it is not prudent and unjust to ask you to cease breaking wind, must be saved for more important and select occasions where it may benefit the team more.'

'Benefit the team more!' Pogo repeated.

'Yes, benefit the team more.'

The huddle had now expanded into a line and they positioned themselves directly behind Nugget in a show of solidarity.

Pogo mulled over his mandate; it was not really all that unreasonable; to fart only in the presence of one's competitors and enemies, all the while paying due care and diligence when in the company of the team and friends. Everybody around the farm was now using that new buzzword: 'Team'.

'Agreed.' he finally consented, not that there was ever any danger of him not. The relief on the faces of his team mates was almost tangible.

Flugal needn't have required the slightest understanding of the quadruped language hitting his ears to grasp the outcome of the proceedings, and once he was satisfied that there was no possible confusion in his understanding, he continued with those morning chores he had designated to fill the time available before he had to prepare himself to leave for his appointment with Bennett.

* * * * *

A hot steamy mug of tea awaited Flugal on the kitchen table for his departure to the bank. He skipped down the stairs exuding a confident air; this was much for his wife's benefit than his, he was concerned not to arouse in her those two demons of gloom and despair and at the same time feeling that if he entered the fray in a cheery, confident mood it would help secure him what he most desired: A small payment holiday. With this he knew he could make good all the payments, just. He simply needed time to restructure any future monies to cover all remaining payments and those he had unfortunately missed, and any advice Mr Bennett could give him in his quest for restructuring his debt would be most welcome.

'You look very dapper my dear.' she said as she handed him his hot mug of tea. 'You're bound to make the right impression.' Mrs Flugal had that rare ability, that enviable talent of disarming people with the most simplest of expressions, and making them feel so special.

Flugal smiled. 'I hope so.'

'I'm sure Mr Bennett is not at all the ogre that we saw the other day. See even I'm beginning to think that we've been giving him a hard time, maybe he was just trying to make some kind of an impression.'

'He certainly did that!'

'Some people do like to gain the upper hand regardless, but I'm sure deep down inside he didn't really mean it.'

That sagacity, which Flugal so cherished in his wife, surfaced again and brought an even bigger smile to his face.

'You're right as always my dear.'

His wife's face mirrored his own and they each sipped their brew in silence.

The tea had the desired effect, and calmed Flugal sufficiently for him to mull over the questions that he expected Bennett to ask, and then examined all the possible answers he could give until he was settled on the most appropriate correspondence in every case.

Finally the time came to leave and he downed the remainder of his tea. Mrs Flugal during this short time had been browsing through one of her magazines whilst partaking her refreshment, and now seeing her husband prepare himself to depart she placed the magazine on the kitchen table and the couple walked slowly out to the car hand in hand, where she kissed him tenderly on the cheek and wished him a safe journey and a successful meeting. Flugal again simply smiled keeping any thoughts, positive or negative, to himself, kissed her back with an equal amount of affection, boarded his chariot and departed with a wave and his continuing smile.

He was watched closely passing through the farm gates by Nugget carrying out his new duties as the team's security chief. He had been out and about partitioning the locals to help out as lookouts. Nugget took an avid interest in Flugal's departure, making a careful note of everything that transpired in order to convey later all the relevant particulars.

Flugal, totally unaware he was being watched leaving the farm, once again, as was his want, ran all possible scenarios over in his head, practising again and again all possible questions and answers.

The journey to the bank was executed respectfully at the designated speed limit, yet Flugal arrived at the bank in what seemed no time at all. He subconsciously navigated the car to his favourite parking spot, not more than five minutes walk from the town square; like most people who have found a system that suits their character and stick to it, so did Flugal. With the car parked he stretched his legs, to help aid his constitution, and strode purposely towards the bank.

On this particular day he knew his constitution would be sorely tested, but happy again with all his responses he could reasonably be expected to give to Bennett's questions, he rounded the corner to the bank to be met by the sight of Bennett in intimate discourse with none other than Mr Williams.

Flugal froze to the spot. He then very deliberately took a step backwards, keeping one eye on the pair at all times until he was totally out of sight. Once happy he had removed himself from any possible chance of detection he carefully began to spy.

Bennett and Williams conversation was obviously very intense; Williams occasionally gesticulated wildly, this was followed by Bennett trying to pacify him. This continuous circle of Williams rising temper and Bennett's pacifying went on for a good number of minutes.

Flugal's discomfort at seeing the two of them together increased tenfold with each passing minute. Williams eventually glanced at his watch, made his farewell and left. Although Flugal could hear nothing of the conversation and could only follow by attempting to lip read, by which he failed miserably, he still satisfied himself that his understanding of what had manifested itself before him was correct.   Once Williams had driven off, Bennett entered the bank.

Flugal remained in the same position for a few minutes after Bennett had gone inside; he wanted to make sure that neither man would return, he definitely didn't want Williams seeing him enter the bank, whether or not he knew the true reason for his visit, and as he could only surmise as to the true motive for the conversation he must, however reluctantly, give them the benefit if the doubt. Flugal cursed his sense of fair play; he could never bring himself to openly accuse anybody unless the facts were overwhelming.

He took a deep breath, quickly reconnoitred the area around him, governed it safe to proceed, then went on his way towards the bank.

* * * * *

Nugget skipped over the yard, he was eager to inform the lads of Flugal's absence; it was obvious to him where he had gone, and everybody needed to know; one to steal themselves in case of the inevitable and two to brace lest Flugal should be in a distemper on his return. The latter was highly unlikely, but you never knew about humans; they behave mightily strange when placed under extreme stress. Animals seem to have an in built pressure relief valve against the stresses and strains of day to day living, they regarded them in much the same way as that precious liquid of life trickling down the spine of our friends in the poultry brigade, or to put it another way like "water of ducks back".

Nugget relayed all he had seen and the general consensus was by the style of Flugal's dress that he was going to make his appointment with Bennett. Then they all in their own time aired their opinions on how they figured Flugal's chances would be with that dreaded bank manager.

Nugget related that, whilst resuming his usual position by the fire one evening, he overheard his master and mistress discussing Bennett; they were not particularly enraptured with him, but she urged her husband to be patient and understanding in any dealings he was to have with him. The conjectures flew in all directions at once, some pampering to their pessimistic side, recounting stories heard down the proverbial grapevine of bank managers from hell tormenting customers at every turn, refusing all entreaties and requests for help, these arguments were counter-balanced delicately by the optimists rallying behind Flugal, extolling his finer points and virtues for which Bennett could not help but be impressed. But by and by the pessimists succumbed to the optimists and calm was soon restored to the group. The morbid few loved Flugal as much as the rest, and there was never any doubt that they would pull their weight when needed and this overriding factor supported the patience supplied by the optimists.

Each to his own kept a vigil on Flugal's return, it was noted that Mrs Flugal face was to be seen periodically peering, inquisitively from behind the net curtains eager for his return. Nugget took it upon himself, as it would not have been untoward to see him venturing into the road, to keep a consummate watch for his arrival. With the exception of a couple of delivery vans for neighbouring farms and a couple of tourists clearly lost, the roads were completely void of all traffic.

As the hours ticked by and the time of reckoning drew near for Flugal's return, the agitation grew on the farm and Mrs Flugal appeared in the yard. This caused much consternation among the animals as her presence surely signalled Mr Flugal at any moment, but he never came.

Rachelle was now by her side; she had arrived earlier on, done all her chores and was now offering much needed support.

Finally Flugal pulled into the yard around four o'clock, and here we shall leave them all to return to Flugal earlier on outside the bank.

* * * * *

Flugal stopped at half-distance to the bank whilst still attempting to fully comprehend the scene previously explained; to the neutral observer it would have appeared as though he was admiring the architecture; the external décor was very much in line with sixties popular culture. He was standing there so long it seemed to him that he had become unaware of the time that had elapsed and not wishing to set tongues wagging and make a scene, approached and entered the bank.

Miss Emily Northern, a cashier, who had worked at the bank only a few short years, and was a former pupil of Flugal's greeted him with a healthy, beautiful smile and affectionate salutations.

'Good morning Mr Flugal. It's been a long time since we've had the pleasure of your company.' He immediately took from that that she was not present in the bank during his last visit.

'It's been a long time.' Flugal said, clearly lying, trying to avoid any reference to his last appointment. 'I have an appointment with Mr Bennett at one o'clock.'

'Mr Bennett is in his office, I think. He left the bank for a while, but I believe he's back now.'

Flugal failed to reply; not through want of manners, he simply followed those basic laws of restraint and declined any comments lest his tongue should run away with him, and dig a hole that he might find impossible to extricate himself from. He only smiled at Emily and took purposeful strides towards Bennett's office.

As he approached the office door his steps became more timid; he quietly, violently chastised himself for his physical action and inability to suppress his inner fears, he still though managed an outward appearance of confidence, calm and self belief.

Bennett sharply opened his office door, anticipating his arrival. He faked an expression of complete surprise at finding Flugal waiting outside.

'Ah, Mr Flugal you're early.' he said striding confidently forward, glancing at his watch.

'Only by five minutes Mr Bennett!'

'Oh, oh, okay. Take a seat then please, Mr Flugal,' he added, gesturing extravagantly to Flugal to enter his office. 'and I'll be right with you.' Bennett never gave him a backward glance and swiftly engaged Emily in conversation regarding the topic covered in the correspondence he carried in his right hand. Flugal watched him, stalling his entry into his office. Emily, for her part, could see Flugal eying Bennett and fought hard not to make any kind of eye contact with him, as this would indubitably cause her boss to follow her gaze and reveal the motionless Flugal.

Flugal for his part could not bear to hold his present circumstance any longer and entered the office, sitting without any ceremony opposite Bennett's desk.

Bennett's arrival was duly signalled by the thudding of his office door closing and he passed by the seated Flugal without volunteering any form of salutation; a psychology I'm sure that is practiced many times over in offices, boardrooms, and exam rooms around the world, in a vain attempt by those wishing to impose their will on their inferiors. Flugal volunteered nothing in reply to this cold shouldered treatment, he simply watched him behind his desk shuffling some papers, while all the time delaying the inevitable eye contact.

'The height of bad manners if ever there was any!' thought Flugal, refusing to be riled and sat patiently awaiting Bennett's opening gambit, admiring or not, depending on your taste, the neutral décor.

'Mr Flugal.' Bennett's opening gambit cut short Flugal's admiration.

'At last,' he thought, 'he deigns to converse with me!' and then immediately castigated himself for his own cheek.

'You know why I requested this meeting.' The opening words were lost to Flugal during his self admonishment, but he got the general drift pretty quickly.

'I kind of figured.'

'Good, then it makes my life a little easier.'

'Go on then!'

Bennett was caught off guard by Flugal's unintentional abruptness. 'We must discuss this very delicate matter regarding your financial affairs.'

'I know that you know that my financial situation is a little rocky at this present time, but I believe that I have a solution to all our problems that will place my family, myself and the bank on a more secure footing.'

'You have to concede Mr Flugal that the bank has been very patient with you.'

He didn't like much where this line of questioning was going to invariably lead. 'Mr Miller has been very kind to me in the past, I agree.'

The mention of Miller unsettled Bennett no end, but he hid his rising contempt for the man remarkably well. 'Yes, yes Mr Miller was well known throughout the bank for his generosity.' Bennett half sneered as he spoke, but his regard for the former bank manager was not lost on Flugal.

'After our last conversation.' started Flugal.

'Yes, our last conversation.' interrupted Bennett, suppressing any caustic comments brewing just below the surface.

'I want to discuss a possible business plan that would be of benefit to us both.' Flugal had no sooner finished than Bennett put an end to this line of enquiry.

'I'm afraid it's a bit late for business plans. The bank, in the present climate, has made the decision, regrettably in your case, that it can no longer support bad debt and must reclaim any outstanding monies.'

'Bad debt!' Flugal desperately tried to hold himself together.

'You fell behind by number of payments; anybody who falls behind over a prescribed period of time, as you have done Mr Flugal, becomes a bad debt. This is bank policy not mine!'

'Only by a couple of months!'

'It may only be a couple of months.-'

'-And I'm trying to make up the short fall.'

'Even making up the short fall Mr Flugal, which is commendable, is invariably bad debt, which makes you still in breach of your contract with the bank. When you signed for the loan you agreed never to fall behind in any of your payments.'

'Works been slow.'

'That unfortunately is not the responsibility of the bank. Due to the missed payments, not one but a number, and you also having the necessity to draw up a business plan, obviously focuses on future payments that must be in jeopardy. This now means that you fall into the bank's classification of bad debt, and in as much the bank has decided, after much deliberation I might add, to demand that any monies outstanding must be paid in full.'

'And exactly what time have you and the bank given me? How long have I got?'

'At a push, time all the paperwork has been drawn up, about sixty days, bearing in mind you continue to make all future payments.'

'And if I can't repay all the payments'

'The bank will be forced to recoup all its losses through the sale of your farm and all its assets on a much earlier time scale, as that is what you placed as collateral for the original loan.'

Flugal sat stunned and found himself unable to make any sort of sound let alone a coherent reply. He had been dreading this scenario and its arrival, however premeditated, but it still cut deep wounds and necessitated Flugal drumming up all his available self control merely to maintain an outward appearance of calm.

'I'm sorry to be the bearer of this bad news Mr Flugal.'

He didn't believe a word. This apparent flippant response snapped Flugal to his senses and he rose from his chair, held out his hand to Bennett and reacted, all the while pressing himself urgently to remain calm and courteous at all times. 'Sixty days you say?'

'At a push.' Bennett now stood and saw Flugal to the door. Flugal exited without another word.

Once in the car park Flugal fought back the tears; he had on one occasion seen his own father cry; the circumstances behind it he could not recollect, but the image of his distraught father had left an indelible mark on him, and stayed with him forever. Not wishing to inflict such a vision on his loved ones, lest someone he should know and should relate this scene to his wife or any stranger unfortunate enough to be in the close vicinity, he choked back the tears and quickened his pace until he reached his favourite parking spot, sat in the drivers seat and slowly, purposefully buried his head in his hands. Any outward displays of emotion would now be furtively concealed within his automobile.

Bennett to do him credit felt no satisfaction at being the bearer of such tremulous news; he made a few phone calls and decided to postpone all phone calls in the short term, until after the fateful appointment was at an end; he simply viewed this part of his job as a necessary evil "it went with the territory" he would say, as way to comfort himself and repeated over and over this simple statement, when pangs of conscience raised their ugly heads above the parapet. His train of thought, which at this time was suppressing the said conscience over this unfortunate episode, was broken by his office phone bursting into life.

'Mr Bennett.' He answered somewhat too abruptly. A familiar tone grumbled down the wire.

'Mr Williams.'

Again the grumbling crackled down the line, only this time the crackling droned on for a number of minutes.

'I hear what you're saying Mr Williams, but my hands are tied.'

Williams refused to let Bennett complete his sentence; injecting his repost like a syringe full of intoxicating liquid into the vein of the conversation. The end result was a non reply from Bennett, if a series of "I don't know" "we'll have to wait and see" and the reiterated "my hands are tied" can be considered worthy replies.

To understand this conversation to its fullest extent we must view the crackling voice first hand. Williams on departing Bennett outside the bank made his way immediately for the office of a one Mr Balshaw. Balshaw was a recognised and extremely well respected architect who had done much of the design work on the surrounding suburbs.

Sprawled majestically over an oak table measuring over twenty feet in length, sat a model of a modern twenty-first century suburban residential development; it had been years in the planning; Williams gave birth to the idea when he purchased his first substantial piece of land: The McKenzie farm. The McKenzie's were childless and so it wasn't too difficult to prise away the farm from the elderly couple with a generous cash settlement. A quick sale ensued.

The seed was sown and the Hickory farm soon followed; Williams was already very careful not to draw attention to himself, so this acquisition was achieved through an intermediary. His master plan, his ultimate goal was now to build a small town entirely designed and owned by him; he would set rental rates for shops and homes, arrange mortgages through his own brokers and generally preside over all as the lord of the manor. The proceeding three years saw Williams gain even more land and grow richer by the day. Only one piece of real estate now alluded him: Flugal Farm.

Williams pernicious, odious assaults on owners of the farms he had acquired were achieved by undercutting whatever business they were in and driving them mercilessly towards bankruptcy. Once out of business they were all too willing to sell their farms to remain solvent, albeit at a knock down price.

In Flugal's case it was the riding school and stables; vast investments were injected into a riding school that would compete with Flugal and therefore achieve the desired results and drive Flugal Farm into his hands. Once the farm was his he intended to sell all the stable assets for whatever he could get, the only horses he had any affection for were his own carriage horses, any others would be disposed of, and then he would shut down the stables for good.

But this had proved a lot harder than he had anticipated. Flugal, totally unaware as to William's machinations, put up a fight and borrowed extra from the bank to cover his stables running costs and build an indoor arena, this ultimately was one of the causes of his undoing, but only after Williams had instigated other more iniquitous measures. These involved the removal of Mr Miller through a series of contrived complaints that held no water, but succeeded in sullying his reputation within the bank, and as he was close to retirement brought about his ultimate removal as Flugal's bank manager and the more ruthless Mr Bennett usurping him.

Williams bowled into Balshaw's office like a captain on a bridge about to bark out orders to his subordinates for an imminent attack

'It won't be long now and then we can then start phase one of the development!'

Balshaw had been studying plans for another up and coming project when Williams stormed into his office; it was a habit of his he had long ago got used to. 'How long is how long?' he replied seeing Williams eying the minute details of the model and rubbing his hands in eager anticipation.

'One month, maybe two. once this last hurdle is eliminated.'

'Last hurdle eliminated.' Balshaw repeated. 'Is this last hurdle still haunting you?'

'Not for much longer!' Williams took time from examining every last inch of his dream only to lift his head from the model and display a fine set of pearly white teeth. 'Have you altered those errors I noted?'

'I have, but you won't see them on the model yet.'

'Good.' Williams again lowered his gaze to his dream totally oblivious to the speed and tone of Balshaw's reply. 'Phase one will soon be a go!' he reiterated.

Balshaw now resulted to give Williams his full and undivided attention. Williams like a bronze statue held perfect stillness, only his eyes twitching, darting from side to side, up and down, examining every line, corner and diagonal of his dream. His inner desire failed to give away any sign of life; in truth Williams already saw, and considered himself lord of the manor and held a posture to effect his vanity.

Balshaw rose and walked around his desk to the far side of the model until he positioned himself directly opposite Williams, and then he too examined every line, corner and diagonal. It was Balshaw who broke the silence.

'All the errors you noted have been corrected.' and then after a short pause, almost as an afterthought 'And I'm sure to your satisfaction.'

Williams said nothing, he simply raised his gaze from the model and smiled that evil, subtle smile that only hints at the odious, execrable traits normally dormant in the human persona, but are always lurking just below the surface waiting for the slightest provocation. Balshaw unblinking held Williams in his line of sight; he could sense his unbending, his unwilling to concede defeat, anything will be accepted as long as the means satisfied the ends and his paucity of benevolence regarded as the norm.

'If you don't like the result of the changes I can make the appropriate adjustments.'

Again no response was immediately forthcoming, just a repeat of that grin and he resumed his inspection of the model.

Williams finally rose to his full height. 'Good! When will I be able to see them?'

Balshaw smiled. 'In a day or two.'

If that was all he was going to get today, then so be it, at least it was another response on the positive side. He informed Williams again that he had noted all the amendments and made suitable corrections, choosing his words carefully, his obsequious replies designed to pamper to the man's vanity. The one thing, the one aspect of his client was he could be taciturn and garrulous in equal measure, and today was a taciturn day.

'I'll be in touch regarding phase one.' Williams spoke half over his shoulder as he made his way for the door. He spoke no more during their brief encounter and it wasn't long before Balshaw once again found himself alone.

13

Flugal pulled into the yard as previously mentioned around four o'clock, his countenance subtly shifting as he tried hard to hide his inner turmoil that would betray him at every turn to his friends and family. His wife took a step towards the now stationary vehicle then stopped, unsure as to when her husband was going to vacate the car or move closer. Happy the car was not going to proceed any further she manoeuvred around to the open driver's side window. Rachelle during this time kept a respectable distance.

'Well how did it go?' Mrs Flugal enquired.

'Just like I expected.'

'We're good then?'

'Absolutely!' the smile on his wife's face reinforced his decision to tell a bare faced lie, and any guilt arising from his actions would have to be dealt with at a later date.

Nugget approached from across the yard while the rest of the crew peered through cracks in the stable walls. A dogs instinct is unmatched in these circumstances and he knew right enough what "absolutely" meant.

Flugal vacated the car, kissed his wife on the cheek, patted Nugget who by now was right beside him, put an affectionate arm around Mrs Flugal and they entered the house in this way followed, still at a respectable distance, by Rachelle. Nugget right at the last minute spun round and scampered back to the stables.

'What did he say?' Chance immediately queried Nugget, who now at a walk entered the block.

'Absolutely!' he replied.

'Absolutely!' queried Nigel this time. 'Absolutely.'

'Yes absolutely!'

'What the hell does absolutely tell us!' Nigel was starting to get anxious, he wanted instant results. 'Sweet nothing, that's what!'

'But what was the question?' asked Pogo.

'Are we good then?' said Nugget.

'Do you believe him?' Chance already knew the answer to his question.

'No!' Nugget looked Chance straight in the eye. 'No I don't. We're still in big trouble. It's the race, treasure or bust for us. That's my take on it.'

'Are you sure?' asked Biff, the concern evident in his voice.

'Absolutely. Look if I am wrong nothing will change, but if I am right we're in training as of tomorrow. '

'We have to assume Nugget's assumption is correct and I for one agree, so let's start upping the anti.' Troy had exited his stables and now took a step toward the centre of the group to emphasise his determination.

During the short break the lads had had from Flugal they had all agreed on their prospective positions within the team and had started discussing training and tactics as best they could, regarding the fact that they had no carriage.

Nigel trotted past Nugget, Chance and the "Boys" out into the yard. 'I don't know about you guys, but I'm going to enjoy what time I've got left here.'

'Yeah, me too.' Troy followed Nigel. After a few seconds pause when the rest all looked at each other searching for any kind of dissension, and when none was forthcoming, exited one after the other.

Nugget took upon his old canine shoulders to exercise those traits in his nature that expressed their desire to have fun and enjoy themselves whenever possible; such behaviour is extremely infectious as can be vouched by the reactions of his colleagues. Nugget placed his pin of choice firmly in the board marked 'football'; when it came to that sport he was a devout

Wolfington Rovers fan. Nigel who seconded the idea was a follower of Dundee United, Pogo and Biff shared a passion for Arsenal, nobody could understand why as they hadn't been within a hundred miles of London, Chance just went with the flow and normally acted as mediator, but leant more towards Brighton & Hove Albion, primarily because his old training ground used to be on the south coast of England and Troy put his faith behind Tottenham Hotspur, another London team; he was once told he was originally from that part of the world and they are the arch rivals of Arsenal. This was the primary cause of Chance exercising his mediator skills.

Nugget pounced on the ball left by the trough during their last sojourn into the world of the beautiful game, and displayed his vast array of dribbling skills.

He swerved, bobbed, danced, jigged and weaved his way through a variety of routines, not allowing the centre of his attention to enter the possession of the spectators. It was Nigel who took it upon himself to provide some good old fashioned centre half play; he dropped his shoulder and body checked the dribbling Nugget head first into a dung heap.

Nigel no sooner admired his handy work than Pogo's hoof proved one obstacle too many and Nigel's senses took a blow hard enough to send even the most hardened campaigner to the 'land of nod', but Nigel undeterred rallied and a few well chosen nibbles on the rear legs of his antagonist wrestled the ball back.

By now the dye was cast and there erupted what can only be described as football mayhem; Chance used all his guile to steal possession from Troy, who in turn pinched Pogo's pocket and delivered a perfectly weighted pass to the emerging Nugget, having only just extricated himself from his pungent resting place. The chequered orb no sooner presented itself at Nugget's paws than again the large frames belonging to Biff and Pogo deposited their hapless friend back into his heap, the guffaws of laughter only added salt to his humiliating wound.

The game continued at breakneck speed; all the combatants, along with a few of the livery horses begging to be let out and join in, offering a challenge of the livery versus farm horses with everybody laughing and cheering in equal measure, with no one really gaining any element of control when they had wrestled the ball away from the previous owner and nobody having any idea what to do with it when they had, as there were no goals of any sort.

Nugget free again to attack the ball holder, now had a secret weapon to aid his quest, he stank to high heaven; anytime he ventured near the ball the combatants scattered in all directions like ants under attack from a size nine boot. Nigel, who above everybody shouldered most of the responsibility for Nugget's condition, voiced the loudest protestations, with his tongue severely in his cheek at the state of affairs.

Nugget could handle most things, but any reference to his present condition bearing any relation to his beloved football team sent him into fits of apoplexy. Now jealousy is a dangerous thing and it had a bearing on Nigel's topic of ridicule. Nugget, not intending to take such a slight sitting down, collected the ball which mystically attached itself to his nose as he weaved his magic across the yard towards his friends, then as he approached the group, delivered a beauty of a pass to Biff and jumped paws, coat and all over the unsuspecting Nigel who, before he knew what had happened, was the proud owner of a dung flavoured jacket.

'At least you smell like a champion now Nigel.' Nugget uttered with no little amount of glee and brought the house down. Everybody laughed; no one louder than Nigel and Nugget.

As the sound of laughter died away and the second half grew imminent, their attention was drawn as always to the crunching of gravel under tyres. On this occasion it was Dave returning, who sprung out of the driver's door and into the house in one dexterous move, once his land rover had skidded to a halt.

From inside the house could be heard the gentle muffled sound of voices, only Mrs Flugal's could be easily discerned due to her strong country accent. After a short pause in their conversation Dave appeared at the door closely followed by Flugal and Rachelle, they all boarded Dave's car and left with immediate effect. Mrs Flugal never appeared. If at any time the three of them noticed the game of football, then they never let on.

The car now out of sight, the six footballers held their positions, nobody uttering a sound until Nugget settled any vexation.

'It can't be that bad if young Rachelle's going.'

And with that there was a collective outpouring of breath and everybody started talking at once, and the game was under way again, injected with even more laughter and mirth.

Dave's car rattled its way along the country lanes, but on this particular journey their direction took them off one of the side lanes that led into a neighbouring village. Along a twisty, dusty road they bumped, Rachelle sitting silently in the back admiring the passing scenery, Flugal and Dave where you would expect them, up front chatting away furiously about all manner of things, none particularly relevant; not much was said regarding the reason for the journey, most of what was needed to be said had been discussed back at Flugal's.

They eventually turned sharply right and entered a drive bordered on both sides by trees that were in dire need of some loving care and attention. Rachelle remarked that the place looked deserted, which was a crying shame as the potential of the place was quite substantial. Dave negotiated the final few yards of the dilapidated driveway and parked right outside a majestic, old style manor house, similar to those erected in Victorian times that mirrored the disrepair the proceeding entry had prepared them for. The house cried out to be lived in; for a tenant to reside within its four walls and share the pride its designer surely had in its conception; to any casual observer its owners had either fallen on hard times or decided on some reason not to inhabit this dwelling anymore and abandon it to the elements.

'Does anybody live here?' Rachelle asked the logical question.

'I don't know.' Dave replied.

'I hope not.' Flugal chimed in 'That roof wouldn't last another heavy downpour!'

Once Dave had brought the car to a rest a few yards shy of a battered old brick wall, which shared the sorry state of the rest of the dwelling and bordered what was once an outstanding garden of natural beauty, even after all these years of neglect it had managed to retain its original charm and grace, Dave and Flugal vacated.

'What a crying shame!' said Flugal admiring what he could see of the garden.

'That it is!' was all Dave could muster, his thoughts were elsewhere; he had made the arrangements for this meet was beginning to get impatient.

He finally caught sight of the person his attention had been seeking. Around the side of the house a frail, old woman in her seventies appeared walking very slowly with a crooked back so severe it made her chin appear level with her waist.

Dave approached the elderly lady. Flugal followed his lead. Rachelle, for the time being, thought it prudent to hold her position in the back of the car, lest the conversation be more of an adult nature.

'Good afternoon or is it evening already?' said Dave looking at his watch. 'Mrs Evening this is Mr Flugal.' then immediately felt ill at lease lest the old lady should think he was trying to be funny at her expense.

'I know Mr Flugal.' said the old lady, completely ignoring any previous reference to her name or time of day. 'He is a bit of a personality around these parts.'

'I am?' said Flugal astonishingly.

'That you are.' And she held out her hand which Flugal gratefully accepted; he could feel her bones crack through his grip and he was respectful not to hold on to tight and hurt the delightful Mrs Evening.

'You have the advantage over me Mrs Evening.' Any humour he had in relation to her surname never surfaced within him, he paid her too much respect for that. 'I don't think we ever met.'

'We did once a long time ago, you were younger then, I was younger then.' she added smiling. 'Do you remember Mrs Dougherty?'

'Funny you should mention her.' Dave chipped in.

'Well Dave my late husband, god rest his soul, and your father Mr Flugal searched for Dougherty's treasure together.'

'You're kidding?'

'Did they find it?' Dave keenly asked.

'They both reckoned they did, but we all thought it was a load of old baloney, one big joke on Dougherty's part to wind up the locals!'

'My father held a similar view, but he did leave me some information as to its suspected whereabouts.' added Flugal.

'That he did.' The old lady looked Flugal straight in the eye and then said austerely. 'But only half the required information, my husband kept the other half. That was their deal: To share the joke.'

'No way!' Dave's excitement and disappointment surfaced in equal proportion and threatened to get the better of him. 'So with Flugal's and your husband's clues we could possibly find Dougherty's treasure, that's if it's not the big joke you say it is. Fantastic! What a result!'

'Maybe.' Mrs Evening said with an air of caution.

'How much did your husband say was there?' Flugal asked with a dead pan expression belying what he really felt.

'Millions!'

Both the men were shocked to silence.

'Millions!' Flugal eventually said once the initial shock had subsided. 'I never knew it was as much as that.'

'I know gentlemen. Shocking isn't it. That a woman would go to such lengths, and see fit to hide her family's inheritance, and so much of it.'

'Just think what could be done with all that money.' said Dave. 'Why didn't your husband collect it?' and then turning to Flugal 'With your dad?'

'Like I said,' started Mrs Evening, 'both men thought it was one enormous joke, but that didn't stop them making regular plans to excavate where they figured it was buried, which amounted to nothing in the end. Ultimately I suppose they thought it wasn't theirs to take, they could never have kept it! If you want his papers you can have them, they're just gathering dust now.' she had answered almost before Dave had finished talking. 'But that's not why you're here is it?'

She looked at the two gentlemen awaiting some kind of acknowledgement, which came finally in the shape of Dave nodding in the affirmative. 'Follow me.' she said gesticulating with her right index finger. The two men duly obliged.

Rachelle, seeing the three of them make their way around the side of the house, vacated the car and followed at a respectable distance; curiosity may have killed the cat, but it positively enlivens a young girl, and she was not going to sit in that car all alone.

Mrs Evening led her three guests down a dusty path, clearly cut between two hedgerows for the purpose of forging a route to whatever the owners had in store in a shed at the far end. And most suitable it was.

Rachelle caught up with Flugal and Dave and made her presence known. Flugal smiled and beckoned her to walk beside him, which made her feel at ease.

'Excited.' he said.

'Very.' she replied.

The path wound its way for a few hundred yards until it opened out into a vast expanse, which seemed out of keeping, size wise, with the rest of the house. In the right rear corner stood that dilapidated shed, with every window either broken or cracked. In the opposite corner sat a tarpaulin covering an object about five and a half feet high by. The frail old lady waved her right hand and mumbled something incoherent. Flugal and Dave shared a look and Rachelle giggled at their reaction; Mrs Evening never broke stride and navigated her way to the tarpaulin. She stopped three or four feet short and waited patiently for everybody to catch up. 'There she is!'

Dave was the first to react to the invitation; he picked up a corner of the tarpaulin and peered underneath, his reaction of raised eyebrows could do nothing but puzzle Flugal and excite his curiosity in equal measure, until he too eventually lifted the covering and examined the object standing under its protection.

'Have you seen it before?' Mrs Evening asked them both. They shook their heads.

'When did you last see it in use?'

'Not for a few years Mr Flugal. It was another of my late husband's passions that lasted all of ten seconds. So you can take it from me it has rarely, if ever, got any use, and has sat under that tarpaulin ever since.'

'Why did he stop?'

'He found another passion!' she replied, and then said 'Golf.' as if to justify her previous answer. 'Remove the cover and have a look.' Mrs Evening grabbed a handful and attempted, as best she could, to remove the cover. In reality she could never have succeeded, it was just a gesture to the get the ball rolling and the tarpaulin removed.

Its removal revealed a black, four seat horse carriage of approximately ten feet in length and standing at around five and a half feet at its highest point, the wheels were covered almost entirely in dust as you would imagine, with rusty hubs for companions, the spokes had traded their previous responsibilities for bracing against the carriages stresses and strains for the borders and boundary markers of a home of spiders.

Rachelle, her curiosity reaching its zenith, ran her finger over the leather upholstery and wrote her name in the dust "this shall be my seat" she thought. Dave and Flugal proceeded to inspect the rest of the carriage, as best they could considering their level of expertise.

'Stroke of luck you found out about this?' said Flugal smiling.

'It was fated that I happen to know Mrs Evening's nephew, who happened to have an aunt looking to sell a horse carriage.'

'Right.'

'Is it to your satisfaction?' Mrs Evening asked without exuding the slightest emotion.

'It's perfect.' Flugal knew he didn't have the faintest idea if it was perfect or not, but it looked the part and he did know she didn't either by the condition of the tarpaulin and carriage; nobody had looked under here in years. He realised straight away that it was the best they could afford and any maintenance would need to be carried out back at the farm, so the sooner they got it back there the better.

'And by the way.' injected Mrs Evening. 'It's not called horse carriage racing, even if the poster does hint at it, but horse driving!'

'Horse driving.' they said together.

'Yes horse driving.'

'Even though it's a race.' said Rachelle quite astonished.

'Even though it's a race young lady. Do you want to buy it? Is it the right size? How many horses are you going to use to pull it?'

Flugal was stumped for words. He realised he couldn't extricate himself without a reply or risk looking a complete fool. 'I have four horses.'

'So did you want my husband's harness? It's a Zilco. I'm reliably informed it's one of the best you can get.'

'Yes please Mrs Evening that would be great, but I would doing you a disservice if I didn't mention to you that I have only a limited budget and you could easily get a higher price if you advertised.'

'I'll accept your offer Mr Flugal, and I'll even chuck in the harness and all of Henry's literature on horse driving. That you can pick up at anytime, Dave knows where to find me.' And with that Flugal produced an envelope from his pocket.

'I've had a few offers, but as Henry and your father were good friends I rather wanted it to go to a good home, somebody I could trust.' Mrs Evening said collecting the envelope off Flugal and putting it in her pocket.

'Don't you want to count it?' he said.

'No Mr Flugal I trust you. Have I made a mistake?'

Flugal shook his head and smiled, he liked the old lady. 'If there is anything you need Mrs Evening, you know where to find me.'

'That I do Mr Flugal and thank you.' she said turning and walking back to the run down house, then added 'There's no hurry in moving it gentlemen. It's survived this long. Collect it whenever you're ready.' She spoke no more and three of them watched her walk slowly and painstakingly back to the house.

'It's fantastic.' enthused Rachelle.

'It's alright for how long it's been out here.' Dave took a step back and examined the carriage from a fresh angle, and nodded vehemently to back up his original assumption.

'We'll come back tomorrow, because first we need to make some room in one of the barns to work on her.' Flugal said running his hand over the dusty seats.

'I've got my tools in the back of the car.'

'Thanks to Mrs Evening we have solved our harness problem.'

'We'll still look on the internet Mr Flugal.' suggested Rachelle.

'Of course.' agreed Dave.

'I'll do it as soon as possible.'

'That would be great.' Flugal said gratefully.

'Yeah great.' repeated Dave. 'There's not a lot we can do here now. Tomorrow it is then.'

'About three?' suggested Flugal.

'Perfect for me.'

'Would you like to come along Rachelle?'

'No, I'll look up that info for you tomorrow Mr Flugal, if you could drop me off at the library on your way through with my grandmother, and then pick us up on the way back that would be great.'

'You too smart to work on a farm Rachelle, but I'm glad you work on mine.'

Nothing Flugal could have said would have made her feel any more happier than she was at this moment, and that thought stayed with her all the way back to the farm, which they eventually arrived at around six in the evening.

As they strolled back to the car something caught Rachelle's eye; she stared intently at a bush not far off from the garden wall, she was convinced it moved or something or somebody was using it as camouflage. After a few seconds hard concentration the bush failed to respond and she abandoned any notion and put it down to her vivid imagination.

Flugal's car slowly navigated the drive back to the country lane, and before they were put out of sight. Nugget poked his head from around the side of the bush; he was in his role as security chief. Nigel had got the tip off from one of his pals. Espying the discovery of the carriage, he was now responsible for relaying this information back to the gang and he made a point of making himself conspicuous thereby allaying any doubts that might be lingering in young Rachelle.

'They got back about six.' panted Nugget as he ran inside the stables. He knew all the short cuts leading off the farm; he had taken a calculated guess as to their time of arrival based on all the information available. They were very carefree, too loose, he thought, in their attitude to concealing such delicate correspondence.

'Was the information correct?' asked Nigel first.

'Yes it was definitely the old Evening place.'

'I know her!' insisted Chance. 'She was looking to buy some horses a few years back.'

'What did they want with her?' enquired Troy.

'A carriage.' said a smiling Nugget. 'She has a carriage, and by the way it's not called horse carriage racing, but horse driving.'

'Sorry guys.' said Nigel 'I should have told you sooner, but I wanted to be sure it was a carriage before I got anybody's hopes up.'

'That's no problem.' Chance replied.

'Horse driving!' shouted an indignant Pogo, failing to grasp the true meaning of the conversation.' No human's going to drive me!'

'Don't get excited.' Chance said calmly. 'It's only a name given to the race, it is still a race.'

'Anyway you can't drive a horse! It's not exactly got any gears!' chimed Biff 'Although in your case Pogo, maybe a reverse gear!'

'And stop.' added Troy.

'Ha, ha very funny.' said a riled Pogo. 'I'll wager my reverse and stop gears against anything you two losers have to offer!'

'A wager.' smiled Nigel 'I smell a wager coming on.'

'You name it dude!' Biff laid down the challenge.

'Go on Pogo, put this young upstart in his proper place. If you don't take him on I will!' Nigel hesitated not in meeting his friend head on, and before Pogo could answer laid down the bet. 'I'll bet two servings of biscuits!'

There were collective "oooohs and aaaahs" Two servings of delicious biscuits was a mighty serious bet and not one to be taken lightly.

Biff pondered the gravity of the wager and after a few seconds contemplation he agreed. 'You're on, two servings of your biscuits against two of pony nuts!'

'Now it's got to be fair!' added Nigel.

'I see, I see. I see you're trying to welch your way out of the bet already.' chided Biff.

'No way man!' reiterated Nigel. 'How can we have a fair race between a pig and a horse!'

'Well you should have thought of that before you challenged me!'

'A hoof race would be in your favour!'

'And an eating contest in yours!'

'Why not an eating contest!' argued Nigel 'It's mutual ground!.'

'Yeah!' chipped in Nugget, and then found he was the only adding to that portion of the conversation.

'You wouldn't challenge Pogo.' queried Biff.

'Hell no! He's the future world eating champion!'

'It's got to be more of a sporting vein.' Chance's calm and revered tones added weight to his suggestion and the group discussed various sporting endeavours that could be achieved whereby no one party had the upper hand; jumping, running, trotting, eating, sneezing, snorting, farting and sleeping were all considered and eliminated, and when they thought they had exhausted all possible alternatives Pogo hit it on the head: Mud sliding!

The time and place were quickly decided upon: The field with the poor irrigation was chosen, with which they were all well acquainted with, and it was duly arranged for the following morning.

The lads slept lightly, as you would expect from anybody not accustomed to so much excitement, but theirs was not the only disturbed nights sleep; while the wager was in its infancy Flugal and Dave's excitement intensified when they visited one of the less frequented barns on the farm, one that was originally intended for dairy use, before the farm became what it is now. The two men inspected the structure paying particular attention to the roof, they were more than satisfied with their discovery that, although the barn had been out of use for a few years, it was still in a sound condition and would be ideal to store the carriage while they toiled away to get it race worthy.

* * * * *

Flugal rubbed his weary eyes and remarked to himself that they had not been this sore for many a year. It was early and the first rays of the new dawn begun to pierce the dark shroud that lay over the land. Slowly, but surely the blue tinted light of morning twilight resumed control and took up the reins of responsibility until such times as she could pass them on to the bearer of the light eternal.

Flugal scoured the yard, not for anything in particular, he just did it as a matter of course to see if he could detect anything untoward that may need his undivided attention before he concentrated on the carriage. The stable block door was open.

He was sure he had closed it, it was never locked in case of emergencies, and with rising trepidation he approached the stables. He was within about fifteen feet when it suddenly dawned on him he had no way of protecting himself lest he should be attacked. His eyed locked on to a pitch fork leaning against a wall, and this provided the ideal protection against any intruder.

He entered the stables, should he call out and give the intruder time to surrender or better still make their escape thereby saving both of them a lot of trouble and bother. Through the dim twilight he became aware that all the stalls were empty. Fear is an emotion that can shroud and colour the most sagacious of dispositions, and Flugal immediately fell to accusation; Williams bore the brunt of his anger. It was clear the stables were completely empty and the intruder had made away with all the occupants. Flugal's grip, on the pitch fork, tightened and he stormed in to the yard, the crisp, fresh morning air filling his lungs. The block was indeed deserted.

He stopped firmly in his track. There it was, a feint sound far off in the distance, his beloved "Boys" calling him and he quickly followed their cries for help. Around the back of the stables he ran and hurdled a water trough until he came to the gate that entered the bottom field. The field curved in such a manner that it was impossible to see the bottom section fully unless you stood on the brow. Flugal pushed open the unbolted gate, a point he would return to later, and ran to the highest point. What met his eyes filled him with a mixture of relief, humour, bewilderment an utter astonishment.

Nigel and Biff were lined up together and would, in turns, take a run at a large section of the muddy field, at which point they would throw themselves onto their sides or back, depending on their preference, and slide as far as they could in the mud; the subsequent slide was then measured by Nugget and Chance, queried it must be said at every turn, but no animosity was present, and then it seemed to carry on again and again and again.

Nigel and Pogo were in constant discussion as to who had achieved the best slide, that was obvious, and the rest seemed to Flugal to be placing bets! The body language clearly insinuated who were the gamblers and that Nugget was the bookmaker.

Flugal ducked down on the brow to observe proceedings a little longer; first Nugget understanding every word he said, then Mrs Dougherty's treasure and now this, these are strange times he thought and getting stranger.

Biff sprinted forward with two or three sharp strides then lunged head first into the muddy strip and slid a prodigious distance to the acclaim of the spectators, including Nigel. He scrambled to his feet, with no little effort, in time to see Nigel hurtling along the same line he had previously trampled; it was agreed between the contestants that there should be parity, and to achieve that aim Nigel would be allocated a larger run up than Biff due to his advantage in size and weight. Nigel hit the mud with the force of a small missile, the spray decorating the coats of all concerned, and skidded a distance equal to that of his equine friend, a draw was announced by Nugget and a re-skid immediately called for.

Lots were drawn, Nigel won and wasted no time throwing himself once more towards his intended target; the upshot was an increase of a few feet on his previous effort and more decoration for the on lookers. Nigel was now barely recognisable as a pig.

Biff took his time to compose himself and collect his thoughts; this was the big one, the winning skid. Nigel had set an impressive target, but it was within his range. He trotted on his toes two or three times, every step had to count, then he sprang forward and covered the ground allocated expeditiously and launched his huge frame airborne into the mire; the splash he made was the stuff of legend and pebble dashed all the spectators while sliding that extra few feet to match perfectly Nigel's previous attempt. Once again Nugget pronounced a draw.

Biff mirrored Nigel in his physical appearance. Troy stepped forward, the tears streaming down his face from the incessant laughter that had accompanied affairs, and put forward the suggestion that all bets should be shared and then thanked them both heartily for the sheer enjoyment they had provided. His proposal was seconded without delay. Biff and Nigel reluctantly agreed to call the contest a draw, although in reality nobody was convinced; all in all it had been great fun and both contestants were utterly exhausted from their endeavours.

Flugal continued to keep out of sight, monitoring the situation to grasp the true meaning of events as they unfolded and relate them back to his wife and Dave.

The group started the slow walk up the field and Flugal, happy now in his comprehension of what he had been a witness, took his leave of the situation and exited the field over the gate. Leaving it unbolted, he left no visible evidence of his presence.

He managed to reach the stables before any of the animals got anywhere near the gate; he felt decidedly like a fool, behaving like a school kid playing hide and seek with his mates at play time, but surprisingly, to himself, he was enjoying the experience. He positioned himself between the stables and the external training arena and waited with bated breath for their arrival, he had also, subconsciously began to recognise and understand certain sounds they made which seemed to him to signify certain words, phrases and meanings and the veil of misunderstanding was slowly and perceptively being lifted.

Nugget as always, it seemed to Flugal was the first to arrive, chatting all the way to the following group. Through the series of barks, whimpers and growls Flugal concluded he was discussing the outcome of the mud slide.

'A fair contest, a fair contest and an agreeable result all round!' said Nugget.

Flugal then heard that familiar snort. 'On average my slides were the superior.'

'It's not the quality Nigel, it's the quantity!' Flugal knew the dulcet tones of Biff very well.

There then followed a long and drawn out series of conversations emanating from every corner of the group, and he struggled to keep tabs on who said what to whom and why, and reference to what. A regular peep through the slit in the stable wall confirmed to him any conclusions he had were correct.

Nigel and Biff remained outside whilst the others wondered into the stables to make arrangements to aid the removal of their extra coat.

Flugal was alerted to the arrival of Dave and Rachelle in Dave's truck, he had picked her up just outside the farm walking along the lane after leaving her grandmother's, by the engine noise and following the eye line and head turn of the two contestants.

Flugal and Dave's eyes met and Dave's offered a quizzical interrogation as to Flugal's present predicament. The sight of his friend furtively concealing himself behind the stables was utterly bewildering. Flugal motioned to them both not to give away his position, and to his astonishment they accepted without question, like it was an everyday occurrence now around these parts.

Rachelle vacated the car and spoke to the combatants, drawing their attention away from the stables leaving Flugal plenty of time to make his escape and reposition himself in such a way that, as he re-entered the yard nobody would automatically deduce that he hadn't been walking this way via one of the neighbouring fields.

'Dave.'

'Yeah?'

'You're early.'

'I thought we could get an early start.' and so ended a rather embarrassing conversation for Flugal.

The two men made for the house. 'Rachelle?' Flugal asked after a few strides. 'Could I ask you to take care of our friends.'

'Sure.' she said skipping over to the stables.

'You're not going to believe this!' Flugal said to Dave as they entered the house. They found the kitchen empty. Mrs Flugal could be heard upstairs singing to the radio.

'Dave I've got to ask you something very important, but mighty strange.'

'I think I know what you're going to say, but go ahead.'

'I don't know how to put this without sounding off my head, a few cards short of a full deck, if you know what I mean'

'Go on.'

'Do you...' here Flugal paused. 'Do you honestly....' he couldn't finish the sentence

Dave answered for him. 'Really think the animals understand everything we say.'

'Yes.' said Fugal with an element of surprise.

'As crazy as it sounds, I think they really do!'

'How did you find out?'

'Nugget!'

'Me too! Nugget looked at me one day in the car when I said something, I can't remember what, and he looked at me real funny.'

'Same here. If you want to make sure why not just set a trap.'

'I know Mrs Flugal has stated quite succinctly that they easily comprehend humans, but there's always going to be a part of me that was going to refute such a claim. I didn't want to upset her by saying as such.'

'She won't get upset, it's your prerogative to be wrong and hers to be right!' jested Dave.

'You've been thinking about this then?' laughed Flugal 'What do you suggest?'

'Simple. We say something important, that's either true or not, in front of Nugget and then we see what happens.'

'Excellent idea! How about we say that we need to inspect the stables to find out who's the messiest inmate, and that individual we be relocated to the new barn.'

'A new barn. Brilliant!'

'They would have noticed us working in that barn for the carriage.'

Mrs Flugal descended the stairs, her feet transmitting her arrival through its creaky steps.

'And what are you two talking about?' she said entering the kitchen.

'Nothing.' replied Flugal, his voice and general demeanour only adding to his wife's suspicion.

'I could hear you both from upstairs!' she saved her husband's blushes by making all present a mug of tea and offering a plate of homemade biscuits and cakes, it was early to be sure, but they were too good to be turned away.

Rachelle entered via the back door and put paid to any opportunity that Mrs Flugal had of asking anymore questions. For now anyway.

'Mr Flugal?'

'Yes Rachelle.'

'The animals are behaving in a very strange manner!'

'How?'

'Well.' started Rachelle, then she espied the biscuits and cakes and couldn't resist attempting to pick one or two off the plate, but was stopped in her tracks by Mrs Flugal reminding her to wash her hands.   Once her hands were washed she helped herself with relish to the delights on offer, and resumed her conversation where she had left off. 'I started to sort out the hose to wash those two dirty scoundrels and Nugget, who stinks to high heaven!' Flugal laughed at her choice of words. 'And placed everything in order to clean them, turned my back for no matter than a couple of seconds I promise, and all hell broke loose.'

'What happened?' said Mrs Flugal with a knowing smile.

'Well, somehow Nugget got a hold of the hose pipe in his teeth and bit on the trigger, the spray hit Chance fair in the face, he stepped back knocking Troy on his back, no mean feat if I may say so, Nugget laughed so loud he dropped the hose, before I could get to it Biff grabbed a hold and ran around they yard drenching everybody from head to foot or paw or hoof and caused utter mayhem.'

'It's nice to see they're in good spirits!' added Flugal.

'Are they clean?' asked Mrs Flugal.

'Oh yes, spotless.'

'Then that's alright then.'

Flugal and Dave thought it best to keep their previous conversation quiet.

'Bu the yards a mess!' continued Rachelle.

'Well they made the mess, they can clean it up!' said Mrs Flugal

'Yes Mrs Flugal. Would you like me to tell them now?' This set off Flugal and Dave in a fit of uncontrollable giggles. Mrs Flugal kept her composure.

'Exactly.'

'I'll do it right now.'

'And I'll start some brunch.'

Rachelle left to do her errand. As soon as the door clicked shut Mrs Flugal put the two guys straight. 'It worries me that it has taken you two this long to even bring yourselves to finally accept the fact that our animals are smarter than the average farmyard folk.'

Dave's and Flugal's curiosity overwhelmed them and they hurried over to the window, like a couple of eager kids awaiting the arrival of Santa, to witness Rachelle admonish the "scoundrels". All the animals looked accusingly at one another, nobody accepting even the hint of any blame; the groups whinnies, growls and snorts sent the observers into raptures, even Mrs Flugal could not resist taking a peak.

Rachelle returned to the kitchen to find everybody as she had left them. 'I told them.'

'What did they say?' laughed Flugal.

'Not much.' returned Rachelle 'Just a series of grunts and snorts is all I could make out. Nugget growled to himself most of the time.'

Dave and Flugal rushed back to the window. The animals had not moved a muscle, but were clearly in discourse with each other.

'Who do you reckon will move first?' said Dave. 'I bet you a fiver it's Pogo.'

'No, it will be Troy; he likes to think he's the strongest, he couldn't stand the thought of anybody getting the better of him.' Dave had to agree with that one.

Rachelle peered over the shoulders of the two men, she could just about make out Chance talking to one of the boys, then they all scattered. 'Where are they going?' she said.

'I don't know.' came the reply from Dave peering through the window, craning his head as best he could to see as much of the yard as possible.

Rachelle, now unable in her present condition to gauge how events were going to transpire, and a little confused as to what really was going on, ran to the back door and opened it a jar. She knelt down and peeked her head around the end of the door only to be met by a wet, sloppy welcome. This mild interrogation brought her reconnoitre to a premature end.

'Hello Rachelle.' growled Nugget.

'Hello Nugget!' replied a shaken Rachelle. 'What are you doing here?' and she sat down on the door mat.

'I was about to ask you the same question!' whimpered Nugget.

Rachelle got to her feet and opened the back door fully. Nugget stood his ground, blocking the doorway, refusing to enter or letting Rachelle leave. Over his shoulder Rachelle watched Nigel and the "Boys" running full tilt back and forth for a number of minutes. Nugget never flinched. This went on for quite a while; Nugget obstinately holding his ground, Rachelle for her part never venturing further than the doorway, never attempting to leave, even though she could have at any moment, so fascinated was she with the theatre that was unfolding before her very eyes.

Once they had all ceased to entertain, the gang scampered to and fro past the doorway.

'You not helping Nugget?' Rachelle squat back down. 'Or are you just going to do your usual?'

'I'm in charge of security!' Nugget said with enviable pride 'And my usual requires me sitting or lounging in one place long enough to get to know the lay of the land so the job can be completed. I can't see the problem can you?' his tone at the finish of the sentence was layered with a hint of sarcasm, but as Rachelle only heard a series of growls, the point was lost on her.

Eventually the hectic pace of life viewed over Nugget's shoulder ceased and Rachelle got to her feet. Dave and Flugal materialised by the door and without a moment's hesitation or ceremony politely passed her and entered the yard. Nugget stepped to one side to let them pass. None of the other animals were to be seen.

'Can you see any difference? laughed Dave.

'Apart from a multitude of tracks, it's still a mess.' said Flugal, his eyes darting along the length of the yard. 'I'll ask Nugget.' he chuckled, and as if by magic Nugget miraculously appeared by his side, making his presence felt by rubbing his wet snout by the side of his leg.   'Hello Nugget.'

'Hi.'

'So can you tell me Nugget, what actually was cleared up?'

'Can't you see the effort the lads have put in.' yapped Nugget.

Flugal made an educated guess as to the track of Nugget's reply. 'I can't really see the effort the lads seemed to have expelled in their application.'

'They applied themselves with much vigour and determination. You should be proud of them!'

'There's plenty of extra tracks.' Flugal continued.

'Tracks to be proud of Mr Flugal. When do we start training in earnest? 'Cos we're ready to go and I can personally guarantee all the necessary security measures are in place!'

'These are tracks to be proud of Nugget; all that effort and nothing to show for it, that I know my furry friend is what it's all about.'

The brief conversation overlapped constantly; Nugget expressed admirable patience, he having the upper hand of being able to translate human more than Flugal could translate dog!

'At least it shows they have an abundance of energy to burn.' Injected Dave,

Flugal nodded.

'My yard started a mess.' Flugal said eying the mess laid before him. 'And has ended up sitting in the same vein, but am I upset. Not a bit of it! Effort Nugget, that's all I ask, effort, and when we start training in earnest it's going to be hard work for all concerned.'

Nugget barked. 'Hey guys, we start training!'

The lads smiling faces manifested themselves around the side of the stable entrance, each grinning from ear to ear and flashing those pearly whites; you couldn't have seen any better in a toothpaste commercial.

'Nugget.' said Flugal 'Are you going to come with us to collect the carriage?'

Rachelle had followed the two men outside, but kept her thoughts to herself, letting events unfold as they will; she was displaying that sagacity once again beyond her tentative years. On hearing Nugget's invitation she hearkened back to their last departure from Mrs Evening's; she was convinced she knew who'd been spying on them 'Come on Nugget you'd like Mrs Evening's place, there are lots of little hiding places to explore and have fun.' she said with a subtle tone of suspicion.

Nugget ignored the leading question as best he could and just laughed it off, exuding none of the traits of somebody whose just realised they've been rumbled.

Dave left Flugal and Rachelle to go and fire up his truck.

Rachelle decided to caress Nugget behind his ear, which sent him into raptures 'Are you going to keep us company Nugget? Someone's got to protect us!'

'I am head of security!' gushed Nugget.

'Yes you are!' shouted Biff 'Yes you are and as head of said security it's your duty to personally guarantee that carriage arrives back here in pristine condition.'

'Pristine condition.' repeated Nugget. 'That is my responsibility. It's not easy Rachelle, shouldering such weighty duties, but I manage without a second's complaint.'

'You're my hero.' chided Troy.

'Only shoulders as old as yours could carry it off Nugget.' added Biff.

'If I could relieve you of such a weighty responsibility I would,' cried Pogo, 'but us mere mortals have to satisfy ourselves with the pulling of said carriage that you will so tenderly deliver into our possession.'

'You're just jealous!' shouted Nugget, but it was all in vain, as they were off in to one of their own private parties.

'I think poor old Nugget is getting a ribbing Mr Flugal.' remarked a smiling Rachelle. Flugal could not contain his mirth and stroked poor old Nugget.

'That's enough of the "old"!' injected Nugget. 'There's plenty in this old work dog yet!' and then laughed at his unintended pun.

Chance poked his head further around the stable entrance. 'Don't you listen to them Nugget. You're doing a grand job!'

'As head of security.....' he didn't have time to finish before a fresh onslaught began.

'Better watch them there family jewels Nugget.' Nigel had been itching to get involved and saw his chance, and grabbed it with both hoofs.

'Ignore them Nugget. You carry on.' Chance said again now fully in the yard.

Rachelle ran up to her favourite, and stroked him on the forehead. 'Can I stay Mr Flugal?' He nodded. 'And anyway I still have some chores to finish and Nugget will take care of you far better than I ever could. I'll get my grandmother to take me to the library tomorrow to get that information for you!'

Flugal assented and Dave called him over to the truck, which was ticking over sweetly. Nugget thrust out his chest as he walked beside his master and they all boarded and left to retrieve Mrs Evening's carriage.

The acquisition of the carriage proved blissfully uneventful and Nugget felt justly proud that he achieved delivery of the carriage unharmed in any further way; we say in any further way, as it was in a less than satisfactory condition to begin with, and utterly impossible to deliver it in a pristine condition due to its years of inactivity and neglect.

Once the carriage had been uncovered by Flugal and Dave, they both took an audible collective intake of breath signalling many disappointments; Flugal himself was quite upset at the carriage's state, but tried to hide it in his usual way from everybody by displaying the overly enthusiastic, but as "necessity is the mother of all invention" Flugal and Dave, who were both totally unruffled by the prospect of many hours work, set about the carriage, without a moment's hesitation to restore it to its former glory.

Nugget, in holding with his position as head of security, kept watch, Rachelle brought out a bucket of warm soapy water, Mrs Flugal polished up the leather and all hands were placed firmly on the pump.

That evening Flugal and Dave placed the carriage into the rarely used barn which they had set aside for the purpose, and where they could guarantee it to remain dry. At dinner the talk naturally turned to the next, most important issues; measuring their new harness for the horses, Rachelle was going to get all the relevant information for them and Flugal would then ring around and try to get a deal on any gear they may still need once he had read those books from Mrs Evening, and gained a better understanding on the fundamentals of horse driving. And last, but not least he had to arrange where they were going to train without being spied upon, plus the small matter of an application form which Dave had taken the liberty to acquire when he had gained all the relevant contact details.

After dinner when all the guests had left and been dropped home, Flugal went for a walk around the farm. Answers to all the above had been agreed and formerly arranged and he was at peace for a short while; his wife never intervened with these walks, their therapeutic value were priceless to her husband.

Flugal meditated long and hard over whether he was doing the right thing; was there a different course of action, but each time he returned to the present; was it fair to build up the hopes of his loved ones and all those who depended upon him; would it have been kinder to find good homes for his horses and livestock while he had the opportunity and sell the farm for a good price; he was never going to be able to bargain for its true value, but he could have relieved the burden of debt from his family's shoulders.

He countered this argument and reinforced his decision to follow the path he had chosen because of the undoubted love and affection with which his wife and family loved the farm, and the enduring memories it will always hold for them being the overriding factor. This in itself was worth the fight; no matter how long the odds were against them succeeding, when compared to losing everything it was a worthwhile gamble to maintain a foothold in the lifestyle they both enjoyed. He personally took pleasure, not from having toys, or from taking expensive holidays, but the living and giving a life to those he cherished above all others.

Then a strange sight befell him. Nigel, of all people, appeared by his side snorting away to himself or was it to Flugal, he could not tell, he was struggling with pig language, and the two of them sauntered around the farm for about an hour or so. Flugal never did find out the reason for Nigel's presence; he was not known to wander around the farm late in the day or night, although he conjectured it was his animal instinct sensing all was not well with his master.

Flugal and Nigel finally came to the gate of the field with the drainage problem he had negotiated when avoiding being rumbled, whilst spying on the mud sliding contest. Leaning on the gate he spoke to Nigel without giving any eye contact. 'This has been in my family for a long, long time, and may it be so for a long time more.'

Nigel snorted.

'If luck is on our side old friend we will be victorious. I have to question my sanity on occasions, placing all my hopes on a carriage race or drive, which I know next to nothing about.'

Again Nigel snorted, but its tone was notable softer.

'You're right Nigel.' Flugal had no idea what Nigel had just said, it just sounded the right thing to say. 'It's crazy and foolish I know, and bordering on total irresponsibility when maybe I should have cut my losses and run and tried to rebuild again, but Nigel, and this is the but, a very big but, this is our home and gentlemen's home is his castle Nigel, and I've never run from anything in my life and I'm not about to start at this late stage!'

Nigel let out a slow, long snort and grunted something inaudible.

'What's that you say Nigel?'

No reply was forthcoming.

'I guess we should be getting back, they'll be worrying about us.' It was a lie really, Flugal had just run out of things to say at this point, and as he struggled to understand a single thing Nigel was saying it seemed like a perfect time to return.

Nigel led the way, a step or two ahead of Flugal, intermittently he chuckled to himself or so it seemed to Fulgal, he was so bad at "pig", his linguistic skills falling so short of the mark that Nigel could have been praising Flugal to the hilt or being extremely profound for all he knew.

Passing the stables Flugal made out the profiles of Chance and the "Boys", their eyes shining like stationary fireflies. Nigel veered of the left towards his friends, gabbing immediately to his comrades. Flugal chuckled at the discourse unravelling before him. The scene of camaraderie he witnessed swelled up inside of him the desire to succeed no matter what the hurdles.

He left the animals to whatever confabulation they deemed to enjoy and entered the house. All was quiet and he made sure everything was locked tight and secure and then made his own way to bed.

Nigel entered the stables chatting constantly to the whole group and not anybody in particular, he mentioned the walk in fine detail; Flugal's unflagging determination to keep the farm against insurmountable odds, this caused a momentary vexation amongst the group, but it quickly subsided as they now accepted this unwanted feeling they had become accustomed to, they just didn't talk about it.

Nigel explained how Flugal spoke of the farm as their home and they should fight for it and do everything in their power to help, and if they all pulled together for a common goal then there is nothing that cannot be achieved. Nigel should have run for government then and there if he could, he would have won by a landslide.

Pogo and Biff added their weight to the ever growing sense of togetherness, Chance chipped in that they should temper any enthusiasm and curb any emotion as that would only harm their progress; to succeed he added they must not let their emotions get the better of them. Troy backed up Chance's observations; everybody must take a backward step and look upon the goal dispassionately. Chance was very impressed by Troy's maturity, if anything, he surmised, these trials and tribulations were going to bring out the best in his friends.

Nugget was the only one not present, he was in the house keeping guard this night, and he was up and about when Flugal returned. He watched his master wander aimlessly around the kitchen, he was sure there was a purpose to it all, but he hadn't quite figured it out by the time Flugal climbed the stairs. He followed a few steps to the rear.

Everybody on the farm slept soundly that night; Flugal slipped into a sound sleep the moment his head hit the pillow, Nugget placed himself in his accustomed position outside the bedroom door, and when contented that his charges were comfortable fell asleep and Chance, Troy, Pogo, Biff and Nigel all huddled or wallowed securely in their respective stables and corners.

14

When morning finally broke, and that dim blue light was once again punctured by those initial golden rays, all remained quiet and at peace. Where on previous mornings the hustle and bustle of Flugal would pre-empt the business of the day, nothing but silence reigned over Flugal farm. The eerie hush, the cold damp air of the crisp late spring morning, the sweet twittering of our feathered friends offspring were the only indications of life buzzing, flittering around the farm as they chirped out their orders to the ever waiting, patient servants.

That familiar sound again of crunching shattered the idyllic postcard setting, and Dave emerged from the vehicle hauling a large brown holdall over his shoulder.

He proceeded straight past the house towards the barn, where the previous night he and Flugal had carefully deposited the carriage, to rest safely and securely away from prying eyes. To the observer Dave's expression was stern and concentrated; his eyes never left the barn, not once did he look around to check whether he was being observed or if anybody else had stirred, he just simply undid the lock and entered like somebody clearly on a mission.

Once inside, the brown holdall, which belied its true weight, hit the floor with a clunk, and without delay Dave opened it and emptied selected contents on to the floor and began his prearranged work.

He inspected every line, nut, washer and screw; those he had cause to remove were greased and returned to its socket; the screws he selected for just lubrication, in order to extricate at a later date due to rusting so fast with age and neglect, were soaked in fluid to aid their removal.

The carriage was then jacked up and both axles inspected, while it was airborne the wheels were rotated.

Placing his ear to the axle he listened to hear of any complaints coming from the bearings; it was not that Dave had any experience with these machines, he simply applied knowledge of other contraptions he had laid his skilful hands upon; for such an antique there were no complaints from the wheels and while the rusty nuts received a soaking, he returned to the brown bag and removed containers of leather and furniture polish. The furniture polish took first attack on the tired old carriage and brought it up to a wonderful sheen in a jiffy. Happy, Dave sent in the second wave in the shape of the leather polish; luckily for the leather it had faired very well under the protection of the tarpaulin; its weight had kept any harmful insects and bugs at bay. Dryness and cracks were the only main threats to its survival. The leather polish was allowed to soak into the cracks and added some much needed tractability to the black covering.

It was time for a mini break and Dave stepped outside to take a couple of deep breaths and soak up the morning, this was his favourite time of day; the world was still asleep and it felt like he owned it, the only other time it was like this was whenever he went walking in the rain or fished.

He meandered over to his vehicle; seated on the back seat sat a transparent plastic box containing his breakfast and lunch, Dave always liked to be prepared, if Mrs Flugal was around you could always guarantee a sumptuous breakfast, but he was not the presumptuous type and so brought his own sustenance.

Box in hand he returned to the barn, only now he took the time to survey the surrounding countryside and outbuildings, still nothing stirred with exception of the chirping of the young chicks. He stopped in the centre of the yard and studied in fine detail the beautiful, crystal clear, blue sky and remarked how wonderful God's omnipotent beauty truly was.

A large stride signalled his return to the return to the barn, but now something was different to Dave. He stopped and looked all around; the birds still chirped, the sun shone brighter yet still Dave felt ill at ease, he was being watched, he was sure of it. The hairs on the back of his neck rose and his heart skipped a beat; he thought of Williams, he was pulling one of his sneaky tricks spying on the competition.

'What are ya doin'?'

The snort made almost Dave jump out of his skin. It was Nigel.

'Nigel! What the hell...You scared the living daylights out of me.'

'Well, what are you doin'?'

'Don't creep up on anybody like that!'

'You still haven't said what're you doin' up so early.'

Dave placed his hand over his heart and measured his heart rate. 'It's beating like a train at full steam!'

'You're mending that carriage aren't you? You're mending that carriage?' quizzed Nigel.

'I've got to get back to that carriage. I've got a lot of work to do, so I'll have to bid you farewell Nigel.'

'I thought as much!'

Here Dave gave Nigel a wave goodbye and walked back to the barn. Unbeknown to him Nigel followed suit.

Dave halted after three or four steps when he realised he was indeed being followed by the pig.

'Nigel, go back to the stables.' he said pointing sternly in that direction. 'Back!'

'No!' Nigel stood firm.

'Nigel I haven't got the time to look after you this morning.'

'Look after me!' Nigel said indignantly 'I'm a pig, and us pigs are the most self sufficient animals around this farm, if not on earth! So there!'

Dave looked Nigel in the eye while he snorted and grunted his way through his mini speech.

'If you're going to come you've got to keep quiet and no interfering.' and then as an afterthought 'And I got no breakfast for you.'

Nigel eyed the plastic box. 'Oh, I don't know.'

Dave didn't wait to hear Nigel's reply, he had already started back to the barn. Nigel broke into a trot to catch him up. 'What do you want me to do?' he said. Dave didn't answer and they both entered the barn.

'Wow!' Nigel was taken aback with the sight of the carriage 'It's a beauty; we all thought it was a piece of junk, but you've brought it up real nice!'

'It's come up real nice.' said Dave 'Better than I could have imagined. It's a real diamond in the rough.' Dave checked the nuts that had been soaking in lubricating fluid; the first nut released with a little effort, it was a good start.

Nigel trotted around the carriage admiring its inherent beauty. 'I never thought it could look this good, you're a magician Dave.'

Dave knew 'pig' language less than Flugal. Nigel appreciated this and just kept talking, not the least offended. His three hundred and sixty degree circumnavigation finally brought him to Dave attempting to release another nut. 'That's a tough one eh?'

'This is a tough one Nigel' Dave's face was reddening dramatically with the effort required.

'Careful you don't bust a blood vessel.'

Finally the nut released. 'Man that was a tough one. I nearly burst a blood vessel there Nigel.' Dave stood up and drank some coffee from a thermos flask he produced from the brown holdall. 'I'll let the others soak a little while longer.' His second mouthful was met with the arrival of Nugget.

'Hey Nigel' he said.

'Hey Nugget.' Nigel replied.

And then Flugal appeared. 'You're early Dave.'

'I couldn't sleep. I needed to do something; I'm one of those people who just can't lie there burning time when their mind is racing about racing!"

'What else was your mind racing about?' asked Flugal

'Oh, nothing.' Dave replied.

But Flugal knew better. 'I know you better than you think.'

Dave knew right away it would be useless to keep up the charade. 'I know a guy who'll give us good odds in the race.'

'Already!' For some reason this news shocked Flugal, he knew it shouldn't have but it did.

'They were too good to be true.'

'How much?' quizzed Flugal.

'A couple.'

'A couple of what?' Flugal's stare never left Dave's eye line, he was waiting for the bombshell. 'Grand!'

'A couple of grand!' Flugal would have sat down had there been any such appliance available for the pleasure. 'A couple of grand.' he repeated in a much kinder, softer voice.

'I know, I know.' said Dave trying to placate any anger coming his way.

'A couple of grand.' whispered Flugal 'Are you mad!'

Nigel and Nugget were both flabbergasted; Nugget looked over at Nigel, whispering, "A couple of grand".

'How much is a couple of grand Dave?' said a now very concerned Flugal. 'Two, three, four?'

Here Dave paused 'Three.' another pause 'Three and a half.' he said slowly.

Flugal took a deep breath.

'We need to win!' said Dave after yet another silence. and realising Flugal was not about to talk.

'What's a couple of grand?' Nugget asked Nigel.

'Don't ask me, but I'll wager it's a lot of money. It's bad whatever it is!' answered Nigel

The two friends stood silent, expectantly awaiting the next chapter of the saga to unfold.

'Ralph!' said Nigel suddenly.

'Ralph, who's Ralph?' asked a surprised Nugget.

'Ralph's a rabbit I know that lives in one of the warrens down by the river; he's a compulsive gambler, he'll know what's going down!'

'He will!' said Nugget eagerly.

'Yeah, from Benny.'

'Benny who?'

'Benny the crow!'

'Who's Benny the crow?'

'Benny the crow, the bookmaker.'

'Benny the crow, the bookmaker.' repeated Nugget.

'Yeah, Benny the Crow the bookmaker. He'll have all the odds!'

'They must be good odds for Dave to bet his "couple of grand".'   Nugget in his naivety knew nothing about odds and betting or anything to do with gambling come to think of it, his life up to this point had navigated a path clear of such a vice.

'We need to win!' Flugal finally spoke.

'She's in pretty good nick.' started Dave, he needed to talk about something, anything that could divert any future questions off the present topic. 'It won't take more than a few days to get her back into a reasonable condition.'

'Where are we going to practice?' lamented Flugal, also trying to change the subject. 'I rang an old friend yesterday to ask his advice, he gave me the low down on the dressage and marathon stages plus the obstacle course. So we need somewhere where we won't bring any attention on to ourselves, and can work at all three. I'm still working on that one!'

'I know a place.' exclaimed Dave.

'Where?'

'The Dougherty's!'

'The Dougherty's!' Flugal frowned.

'The Dougherty's have a dirt track that runs around the farm. It was used to move hay and stuff.'

'I don't really know them that well.' Flugal said, unsure as he was in letting any outsiders in on his plans.

'I do. I've done some work for them recently; like everybody else they've fallen on hard times, so they asked me for a few favours. I don't charge you see because they are nice people. I'll ask them if we can use their track. They won't mind.'

Flugal nodded; he didn't have a better idea and it would keep them out of the public eye. 'I didn't realise they had their backs to the wall.'

'Williams!' replied Dave.

That name again. They could definitely do with finding that treasure if this race falls at the first hurdle, thought Flugal.

Nugget and Nigel had furtively removed themselves from the barn and scampered across the yard to the stables, both eager to relay the latest gossip.

Flugal didn't waste any more time getting stuck into the job at hand, worried now about his friend losing all that money placed on an outrageous bet; this extra stress he definitely didn't need, he must have got fantastic odds he thought, them being unknowns and all in this line of work.

Dave kept quiet, he realised he had just added to his best pals stress levels, unintended as it was, but that failed to make him feel any better.

* * * * *

Nugget looked left then right. The coast was clear and he gave the signal for Nigel to run across the lane bordering Flugal farm, through a hedge and across the field, closely followed all the time by Nugget himself. Ralph's place was a good ten miles away and it would take at least two hours to reach him over the open ground.

Such was Flugal's trust in young Rachelle that he never looked in on the horses except at first thing in the morning to check on their well being, then he left everything to her care, which was considerable. This allowed Flugal and Dave time to concentrate on the carriage, and to be unaware that the two of the farms inhabitants were missing. The only interruption being whenever Mrs Flugal needed to announce to her husband, and any visiting friends, that food was on the table and would ring three times on a large hand bell that had been in her family for years; the origin of the bell she had no idea, but it suited her purpose admirably.

The peeling reached the ears of the two men and they immediately downed tools. Rachelle met them half way across the yard as she to answered the call. 'The "Boys" are well today Mr Flugal.'

'Excellent.'

'But I can't seem to find Nugget or Nigel.'

'Oh.'

'I've looked everywhere for them.'

'They were around earlier. They'll turn up sooner or later. Nugget always had a tendency to go wandering, even as a pup.'

Nugget knew the way to the river, then Nigel would direct them to the warren.

'How come you know this Ralph?' asked Nugget.

'I saved his bacon once.' Nigel laughed at his won joke. 'Get it. I saved his bacon.'

Nugget smiled sheepishly; he wasn't sure whether to laugh or not considering Nigel's past.

'He got in a pickle with a couple of ferrets over at Willoughby's. They were putting the squeeze on poor Ralph with whom he placed a certain bet with. I had to smooth things out for him.'

'Why?'

'Because Ralph gave me a hot tip in return.'

'Did it pay out?'

'In bundles.'

'Wow!'

'Ralph will know what's going down.'

'You kept that quiet.' said Nugget looking sideways at Nigel for his reaction. His friend failed to answer and he didn't feel like pushing it; Nigel a closet gambler was enough to be getting along with.

Nugget was excited at the prospect of a great adventure and admired the alacrity at which Nigel was prepared to set off. He had wet his appetite and he longed to make this Ralph's acquaintance.

Nigel led him down a rarely trodden, dusty old path that ran parallel to the river. They approached the spot where Ralph had bumped into Flugal and then into a bushy area surrounded on three sides by grass covered mounds. Here Nugget stopped and peered through a gap in the hedgerow; this was near the site of his spying old Williams with his horses. Pulling a carriage no less! This recollection made the hairs on the back of his neck stand on end, why had he not thought of that before. Williams was behind the race, it was logical, he wanted everybody to enter, gamble all their money and then take all the winnings for himself and leave them all vulnerable to his taking all their land. Unbelievable as it sounded to Nugget, he believed it all to be true. He had to let the gang know, but only when they were all together.

Nigel called to him to catch up and he sprinted off in the direction of his voice without a backward glance and caught up with him standing outside the entrance to a large warren. They could hear voices emanating from the depths of the burrows, growing louder and louder every second, somebody was complaining bitterly about being disturbed during his dinner.

A young male rabbit hopped out of the warren with a look of utter disdain, which evaporated as soon as they espied Nigel.

'Nigel old boy, what a pleasant surprise, what brings you down my neck of the woods? What can I do for you?'

'Ralph, we need your help!'

'You do.'

'Well your advice actually.' Ralph looked suspiciously over at Nugget.

'This is my pal Nugget from Flugal farm.' said Nigel offering some kind of introduction.

Nugget could tell he was trying to place him; it would only be a matter of time, but he stopped short of putting him out of his misery.

'Any friend of Nigel's is a friend of mine.' Ralph finally said placing a foot on Nigel's shoulder to emphasise his deep felt friendship for him.

'Nugget and I were wondering what can you tell us about a certain carriage race or drive due to take place within the next month or two?'

'Oh.' Ralph was surprised at the request, which in turn surprised the two visitors. 'You want to place a bet?'

'Might do.' said Nigel and Ralph shuffled closer in order to keep the conversation strictly private. 'But is it worth my while?'

Nugget kept his counsel.

'It is at that!' Ralph smiled. 'Benny the crow's giving mighty fine odds at the moment; you can get up to 25 to 1 on some entrants depending on what part of the race you're betting on.'

'What part are you betting on?' asked a surprised Nigel.

'You do know there is three parts to this carriage drive?'

Nugget and Nigel both nodded.

'The first part of the event is a dressage section; they mark the team's ability to walk, trot and general control, then there's the marathon section; this involves competing over a per-designed course against the clock, which they are building as we speak, lastly and by no means least comes the obstacle section; where the teams have to negotiate man-made and natural obstacles again against the clock. There will be teams of one, two and four horses. I take it you'll be interested in the four-in-hand class?'

Nugget and Nigel again both nodded.

'The support races will involve single and two horse. You're not interested in placing a wager on those?'

This time the friends shook their heads.

'This 25 to 1?' said Nugget 'On who?'

Ralph rattled off the entrants he knew about from the main event, now warming to Nugget now, none of which included Flugal.

'Are those all the entrants?' said a concerned Nugget.

'As far as I know.' replied Ralph 'Why you expecting more?'

'No, I just thought the field might be bigger.'

Nigel and Nugget looked at each other; a horrid thought ran through both their minds; what if Dave had placed a bet on Flugal and Flugal wasn't even registered as a contestant. Surely that wasn't possible, unless he had gone to an independent bookmaker. Dave was supposed to enter him, as he had the application form.

'When is the closing date for entries Ralph?' enquired Nigel.

'I dunno! Soon though. You expecting someone to enter late?'

They both shook their heads. Ralph was not convinced. 'You wouldn't keep any hot tip from your old friend would you?'

'Ralph, if we hear anything you will be the first to know.' Nigel tried hard to placate him.

'I hope so.'

'You can count on it. When we come to place a bet we'll do it through you okay.' This did the trick and Ralph visibly relaxed.

Nigel and Nugget thanked Ralph for his advice and said they would be in touch sooner rather than later, and they left on friendly terms.

The journey home seemed to take forever, much longer than the two hours it took to get there, but Nugget and Nigel finally arrived back at the farm to see Rachelle going about her chores and hear Dave and Flugal still working studiously away in the barn.

They entered the stables unseen and relayed what had transpired at Ralph's and their new fears to the lads. It was quickly agreed upon that their concerns were not without merit and plan of action was expeditiously drawn up to ascertain if Dave had indeed failed to enter Flugal in the race. Dave it was conjectured kept all his paperwork of any importance in the glove compartment of his land rover, and they had to somehow gain access to the said compartment. It was agreed Nugget, as head of security, should be the one to enter the vehicle the very next time Dave gained entry. The only problem they could see with the plan was that they had no idea when that would be, and time was of the essence. It was then decided that Nigel would lure Dave out to the land rover allowing Nugget the opportunity to surreptitiously open the glove compartment and retrieve the said application form, which they could then present to Flugal, who would soon recognise the error and all could be rectified to everyone's satisfaction. This master plan was unanimously agreed upon with the lads adding valuable back up in the distraction department. On the subject of the luring out of Dave, after much debating, it was Nigel himself who suggested and concluded the debate by remarking he would simply remove Dave's plastic lunch box.

Wasting no time, Nigel advanced on the barn, the horses lined up, not in particular order, to help with the distracting and Nugget hid himself around the far side of the land rover.

'OI!' echoed around the yard.

'Brace yourselves lads!' said Chance.

Nigel then came flying around the corner of the barn with Dave in hot pursuit.

'You greedy pig, come here!'

'Nigel!' shouted Flugal bringing up the rear. 'Nigel!'

Nigel continued on running towards the car; here it suddenly dawned on some of the group that their plan had one fatal flaw.

'How are we going to get him to open the car door?' asked Pogo. As you can imagine there was not much forthcoming.

Nigel reached the car, stopped, and was nabbed by Dave. 'Gotcha!'

'Nigel.' said a panting Flugal. 'What are you up to? Sorry Dave, he's never stolen food before, not in the whole time I've known him.'

'That's okay.' Dave said examining the box. 'I know it's out of character, but these are strange times.'

Nugget stayed hidden.

'Now we're here you fancy tea and cake, that run's given me an appetite?' offered Flugal.

'Do I!' smiled Dave, and both men approached the house. Just then an almighty crash stopped them in their tracks. They spun round to see Nigel staring blankly back at them, with Nugget not knowing what or who to look at, Chance staring at the back of Troy's head, Biff and Pogo in hysterics, and Troy standing in a pile of chipped and broken glass that once slotted neatly into the passenger side front door. Troy whistled nonchalantly as if he didn't have a care in the world.

Dave was speechless as he examined the damage, Troy still whistled, and Flugal was too lost for words.

Dave opened the passenger door and inspected the glass littered over the passenger seat then turned to face the whistling Troy, just in time to see Nugget spring by his right hand side, nearly sending him flying, and attack the glove compartment.

'What the….' Dave never finished the sentence; Nugget had the compartment open and the application form, which was exactly where they feared it would be, in his mouth and was out of the door and presented it to Flugal.

'Thank you Nugget. What's this?'

'My car!' Dave finally uttered.

Flugal opened up the piece of paper Nugget had given him and it quickly dawned on him its significance. 'Dave. You did send off my application right?'

'Yes.' Dave paused and he tried to recollect. 'I'm pretty sure I did.'

'Then this must be a copy.' Flugal showed Dave the form.

Again Dave was speechless, his eyes widened and Flugal knew he had forgot.

'The post office shuts in just under an hour; we can send it recorded.' said Dave with just a hint of panic.

Flugal smiled; he could sense the urgency in Dave's voice. 'I'll get my car keys.' He returned in a matter of seconds and the two men departed pronto.

'Don't you think it's kind of funny?' said Flugal after about five minutes driving or so.

'No, but I did wonder why you smiled. And my car's a wreck.'

'It's only a window! And you can easily get a new one for that model at the beakers yard. No, I mean Nugget giving me the form.'

'Yeah.' Dave nodded; he had nothing to say or add so he just nodded.

'How did he know it was there?'

'I dunno. Maybe you now have a psychic dog!'

'Maybe. Makes you feel good though doesn't it?'

'Does it?'

'Knowing those boys are behind us all the way and looking out for us.'

'I suppose.'

'Come on Dave, I know you've finally come round to the idea that they understand everything we say?'

'Scary isn't it!'

'I'm just starting to finally accept it, even with what happened in the yard, but there's just too much going on to ignore the obvious.'

'I'm with you there! I didn't want to sound like a nut, bit this has convinced me though.' added Dave.

'I can associate with that!' Flugal said in a jocular tone. 'I didn't want to say anything stupid. Like you know Mrs Flugal said she's always known and how come we hadn't figured it out sooner.' and then after the briefest of pauses, added. 'Women's intuition I guess.'

Flugal turned into the street off the high street, heading for his favourite parking spot.

'They want us to win!' Flugal added as he started to park the car.

'Yeah!' Dave smiled again.

'But how did they know you had forgot to post it? Somebody's told them!'

'Who is going to tell them!'

'That is worrying!'

'I don't care!' Dave said. 'Whoever it was saved my bacon and blushes.'

'No, neither do I!' Flugal finished parking the car, and the two friends filled in the application, paying particular attention to the different sections of the drive, and posted the form recorded delivery. Two days later Benny the crow gave odds on Flugal at fifty to one.

'I don't believe you did that! It was great!' enthused Pogo as he slapped a hoof on Troy's back. 'Fantastic! What do you reckon Chance, thinking on your feet or hoofs or what?'

'It got the job done.' Chance was clearly impressed. 'Sure was thinking on your hoofs alright!' and they all laughed.

'You're the horse today Troy!' continued Pogo.

'I'd have kicked both windows in to increase my options!' Chance winked as he turned and walked towards the lower field 'I'm going for a walk while we got some free time.'

Rachelle who, as is her want, kept quiet, now pressed Chance. 'Where are you going Chance?'

'For a walk.'

'You going for a walk?'

'Sure, you want to come?'

'I wish I could go with you, but there's nobody left to look after you lot! I could ask Mrs Flugal.'

Biff trotted over and nudged Rachelle towards Chance. 'Get along Rachelle. We'll be okay.'

Rachelle, confused, looked at all her friends in turn searching for some kind of explanation. Nugget tugged at her trouser leg, pulling her in Chance's direction, Nigel bumped against her gently with his belly. Biff nudged her again.

'Okay, okay I get the hint; I'll go for a walk. You boys behave.'

Chance waited for her to catch up, she stroked his neck and patted him affectionately 'If I didn't know any better Chance I'd swear they were trying to get rid of me!'

Chance chuckled. 'No Rachelle, they love you too much for that.'

They wandered down to the lower field. Rachelle unlocked the gate and at their leisurely pace enjoyed each other's company and the day.

'Hey, show me that kick!' Nigel shouted over to Troy.

Troy kicked out displaying all the power and prowess he could muster.

'Wow!' said Nigel.

'Want to see it Nugget?' boasted Troy.

'Go ahead.'

Troy gave his all, displaying the now infamous kick and smashed in the rear passenger window.

'Wow!' said Nigel again.

15

Williams burst into Bennett's office with his now all too familiar habit of entering in without invitation, and it annoyed Bennett no end, but he took great pains not to show it.

'Flugal farm!' shouted Williams; he had also taken to shouting whenever Flugal farm formed part of the conversation 'Flugal farm, what's the score? When is it up for sale?'

'Mr Williams!'

'Mr Bennett.' answered Williams refusing to grant Bennett time to reply 'I have been reliably informed that Flugal farm will be imminently up for sale!'

'Who may I ask told you that?'

'That's confidential.'

'I can assume then Mr Williams that nobody in this bank gave you that kind of information, and if I find they did they will no longer work in my bank!'

'All I need to know Mr Bennett,' asked Williams calmly, but secretly livid that an upstart like Bennett dare talk to him in that way, 'is when the farm is up for sale.'

'If the farm goes on sale and only if then, you will be notified in due course Mr Williams. Those are the procedures.'

This could only have one outcome. It irritated Williams immensely. 'I expect to be the first to know!' Williams had remained standing and his agitation manifested itself in his pacing across Bennett's office. 'I expect not only to be the first to know, but to have the only offer accepted.'

'Mr Williams.' said Bennett now standing.

'Please tell me you're not going to tell me something I'm not going to like.' countered Williams.

'Mr Williams, procedures will have to be followed and observed.'

'Yeah right.' Williams stopped pacing. 'We'll see about procedures. There's too much at stake here Mr Bennett, as you well know!' And with that he left. Bennett sat back down in silence.

Williams agitation had not abated by the time he reached his car and slamming the driver's door shut, he gunned the engine into life at high revs and wheel spun away, which did little to quell his rising fury; Bennett to him was a dogsbody and should bow to his masters, when he was lord of the manor Bennett would bow to him and not be in a position to answer him back in the manner that he just did.

Arriving home he pulled the car up sharply outside his mock Tudor house, he slammed the door shut again without bothering to lock it and made straight for the rear of the house where he kept his stables.

Four magnificent black stallions who went by the ominous names of Thunder, Lightning, Tank and Storm, their black coats glistened in the bright June sun, waited patiently for their master.

'Here he comes.' said Storm, he was the most garrulous of the quartet. 'Better look lively, he looks in a real foul mood!'

'Great.' said Lightning gleefully 'We'll go for a run and maybe get a chance to steamroll somebody.' This then brought on a serious case of the fidgets for just thinking about the prospective steamrollering. 'Who do you reckon is going to give us a race? What do you think Thunder?'

'I don't care!'

'What!'

'I don't care who enters. WE'RE GOING TO STEAMROLL THEM ALL!'

Thunder and Lightning laughed their heads off.
Williams stood with his hands on hips filling the doorway of the stables, his outline in silhouette.

'Steamrollerin!' sang Lightning.

'Okay my friends, let's see if we can break our existing record.' Williams said.

'Steamrollin 'em pretty good!' added Storm.

The quiet one of the group as you might have guessed by now was Tank; he wasn't named Tank without reason; he and Troy were two peas from the same pod.

In no time at all Williams had the team rigged ready to go, the carriage secured with the help of his stable lad, and was on his way on a wide circuit around his estate that bordered the river, where Nugget espied them before "steamrollering".

* * * * *

You could have cut the tension with a knife, the expectation was tangible. The barn doors slid open; this was the grand unveiling of the new carriage. Mrs Flugal had laid on a veritable feast yet again with what little they had, but it still looked magnificent, and she issued instructions to young Rachelle to make sure the animals were lined up to inspect and view their new carriage.

Dave steered while Flugal positioned himself to the rear providing the horse power, and between them the carriage paraded itself to its audience.

There were lots of admiring glances and comments; Mrs Flugal congratulated them all on their hard work, the horses bustled and jostled to get a better look, and it was universally agreed that they had only to turn up in such a majestic piece of machinery to win; the confirmation of Flugal's entry had been received that very morning, arresting any fears. Dave paid the entry fee, which included registering themselves with The British Driving Society, and resolutely refused to accept any reimbursement. He had also collected all the relevant literature regarding carriage driving from the wonderful Mrs Evening, to go along with that sourced by Rachelle. Flugal now had a surprise in store for his little helper.

Mrs Flugal then added that it would be a shame to waste any more time and that everybody should enjoy the feast, then commence training as soon as practicable. Nobody present could think of any good reason not to partake of the goodies on display, and so they did. Afterwards, without any delay, once a satisfactory amount of time had passed after the victuals had been consumed, the decision was made to take a leisurely trot down to the Dougherty farm to use the track, but before they left Flugal approached Rachelle.

'Rachelle!' he called out, as she started to make her way across the yard.

'Yes, Mr Flugal.'

'I've got a request of sorts to ask you. You can say "No" if you want and I know you'll need your grandmother's permission, but would you like to be my groom on the carriage?'

'Would I!'

'I'll take that as a "yes" then!'

Rachelle nodded enthusiastically.

'Good, glad that's settled.'

'I thought you'd ask Uncle Dave.'

'We both agreed it should be you, your over fourteen, so your old enough to compete on all sections and I'll get you registered with IHDT.'

Rachelle beamed back a huge smile.

'We're going to check out the Dougherty's place, so you be ready to go tomorrow.'

'Okay.'

Mr and Mrs Dougherty had agreed without reservation to allow Flugal and Dave to practice as much as they wished; understanding the position he found himself in all too well. Flugal offered to pay, but they refused, and as no one used the track much these days they kind of felt to charge anything was not neighbourly; Flugal secretly promised himself that if they ever found the treasure it was only right and proper that it be turned over to them, as it was their true inheritance.

* * * * *

Nostromos Global Industries weekly meeting had gone much as planned and all necessary business and arrangements had been sanctioned to allow a smooth operation of the planned drives; Lucy had added the suggestion, a couple of days after the original meeting, of expanding the occasion to include more events, as that would guarantee more exposure.

There were still a few dissenting voices to the sagacity of such a peculiar undertaking, bearing in mind the costs involved, and as to why they could or should not have sponsored a horse race at a respectable meeting, but these were quickly dismissed without to much trouble due to the increased publicity such a strange event had produced. The carriage races or drives were most definitely on!

Charles during all this time had settled into his post at Global, securing his position at every turn, wheedling out those who do and those who may oppose him at any future date. One such measure was to ensure that Lucy was definitely on his side, he made sure that she was aware that his door was always open to her if at any time she had a grievance to air, but he also had an ulterior motive for his offer; he had first become aware of its existence during that fateful meeting when the drive was agreed upon. He liked Lucy; she was pretty, that there was no doubting, and funny, they shared the same taste in humour, she was sporty, he liked that in women, and just recently he had the first indication that any feelings he may have for her could be reciprocated; he wasn't too sure at first, but any doubts were dispelled one Monday morning over the coffee machine, the signs were there for all too see and Lucy showed herself not to be the retiring type in these situations. All that was needed now was for him to summon up the courage and ask the fateful question, then pray the answer to be what he most wished.

The team stood proud with Chance front right, this was due to the propensity of right hand turns expected around this clockwise course. Biff was chosen to partner Chance as a leader; he was considered the more agile between him and Pogo, and if steering around tight turns was to be an issue then agility was your best friend.

That left Troy and Pogo, as the wheelers in the power house at the rear; their job was to get the carriage rolling, especially on any inclines or hill starts negotiated, as this would involve the pair of them taking the initial strain, but more importantly these two, it was agreed, would be the best pairing to provide the braking during descents, Chance and Biff being ahead of the pole that separated them were unable to provide any braking assistance at all. Also as wheelers their harness was different; they were 'breeched' so to be able to pull against the pole in order to brake.

Flugal had decided in his own mind the correct order; he attempted to lead his horses to his chosen position, but finding stubbornness resistible to his efforts reluctantly left them where they stood. 'So be it.' he muttered.

'Looks to me like they know more than they let on? More than we do anyhow?' said Dave smiling.

'It seems that way.' Flugal replied standing hands on hips contemplating his next move. 'You coming?' he said finally climbing aboard.

'You bet!' Dave jumped sprightly on to the carriage belying its years of inactivity. 'Do you shout "Yeehaa!" or "Giddy-up"?'

Flugal stared blankly back at Dave. 'I'm going to make that "clicky" sound and see what happens.'

'Shame you can't ask them or more to the point ask them and understand the reply! Isn't that right boys?'

'If he shouts "Yeehaa" I'm off like a bullet out of a gun! That'll teach them!'

'Easy Troy.' Chance said calmly. 'If we get a "Yeehaa" we'll just jerk the carriage forward, knock them off balance a little and stop.'

Troy tutted.

'That will be sufficient.' Chance continued.

'And if a Giddy-up?' asked Biff

'We'll go backward.' laughed Pogo.

'Yeah!' agreed Troy. 'Like a bullet out of a gun!'

'See.' said Dave, beaming a huge smile. 'They're discussing the most logical way to get us underway!'

A little alarm bell started tinkling inside old Flugal's head; he wasn't convinced by the tone of his teams conversation, so he erred on the side of caution and let out a slow, deliberate "clicky" sound, then grit his teeth awaiting the maelstrom. Nothing happened. After a short pause he tried again.

'Shall we?' whispered Chance.

'Like a bullet out of a gun.' chuckled Pogo silently, and the carriage rolled gently forward, slowly but surely picking up speed as they negotiated the old dusty track.

Over the period of an hour, until everyone reached a state of exhaustion, the carriage sped up, slowed down and took all the corners at differing speeds. Flugal did his best to simulate some kind of dressage routine shortly after, but he knew that they would need a much sterner test than this in time.

'Hey Chance?' panted Troy. Chance was too short of breath to answer. 'Hey Chance?' he said again.

'Yeah?'

'You said carriage pulling was a piece of cake!'

'When did I ever say that?' gasped Chance, swallowing great gulps of air.

'I dunno, but you said it'

'Water!' croaked Biff.

'Water!' repeated Pogo indignantly 'We're doing all the manual labour around here!

'Damn right Pogo old boy, damn right.' agreed Troy.

Chance looked disdainfully back at the two of them. 'If that was manual labour I'm Nugget's uncle!'

Pogo looked at Troy then Biff, then Chance and smiling said 'There is a family resemblance.'

Chance deigned not to reply, he just swished his tail in Pogo's face 'See the family resemblance now?'

Biff cracked up, Troy forgot his moans and laughed 'If only Nugget could see himself!'

Nugget, all the time the lads had worked their socks off, lounged around the yard either playing with Rachelle or sleeping. Nigel just slept. It was a beautiful spring day.

Mrs Flugal did her spring cleaning all the while cooking her delicious wares, it helped her relax; she had found recently that cooking was a great stress reliever, and it was distracting her mind sufficiently from the problems at hand to allow her to recharge her batteries.

Nugget opened one bleary eye and tried in vain, not that he wanted to, to lift his head in order to view the weary return of the lads; once uncoupled, with the help of Rachelle, Biff crashed into his stall, Chance stood motionless trying to gauge which muscle hurt the most and decide on the path of least pain to his bed, Pogo zigzagged off each stall wall on his way to a well earned slumber and Troy, once in his, just refused point blankly to ever move again come rain or shine and promptly keeled over.

Flugal and Dave left the carriage in the yard and staggered into the house with a few unintelligible, caustic comments from the livery horses ringing in all their ears.

'My back!' exclaimed Dave hands on hips and arching his back.

Flugal gave his wife a hug and a kiss and slumped into one of the chairs surrounding the kitchen table.

'Good day then?' said Mrs Flugal cheerfully planting a pot of brew on the table. Never had two men been more pleased to taste a hot steamy cup of tea. 'How'd they do?'

'Great.' said Flugal sipping his tea. 'Just great. The problem is the driver, he's an idiot.'

Dave shuffled his feet in that embarrassing way when you feel you're imposing on a personal moment.

'An idiot!' repeated Mrs Flugal.

'Yes an idiot. I've no idea what I'm doing!'

'Maybe it just feels like that.' she kissed him on the forehead.

Rachelle came in from the yard.

'Did you crash?' continued his wife.

'No!'

'Did any of the lads fall or get hurt?'

'No!'

'Did they display any weakness or incompetence?'

'No!' he knew where this was going and he felt like a log running down the rapids of a mighty river: At its mercy; Flugal knew where the final destination this discourse would lead him, and he accepted it gratefully.

'Then what are you worrying about?'

'I don't know.' He had said it before he even thought of it, and instantly felt himself rising to those heady heights of idiocy.

'Troy's keeled over, I've never seen them so tired!' Rachelle interjected.

'Is he?' said Dave, just glad to say anything.

'He's okay.' laughed Rachelle. 'He's been chatting to the others in the stables, returning any compliments from the livery horses. Although some of the owners are a little concerned at finding on ours flaked out; they all think they've got the colic!' Mrs Fugal gave her a cup of diluted orange squash; it lasted all of five seconds. 'I give him five minutes more and he'll be up looking for his fresh hay, pony nuts and hard feed!'

'Oi!' hollered Nugget.

'Whhaaaattt' answered the prostrate Troy.

Pogo, Biff and Chance chomped on mouthfuls of delicious pony nuts.

'Nuuuttss!!!'

Still no input came from Troy's team mates.

'I'm too tired!'

'Yeah, but you know...you know.' Nugget was relishing dragging out the punch line 'it's kind of different today.'

'Different. How?'

'You know.........you know.'

'No I don't know. I'm too tired.'

Chance took another huge mouthful of the delicious nuts.

'What's different?' Troy could feel himself getting a little impatient at the lack of response. His left ear perked up awaiting eagerly Nugget's response.

Pogo and Biff joined Chance and gulped down nuts as loud as they could.

'These nuts of yours.' came the response, finally.

'But what's different about a bag of nuts when I can lounge in my nice warm stable.'

'There delicious.' And Nugget buried his head deep into the sumptuous bag. A mouth full of dirt and grit met his efforts. Nugget raised his head to be met by Troy's icy stare. 'Miraculous. And there was I about to call the vet.'

Troy looked down on his less than full bucket.

'Anybody got a mobile handy.' added Nugget.

Troy took a tentative nibble 'You know what these need............gravy!'

'You want that as a take out? I'll take them out for you!' and Nugget grinned his cheesiest grin.

* * * * *

Tank swung all his sizeable weight onto his right side in order to drag the carriage around the sweeping right hand bend, he had for his partner in the boiler house at the rear, Storm. Storm chatted constantly; sledging anybody and everyone who came within his line of sight. Tank grunted his approval at basically everything Storm sledged. Thunder and Lightning led the team, guiding the quartet around the twisty track specifically designed by Williams to bring out the best in his horses.

Williams never did anything without having an ulterior motive; he opened his track to any outsiders who wished to use it to exercise their horses, run or ride a bike.

On this hot spring day Williams and his ream of "steamrollers" knew they should receive a fair share of victims, and they were not to be disappointed.

Lauren Dancing, a fifty year old retired school teacher, was riding her chestnut mare Shandy. The day was beautiful; the weather perfect for riding, with just the hint of a breeze. Shandy had recently recovered from an injury to her left foreleg and was looking forward to getting out and stretching her legs.

Thunder was the first to espy Shandy and her owner walking sedately around the track. His personal favourites were cyclists and joggers. Shandy threw her head high in the air catching all the smells, sounds and sensations associated with such a gorgeous spring day.

'There she blows!' yelled Thunder quickening his pace, and so loud it was miracle Shandy never heard.

'Yeehaaa!!' bellowed Storm, raising his game to match the team's acceleration. Shandy heard that alright!

Williams, irked by all that un-commanded increase in speed, ordered his team to slow. It was all in vain, they had their prey "banged to rights" and nothing was going to prevent them from enjoying a little sport.

'We'll give them the old one-two to start.' suggested Lightning.

This entailed the lead horse nearest the victim nipping their hind quarters, followed by the rear horse swinging the carriage in a body checking motion, forcing them off the track and into the surrounding hedgerow. About three months ago one unsuspecting jogger received the "old one-two" and ended up being deposited through the hedge and head first into the river.

Shandy's superior hearing made her ears prick up at Storm's outburst and she immediately broke into a trot. Lauren, once the initial shock had wore off, grew steadily excited, commended Shandy on her endeavour and courage to dare to trot first day out, and decided to remain oblivious to her taking matters into her own hands. Shandy felt the warm glow of affection from her owner, who stroked her neck with her right hand; Lauren was an extremely accomplished rider and never lacked confidence when it came to her horses.

Thunder and Lightning realising they had been rumbled sounded the general charge: The race was on.

Williams continually ordered them to obey, chastised them when they ignored him and made many pathetic attempts to bring his horses under his direct control. All to no avail.

Shandy's trot broke into a canter. Lauren, to her surprise, discovered herself accepting the canter, unquestioning her position; subconsciously she realised she was really just a passenger and so enjoyed the ride, knowing she could halt their progress at any time.

Tank let out an all too rare call for more speed; such was the rarity of Tank's exclamations that his request for added speed led to an initial reduction! But this was short lived and the chase was renewed with increased vigour.

Shandy could hear and feel the carriage bearing down upon her and she wondered, hoped and prayed that her leg would hold under the strain; she had heard from the other horses the antics of Williams team. If you could get a head start, she was informed, and you can keep them at a safe distance because they could only maintain the charge for a couple of miles.

Lauren heard Williams cussing his horses disobedience, glanced over her shoulder and saw the real reason for Shandy's sudden departure from their sedate walk in the sun.

'Come on Shandy!' she shouted without a moment's hesitation, the thrill of the chase evident in her voice, 'Come on!'

Shandy bent herself against the chase, knowing that Lauren was now fully aware of their predicament, and it only added to her strength and resolve to outlast the "quartet of cruel", as they had been nicknamed by one of her closest friends.

Around the track they went, circumnavigating its every inch, each fighting to gain some tangible sign of superiority. The track was two and a half miles in length, quite a size for a private practice facility, but Shandy accepted that one lap and a bit would be all she required to get them to safety. Her lungs now were starting to burn under the effort; it had been a while since her last outright gallop, but gallop she now did, for she felt the claustrophobic effect of them closing in on her, but her leg was still holding. So far so good.

Storm shouted, yelled, cajoled, steered and bellowed instructions seeing them gaining slowly, but explicably on Shandy and her rider.

Williams also had begun to realise the true meaning of events, and he too now joined in encouraging them on to greater toil.

Lauren on hearing Williams roar on his team called on Shandy to equal the team's output.

Shandy could feel the panic rising within; Williams was definitely beginning to close and her injured leg was displaying the first symptoms of complaint. She held her nerve and her speed as best she could, Lauren's encouragement helped enormously. They began to exit the fast right hand bend and a lengthy straight followed; her leg accepted the straight, the turns were causing all the bother and she would have to slow by the end of this straight to negotiate the next bend, or so she figured. The only comfort was the "quartet" would also find the going harder. She constantly allayed any fears by telling herself this undeniable fact and that the straight marked the two mile barrier, she prayed they would start to show signs of slowing by then.

Thunder was the first to start breathing heavily. Lightning feeling the weight increase on his shoulders, as Thunder slowed, took up the slack, but this would and could only be a temporary solution. Tank and Storm displayed no signs of wavering and only had eyes for Shandy.

On the straight Shandy's leg failed to ease and Thunder's energy levels rose again at the perceptible closing of the gap. Shandy realised she had one last full on sprint in her leg and then all would be lost or she could maintain her present speed and take her chances at the two and a half mile point, hoping that their stamina might wain. The straight was now nearing its end, but Lauren had remained mute for a few minutes, breathless in the chase.

Lightning realising the load on his shoulders had eased pushed on harder, but his push exhausted him to point of no return and he too began to gasp for air, Thunder's resurgence evaporated and at last there was a reduction in forward speed.

'Damn!' shouted Williams, he knew the game was up. Even Tank and Storm were now flagging badly, but valiantly still pushing on; Storm had not said a word for a number of minutes, which under these circumstances was always a bad sign.

Shandy and Lauren heard Williams outburst and both smiled independently of each other. Shandy never let up her speed, out of the corner of her eye she could see the carriage falling back. A left hand bend met the end of the straight and she pushed hard round it knowing the carriage would slow even more, and she had escaped the "old one-two".

By the time she did slow the pain in her leg had risen to uncomfortable levels and she knew it would stiffen considerably. She tried to stretch it as best she could.

Lauren reined her in slightly, telling her to slow, patted and stroked the side of her neck congratulating her on her brilliant effort, she knew it would be a while before she rode Shandy again, but the love and pride she felt for her horse filled her heart to near bursting. Lauren dismounted once they were out of sight of the "quartet", but kept Shandy moving at a walk and they continued on sedately back towards the stables. Shandy secretly prayed her pursuers felt as tired as she did. She needn't have worried.

Williams cussing continued on after his charges had come to a complete stop. Thunder and Lightning looked sheepishly at each other; not really wishing to express any views on the chase, Tank grunted, the garrulous Storm aired his many assumptions on their failure, and was politely informed where he could place them. Williams kept on cussing; he could never conciliate the thought of losing with the actual event; it just was not acceptable to lose in any way, shape or form.

16

Flugal exited his bedroom stretching and rubbing his aching back. Nugget mirrored his actions.

'Morning Nugget.' said Flugal looking down at his furry friend. 'You ready?'

'In a minute or so, just got to loosen up a bit.'

The two old pals staggered down the stairs like a couple of geriatrics. Flugal reached the bottom first and turned to see Nugget standing two steps from the bottom, shaking his rear end in a pendulum fashion.

'A bit stiff eh?' inquired Flugal.

'As a board!'

'Stiff as a board I bet.' Flugal laughed at his own joke.

Nugget stared back blankly; he was used to the conversation taking this track. 'I know you can't understand anything I say, but there are days...' Nugget cut himself short. Flugal kept on chuckling and muttering to himself on how funny he could be. 'Yes, there are days!' Nugget descended the last two steps. 'Hello.' he barked to prove the point to himself.

Flugal stroked old Nugget around the ears: he loved that. 'Hello.'

He barked again louder than before.

'I here you Nugget. It's going to be a long day!'

'Why?'

'A long day Nugget.' Flugal said very slowly, over pronouncing every syllable.

'It's a good job I like you.' replied Nugget.

'Yes Nugget, you and I have a good understanding. We better get started.'

'Whatever you say boss.'

'See Nugget my knowledge of dog is improving.'

'I hope your carriage driving is not improving as fast.'

Nigel was the first up this morning; a rarity worthy of a number of comments from his friends, which were usually totally ignored by him.

Nugget and Flugal came across their curly tailed friend. 'You're up bright and early Nigel.'

'Don't start Nugget....I can get up as early as anybody!'

Nugget thought it best not to pursue this line of questioning lest something had happened during the night.

Biff and Pogo limped out of the barn, looking like a couple of drunks after a heavy night. Flugal didn't bat an eyelid at seeing his horses wander unattended in the yard.

'Oi!' hollered Nugget 'You ready for a few more laps?'

'Like I was born to it!' replied Pogo sarcastically.

'It was written in your stars.' Injected Biff 'Your life will be an ever increasing series of circles, each leading to an entire different connection of emotions.'

'Somehow I don't think they'll be the only stars you'll be seeing today.' Nigel added gleefully, holding onto a mischievous grin as he did so.

After the morning feed was over, Flugal pulled out the carriage, with no little effort, from the barn, arranged the tack and harness, then collected and connected each horse in turn; all but Chance complaining bitterly as he went about it, but even if Flugal had been able to understand horse, he would have quickly realised that there was no intent in their groans and moans. It was purely banter done for the sake of it.

Chance was the last to be bridled and connected to the carriage, and as you would have expected of a former professional, it was completed quickly and efficiently and in utter silence.

Nigel and Nugget hopped onto the rear of the carriage as it pulled out of the farm, they were surplus to requirements on the farm today and had decided to join the boys in a show of solidarity; Nigel required a little extra patience in boarding, but he was determined to experience firsthand practice day and to add any suggestions that might seem appropriate. Along the way they took a small detour to pick up Rachelle, as she was going to make her debut as Flugal's groom.

Once at Dougherty's track Flugal steadied the four friends, speaking words of encouragement, urging them on to greater effort than the previous day, and offered any advice he could think of. Chance took the opportunity to add a few well chosen words of his own. Rachelle, who had been briefed on the way there as to her job, showed her dedication to the task at hand, that she had done her homework thoroughly, and now sat, fidgeting with nervous anticipation. Nugget and Nigel decided to stay board and add some valuable extra ballast.

The team each took a deep collective breath, scraped their front hoofs over the ground; seen sometimes as an act of impatience or boredom when seen through human eyes, though in the equine world it is also an instinctive habit similar to the sprinter psyching themselves for a ten second dash to glory or ruin or the intrepid explorer testing the soundness of the foundation before venturing forth on another desperate tale of derring-do.

Flugal ventured another "clicky" opening to begin the training circuits, and braced himself on its outcome.

They rumbled ungainly at first around a couple of circuits, then as like yesterday, gradually gathering speed as the stiffness wore off. Flugal had doubted the team's positioning at first, and subconsciously he realised Chance had played a big hand in affairs, but he was content and accepted their decision; Biff was indeed proving to be a leader, Chance was seen to give him his rein once they had successfully navigated a few more circuits. Pogo and Troy, two complete opposites, worked well in harmony as wheelers. Rachelle moved expeditiously and with great agility when called upon to help balance the carriage.

Circuit after circuit they practiced; some at a trot, others at differing speeds and slowly, but surely each individual friend started to learn more and more about his compadre.

Half an hour later, with all the horses tired, but not exhausted, Flugal thought it best they all take a breather and some refreshments. Nugget and Nigel maintained a respectful silence in the back throughout the circuits.

During their replenished thirst Dave arrived in his old truck, the land rover having given up the ghost the previous day, beaming a huge smile, desperate to offload all the latest gossip.

'This event is going national!' he said approaching the team.

'I kind of figured.' frowned Flugal, gulping down a mouthful of water, 'With dressage and marathon on the Saturday, the obstacle section on the Sunday, we've got a lot of work to do!' This was all bad news to the confused Flugal; he had three disciplines to teach his " Boys" and not a lot of time.

'Yeah! They've had plenty of entries, more than they anticipated.'

'How many?'

'I don't rightly know, from all over the country though!'

The thought of professional out-of-towners entering a local carriage race troubled Flugal; they would have to have a complete rethink in terms of training, on this subject, he prayed, Chance was one step ahead of him.

'These circuits have run their course, if you'll pardon the pun.' said Chance quietly.

'I reckon so!' answered Biff 'We've gotta improve our overall fitness if we're gonna get anywhere near winning this thing! I don't know about you guys, but I'm really whacked and it's only been half an hour.' None could argue.

'I don't know which part of me hurts the most!' said Troy stretching his back. 'It was easier giving them riding lessons.'

'By my reckoning.' stated Chance 'This obstacle course will not be a simple track like this one. There's got to be some tight twisty turns through bollards, with penalties for hitting them, plus a few undulations to sap the energy out of you. Stamina is the key!'

'I once saw a jogger.' began Pogo 'running between lamp posts. He would sprint to one, then jog to the second then sprint again. What d'ya reckon.'

'It's an idea.' said Troy, realising that they were starting to think and act as a team.

'A good idea.' smiled Chance.

'Well if nobody's got a better one.' stated Biff, 'Then we'll knock ourselves out giving it a try!'

Flugal dismounted the carriage and with hands on hips stared intently at the ground; his mind was wandering in all directions, aimlessly between continuing with the circuits, their purpose, how many to do if he held them as adequate, and could he really ask them to give their all for him, his wife and the farm when all the responsibility for this catastrophe should be laid firmly at his feet.

He caught Chance sneaking a peek in his direction and he smiled a smile of reassurance; their worry was another piece of the jigsaw that made up this tragedy and only added to his ever increasing stress levels; he cared deeply what they thought and how they felt, not only were they his horses, dog and a pig, which always brought a smile to his face whenever he grouped them together that way, but his friends and family as well.

Rachelle followed him off the carriage, and gave them all a drink of water from a large container they had unloaded before starting practice.

Dave broke his train of thought with this usual well timed bombshell. 'You know Williams has his own track to train on!'

'No! But I'm not the least surprised.'

'Yep, and his team some are saying are the ones to beat.'

'When was Williams ever interested in carriage driving?'

'I've seen his team in action.' growled Nugget, which was missed by Flugal and Dave, but not the rest.

'Where?' quizzed Nigel.

Nugget felt all the eyes fall upon him; he took a deep breath, steadied himself and gathered up his thoughts. 'Down by the river.'

'Down by the river!' half the group spurted out together.

'When Flugal fell in, that's probably why he didn't see him.'

'What were they like?' Chance said.

'Beautiful.' Nugget had said it before he realised what he'd let himself in for.

'Really!' Biff and Troy gibed together and eyed Nugget closely.

'They run pretty good too!' Nugget raised his nose in the air; he was going to give as good as he got.

'And you never thought to mention it?' said Nigel very seriously.

'Never occurred to me until now! Would it have made any difference?'

Chance came to Nugget's rescue. 'No it wouldn't. At the end of the day we will have to beat everybody that is put in front of us, regardless. Williams has his man made track that he uses regularly for riding and now driving his horses; they will be very well prepared and so must we.'

'We're gonna beat them, beat them all!' Pogo's outburst was appreciated as much as it was unexpected, but he said it with such conviction, brimming with confidence that it could not have but rubbed off on them all, and they all agreed that victory could be theirs and was well within their reach, as long as they all supported each other, pulled together and watched each other's backs.

'You bet.' smiled Nigel having lost any air of seriousness, which he secretly regretted and made a mental note to apologise to Nugget later. 'There isn't a team entered we can't beat.'

'That's the spirit.' interjected Flugal, as stood trying to decipher all as it transpired before him.

'Would that be the royal "we"?' laughed Biff.

All the lads ribbed poor Nigel and old Nugget mercilessly in a friendly way, but they could see the joke clearly and laughed along to.

While the animals were in discussions and jesting with their friends, Dave climbed aboard his battered old truck and left. Flugal allowed the group to rest some more and replenished their sustenance. The animals made the most of the extended rest period, lying around, laughing and joking constantly, relieving any tension, that they lost complete track of time, so by the time Dave returned they were all totally unaware how long he'd been gone.

Dave unloaded eight large sets of cones from the back of the truck with the help of Flugal. The group grew silent, fascinated, watching the two men position the eight pairs of cones at various points around the track.

'This should be interesting!' said Troy getting to his feet. 'Hope you're feeling fit Pogo!'

'Yeah.' replied Pogo, rising also, as his curiosity got a better hold of him.

'I can suddenly feel a bout of lethargy coming on!' interjected Biff, walking past his two friends to get a clearer look.

'Better sharpen my size nine hoofs then!' Troy said finally.

It became obvious relatively quickly as to their intentions; the sharpness of the angles between the pairs of cones and their close proximity to one another clearly indicated the sharp turns Chance had been talking about earlier.

'I tell you what.' started Troy, with a customary cheeky grin and looking straight at Chance and Biff 'You two lead off and Pogo and me will provide the moral support!'

'That's my speciality.' chuckled Pogo 'Moral support. Did I tell you about the time way back when I was a foal....'

'Yeah, yeah, yeah.' interrupted Biff 'When you were a foal. I'm surprised you can remember back that far!'

'You remembered it though.'

'You talk in your sleep.' continued Biff.

'It covers your snoring!' grinned Pogo. He was having the better in this encounter and loving every minute.

Biff snorted loudly and instinctively everybody stared at Nigel.

'What!' Nigel exclaimed, feigning indignation, then he too snorted as loud as possible to make a point.

The two men, their cone placing completed, approached Rachelle and the jocular six and explained to them fully their new plan whilst harnessing the "Boys" back up to the carriage. Nugget and Nigel took the opportunity to resume their positions behind Flugal and Rachelle. Both of them found little surprise or embarrassment now in talking to the animals in a human way when the need arose, whilst Dave became an interested spectator.

Harnessing complete, Flugal drove them out to the starting place on the track, and after giving the team a quick recap and advising them as to what was required this time round, which brought about a quick, witty series of wise cracks, they sped off towards the first set of cones.

The turn was sharp, perhaps too sharp for a first attempt, but the lads never slowed; Chance talked them round the initial part of the turn, with Biff adding support at every interval. Pogo and Troy clenched their teeth as the weight of the carriage dragged down on their shoulders. They all turned right on Chance's command, which coincided exactly with Flugal's, and the carriage veered into the tight right hander and exited with only a marginal loss of speed and never once touched the cones.

'Brilliant!' praised Nugget.

Rachelle shouted encouragement every step of the way; where before she had kept quiet in order to concentrate on the job-in-hand, now her natural confidence rose to the surface.

Nigel joined in, sat up and hollered encouragement deafening Flugal in the process.

The team's hearts filled with a mixture of pride and joy and they clattered onto the next set with great anticipation. The next turn was to the left. Again Chance led the chorus of recommendations and instructions; he was falling back on his years of training as a professional athlete; there was nothing he could not figure out that a professional horse could do. He had no experience of carriage racing or driving, but with a little imagination and a lot of application he would, and had found a way.

They entered the tight left hander, the driver, groom and passengers leant into the turn to aid its progress. Pogo and Troy grunted audibly as they swung the great weight to the right. Chance and Biff chose the best and most expeditious line through the cones, bearing in minds the strain the rear two friends would have to bear in order to satisfy their choice. Again another successful turn was negotiated, no drum hit on either side. The third corner went much the same way and Flugal began for the first time to believe that his team were at last acting and working in unison and they might just stand a chance, a remote chance accepted in the obstacle section, but a chance none the less. Even Dave was making complimentary noises; he was no doubt eying a tasty return on his investment.

Chance and Biff navigated them up to the fourth turn, a right hander, the passengers leant right, Troy and Pogo swung the carriage into the corner, but the ground on this portion of the track was different; it had a loose top surface like gravel, nobody had taken it into consideration. The two horses slipped at a crucial time; Chance and Biff felt the tell tale rearward pull on their harness and instantly knew the turn was doomed to failure. Troy and Pogo regained their footing and balance, and made a desperate attempt to manoeuvre the carriage around the last remaining cones, but to no avail; that slip relegated them to failure and they struck the left-hand cone a broadside sending it cartwheeling through a hedge.

The carriage now righted, the team slowed to a trot and finally came to a halt from whence they had started. They all remained silent.

'Sorry guys!' Flugal was the first to speak 'That was harder than I thought.'

'You're telling me!' butted in Troy.

'You were fantastic!' shouted Rachelle.

'That last set of cones was too much to ask of you, I'm sorry.' Flugal sat contemplating the lap and his decision which pushed the team over the edge.

'No way!' said Pogo, looking over his shoulder at Flugal, Rachelle, Nugget and Nigel. Flugal's and Pogo's eyes met with a mutual respect 'We need to train harder, we lost concentration, the loose ground caught us cold, but that's no excuse, there's no reason we should not expect the same on race day!'

'Thank you Pogo.' Flugal knew horse about as well as pig, but he understood Pogo on this occasion perfectly.

'Pogo,' said Chance, 'that was well said. I did get caught cold.'

'Me too.' agreed Biff.

'We led you two in at the wrong angle and speed for the conditions. We've got to run that set again.' They all unanimously agreed with the senior member of the team.

The horses moved forward a few paces without any command from Flugal; he knew what was going to happen and kept his counsel.

'Let's go.' Nugget said quietly and reverently.

'Better hold onto your hats!' Nigel added.

'They want to go Mr Flugal.' said Rachelle, and he adjusted his seating position in readiness.

'Then turn them loose old friend.' Dave shouted in eager anticipation, and Flugal gave the command to go.

Confidence as anybody will tell you is a many splendid thing, although invariably tempered with fragility; the first three turns were executed in an equally efficient manner and the team turned for that final right hander. Flugal sensed the tension rise as they approached the last set of cones: Chance and Biff were silent, concentrating on achieving the perfect line and speed through the turn.

The line chosen, they accelerated right, everything followed as before albeit this time they adjusted correctly for the loose top surface, and the carriage made a perfect entry. Around the turn they held the carriage, it made a perfect slide, apart from a minor jerk which was quickly corrected, and they exited faultlessly on line and speed.

Nigel, Nugget and Rachelle roared their approval on the successful completion of an impeccable lap and that if there was any doubt as to who was the best, it was team Flugal, and nobody, not nobody was going to beat them. Poor old Dave was drowned out on the sidelines by the joint growling and squealing of the three cheerleaders.

Flugal let out a huge sigh of relief. His joy though was to be short lived; the carriage slowed to a walk, the horses were chatting constantly to each other and he became painfully aware that Chance was limping. That explained the jerk mid way round the turn he thought, and he never pulled up, the poor fella' must have been in intense pain. Flugal brought them to a halt and dismounted the carriage. It was that leg, the left foreleg Flugal and Rachelle found on closer inspection; it had swollen quite considerably around his tendon.

'It's that injury again old fella!'

'Injury again?' quizzed Dave now squatting beside them both.

Flugal ran his hand delicately down the back of Chance's leg; the horse twitched nervously when his hand came near the tendon, and the tiny scars that had resulted from the pin-firing that had been performed on him to help cure his original injury. 'Steady old friend, I'm not going to touch it, we need to get you home and some ice on that!'

The sight of his lead horse injured depressed Flugal immensely, but he consoled himself with the fact that the race was still weeks away and Chance would have time to rest. 'When I bought Chance from his previous owners he had a history of tendon trouble, it was the cause of ending his racing days!' Chance stood, head bowed, utterly dejected. Rachelle stood silently stroking his head.

The other three held their gaze on Chance; each in turn had apologised for his bad luck and as a group offered to help him as much as possible. Chance thanked them all. Each secretly though wanted to know more about his racing days; their curiosity growing immeasurably with each passing minute, because this was one topic Chance forever stayed mute on.

'At least we can give him some rest before we need him to take another run.' Dave said standing.

Slowly and painstakingly they made all their way back to the farm. Chance was led some of the way by Rachelle, until Dave returned pulling Flugal's horse trailer so by the time they reached home Chance was a full fifteen minutes in arrears to the others.

17

Williams surveyed his latest acquisition with the air of a man who's just completed a business transaction, knowing full well he's screwed his opponent for all he can get. The apple of his eye was a brand spanking new, glossy black, four seat racing carriage; the paint work glistened in the bright sunlight and Williams admired his own reflection on the body work. He adjusted his hair and straightened his tie.

Williams mobile phone sprung into life inside his jacket, he removed it muttering that there was no peace for the wicked, and answered it in a surly manner. On receiving this conversation he stood with one hand in his pocket, alternating his expression between disdain and contempt. The unknown recipient was Bennett.

'Unbelievable!' Bennett muffled his cry in utter disbelief on the other end of the phone, hiding his voice as best he could with his left hand over the receiver.

Williams exhaled deeply, his anger rising in direct proportion to his own words. The gist of the conversation was that Flugal would be given sufficient time to settle any outstanding debts, then if he is unable to meet the payments the farm would go into receivership and ultimately be put up for sale. This was not what Williams wanted to hear; through his end contacts he had expected the heads up and be given first refusal and demanded Bennett to be good to that word, but he would now have to bid along with everybody else should it go on sale; this insulted his overblown sense of vanity and he voiced his discontent with no end of hidden malice, and after venting his spleen to his desired taste, he hung up on Bennett.

Bennett stared incredulously at the phone as if he was expecting it to suddenly admit it had played a practical joke on him, but no Williams had hung up and after he had gone out of his way to personally advise him on the turn of events; everybody else would have to make do with reading public notices or be lucky enough to visit the respective estate agents or auctioneers. What an arrogant and obnoxious man, thought Bennett, and deliberately replaced the receiver with much care lest he should damage it with some latent anger. He leaned back in his chair and stared at the ceiling mulling over the phone call and his unenviable position with Williams. Finding himself unable to quell or quash his temper, which was about to run wild like a stallion free of his reins, he realised there was only one solution at a time like this: Mint choc-chip ice cream. Bennett informed the assistant manager of the bank that he was going out for a while, and kept walking straight for the exit, not worrying to acknowledge any response or guarantee for when he should return.

Bennett exited the bank and turned left; he was a man on a mission and he knew his destination well. He had deduced quite early on in his life that whenever he was down or depressed he must indulge himself in a special pleasure to help revive his flagging spirits. He was lucky, he had many simple pleasures he could fall back upon; today was mint chocolate chip ice cream day and within minutes of vacating the bank he arrived at the desired shop. Inside he ordered a large double scoop cornet and then proceeded to slowly saviour the delicious flavours whilst meandering down the high street. At the far end, a section of the shopping precinct he was totally unfamiliar with, he came to rest outside a bookmakers going by the name of Whittakers; there were pictures of race horses in full flight and sportsmen and women in various attitudes of competition then something caught his eye. In the bottom right hand corner of the window sat a newly erected poster, quite inconspicuous really, of size and dimensions guaranteed to infuriate young Charles, advertising Nostromos Global Industries sponsored carriage race with all the entries listed below. One competitor captured his attention: Williams.

Benny the crow shook his head in that inimitable style inherited by all bookmakers around the world, sucked a huge mouthful of air through his beak and muttered something incomprehensible.

'Carrots!' he finally said after a moment's silence. 'Carrots!'

Ralph, who was the closest to Benny, nodded vehemently.

'When was the last time you saw a crow eating carrots?'

'It would be a first I agree.' Ralph said nodding again.

'A first!' assented Benny

'A first.' repeated Ralph.

'Let me get this straight, so as to properly gauge the level at which to pitch proceedings. You want to bet carrots on the upcoming carriage races?'

Ralph only smiled this time, his neck was starting to ache from all that nodding. 'And maybe some cabbage!'

'Cabbage!' Benny couldn't quite believe his ears; he had heard many things and propositions during his bookmaking years, but carrots and cabbage to a crow was a new one.

'Yeah! Crows eat cabbage, yes?'

Benny shook his head.

'Oh. What then?'

'Got any corn or wheat? I'm very partial to corn or wheat.'

'How much?'

'How much can you get me?'

'A couple of bushels of wheat!'

'A couple of bushels eh.' This shocked Benny, but he wasn't about to weaken his position by revealing it. Ralph didn't quite strike him as a bushel thief or collector come to think of it.

'Can you get them?' It was a logical question considering Benny's suspicious mind.

'Sure!'

'How many?'

'Three maybe four!' boasted Ralph.

Jed, Ralph's partner in crime, a rabbit of a slightly smaller build, came and stood beside him. 'I'll...we'll guarantee three!' he added, smiling confidently at the acknowledgment of his boast. He felt good that Benny had noticed him and been included in the negotiations.

Benny digested all the information presented him like a poker player trying to deduce whether his opponent is bluffing. 'Okay. You boys deliver me at least three bushels and I'll give you eight to one on carrots and cabbage on any contender except Williams. He's three's! I can't say fairer than that!'

'We want Flugal!'

'That loser! He's twenty five's. That's outside the proposal.'

'I know.' Ralph felt that finally he had the upper hand.

'You can have fifteen's on Flugal.'

'Fifteens!' Jed blurted out. 'He's not that good and anyhow Chance is injured.'

'Yeah, Chance's lame.' backed up Ralph.

That's news, Benny thought. 'Okay, you two can have twenty-five's on Flugal, but you keep it to yourselves, anybody approaches me about Flugal and Chance at that price and I'm going to know it's you two and you drop back to twelve's tops!'

The deal was struck. Benny was to pay them within three days of the race if they won, and for his part he made one last demand and that was that one bushel was to be in his possession by that Friday evening. Jed and Ralph consented eagerly.

* * * * *

Flugal and Dave drew up a training programme for the three remaining fit horses, whilst Rachelle put her groom's responsibilities on hold and took upon her slender shoulders the responsibility of nursing her Chance back to full health with the help of Mrs Flugal and some of her wonder remedies her grandmother had passed down to her; a job his wife dedicated every available hour to fulfil. Flugal had no hesitation in giving such a hefty responsibility to Rachelle, for one they had decided to give the old man of the team a couple of days to see how he recovered, before calling the vet and two he knew that love is a very powerful healer.

Chance gave himself up to her care; she gently chastised him whenever he stepped out of line or she perceived him to be leaning towards the disobedient. Chance just laughed at her playful tone coupled with words of remonstrance, but thankfully the swelling reduced after a day or two and he started to recover nicely.

The three weeks that passed since Chance's accident seemed to evaporate into time; Chance's leg improved greatly, Mrs Flugal's medicines working a treat, and greatly aided his rehabilitation and general well being. So much so that Chance wished he had had them back when the original injury occurred, for he was now managing to walk and trot a few miles every day, with a short canter with no ill effects.

The rest of the bunch kept up a strict, though not too punishing, training regime, as all riding lessons had now been suspended until after the meet and they were well aware that their terrible secret regarding Chance was out; on Mondays and Wednesdays they practised dressage in the barn that held the carriage, and for the last week Chance had thankfully returned, but just for this discipline. The barn kept them out of sight and its confines helped tighten their control. Tuesdays and Thursdays were obstacle days at the Dougherty's and that left Friday and Saturday to practice the marathon around the farm, with occasional forays down the country lanes. Sunday was a day of rest. Finally with about a week to go Flugal backed off the training, he was very wary about tiring out the younger horses with the race now only seven days away. He was also hoping to get the last week with all four of them back together running obstacles and the marathon. During Chance's enforced absence Biff had grown into a fine lead horse; Pogo and Troy trusted his judgement and their runs around the obstacles had become smoother if not faster, albeit being one short. Pogo and Troy enjoyed each other's company in the boiler house at the front of the carriage and this only aided practice times no end.

Nigel and Nugget had also not been lazy during this time; Nugget as head of security made sure that any further information could not leak out; Chance's accident had been unfortunate and he had been spied limping back to Flugal farm by the two rabbits, so he found it impossible to keep a lid on it with those two. All other operations were conducted under a veil of high security.

Nigel used all his available resources, friends and favours to gain any valuable tit bits that could be of benefit to team Flugal.

It was late on the last Saturday before the race, when the team of three plus Nugget, and Nigel were led by Flugal through the gate to the farm. They chatted and laughed away to themselves clearly enjoying an in joke that Flugal was not in on. It had been a very productive day; the times were stable, a couple of seconds had been shaved off the previous best, they had accepted that without Chance they would only improve marginally and this was achieved through slickness of the run. The closer the race came the more the anticipation and excitement grew within them all until it reached near fever pitch.

Any outsiders witnessing the banter between them, could not understand how they remain so close when it seemed so fierce, but that was the secret, because they were so close now, closer than they had ever been, nobody ever took exception and any and all opportunities to "get one over" were gleefully accepted.

Nugget jumped off the carriage and ran up to Rachelle and Chance standing in the stable doorway. 'Hey Chance you ready to rock and roll on Monday?'

'Sure am!.'

'My Chance needs a couple of more days!' said an over protective Rachelle, once she got the gist of Nuggets questioning.

'I still got to do what my nurse tells me Nugget.' and he took a tentative step into the yard. Nugget and Rachelle watched him closely, both for different reasons; Rachelle was concerned his achilles wasn't quite healed sufficiently, knowing Chance would jump at any available opportunity to run with the team without giving due care and attention to his injury, and Nugget with eagerness to get the team back as four and get in some valuable practice.

'Tuesday will be a good day to train.' said Chance stretching his leg, and then seeing Rachelle's growing concern ' My leg will need a good run by then! The dressage is good, but it's not a run!' and he ventured out into the centre of the yard. The day was overcast, but clammy and the warmth soothed his leg.

Flugal led the team over to the stables and with Rachelle's aid unhitched the team and prepared them for the evening. It gave him great joy to see the old trooper up and about and showing no outward signs, bar a few first tentative steps which were more a precaution than anything. Even Pogo, Biff and Troy voiced their pleasure at seeing him pain free, but these were punctuated with the obligatory banter. Chance as always gave as good as he got; it had become quite apparent to him during his enforced absence that they had inherited some independence and maturity, and this pleased him.

The arrival of Bennett brought an abrupt end to the banter and comically they all turned in unison to espy his arrival.

'What does he want? And on a Saturday!' said Rachelle cuttingly, totally oblivious to the level that she had pitched her outburst.

'This'll be interesting!' Nigel said moving to the front of the group 'Nugget you reckon you can get close enough to get the low down?'

'Consider it done.' and he scampered to catch up Flugal, who had gone to greet Bennett as he exited his car.

Flugal felt uneasy; his fear and trepidation had grown in intensity on seeing this man and it angered him. On approaching the car he was convinced, with every step, his adversary could sense, smell his fear and this only added to the cold chill that crept down over him. Flugal knew Bennett saw the fear etched over his features and he instinctively rubbed his nose to hide it. Bennett for his part held out his hand smiling, saying nothing as yet.

'The smiling assassin.' thought Flugal, as he shook him firmly by the hand; he wanted to make a point to him that any external references to weakness must be quashed by this handshake. Bennett grasped Flugal's hand just as hard.

He then led him into the house via the kitchen, with Nugget in close attendance. Mrs Flugal inquired after their thirst, as she always did, refusing to break her habit just because the guest was less that welcome, and it was answered in the positive.

Bennett sat down by the kitchen table, placed the briefcase beside him, opened it, and removed some documents. 'Mr Flugal.' he started.

'Yes.' He had answered without giving it a moment's thought and would have kicked himself for it given the chance.

'Mr Flugal. The bank have asked me to convey their sympathies to you in your present circumstances.'

'Yeah, right.' thought Flugal.

'And they thought it would be nicer if I visited you at home rather than discuss over the phone or in my office.'

'That was thoughtful of them!'

Bennett was riled but, bit his lip; he gave Flugal the benefit of the doubt considering his opening gambit and stressful situation. 'Yes it is, but given your present circumstances, that business has been very slack for you recently, and taking this into consideration, I am here to inform you that I'm going to give you a payment holiday of a couple of months, in order to pay any outstanding monies.'

Flugal fidgeted nervously. It was the best news he could have had at this juncture, and the most surprising.

'If you are unable to pay by the time the holiday finishes Mr Flugal, then the bank will be forced to try and recoup its money,' Bennett made sure he emphasised the word "will", 'and this will regretfully involve them repossessing and selling this farm, as you put it up as security.'

'Do you have any buyers lined up?' Flugal inquired. Bennett remained stony faced. Before he could muster a reply Mrs Flugal came with the refreshments, sat them down on the table, within easy reach of all, and seated herself by her husband.

'The bank thought it nice to have this little discussion at our home dear.'

'I heard. And thank you Mr Bennett, that's very considerate of you.'

'That was my sentiment.'

'I was explaining to your husband Mrs Flugal the unfortunate circumstances we now find ourselves in, but we'll give you both as much help as we can. Like you said once before Mr Flugal, you have been with us for a very long time.'

'We've got a couple of months.' Flugal added in order to try and calm his wife, in case she hadn't quite picked up that part of the conversation.

'Thank you Mr Bennett, it gives us something to work with.' Mrs Flugal now said gratefully.

'That's exactly right!' Flugal said, selecting his tea and taking a sip.

'Unfortunate circumstances Mr Bennett.' Mrs Flugal said, in a manner not exuding any emotion which unnerved Bennett. 'Unfortunate for us!'

'I'm sorry Mrs Flugal, but my hands are tied over this. If I could help you more I would.'

'It's not your fault Mr Bennett, our anger and disappointment is levelled firmly at your bank, you are just their messenger. Loyalty doesn't count for much these days does it?'

Bennett sought solace in his tea using the time to think up a suitable reply. 'No I'm afraid it doesn't!' he finally said almost without thinking; his response shocked and unnerved him further, but he took a small crumb of comfort from the thought that at last he had let go those shackles he felt restrained him from openly admitting his position, which was at times itself untenable.

'The banks always win!' and with that Mrs Flugal rose and left the room.

The two men sat in silence. Flugal felt the weight lift from his shoulders; was this a sign that their luck was about to change.

'You know the only way we had open to us to pay the arrears was to sell our belongings!' he hated to openly admit his impending failure, but it did him the world of good and it brought him immense relief to bring it out into the open.

'I did recognise this.' Bennett said.

'Why did the bank allow me to borrow more money if it thought me a bad risk?'

'I don't know!'

'I've borrowed before, fallen behind some I admit, but always paid it off in time. What's so different this time?'

'Economic climate.'

'Economic climate!'

'Your loan was before my time Mr Flugal. You need to talk to Mr Miller to get the definitive answer.' Bennett breathed a sigh of relief at extricating himself from such a corner and placing all the onus on Miller, but Flugal was not about to let him off the hook that easily.

'I think the bank has behaved very irresponsibly!'

'Maybe Mr Flugal,' answered Bennett slowly, 'but the bank is still after all a business and will operate as such, and this is the position we now find ourselves in.'

Flugal could have returned with a caustic comment, but he meditated on what really was the point, and as he had been given extra time to pay, simply smiled politely and kept any thoughts to himself.

Nugget throughout this discourse had laid down on the floor beside his master facing Bennett, he now gave Flugal a look of respect and held him in awe at facing the enemy head on, not retreating an inch; he was giving it to them. He didn't quite understand the entire gist of the conversation, but he was putting up a fight to the bitter end; Nugget didn't like the sound of his own use of the phrase "the bitter end" but it somehow seemed apt.

'I have these papers I have to give you.' Bennett said with genuine regret. 'I'll leave them here on the table Mr Flugal, explaining all that I have said and more.'

Flugal nodded, sipped his tea and stroked Nugget around the ears.

'And here I thought he didn't know I was here.' whispered Nugget to himself.

'Well thank you for you and your wife's hospitality and I do sincerely wish we could have had this meeting under more pleasant circumstances.'

'And not unfortunate ones!' Flugal replied, keeping his temper in check.

'You tell him.' growled Nugget, wishing for once that his master truly understood him, so he could give the pernicious Mr Bennett a piece of his mind.

'No, quite!' and Bennett closed his briefcase, drank the last of his tea and rose. Flugal followed suit, holding his cup in his left hand and escorted him, with Nugget, to his car. Bennett climbed aboard, leaving his case on the passenger seat and left. No other words were spoken. Flugal returned to the house leaving Nugget to run over to the stables and relay the course of events, even those he didn't quite understand the meaning of, as best he could.

The group all expressed relief that things were starting to alter in their favour at last, but it still left the race as their only real chance of salvation now; not that this came as any great surprise, it had become the accepted norm over the past weeks, but as everybody was concentrating on the race it felt inappropriate to mention it. Nugget brought up the buried treasure he heard about, but they dismissed that as pure fantasy, still Nugget thought it prudent to keep it as an option. He had heard all the talk between Dave and Flugal and knew deep inside himself that they had found something big, and the race, albeit of great importance, was stalling their search. He therefore secretly decided to make some investigations of his own whenever he had the time to spare, and help Flugal find those papers he had promised to recover from storage.

Rachelle ran through her chores in a dull, solemn, mood; she was now reasonably fluent in her understanding of the many nuances in horse, since she had been taking care of Chance, and her depression sank over her like a veil, clouding her view of the future. Among her extra chores now included catering for Nigel, previously Flugal had taken to accommodating him due to his habitat, but Rachelle had argued that it would appear unfair if she didn't shoulder the responsibility for Nigel, seeing that she cared for all the other animals. Flugal agreed with her; her maturity seemingly surprising him now at every turn.

'All we can do is apply ourselves as best we can, try hard and pray that it is sufficient to bring about our salvation!' Rachelle interjected between any verbal responses from her friends.

'And if it's not?' asked Biff.

'Then let us have the strength to accept our fate. But we are in a position to control and alter our own future and that makes us special. We need to remember that and make it count!' continued Rachelle mucking out the stables, the occupants sidestepping her when it was their turn to be cleaned out.

'We have two months to the end of our world as we know it!' Nigel's statement may have sounded slightly on the melodramatic side, if not true, but it rang through the group, disturbing them once more from their routine lifestyle and focusing their efforts for the next few days.

Rachelle finished up and made her way back to the farmhouse with a heavy heart; even in the hardest of times you always hope and pray the blackest of days will be lined with silver. To think of such bad news dealt a major blow to Rachelle's cloud.

In the kitchen the mood was slightly more upbeat and Mrs Flugal was at her pragmatic best, dishing out sound, practical advice and options that they could use, which didn't include visiting any antique dealers; she had her hands burnt once already going down that road.

All three sat down for a bite to eat. as Mrs Flugal had always stated "Nothing can be achieved on an empty stomach!"

You could set Dave's daily routine by the meal times at Flugal Farm, and sure enough he appeared right on cue.

'I've got the low down on all your competitors and how the sections I believe are going to pan out. I know you didn't ask me, but I knew you would eventually.'

Dave sat down, adjusted his cutlery, being a lefty, and as if by magic his meal appeared before him, courtesy of Mrs Flugal, and he tucked in without delay. This brought a smile to the Flugals; Dave was after all one of the family. A few quick mouthfuls and he continued. 'Williams is one of the favourites.' and then realising a possible error 'I think.'

'You think?'

'Astonishingly, he's been at this for a few years, off and on, so we have to take it that he's going to be able to train whenever he feels like with the very best of facilities. How's our training going?'

Flugal gave Dave a brief run down on the team's performance and the advancement they all made in the training runs, dressage and over a make-shift marathon course, considering they were down to three, and how he was looking forward to the return of Chance so they could all run as four again in the lead up to the race.

'You're currently twenty-five's!' said Dave after hearing all the news.

'Sorry?' Flugal was caught off guard. Even Mrs Flugal stopped eating to listen to this thread of the conversation more clearly.

'You're twenty-five to one to win!'

'Seriously!' Flugal ate slowly digesting this information; he hadn't even thought about his odds in the race, only the winning of it. Rachelle was the only one now still eating; this was all gobbledegook to her.

'Yes, seriously.' Dave emphasised 'Twenty five-to-one, and before you ask, that was where my sizeable bet was always going to be placed, on you to win!'

'Oh.'

'Don't worry.' Dave could see the worry etch itself in Flugal's very pores.

'I've got it covered.'

'How much did you place on us?' asked Mrs Flugal.

'Please!' pleaded Flugal 'I don't want to hear it. If you must discuss it I'll leave the room for a minute or two.'

'Don't panic. That won't be necessary. I can ask Dave later.'

'I've seen some of the other drivers and their teams, apart from Williams.'

This news Flugal really wanted to hear, practicing is one thing, but one needs to know what kind of opposition to expect. 'And'

'And they're good, but not as good as us.' then quickly added 'In my considered opinion that is. We stand a good a chance as anybody.'

'Really?' Rachelle now inquired, this lifted her mood; this was the silver lining she wanted to hear.

'I didn't see them run,' Dave started looking directly at Rachelle, then turning to the table as a whole. 'but the horses are not looking all that fit, and I'm pretty sure they're not putting the hours in we are.'

'You must have done some driving to see all those entrants in so short a time.' asked Mrs Flugal.

Dave took a mouthful of food, and just waved his hand in that time honoured fashion to signify it was no big deal and nothing to worry about. 'We've all got to do out bit.' he finally said.

* * * * *

In the late afternoon Williams gave his "quartet of cruel" a run around his track. Once warmed up, the four miscreants espied in the distance the lone figure of a jogger; he wasn't so lucky and they notched up another victim to "steamrollering'.

18

The build up of interest in the carriage drive had been worryingly slow by Nostromos Global Industries standards; all the hype and money they had injected into advertising yielded very little return, but in the three to four weeks leading up to the race public interest gathered momentum, finally exploding into their consciousness. A real buzz was now felt throughout the local community when they became aware that one of their own had entered the main event, and seeing a possible head to head with among other people Mr Williams.

Flugal received many callers during this period; Mrs Flugal entertained most, although it put a strain on their already beleaguered resources, but this was offset to some extent by the promises of their returning students once the race was over. Throughout it all she insisted in keeping up appearances. They were both offered all kinds of help, some from those whose horses were liveried at the farm plus others from quarters neither knew ever existed. Flugal politely declined most, as it was an anathema to him to accept favours from people who he had no hope of ever repaying, but over time the tide of good feeling and well wishers with offers of help became unstoppable and so he accepted only those he considered would be of benefit to his wife, and she without his knowledge did the same for him.

In the animal kingdom news reached the group that the other contestants were far from "unfit", as Dave had described them to Flugal. On the contrary there were many professional outfits entered and driven by some very accomplished racers, whose track records were the stuff of envy. This didn't seem to affect anybody around the stables to any great degree; they were buoyed by the return of Chance and looking forward, with relish, to attacking the obstacle course once more in an attempt to set a new faster time.

Williams quartet were as popular here as Williams was with the humans. The stories had been steadily filtering back to the farm about their antics on his track; these had the effect of giving rise to a now growing indignation towards the man and his beasts, the advantage being to allow Nigel to gain access to their training routine and his spies made mental notes of all the times. Williams had for some time been waging a war against the starlings nesting around his estate, regarding them as vermin. Nigel took the opportunity to become very friendly with Sammy, a starling of junior rank in the flock. He kept a close vigil on Williams, and every time the "quartet of cruel" upset any locals he would report back to Nigel, who used these as a means of building the team's competitiveness, enflaming their passions to right such wrongs, and show them how they can expect the worst of the teams to behave. "There can be no prize for us" he would say "for a second place!"

It was decided that Tuesday would be the day when they would all run again together as a foursome. Chance had taken advantage of an extra day to rest up, used the dressage practice to stretch his legs and enjoyed the healing powers of Mrs Flugal's medicines under the continuing care of young Rachelle Perkins. The four friends would once more become united under the banner of "Team Flugal", a phrase rapidly being adopted. Flugal took the opportunity of a walk, rather than a trot, to the Dougherty's to allow Chance to warm up slowly.

Here finally they now all stood, Dave being the only absentee, Nugget and Nigel sat on top of a grass bank overlooking the track with Rachelle in her position as groom. Flugal inhaled deeply, praying that there would be no recurrence of the injury, otherwise any chance of success would surely evaporate. He could see the horses were eager to get going, the tension displaying itself in lots of tiny ticks multiplying across their backs.

'How's your leg Chance?' Biff whispered.

'Okay. We'll soon find out after this run!'

'We'll try and take as much of the strain as "equinely" possible until you feel comfortable.' comforted Troy.

Pogo nodded.

Chance smiled back at his rearmost pals. No words were necessary.

'Okay, let's do it!' Chance said firmly, and they marched on at a steady pace to the makeshift starting line.

'You say when Chance.' Pogo muttered as they approached the line.

Flugal spoke constantly, trying his utmost to calm Chance, believing him to be under great stress. He could not have been further from the truth, Chance in fact was the calmest one among them; again his professional training and background had taught him one important factor: To know your own body, and although there are no guarantees in this world or any other, Chance was ninety percent sure his leg would hold up this day. He had further decided to rest it fully tomorrow. He daren't share this knowledge until the day ended in case he might tempt fate, he did not want to get their hopes up only to dash them later, and as most professionals carried varying degrees of superstition, Chance was no different.

'Ready?' Chance said, tightening his shoulder muscles for that initial strain to help break the carriage's resistance to any increase in forward movement and momentum.

'Ready.' they all replied.

'Then let's go!' And the carriage flew instantly onward to the first corner.

Flugal was taken aback by this expeditious beginning and clenched his teeth, expecting imminent catastrophe.

The team led again comfortably by Biff and Chance careered down to the first bend; they chose a line that Flugal immediately knew to be right, he tried to suppress a grin, instinctively there line and speed were perfect. The exit was no less spectacular and Fulgal was shocked to feel the positive acceleration along the straights, and flying around corners with no discernible loss of speed and before he knew it they had crossed the start/finish line and they were decelerating to a comfortable trot.

'Wow.' was all he could say, it had been that exhilarating; he had forgotten how quick the team could be when under the power of all four. Rachelle simply laughed; she was so proud of all of them.

Nugget and Nigel exuded similar feelings, making them known to their friends as best they could.

The trot was maintained for the second lap; again Flugal had no input in the decision, he was acutely aware of his lack of concern and he bore them no malice only giving regular encouragement during this time of recuperation. The horses discussed the lap, dissecting every inch.

'I took the second right hander too wide.' Biff said looking sideways at Chance.

'We took it to wide.' Biff felt relieved at not bearing sole responsibility in their loss. 'We can shave a second off the lap times. Any suggestions?' Chance looked back over his shoulder.

'None to add.' Pogo said shaking his head.

'None from his corner!' added Troy.

'Okay then let's keep it tight around the first three, don't hit any barrels, and kill the faults around the last and set a record time.' Chance stretched his leg at the end of his mini speech.

'How's that leg of yours?' asked a concerned Biff before the other two could.

'It's holding up just fine. I want us to give this lap some serious speed and test my leg to the max, I'll rest it after and then we'll have a better idea if I should be in the team or not!'

'We ain't going to run without our main man Chance.' And Troy nudged him in a sign of equine machismo.

The team trotted to one hundred yards short of the start line then slowed to a walk after a request from Chance, the trot resumed thirty yards short. The line was the catalyst, the spark that ignited the carriage into the flying lap, they knew that on the day the clock would run once one of their noses crossed the start line and end the same way; its forward motion never diminishing for a second, no let up would be acceptable. The corners one by one flashed past, Flugal was truly speechless for the first time during training. It soon became plainly obvious to all concerned this was something special.

Nugget and Nigel both started their mental stopwatches, Rachelle had hers running on her wristwatch; the two spectators would consult the other with their time for the lap at the end and then the mean time would be adjudged to be the agreed lap time. Both had made a record of the fastest three and four horse lap times and the first, unbeknown to the lads and Flugal, had already broken the four horse lap record. And this was run was quicker still.

The last corner appeared on the horizon, the one that had caused such consternation earlier, and in an instant it rushed past and the run was over to be followed by yet another cooling down lap.

Nugget and Nigel compared times, the result was never in doubt, the time was spectacular, and better than they could ever had wished for and the two couldn't wait to tell their friends, falling head over heels as they clambered down the bank to get into earshot. Rachelle stopped her stopwatch and marvelled at the time.

The two timekeepers fought each other, as well as gravity, to be the first to spread the great news. The scene was farcical to behold and no less funny to take part in; Nigel and Nugget cracked up as they desperately tried to get the upper hand and holler over to the lads whose attention either had yet to attract. Gravity though finally won the day and eventually the two friends fell on their backs, slid down the bank and keeled over with raucous laughter, rolling from side to side with their legs in the air.

Finally Biff noticed them. 'Now what are they up to?'

'Who?' asked Troy his head darting from side to side and coming to rest looking directly at the two figured rolling in hysterics. 'Oh, those two layabouts!'

'Our head of security and intelligence.' added Pogo sarcastically 'Maybe they're reviewing the latest intelligence reports!'

'It doesn't look good! Chance said 'Unless the rest are that bad!'

'They've just set an incredible time Mr Flugal.' whispered Rachelle.

'I know I could feel it.'

The team halted a few strides short of their timekeepers final resting place. Nugget tried to focus through watery eyes, Nigel just plainly refused, and just waved a hoof in their general direction as an acknowledgement.

Flugal was astounded at the sight presented before his very eyes; his normally reliable Nugget and his trusted Nigel enveloped in a bout of uncontrollable jollity. 'Nugget!' Flugal said, feeling that he should be seen to do something before the situation becoming mightily embarrassing, but his remonstration set them off even more. Still they laughed. They can't laugh for much longer, he thought, viewing the histrionics. How wrong he was.

Nigel's and Nugget's predicament was being enflamed by Flugal and the lad's dead pan and confused look; the more the two viewed them the more they descended into chaos.

Flugal decided enough was enough and jumped off the carriage, approached his two trustworthy timekeepers and tried to gain their attention. Again this only had the effect of tickling the two even further, and the laughter increased notably by a couple of decibels.

Chance led the team, who had now started to giggle themselves, carefully around to Nugget and tapped him on the shoulder. Nugget looked up and saw the giggling Chance and then tapped Nigel on the shoulder and futilely tried to explain that the team were here; there could only be one outcome to Nigel seeing Nugget and four giggling horses, plus Flugal's and Rachelle's straight faces, the only ones remotely maintaining their dignity. He cracked up again.

Flugal now, for all his powers of self control, succumbed to the moment and everybody, including Rachelle, descended to Nigel's and Nugget's level.

It was Nugget who ascended to his previous dignified persona first and began to share the glorious news, but Nigel was not far behind and beat Nugget to the punch with the ecstatic piece of news.

'Fantastic!' hailed Pogo and the four literally jumped for joy.   Flugal stared mannequin like at the four happy horses,

'What's up?' he said, trying now to comprehend this sudden change in mood and chastising himself for not better understanding dog, pig and horse.

'What's up?' he asked again.

'Maybe they know they set a fantastic time Mr Flugal.' whispered Rachelle,

'I reckon so.'

'We set a lap record!' Nigel was beside himself with joy.

To Flugal this meant nothing, but a series of grunts and snorts. 'Sorry.' he said tapping the side of his head 'I don't understand.'

'He doesn't understand.' Nigel repeated.

'Talk slower.' suggested Troy and he leaned towards Flugal and repeated Nigel's last statement very slowly. 'Weeee sseeeeettt aaaa llaaaaaaapp rreeecccooooorrddd!'

Flugal was none the wiser and simply shrugged his shoulders feeling a complete melon.

'I give up.' said Troy 'He'll figure it out. Just keep laughing.'

Flugal decided to take a gamble 'Did you set a good time' the horses nodded.

'How good? Very good?' They nodded again, he could feel the elation building inside, he dared not ask the next most obvious question in case all his hopes were dashed, but he couldn't resist 'A lap record by any chance?' he got the nods. Flugal let out an ecstatic hoop for joy and started dancing.

'See I told you.' said an ecstatic Rachelle.

'There you go.' said Biff.

'Yes!' he shouted 'Yes, yes, yes.' He didn't care who was watching, and turning to the team of seven he said 'We can win, we can win!'

Now it was Flugal's turn to inject a little happiness into the team with his enthusiasm, and now they all jumped and hollered for joy with Flugal and Rachelle leading the chorus.

The scene surveyed from afar left a feeling of bewilderment and amazement and Williams lowered his binoculars and stroked his chin pondering what on earth Flugal was up to; a new training regime maybe? He left after a few minutes, as soon as he was satisfied there was going to be no further developments, none the wiser. Neither was Nugget, he was blissfully unaware that his security had been breached; his lookouts had been unable to pick up the intruder.

Williams dialled out on his mobile as he opened the door to his Mercedes; he called Balshaw, he wanted another look at the plans for his manor. The mere thought of his being "the lord of the manor" had gripped him more and more like a plague, and absorbed his every waking moment, lurking in the background, subtly nudging him towards certain decisions. It coursed through his veins and he needed his daily fix admiring his model, dreaming of the day when he would indeed be lord. It would help keep him calm for the rest of the day, until it was time for a training run himself.

* * * * *

Bennett slumped down in his office chair; the walk for the ice cream the previous day had the desired effect and done him the world of good, and now he saw everything more clearly. Yes Williams was a trusted and valuable client to the bank, but he had responsibilities to the many hundreds of clients in his particular bank and why should he get preferential treatment. He mused over his many other troubles that day, and his staff furtively accused him of being surly and disagreeable, but they couldn't possibly have known or had the slightest understanding of all the troubles that cursed through his soul. It was not common knowledge to them that Williams eyed Flugal farm enviously and already considered it his own, he could buy it many times over, and Flugal to him was an unwanted tenant who should be evicted. Bennett hated having his hand forced; he should be allowed to make his own decisions locally within his bank and this was a local decision regarding one of his customers. Williams regarded him as one of his!

At the end of the working day, the afternoon sunlight filtered into the office, sadly his only connection to the outside world. Bennett didn't want to be disturbed and the light warmed him sufficiently to allow him to decide to begin the long journey home; he was among the growing army of eco-friendly commuters making the most of the free gymnasium right outside their door and walking to and from work agreed with his constitution.

Strolling languidly down the main high street, once he had locked up the bank for the night that dissected the heart of the shopping precinct, he laid a critical eye over all the shop fronts that took his fancy; it helped him raise his flagging spirits, but it was a short term fix, he would only end up correcting himself for being so odious against people, merchants, hard working people like Flugal, who struggled daily to make ends meat and to live their dream of owning and making their own business a success. This correction dulled his spirit even more. No ice cream today; thinking about what he would have for his tea brought about even greater melancholy of his living alone, and having no loved one to share life's little adventures with and to grow old by the fire together. He was a successful a bank manager, but he lived alone, did his own thing whenever he pleased, the perfect existence for some, but he was definitely alone and he secretly longed for a partner, and his present circumstance only highlighted the omission.

He halted his progress by the local butchers, not through choice, he was giving himself a severe talking to; he shouldn't be so sad, he was one of the lucky ones, he always wanted to be a bank manager, he enjoyed his job, so what reason did he have to be so sad and sorry for himself?

Mr Marlow, the butcher, watched curiously from inside the shop his own bank manager giving himself a serious ticking off. Bennett took one pace forward, cleared his head happy that he had straightened himself out and then realised where he was. Steak, he would have steak for his tea.

Mr Marlow did his butchers proud and furnished him with a prize of a fillet steak; food the great reliever had once again come to his aid thanks to Marlow's butchers. He now strode purposefully home, his steak warm and comforting in his hand, the aroma of the butchers still fresh in his nostrils. At the far end of the street, again he came to the bookmakers and took time to read the list of entries in the up and coming carriage drive. The poster was bigger now that interest was increasing, but now something else struck him, the addition of another name: Flugal at twenty five to one. Bennett entered.

* * * * *

The day before the opening day of the meet, Flugal's nerves, which had remained intact up to this point, showed the first signs of wear and tear even though Chance's leg had shown no after effects of the previous days training. Mrs Flugal recognised the symptoms, and furtively softened any harshness in his environment.

Nigel and Nugget had stepped up their efforts; Nugget received the first inkling that their training sessions may have been compromised; Sammy had relayed to him that one of his spies had followed Williams to Flugal farm and then onwards to an unknown destination. From the description that he gave it could only be Dougherty's place.

Nigel had set about sourcing all available information left on the other contenders; this was very time consuming, he had been forced to send away weeks before for those "out of towners" and now that information was in his greasy hoofs. Williams was the favourite, even with those in the know, which surprised and comforted him; if they could beat Williams then they could beat the rest, but running him close were three others.

First was a guy named Fulton; he was a keen amateur of vast experience and a farmer like Flugal. He ran his carriage like a professional, entering competitions all over the country and placing any prize money he won into a trust; a year or two ago he won every drive he competed in and this year he had great expectations for his new team. Second came Lyndsey; Lyndsey was a past champion, had won everything there was to win, with a fine reputation for breeding and training horses in the sport of carriage driving, so you just knew his team would always be well prepared. Third came the young pretender; there had recently arrived on the scene a young arrogant driver by the name of Michaels, whose father had lent him his horses to drive. In his opening meet he won hands down and this ignited a fire in his belly; he entered every meeting available after that and the thought of a such an unprecedented large purse was too much to resist; he had boasted to all who cared to listen that the prize money was as good as in his account.

Michaels always paraded his horses to his guests, extolling their virtues and strengths, lauding them above all others.

Nigel passed on any intelligence to the lads. Chance was as always phlegmatic, Troy bustled with eager anticipation for the forthcoming contest, Pogo pranced about imitating landing the knockout blow in a boxing match, marking his victory with exuberant celebration, Biff said and did nothing, he simply enjoyed being a spectator on the antics of his fellow teammates, it got so that he positively relished Nigel bearing more news.

Training had relaxed a little for the rest of that day; earlier Chance had thought it wise to kick on during some laps, in order to test his leg, and just go for a warm up on others. Flugal had obviously come to the same conclusion and did just that. Now he appeared at the door of the stable sporting a huge grin.

'It can't be a Wednesday!' said a sceptical Biff, 'He's smiling!'

'Have we not got a lot to smile about?' Pogo said in Flugal's defence, then realised in hindsight maybe they didn't actually.

'What's so funny boss?' Nigel enquired, stopping a few feet short of the entrance.

Flugal looked down at his faithful pig with all the understanding of a five year old hearing Latin for the first time. 'I've got you all a present.' A cacophony of noise met Flugal's offer of a gift and he was momentarily knocked out of his stride. 'I...er..I....er thought you might like these.'

What? They all asked together; more food, clean blankets, fresh hay, sugar, they were all partial to a little sugar, mints and strong ones at that. Yes they agreed, it was mints, a luxury long time coming, and after all their hard work what better way to reward them. Each argued that theirs was the worst breath and consequently they deserved the lion's share of the mints.

'I've got new bridles, harnesses and reins!' announced Flugal.

There was stunned silence. Nugget said he was going to look for buried treasure, it was infinitely more pleasurable than bridles, harnesses and reins, and slipped past Flugal into the yard.

Nugget for a long time now had been planning to search for the treasure, but various other adventures and responsibilities had taken precedence and invariably interrupted this one, but now he could take some time out and explore this opportunity to indulge his curiosity and find the all important clues to discovering Dougherty's hidden fortune.

The lower field was his favourite spot, he had spent many a long hour dissecting all the possible places on the farm where it would be logical to hide any treasure. The lower field had many advantages; one it was hard to access, the drainage was terrible, what a perfect place to hide it: two nobody ever went there for that very reason, and third, he couldn't think of a third, but he was convinced it would reveal itself to him in due course.

Down at the far end of the lower field Nugget felt very uneasy; he was convinced he was being watched, his natural instinct for self preservation sensed it, as all dogs do, but he would have to wait for them to show, so for the time being he had to be patient and hold his nerve, busying himself with deciding where to look first, but it was proving impossible. He knew where to look and now here he was down in the field none the wiser, wandering aimlessly through the sodden mud.

Nugget grew more and more frustrated the more he walked in pointless circles; this was ridiculous, he thought, where does one start to look for treasure. His eye ran along the line of the fence up to the higher side of the field near where the lane ran along to the entrance to the farm.

He was soon startled by the pair of eyes that had been following him, inspecting his every move. 'What are you doing down here Nugget?' Dave's voice brought about a mix feeling of startled fear and comfort.

'Who me?' This stupid answer he realised way too late, as there's only two people here and one's asking the question. 'Oh just admiring the view!' A second dumb reply, he was making a pretty good show of being a complete fool.

Luckily for his canine friend Dave, like Flugal, couldn't decipher a single word Nugget said, and so carefully navigated his way through the mud and gave him an affectionate stroke.

'Looking for buried treasure by any chance Nugget?'

'Who me? Oh no just....just seeing how deep the mud is around here!' What the hell are you talking about Nugget, he thought, and chastised himself for behaving like a complete idiot. "How deep is the field?" Oh come on Nugget! Dave was still none the wiser and just carried on as before.

'No one's going to bury treasure in mud Nugget!'

'I know that!'

'If you're going to bury treasure you'll need much firmer ground like under the one over there beside those tree trunks or something.'

You've been giving this as much thought as I have conjectured Nugget.

'Not that I've been giving this any thought Nugget, you understand,' said Dave seemingly forgetting that Nugget could understand everything he said, 'but still there's no harm in a little exploring. And anyway Mrs Evening gave me all her late husband's notes and they all point to this place.'

'Exactly.' agreed Nugget 'They say great minds think alike.'

'Where do you think we should look first?' Dave surveyed the line of trees that marked the boundary of the field, his feet squelching in the mud.

'Did I ever tell you why I thought it might be buried in this particular field?' Nugget shook his head. Dave laughed seeing a dog using a human trait.

'You make me laugh Nugget.' They both smiled, each for his own reason. 'Well this part of the field originally used to belong to Dougherty's farm. Did you know that? Nugget shook his head again. 'Well it did. They sold it because, believe it or not, the drainage was poor and nobody ever visited this section of the farm. What a perfect place to hide buried treasure. For all we know Nugget we could be standing on the very spot!' Nugget looked down at his filthy paws.

'We could be millionaires.' he growled.

'You better believe it old friend, millionaires.' Dave believed he understood him that time. 'Where should we start first?'

Nugget scrambled, slid through the mud to the first in the line of trees, barked at Dave to join him, and the two companions started their exploration. Dave had seen fit to bring a spade to aid his search and before long they were both digging exploratory holes before they were aware that over half the day had vanished, and the late afternoon shadows began to creep across the field.

They finally reached the last tree in the line and sadly both had to admit defeat and what a fruitless exercise it had been although essential none the less. Neither, to be honest, had the remotest idea what they were looking for; each had hoped the vital clue to the treasures whereabouts would reveal itself during their search. They were both, sadly, to be bitterly disappointed.

Dave pulled some lunch out of his knapsack and shared it with Nugget. 'That's eliminated the trees. I really thought it would be here; old Granger, their gamekeeper told me that old Mrs Dougherty frequented this part of the farm often; why else would you come here, to a sodden field that's good for nothing. It's definitely not for the view!'

Dave and Nugget gave the view and the lengthening shadows their critical eye; the shadows of the branches painted eerie images over the muddy grass, making further and further inroads the lower the sun set to the horizon. Nugget's fur stood up along his back; he imagined gargoyles and monsters springing out of the eerie shadows.

'Got to move them boulders.' Dave said to himself, lost in his little world. 'Maybe it's under those.'

'Maybe.' answered Nugget.

'No Nugget, I've inspected every one, they haven't been moved or tampered with in generations.'

Nugget ran over to the boulders and jumped up on the largest and played at being the king of the castle, master of all he surveyed. Dave was right, they hadn't been touched in a very long time. One thing struck him though, the shadows never touched them, they seemed to bypass the rocks, to afraid to interfere with their final resting place, and this gave them special significance to him; no shadows, no gargoyles, he could defend his position from the rocks. He was king.

Dave walked around the boulders, not for inspection rather introspection, it troubled him that he was wrong; he had been naïve enough to think that all he had to do was visit a few trees and bingo the treasure would reveal itself to him in this very spot, dying to be discovered and then all their troubles would be over.

Nugget snarled at the advancing shadows, their spiky tentacles inching toward the outer periphery of the rock. Dave was lost in his own wee world, gazing at the blue sky and the few paling translucent clouds.

'I know it's here. We are so close Nugget!'

Nugget didn't hear Dave, the tentacles were getting a little too close to comfort fading in and out with each passing cloud. If only Dave had only climbed the rock and seen the view Nugget had at this time, it would have shown him a beautiful "X" marking a spot.

Nugget's fur tingled with excitement; he danced around the top of the rock, hopping through ninety degree turns; the "X" had grabbed a hold of his consciousness and his imagination refused to let go; could it be that simple. There it was, there was the treasure, the answer to all their prayers, calling out to them, asking to be dug up, there laid perfectly across the field were two mighty fingers crossing at their mid points. How can Dave not see this, but he hadn't and the closing of the day marked Dave's retreat back to the house, his tail sagging somewhere between his legs.

Nugget didn't waste any time and overtook Dave by a few yards, spun around and spoke to him while walking backwards.

'Never mind, we've got to look at the positives in all of this.' He could see Dave had not seen the "X" therefore failing to realise its true significance and thus taken their failure very badly, the disappointment was etched across his face. Dave grunted.

'At least we know it's not in the trees, but did you see that big juicy, wonderful "X" formed by the branches. Surely it can't be that simple! "X" marking the spot.' Dave sadly could never understand and was totally oblivious to Nugget.

Nugget knew he had to get Dave back to the field and at the right time of day; he tempered his enthusiasm, surprising himself at his own self constraint; his normal tactic was to go well over the top, jabbering on at over a thousand miles an hour, but here he was the model of self control.

'Dave?' he started eagerly 'We still have to go back and make doubly sure we didn't miss anything this first time and Monday afternoon I've got nothing planned.' Dave ignored him. 'Okay how about Tuesday?' Still no answer. 'Saturday and Sunday are out, that's race weekend, but we can make a date of it on that Monday after, what d'ya say?'

Dave stopped short of the gate and took a second to mull over Nugget's growling single sided conversation; he apologised to his furry friend for his bad manners. Nugget accepted his apology and Dave asked for him to kindly repeat it all again, Nugget duly obliged. It was a pointless task really and

Nugget knew it, but this did not stop him repeating again the previous discourse with an equal amount of passion. Come the end Nugget resigned himself that Dave was just as equally in the dark as before.

'Oh well Dave, you just let me know when you want to go dig up some treasure 'cos I'm your dog!'

Dave strode silently through the gate, feeling utterly dejected and embarrassed; he didn't know what to say to old Nugget, so he just gave him a pat and that had to make do right now.

Back at the house a concerned Flugal met Dave coming up his path and enquired into the long face and morose behaviour. Dave was too ashamed to admit to his friend where he had been and how he felt.

Nugget on the other hand reacted in the complete opposite and told all his pals in the stables, but they had the benefit of knowing about the "X". Nigel was all for leaving there and then and digging up the treasure; pigs according to him are excellent diggers, better than dogs, better than anybody. This was red rag to a bull and Nugget fought the dog's corner vehemently; dog's reigned supreme in the sport of digging, whenever, he pointed out, did you ever last see a pig burying a bone or anything?' This was a solid point.

'Wild pigs.' countered Nigel 'Are among the upper echelons of diggers.' Nigel stood his ground valiantly; it was the classical irresistible force against the immovable object.

'I tell you what.' said a frustrated Troy 'Why don't we both go down to the field, find the "X", and organise a dig off.' Troy laughed at his use of his phrase "dig off".

'We can judge the winner on the amount of earth amassed by each of you!'

Troy had struck on a most excellent idea. Many hands, hoofs and paws make light work, and then the treasure would be theirs.

'Yeah!' agreed Pogo 'But what are we going to do in the event of a tie?'

'You have to put all the earth back, and the first to complete wins!' Biff said slowly, half mockingly, knowing his suggestion was ludicrous. To his complete surprise it was immediately adopted.

'We're missing the big picture here everybody.' It was Nugget's turn to be frustrated. 'We know where the treasure is buried.'

'You think you know.' Nigel said sceptically.

'I know I know, and I'll win the dig off to prove it!'

'Anytime!' smiled a confident Nigel. The game was on.

Flugal thought it wise not to press to hard on poor old Dave; his melancholy hung over him like a cloud, raining down on his parade. He had never seen his friend quite like this before.

Dave slowly recovered his good humour. Friday afternoon had been designated a time of rest with two days of hard racing ahead; they would have loved to get some more practice in and improve on Chance's fitness, but they had to be practical, Chance needed to rest up. When finally they had both been fed and watered they parted company, agreeing to meet early the next day to prepare everything for race day, but not before Flugal presented him with an eagerly anticipated gift: His father's notes on Dougherty's treasure.

Rachelle finished her chores, guaranteeing all the animals spent the night in relative luxury. Funds were now dangerously low and she knew it. She was now spending her own savings to assure her friends did not go without, she kept it a secret from Flugal, but he knew and secretly vowed to repay her as best he could.

19

The morning of race day brought a sense of relief to Flugal; the release of tension that the day of the event initiated manifested itself into good humour. Mrs Flugal kissed him on the cheek as she prepared breakfast, and lunch for all to take with them. Dave was due to appear at any time.

The previous day Mr and Mrs Flugal, Dave, Rachelle and all the gang had a productive day of organisation. Chance's leg had held up well after the Thursday and Friday morning runs, he had the occasional twinge, as you would have had expected, but nothing to much to worry about, and he felt felt no other side effects other than a few sore muscles for being out of action for a couple of weeks. The carriage was polished top to bottom and all the travel arrangements, equipment and supplies were checked and re-checked until they worked like a well oiled military machine.

The animals thankfully had slept well. Flugal also enjoyed a unbroken night's sleep. Nugget was the first to rise; he slept in the stables this night and he took the early rise as a time to examine all their equipment. He saw Dave arrive in his newly cleaned truck, and enter the house, and continued his checks, looking in on the horses and Nigel still sleeping enjoying sweet dreams.

Dave was in extremely good spirits this Saturday morning; it had taken him less than twenty four hours of recuperation and self reflection with something as simple as a failed treasure hunt to highlight to him how his misanthropic tendencies blighted his way of life. Loneliness is a waste of precious time he decided and this Saturday was going to be the first day of his new life.

His good humour was infectious and the Flugals eagerly fanned the flames of friendship; breakfast never tasted so good.

Rachelle turned up with her grandmother, both were coming to the races to add vital support. Rachelle set about her chores, her grandmother joined Mrs Flugal and the two thoroughly enjoyed each other's company, remarking why it had taken so long for them to get together.

The lads all awoke within minutes of each other, Rachelle acted as their personal alarm clocks, and eagerly discussed how they were going to run each race and the tactics to be used against each contender. Chance felt a tingle run through his muscles, spreading to his every nerve end; he had not felt this way in many a year and he realised how much he missed the thrill of competition. He couldn't wait.

Nigel's job was done, and a good job it was too. He too was going to savour every second.

* * * * *

Ralph and Jed on this day duly delivered Benny the crow his bushels of wheat. That had been a mission in itself.

Ralph had a buddy, a quite unscrupulous fellow who would do anything for a quick profit and as he himself was heavily in debt and needed a way out of the fix he presently found himself in, so stealing a few bushels of wheat fell within in his own bounds of acceptable behaviour.

Ralph's buddy let him know that 'Old Farmer Littlehorn' was harvesting some of his wheat early, about two weeks prior to the big event, and his security was non existent. Littlehorn's farm was huge, so he would not miss two or three bushels. There was though one problem: Larry.

Larry was a great dane and as great dane's go was as thick as a redwood. The difficulty Ralph and Jed faced was Larry slept in the bushel barn, as the two rabbits came to calling it, and found it nigh on impossible to keep his mouth shut; the slightest provocation and Larry would shout and scream with such delight at having a new friend to play with and would undoubtedly awaken the whole farm.

Now a bushel of wheat to a rabbit is enormous and to overcome this obstacle Jed would pull a wheel barrow over to the barn, load it with the booty while Ralph would keep watch, then on the return it was decided that both miscreants would work in tandem to remove the bushels.

Now Larry was no exception in the canine world in as much as he loved bones, steaks, in fact any food stuffs remotely resembling meat, he loved them to bits! Ralph and Jed were stuck on the idea of feeding Larry drugged meaty chunks to help to send him to sleep, and to this end Jed's mother mixed up an old family recipe guaranteed to invoke somnolence.

Once at the farm Ralph crept ahead of Jed by a few yards, armed with his drugged meaty chunks, keeping a vigilant look out for Larry. The bushel barn now lay dead ahead and Jed called out to Ralph in a whisper just to confirm this. Ralph raised his foot to acknowledge then held it to his lips and let out a gentle 'Shshshsh.'

Jed 'Shshshshsh'd.' in response.

Ralph 'shshshshsh'd' a second time and a near farcical "shshsh" and counter "shshsh" erupted. Jed started to get an attack of the giggles, fatal in the circumstances, but bit his bottom lip and managed to keep a lid on his emotions

The creak of Littlehorn's back door signalled Larry's departure for the night into the yard and the bushel barn. Ralph and Jed tip-toed slowly forward paralleling Larry's progress toward the barn. Larry stopped and smelt the air and for a split second the two rabbits hearts stopped; was Larry about to explode and pounce upon them? Ralph's grip tightened on the meat. He was ready.

No, Larry walked on filling his lungs periodically with the warm, balmy air of a late spring evening and disappeared into the barn.

Ralph and Jed reached their objective and peered through a slit in one of the side panels which gave a perfect view of Larry and the interior. Larry had laid down to sleep in the far corner against some bushels collected that day.

'Give it a few minutes and he'll be fast asleep, then we can save the meaty chunks for later.' said Ralph.

'Who for?'

'What?'

'Who for?'

'The meaty chunks, who for?' Jed finally explained. 'Who are we saving them for?'

'For Larry!'

'But Larry's asleep!'

'In case.'

'In case of what?' Jed was now confused; not hard if you knew him well enough.

'In case he wakes.'

'Ooooohh.'

'See?'

'Who's going to wake him?'

'Shut up Jed!'

'Okay.'

Ralph confirmed that Larry was indeed lying down to sleep for the night, and after a gap of a further fifteen minutes or so during which time Larry had not stirred, Ralph decided it was time to go.

'Follow me.' he whispered, and he expeditiously circumnavigated the barn, arriving at the barn entrance in a flash, eager to liberate some of Littlehorn's stash of bushels. He turned to reaffirm the plan of attack to Jed. Jed was nowhere to be seen. 'What now!' said an exasperated Ralph and retraced his steps until he eventually came face to face with a panting Jed, dragging the wheelbarrow.

'The wheel got caught up in a hole. This guy Littlehorn should have more consideration for night prowlers walking around his yard!'

'Is that so! Any more catastrophes awaiting you?'

'I've only had the one so far tonight.'

'So far!'

'Yep, but the night's still young.'

'Tell me about it. Okay here's the plan again; I'll keep a watch over Larry armed with these meaty chunks.' Ralph continued dangling the bagged, spiked meaty chunks right in front of Jed's nose. 'And you light finger two or three bushels. If he should arise at any time I'll give these to him and Bob's your uncle we'll make off with Benny purchases. Any questions?'

'No'

'Good.'

'You thought I was going to say I haven't got an Uncle Bob weren't you?'

'No.'

'Yes you were, admit it!'

The two rabbits reached the entrance. 'Go on admit it you were.'

'No I wasn't, now keep quiet.'

'I don't believe you.'

'I don't care.'

'I have got an Uncle Bob, he lives in Sussex.'

'Jolly good.'

'He grows his own cabbage you know, won many prizes, they say down in Sussex that Bob's cabbage provides the best roughage south of London.'

'Fascinating.' Ralph entered the barn ignoring Jed's every word.

'I've never tasted roughage, have you?'

Ralph could not hear him, he was now about ten or so feet from Larry.

Jed started to collect the bushels; he examined them all very closely, picking out those that could be easily removed from the barn; he wasn't too impressed with what was initially on offer. He examined the bushels more closely and discovered to his great delight, just behind the first row, five or six juicy looking ones, which in his humble opinion and limited experience in these matters, matched the description Benny had supplied them with, as to the desired quality he most requested. He would love to get his beak into those, thought Jed, and peered over to Ralph to gain his approval. Ralph had his back to him eying the sleeping Larry as a detective would, hunting for clues. Oh well, he thought, Ralph won't mind and he was sure he would agree that a juicy looking bushel is far better than these tatty, tired looking ones at the front. Jed put down the wheel barrow and fingered the first row; they were tightly packed, but with a little effort one could more than sufficiently get a decent grip on the juicy ones.

Jed reached over the outer bushels and frustratingly found that his original assumption had been sadly lacking, and he could only get a few fingers on the ones he had selected for removal. He took a step back and looked over again at Ralph. This time their eyes met and Jed quickly interpreted the inner meaning of Ralph's icy stare. He pointed to the juicy ones mouthing 'bushels'.

With a cheesy grin he diverted his attention back to the conundrum.

Ralph began to sweat; Jed was starting to do his head in, his neck was starting to ache with the constant jerking between Larry and his direction.

Jed squeezed open a large gap to get a much better grip, and now with both feet planted firmly on the ground he attempted to lift the bushel and hey presto, it fell forward through the gap and straight into the wheelbarrow with a thud. Ralph nearly died. Larry remained asleep.

Jed was now onto a winner and leapt straight through the gap for number two. With great alacrity bushel number two thudded into the barrow. Jed was feeling mightily pleased with himself. Ralph's heart went into palpitations.

Jed could do no wrong, the bushels were at his mercy and he chose for his "piece de resistance" a large bushel just begging to be appropriated. The best of the bunch he decided. Ralph watched open mouthed, willing Jed to change his mind, gesticulating madly to get his attention and divert his master plan, but there was nothing he could do to prevent certain catastrophe.

Jed reached in and plucked the bushel with all his might. It freed itself from the confines of the surrounding bushels, collapsed forward, grazing those ahead and fell into Jed's outstretched arms. Jed beamed a smile of shear ecstasy over to Ralph whose colour had flushed completely away. Jed laid the third bushel into the wheelbarrow, and when satisfied all his wares were secure, bent his back against the barrow and inched his way to the barn door.

Ralph now looked on Larry as a vanquished foe, flipped back his head, turned sharply and sauntered out of the barn.

Jed had reached the yard, but was panting and puffing wildly; he requested a little assistance from Ralph, but it was all to no avail. Ralph with the air of a rabbit that just broke the bank strolled by, swinging the bag of meaty chunks with gay abandon, as a city gent would an umbrella.

Jed by now had made his way half way across the yard, but was exhausted.

Ralph spun round and decided to impart some pearls of wisdom to his fellow miscreant, but suddenly became acutely aware that the bag of meaty chunks was not as heavy as he would have wished, and this was confirmed by one of them clobbering Jed firmly between the eyes. Stunned and exhausted he fell back against the wheelbarrow.

Ralph now looked down at the half empty bag; he felt a lump plummet deep into the pit of his stomach and lifted his head just in time to witness a shower of meaty chunks rain down and pepper the sleeping Larry.

Larry recovered his consciousness with a start and let out an ear piercing whine. 'What the……..cool meaty chunks!' Which he then devoured instantly.

Ralph and Jed did not wait to see Larry's next move and by now had the wheelbarrow travelling like it had wings, but it still seemed an age for them to get anywhere near the hedgerow they had chosen to enter and exit the farm, and provide a hole large enough to cater for their barrow full of bushels.

Larry was now fully awake, spied Jed and Ralph closing in on their escape, and heard his master Littlehorn shouting out his name after he had woken up the household, but his attention was now naturally drawn to Ralph and Jed, and without a second's further hesitation, bounded, bawling out of the barn.

Ralph helped the now invigorated Jed and the wheelbarrow onwards to the gap in the hedge, then turned with shear fright at the slobbering, whaling Larry bearing down on him and spent the last of his meaty chunks, aiming straight at Larry's head, praying the sleepy drug would kick in at any moment and send this behemoth to sleep.

Larry gobbled up the meaty missiles, laughed at the height of his lungs, ecstatic at having found an unexpected couple of best buddies, and closed in on poor young Ralph and Jed.

Ralph said his last prayers and goodbyes, whilst exhausting the last of the missiles. Larry gained ever closer; he could clearly see the white of his eyes, smell his meaty breath, feel the wetness of Larry's slobber.

'I'm through!' shouted Ralph, letting go of the wheelbarrow and standing frozen, chunk less, resigned to his fate. 'The end is nigh.' he reiterated, twitching with nervous expectation, his every sinew taut with adrenaline, fuelled with fear. He slowly raised his right foot and waved goodbye.

Larry pounced, tongue slopping vertically down from the right hand side of his mouth, shut his eyes and launched a huge lick at Ralph with Littlehorn's raging, at his antics, echoing in his ears. And then nothing. 'What!' Larry opened his eyes and the tuft of grass where stood his new furry friend was now but a few trampled blades.

Jed dragged a stunned Ralph and the wheelbarrow towards the hedge.

Larry recovered his senses and took off again after his two fluffy bushel thieves; their head start evaporated in an instant. Ralph let out a cry, Jed quickened his pace with all the strength he had left and Larry leaned forward after a particular long stride and slapped a big wet one on Ralph. He cried out in pain, Jed thought his pal was dying 'NO!' he screamed and desperately jumped for the hole in the hedge. The un-restriction of freedom quickly enveloped them and they made it to the far side of the hedge sprawled in a heap beside the upturned wheelbarrow.

Larry, longing for another taste of furry rabbit, lunged a second time, panicking at watching them disappear and plugged the gap, but Larry was no rabbit and the wheelbarrow hole was never going to be capable of letting Larry free, no matter how hard he tried, once he'd shuddered in the hedge like a cork in a bottle.

Littlehorn arrived just in time to pull Larry free of his imprisonment and to miss the rabbits escape into the woods.

'Larry, when the hell are you going to give us a little peace and quiet, chase them there poachers will ya' not a couple of floppy eared miscreants!'

Jed and Ralph finally came to a halt completely knackered. Ralph jittered uncontrollably, his neck muscles twitching at every sound in the woods and the thought of the smiling, slobbering Larry.

'Ralph?'

'Yeah Jed?'

'Ya' think we got enough bushels. I mean if Benny don't like the taste of these...'

'You know something Jed?'

'What's that?'

'I don't care.'

'I hope they're up to his extremely high standards.'

'Want to know something else?'

'What's that?'

'Gambling don't pay!'

'Unless you're Benny!'

'Yes Jed, unless you're Benny.' Ralph checked the coast was clear. 'And Benny won't care.'

Jed lay back on his elbows and inspecting their haul. 'They look juicy enough for me.'

'Jed?'

'Yes Ralph?'

'Thanks.' Jed looked embarrassed. 'You saved my life mate and I'll never forget it!' The smile that erupted across Jed's face would have required a hammer and chisel to remove.

In the early hours they reached Jed's mother's, parked the wheelbarrow in a safe place away from prying eyes, and made the most of the remaining hours until Benny could relieve them of the bushels.

Jed was the first up later that morning and his initial duties involved inspecting their haul. It was fine. He came back inside to find Ralph tucking into breakfast. 'Bushels okay?' he said between mouthfuls.

'Did the fox sleep well?' Jed's mother interjected before her son could speak.

'Fox?' queried Ralph.

'The fox the meaty chunks were for; I mixed just the right amount to send that fox Larry to sleep with no bother.'

The two bushel thieves looked at each other. 'Larry the fox.' Ralph finally said real slow and he shivered at the very thought.

Jed and Ralph made their way to the race meet in eager anticipation of a good days sport. Just a few miles from them team Flugal departed the farm and hit the road.

* * * * *

Williams packed the last of his essentials; blinkers for Thunder and Lightning; they had recently developed a bad habit of biting one other and not getting along quite as they should, so he thought it best that they couldn't see each other, and decided as an extra measure to fit a curb chain to help him steer the two combatants and cancel out any belligerence and disobedience that should raise its ugly head. Flugal needed no such devices.

* * * * *

Bennett stopped by the bookmakers of the morning of the first day of races and took one last look at his betting slip then made his way, at a sedate pace, to catch the bus that would transport him to the course; his mood had lifted considerably over the past few days, primarily due to the blissful lack of business he had to conduct with Williams, and he found himself whistling during his walk, something that had been amiss for many a year.

20

The hustle and bustle of a large sporting event came as a complete shock to most of team Flugal. It was colossal. Mrs Flugal immediately felt ill at ease among the throngs of people of all ages who had taken the opportunity to witness something out of the ordinary in sporting circles, but there were also many additional attractions to entertain the.masses; a travelling fair had made its temporary home in an adjoining field, offering all the traditional and a wide variety of rides and stalls, local farmers and traders set up stalls to sell their produce, everywhere could be seen marquees of all shapes and sizes offering everything from horse harnesses to riding gear to sporting goods and memorabilia, CDs, DVD's, books, all manner of refreshments, including ice cream sellers catering for those with more sweeter pallets, there were vendors selling clothes of various brands, amusement arcades, hot air balloon rides and of course horse riding schools promoting themselves to all and sundry.

Flugal secretly kicked himself for not thinking of that, as he witnessed for the first time this maelstrom of human activity and it invited concerns that they might not be able to make the competitors enclosure and that would inevitably involve them missing their start time. He needn't have worried; his fears were allayed by a marshaller who examined his pass, a pass sent by courier three days earlier, and personally escorted him and their horse-box through the crowds.

Nugget by contrast couldn't wait to get out among the hordes of spectators, he already had an eye on a couple of burger and hotdog stands and the smell of cooked burger meat, hotdogs and fried onions, was sending his taste buds haywire.

Nigel sided on Mrs Flugal's side; nobody was going to appreciate a pig roaming around.

The lads were wide eyed and a little gob smacked at the size of the event, all that is except Chance who viewed the event as a minor sporting occasion, his judgement would always be clouded by the grandeur of the Derby. He was though mightily impressed at the organisation; it could easily have been allowed to deteriorate into chaos, it would not be the first time, even much larger events he had participated in had been reduced to a farce. He pointed out things of interest to the other three; their excitement was certainly catching, but he was well aware that they must remain focused.

Team Flugal were led to their allocated section of the enclosure and immediately set about preparing themselves for their dressage heat; they were all quietly confident that they could pass the first section without trailing the leaders too much. Chance had stressed the point that they could not win this event on day one, but could certainly lose it. The marshal gave Flugal the agenda for that day; their dressage was near the end of that section at 11am; the marathon, over a difficult multi-phase course measuring fifteen kilometres, was for 3pm, each would be run after the sections for the smaller two horse carriages. The Sunday was to be a slightly later start with just the obstacle course to run, against the clock, over a technical figure of eight course, which in the words of the marshal "Would then separate the men from the boys!"

Rachelle and her grandmother took it upon themselves to buy everybody drinks and snacks from a nearby vendor, Mrs Flugal as always had provided adequate sustenance, but Rachelle's grandmother was equally as stubborn and insistent they would help out as best they could. Rachelle, as always, didn't forget about the six other members of the crew and promised them their treats at the end of the day.

Williams had beaten Flugal to the enclosure and secured the top spot for himself and his team; it was nearest the entrance to the course, there nobody could spy on anything untoward that he was up to, but he could keep tabs on them.

Flugal, by comparison, was at the far end, he didn't see any disadvantage to this arrangement, on the contrary it was as far away from Williams as one could possibly get.

Dave during all of this was not allowed entrance to the enclosure with his truck, so once he had secured parking for the day he joined up, carrying as many essentials as was humanly possible. His cheery grin and demeanour a vast contrast to only a short while ago, only added to the general air of excitement.

Over a loud hailer system announcements came thick and fast.

'Somebody likes the sound of their own voice!' complained Pogo.

The voice informed everybody of the start times of the initial runs and anything else that the announcer thought might be relevant; which amounted to nothing to the contestants.

The lads had decided in advance who their nearest challengers would be by the conditioning of the teams; Fulton's and Lyndsey's were immaculate and would have easily won any prizes for best turned out, Michaels team kept a low profile, but didn't fool anybody and did nothing to dispel then as serious contenders.

The day seemed to evaporate before their very eyes and not before long the first events were concluded, and the first team for the four-on-hand event was called forward to the dressage; this brought on a few palpitations in some of the contestants as they slowly made their way with much trepidation out of the enclosure.

'Good luck.' called out Nugget.

'Piece of cake!' the lead horse said arrogantly, trying hard, but failing to hide his fear. The other three turned their collective noses up at Nugget. 'We promise to go easy to give you no hopers a fighting chance!'

Nugget considered making a reply, but decided on the better side of caution.

'Is this charity week? Did I miss something?' came the call from a team further down the field.

'The only charity their going to get is my leftovers!' came another.

'You need to keep your energy up buddy 'cos that slop you're getting ain't making it!' replied the lead horse to one of the antagonist.

Team Flugal were stunned, momentarily, to silence at the banter exchanged by the surrounding teams.

'See what you started Nugget.' said Nigel trying to get a rise out of his friend 'Don't wish anybody else good luck again, whatever you do!'

'I'll just tell them to break a leg.' And they both laughed. Nugget walked out into the walk way that separated the teams on either side of the enclosure 'Seems to be the norm around here!'

The time to Flugal's first run was soon upon then and they watched as the teams passed them by or moved out from further up; some were cocky, the really overly confident ones shouted their intentions as they vacated, but all were a little subdued on their return, a clear indication that the standard of dressage was high, and this was supposedly easier than tomorrow's "separating the men from the boys". Only Fulton's and Michaels teams, of the front runners, were content with their performance's.

Flugal's name was called and the team moved out with a chorus of sarcastic "good lucks" and derisory "break a legs" ringing in their ears; those left behind in team Flugal quickly made their way to the spectator area to get the best seats available, only Nugget and Nigel remained; these two had decided earlier to sneak around the outside of the enclosure, undetected and watch the run from an advantage point Nigel had spotted.

Flugal and Rachelle carefully adjusted their seating positions, as they walked to the entrance to the arena; his heart was racing, she visited nervously, he could feel it pounding under his shirt and coat, and was instantly, equally filled with excitement and trepidation, and could only imagine how they must have felt ahead of him. His attention was suddenly drawn to neighing horses.

'Hey hobos...'

'Shut up big nose!' Troy cut them off before they could get any purchase on their sledging.

'Now, now Troy.' butted in Chance. 'We got to remain focused; they're only doing it to get us rattled.'

'Yeah, sorry lads.'

'That's okay Troy.' Biff said then shouted at the antagonist   'Right back at ya' kiddo!'

'You just take it on the chin. You got plenty of them to spare.' It was Pogo's turn to get stuck in.

Chance shook his head in resignation.

'Hey you guys don't give up on the milk round!' exploded a voice: It was Thunder.

Troy was all for having a pop there and then, but the calming, sensible tones of Chance prevailed at last.

'We'll get them on the way back.' Pogo said quietly, so only the four of them could understand.

The enclosure opened into an arena three to four times the size, which held in its centre the dressage area, which itself was approximately forty by one hundred metres in size with marker boards to signal where transitions in speed and gait were to take place. The dressage test itself was a series of circles, figure of eights and diagonals all executed at either working trot, collected and extended trot and a canter, and including at one point a halt and a rein back. The whole sequence was to be judged by a panel of three whose joint marks made up the final score, but not before they judged Flugal on the turnout of his carriage and team; the rig was spotless, totally unrecognisable to the carriage they originally bought, the "Boys", his and Rachelle"s appearance was beyond reproach, the harness was made to look brand new, the whip had been double checked to be the right length for a team of four, and any and all preparations we're checked and double-checked so as not to lose the event on the first day.

'Blimey!' exclaimed Biff eyeing the growing thong of spectators.

'Let's show them how it's done guys!' added Troy.

'You bet.' said Pogo.

Chance broke in. 'There's nothing here we haven't seen before or discussed and practised, so let's just go out and do our best.'

'Flugal will see us right.' Biff said with real conviction. Chance broke the news to them that Flugal had received the course plan that very morning from the marshal who guided them into the enclosure; this was deliberate so to prevent contestant gaining an upper hand, and Flugal had spent as much time as he could allow studying it. Troy doubted whether Williams would have found himself in their position.

'Just how I pictured it!' Pogo stated. 'I wouldn't want it any other way!'

'Well said Pogo.' answered Chance.

They all agreed. Chance added he had all the confidence in the world in everyone's natural ability and determination to succeed, because that after all is all that was needed.

Flugal made a mental picture of what was required; he wasn't used to memorising facts and figures at such short notice, so the whole team dissected the plan and added suggestions and now it was time to put it all into action.

The bell finally sounded to signal for team Flugal to begin their dressage once they'd been inspected, and without a moments hesitation begun their routine.

From far off Flugal heard all too familiar sounds and one he never thought he would; Nugget and Nigel were voicing their support for team Flugal and causing all kinds of mayhem in the process alongside, what seemed to him, a chorus of rabbits.

Nugget and Nigel had in fact ran into Ralph, Jed and their friends, who had adopted Flugal as their team.

Slowly and methodically they displayed a dressage routine that belied their inexperience, and apart from a few occasions when they forgot to stay on the bit, were responsive, obedient and made a very good account of themselves. At the end, which seemed to come upon them all too quickly, they had achieved the first objective: Not to lose it first out. Then came the marks: They were fifth overall.

Flugal guided them into the enclosure only to be met by Williams going the opposite way.

'Only fifth!' sneered Williams with utter glee.

'You want to see dressage Flugal then watch the professionals!' shouted Storm, then rubbed salt into the wound by calling the lads a bunch of cart horses better suited for the rag and bone man.

'Ignore them.' Flugal said not even making eye contact with Williams, realising the banter between the horses was not of the pleasant variety. 'We did good.'

Back at their site they were met by a running, smiling, utterly ecstatic Mrs Flugal and Rachelle's grandmother. 'You were fantastic!' they shouted. Dave was absent.

'We are only fifth.' Pogo interjected before anybody could get carried away.

'Fifth is still competitive, and I don't rate the rest that much, bar the Lyndsey and Fulton teams of course, they'll get in the top ten.' Nigel appeared out of nowhere breathing heavily. 'Fifth is good.' he reiterated 'A steady run, we'll improve on that fifth before the day is out. The marathon's next and nobody tops us for speed!'

Rachelle tapping into the gist of the conversation agreed whole heartedly.

Flugal and now Dave, who like Nigel miraculously appeared, helped to remove the bridles, harnesses and tack and allowed the horses some freedom; Flugal had openly objected to tethering his horses, they were safely ensconced in his section and he trusted them explicitly so if anybody didn't like it then stuff 'em, that was his attitude, but he still fidgeted uncomfortably lest any marshal should come by and demand that they be tethered or face being banned from further participation. He didn't concern himself for long; it soon became apparent that the other contestants had followed suit.

'Where's Nugget?' asked Rachelle.

Everyone looked high and low, Nugget could not be located. Panic started to set in and overtook all emotion and other concerns at the absence of their friend; there's was always a close knit community and now closer still because of the predicament they now found themselves in, and the loss of one of their own around a strange place perturbed them all.

During this time of consternation, with friends of the absentee running around looking in every conceivable hiding place and more, a familiar voice punctuated the panic. 'Ralph's got a bet on us!' It was Nugget. 'Ralph's got a bet on us!' he repeated.

Everybody came to a standstill. 'Where have you been?' they chorused. 'Where the hell have you been?' Nugget didn't know which way to look. It caught him on such a hop.

'We have been worried sick over you. You could have been hurt in an accident, these horses don't know you like we do, they only have to kick out and that's you done for!' Nugget hung his down sheepishly on hearing Flugal's admonishment; he hadn't done that in years, but it was also showed the deep concern for his welfare that filled him with a warm, joyous sensation.

The lads wanted to know who Ralph was. Nigel and Nugget were now in a position to relay their mini adventure.

'What are they talking about?' Flugal asked.

'No idea.' his wife answered. 'This conversation's got me beat!'

'Don't know dog or pig. God knows I've tried to understand every word they say.' replied a laughing Dave.

'Knowing them two they're telling a ripping yarn.' Rachelle leant forward and stroked Nugget, his side of the story now being briefly interrupted by her.

'Hey Nugget!' called Ralph from behind some trees. Nugget made his apologise, halted his commentary, and ran over to his fluffy friend.

'Where's he going now?' Mrs Flugal was fascinated by the dog's antics and followed at a respectable distance, but Nugget was back before she even went ten paces.

'Williams lies first' cried out an exasperated Nugget.

'No way! Him in the lead?' Nigel was shocked, but he knew he shouldn't be.

Flugal's eyes darted from Nugget's growls to Nigel's snorts to the neighing of the horses. 'What? What? What's going on? Somebody tell me!' Flugal kept looking at the animals.

Mrs Perkins pointed to a board standing at the far end of the enclosure, which all of team Flugal had ignored until now, but had become the centre of a great deal of commotion. 'That might be your answer Mr Flugal.'

They all turned just in time to see Williams name go top of the leader board.

'I don't believe it.' Dave said what they were all thinking. 'You'll never keep him quiet now!' The team were crestfallen; they had judged themselves against their bitterest rival and had failed at the first hurdle. They now found themselves relegated to sixth, and the prospects of further reductions were considerable.

'We knew from the outset.' started Troy, 'that we weren't going to top dressage, it's very technical and these teams have the edge on us in this discipline, so let's not get carried away just because he's currently sitting top of the tree.'

Flugal unwittingly repeated Troy's words verbatim. 'That makes us sixth.' He added at the end.

'The odds would have widened on us, excellent.' added Dave, and with that attempted to disappear off on a private mission, but was halted by the continuing conversation.

'Oh great, that'll build morale.' Nigel was beginning to let everything get the better of him until he realised his error, and took deep breaths to calm himself down.

'We're going to be thirty-to-one at least. Fantastic!' said Dave in that cheery fashion adopted by those who had resigned themselves to accepting their fate and are determined not to let the adversity get the better of them.

'Why Dave?' Rachelle's grandmother was not the gambling kind.

'Because we can make an even bigger killing Mrs Perkins!'

'That's what I meant to say!' Nigel proclaimed proudly.

'We're capable of winning this.' Dave continued. 'And at thirty to one! That's a great price!'

'Can't say I agree with it, but under the circumstances if you say so I'll place a small bet for Rachelle and me.' And she motioned to Dave to show her the way; Rachelle was astonished, but pleasantly surprised in the change to her quiet, sedate grandmother

Williams re-entered the enclosure. 'Look at him.' growled Nugget. 'He thinks he's won it already.'

Williams beamed satisfaction with that air of arrogance guaranteed to infuriate anybody that crossed his path. He found to his annoyance though that only his servants came forward to congratulate him, so he walked to the outskirts of his section in a vain attempt to make eye contact with his competitors, marshals or spectators. These tactics were spotted and easily understood and for many minutes he stood alone, reluctantly accepting his snubbing and finally stepped back to his carriage and team, quietly seething, vowing the most hideous of retributions on everybody and every creature.

Flugal watched all from behind his carriage and vehicles, deciding on a more furtive approach. 'What are you doing?' Mrs Flugal inquired.

'Watching Williams'

'You've become fixated with him!'

'Just adopting a more prudent approach to my competitors.' he replied not removing his gaze from Williams.

'When's your run in the marathon?' she asked.

'About three!' and he turned to face his wife now satisfied his adversary was not up to anything untoward.

'Good let's relax with a pleasant stroll through the fair, it will take your mind off everything.'

Flugal reluctantly consented although he needed to familiarise himself with the marathon course, but what could he do! Before they left they collected Mrs Perkins leaving Rachelle to stay with the animals, as Dave had decided to disappear on his own to conduct some more personal business. Rachelle had after all Nugget and Nigel for company.

The lads relaxed and chomped into a light snack; neither of them had much to say; the mornings exertions had manifested itself into ravenous hunger.

Chance tried his best to keep on boosting morale for the afternoon run; the three younger ones were beginning to grow more and more concerned about it, for as the day progressed team Flugal dropped slowly down the pecking order, finally finishing in tenth place.

'We got to know, I've got to know how we stand with the others.' Pogo could feel his frustrations turning into anger.

'We're tenth.' reminded Biff.

'No I need to know what they're thinking. Nugget your head security, check on this will 'ya.' Nugget needed no second invitation; he was off. 'Nigel see if you can source some intelligence. I...we need to know!'

'At such short notice?' Nigel said.

'Somebody's got to get it!'

'We'll get it! I'll get it!' said a determined Troy. 'I'm not hanging around here waiting.'

'Hang on a minute; what are you going to find out?' Chance was trying to see reason.

'Listen Chance.' shouted Biff. 'All of these are not facing eviction, their whole existence destroyed, taken away, with severe servitude their only prospect.'

Chance had no answer. Biff was right.

'Any information that we can use to keep our cause on track has to be worth the risk. It's not cheating, its survival.' added Troy.

Rachelle had been a spectator, but now added her weight to the cause; from the horses intonation she understood everything this time.

The plan was hatched, which they valiantly tried to relay to Rachelle, hoping she would comprehend; Rachelle would lead the horses, Nigel took an age to explain that one to her, and he would take charge of their rear, as they would use light exercise around the enclosure to basically spy on their competitors. Nugget had flown off to talk to Ralph to get the latest betting news in case it could shed light on anything, and as a backup Nigel was to act as a diversion, if required. He was the only pig around and this made him ideal to create a stir.

Rachelle led her beloved Chance out into the enclosure, Pogo, Biff and Troy followed in that order loosely tethered to one another, whilst Nigel took up the position of shotgun; he was their wingman keeping a beady eye on everybody.

Rachelle whispered in Chance's ear to fake a limp; she hoped Chance had understood her request, and he could have won an Oscar for his performance that followed; anyone passing by would easily have thought his leg was about to drop off. Rachelle knew now, without a shadow of a doubt that they were special.

Pogo then took the opportunity to drop back from the pack; Troy and Biff shielded his retreat and he furtively tip-toed around the rear of a couple of teams, hugging the tree line to hide his presence.

Chance limped on; Biff and Troy gregariously acted out passers-by, examining all the other teams with great scrutiny, making mental notes of anything that might be of use.

Pogo now crawled along as low to the ground as any horse possibly could and finally managed to get himself in a position to be able peer around the outside of one of their competitor's horse boxes, only to came face to face with the equally surprised Jed, munching on a juicy carrot. 'Nice down here isn't it?'

'It's.....it's different.' stammered Pogo.

'So tell me Pogo?'

'Yes?'

'What are ya doin' anyhow?'

'You know me just loafin' around! And anyhow how come you know me? I don't know you.'

A few of the surrounding horses started to become very interested in who Jed was talking to, as their view was severely restricted by the horse box.

'Are you on a mission Pogo? I'm Jed, Ralph's friend.'

'Shshshshshhshsh!...........No, no just loafin. Who's Ralph?'

'It's top secret eh? A friend of Nugget's.'

'No, like I said I just fancied a bit of loafin' around between runs.'

Jed was having none of it. 'I can help; I'm good at spying, you're spying aren't you? Loafin' around is just the code word for it right? My uncle taught me, he's a master rabbit spy! Or I can loaf like you, call it whatever you will.'

Pogo knew his time was quickly drying up and he had to get out pronto. He searched desperately for Nigel.

'Hey Pogo who's top of you loafin' list?'

'Er....'

'Lyndsey?'

'Er....'

'It's Lyndsey isn't it?'

'No, not quite.' Pogo said, inching backwards towards the rear of the horse box in a vain attempt to remain out of sight.

Jed took an equal pace forward to maintain the equidistant gap and continue their confabulation.

'Michaels. Yes I thought so.' Pogo hadn't even answered. 'Michaels is a dangerous customer.' Jed scratched his chin. 'Yes, you're right to watch him.'

'If you say so.' Pogo was now in grave danger of being discovered, the horses had positioned themselves in order to gain a better view of Jed.

Biff and Troy became alerted to Pogo's predicament when he failed to reappear and they searched the general area for his whereabouts. They quickly realised that the situation called for a diversion. Chance agreed, but being concerned for young Rachelle's safety, was unable to pinpoint how the diversion should start.

Pogo now found himself between a rock and a hard place and resigned himself to his being discovered. This was going to get messy.

They needn't have worried, Nigel was already on the case, and in true pig fashion ran headlong into the Fulton camp attacking anything remotely edible. The fur-or he stirred up could be heard at either end of the enclosure and achieved the desired results; everybody's attention was drawn to Nigel and Fulton's team. Pogo seeing his opportunity, while his potential pursuers were distracted, made his getaway.

Poor old Nigel received numerous kicks and shoves, fending of all attacks from all corners, never once ceasing to munch away deliriously at whatever sustenance was nearest to hand.

Poor Rachelle tried in vain to save Nigel, but she had Chance and the boys to care for; they could do nothing unless of course they wanted to be embroiled in a team fight and that would get them disqualified. She was also puzzled by the "Boy's" lack of concern for their friend, unless she had totally misread the situation, and she was priding herself on her ever expanding knowledge of her friends. They were actually egging Nigel on.

'Leave us Rachelle and save Nigel, we'll be okay.' said Chance tugging gently at the reins. Rachelle read these signs; they were now getting concerned and she sprinted over to Nigel.

The horses turned for their section, heads held high, mission accomplished; they had seen enough and anyhow Nigel was still creating havoc and as much disruption as necessary.

The attitude in some quarters, not all it has to be said, is that they were rank amateurs and how dare they challenge such existing teams as these, and here they were now causing merry hell around the enclosure. These teams held team Flugal in utter disdain, that they should have to lower themselves to be seen to compete in the same arena.

None more so than team Willliams, who led the chorus of calls for them to be disqualified; the lads started to get the first idea that they had possibly overstepped the mark on this occasion.

Rachelle managed to get a hold of Nigel and attempted to drag him clear. Under normal circumstances she wouldn't have stood a prayer. Nigel fell back, restrained by the force of Rachelle, goading them that this was their lucky day, and that their continued good health and safety was the direct result of Rachelle's intervention, and they should be down on bended knee thanking her. Nigel always had a bad habit of over exaggeration.

'Nigel!' Rachelle exasperated, after checking the horses were safe. 'What the devil do you think you're doing? If Mr Flugal here's of this you'll be banned from the meet!'

Nigel retreated hastily enough to get out of their reach, but not enough to look chicken.

The lads all congregated back at base and discussed any snippets of information or useful tips picked up on the brief sojourn across the enclosure, and what excuse they could possibly imagine up when the inevitable inquisition should start. The discourse was broken up by the arrival of the large shadow of Mr Williams. 'Well, well you have been busy Flugal.' he said stepping uninvited into the camp.' And very careless may I say so allowing your horses to wander aimlessly unsupervised.'

'Unsupervised my.............' Biff was cut short by Rachelle.

'They were not unsupervised.'

Williams, caught unawares, turned to confront the now angry Rachelle, hands on hips, glaring at him. This offended his ego.

'You, you're only a child.'

'I'm old enough and quite capable of looking after these horses, who I have you know are some of the smartest around!'

Chance moved around to be by her side knowing Williams was not going to take that lying down.

Williams still took a menacing step forward only to be greeted by the fearsome growl of Nugget, returning from his security reconnoitre; he decided on the side of caution; Nugget to him was this vicious, rabid, snarling, evil dog that needed to be put out of its misery.

'Nugget!' Flugal's voice boomed over the snarling and Nugget instantly fell silent 'What are you doing?'

'Your dog nearly attacked me!'

'That's a lie.' said Rachelle.

'Alright, alright.' Flugal calmed her down and her grandmother, who was no more than a step or two behind, gave her a reassuring hug.

'What are you doing here Mr Williams?'

'Making sure your horses and especially that pig of yours don't run riot again.'

'What's he talking about Rachelle?' her grandmother asked.

'I took them for a walk to loosen them up for this afternoon and Nigel ended up.....kind of ended up....causing a stir.'

'A major disturbance more like, ask Fulton if you don't believe me, your pig ransacked his teams supplies.'

Flugal looked over to Nigel, who skulked behind the horse box. 'I'll straighten this out with Fulton, and from your statement this clearly has nothing to do with you, so I'll kindly ask you to leave.'

'With pleasure, but you haven't heard the last of this.' And he did just that.

'Rachelle.' Flugal called her over after Williams had left 'Is it as bad as I'm being led to believe?'

'He did enter the Fulton camp.'

'I'll go and have a chat.' Flugal spoke in that grave tone, this was not going to turn out well, and he too left.

Mrs Flugal and Mrs Perkins still had in their possession the bags of goodies and gifts to be enjoyed at the close of play today, and they were now used to entice everyone away from the sombre mood. Nigel peered into the bags. He thought his antics at Fulton's were enough for one day.

Flugal returned fifteen minutes later and confirmed his worst fears that Williams not Fulton, who was okay about the whole affair as he owned pigs himself, had logged a complaint and asked for Flugal to be disqualified. A deathly hush descended over camp.

'Damn!' whispered Nigel. 'I've gone and done it.'

'No you haven't.' Nugget replied 'We're a team remember, we've gone and done it!'

A little while later a marshal approached and spoke to Flugal in private; Flugal pleaded his case, as was witnessed by his body language. The animals felt guilty that their master should have to do this; they meant well, but it had all backfired catastrophically.

Flugal returned looking exhausted. 'We're not going to be disqualified.'

'Hooray!' they all shouted.

'But Nigel has to go; today he can stay, but tomorrow is a no go.'

'What!' Nugget wasn't happy.

'No, no he's right Nugget, I can't be seen to be part of the team anymore. We should just be grateful Fulton didn't push it, but I won't be to far away lads. They can chuck me out, but where there's a will…!'

The time was nearly upon them for the beginning of the marathon section, he was confident as to the courses layout; the roads along which it wound he knew really well, and the cross-country section held no fear for him, but what Flugal really needed right now was Dave to reappear to help out, but in the end his luck held firm, as he always secretly felt it did, in the shape Rachelle. There now wasn't an equine task she didn't prove to be a dab hand at. Dave materialised ten or so minutes before Flugal was required to make his way to the start, breezing into the camp without a care in the world.

'What did I miss?'

'Nothing much.' Flugal said adjusting his dress.

'I heard Nigel caused a real stink with Williams down at Fulton's.'

'Well you missed that.'

'He's horrible that Mr Williams!'

'Yes he is Rachelle, he's definitely not flavour of the month around here. In fact Nigel is now a bit of a celebrity!'

'That's me!' jumped up now a proud Nigel. 'An A-list celeb!'

Dave quizzed Nigel's reaction without any success; he still even now, for all his worth could not decipher pig. 'Anything you say Nigel.'

The joke was not lost on the others.

'Give us a hand.' Flugal asked Dave as he and Rachelle led the horses and carriage out into the main drag of the enclosure.

'Sure.'

'Dave?' started Rachelle.

'Yep!'

'Where do you go all the time?' Rachelle broached that awkward question as only a kid can do and adults wish they could.

'Seeing friends!' It was a lie and they all knew it. Dave re-evaluated his position. 'Nothing for any of you to worry about; I'm not grassing you up if that's the worry.'

'No, no, we never thought that, not that we've got anything to be grassed up about.' Flugal said shaking his head.

'I'm just having a bit of fun. Hey guess who I bumped into just now?'

'I dunno.'

'Bennett.'

'Oh!'

'No, Bennett was lambasting old Williams. It seems he's not being playing him with a straight bat!'

'Oh.'

'Obviously he couldn't tell me any of the details; client confidentiality and all that.'

'Sounds like he shouldn't have told you that!' said Rachelle.

'I think all he wanted was for you to know he wasn't on Williams side, and the best way doing that, without bringing any attention on himself, was to talk to me.'

'Interesting.' Flugal said in a low tone.

'Very.'

Flugal and Rachelle boarded the carriage 'I still can't bring myself to trust him.'

'Maybe your judgement has been a little coloured.' replied Dave. 'You should cut the guy a little slack.'

'Possibly.' Flugal replied making himself comfortable, without making eye contact with his friend. 'Okay guys let's give them something to remember us by other than Nigel's escapades.'

The "Boys" all laughed; it was rare for Flugal to crack a joke, but it showed he was relaxed and in good spirits and a good run was on.

Dave and Mrs Flugal, accompanied by Mrs Perkins, Nugget and Nigel all waved and shouted good luck.

The four horses, with Flugal and Rachelle aboard the shiny black carriage, now departed whilst the remaining five split into two with three heading for the spectator galleries again, leaving Nugget and Nigel to scamper off to their chosen hiding place behind some trees Nugget had spotted on his return from talking to the rabbits; Nigel thinking quite rightly it prudent to stay out of sight and mind.

On the way to the start Flugal began to encourage the lads to even greater effort; his words could be heard coupled with those of old Nigel and Nugget hollering from outside the enclosure perimeter, abandoning immediately his cautious approach to inconspicuousness. They were still within earshot as the team came to a halt short of the start, and their vociferous support raised their morale to new heights. Flugal on hearing the continued snorts and growls couldn't help smiling, because he was aware of the effect this would undoubtedly have on the team

Nugget and Nigel watched with pride as team Flugal was announced, the voice bellowed out their score from the dressage and their present position.

The two friends had settled on a spot that ran along the side of the first long straight, and gave excellent views in either direction. Yet again they were joined by Ralph and Jed and the whole gang of betting slip wavers, who had all agreed to show solidarity to their animal friends.

'Come on lads!' Nigel could not contain himself any longer, knowing the importance of this run, the nervous tension had been growing inside him and he suddenly had the overwhelming urge to expel all that pent up pressure, even if that meant giving himself away.

Bennett, who had missed Flugal in the dressage, had managed to get to the front of the galleries and surprised even himself by calling out his name along with the hordes of spectators now viewing the day's second section. He immediately slunk back into the crowd fearing the embarrassment, not wanting to make a fool of himself in front of any of the bank's clientele. Flugal failed to notice.

Williams could feel the envy slowly eating away within; why should he feel jealousy for a man like Flugal; his team were better trained, looked smarter and chatted nonstop among themselves, scattering derogatory remarks like confetti about the other horses and competitors coming and going this afternoon.

Dave, Mrs Flugal and Rachelle's grandmother made themselves comfortable; they had managed to get good seats as the excitement steadily grew as the competition closed in on the thrilling end of the day; everybody enjoyed the marathon and they sensed that there existed only a fine margin between success and failure, any mistakes made in the dressage could be cancelled out now and visa-versa.

Already the crowd had witnessed a couple of excellent runs that had resulted in that team undoubtedly shooting up the leader board. Flugal had deliberately avoided looking at the board, preferring to concentrate on his own run. Williams by contrast was the complete opposite; he found it impossible to take his eyes of it.

21

Charles Nostromos had had a restless night; these recently had rapidly becoming the norm, for a peaceful repose is not the domain of a mind troubled by self doubt and there was now a constant chorus of disapproval emanating from his board, that these carriage drives were being derided at every turn as irresponsible and a waste of valuable company time and money, and why had they not sponsored a more recognisable sporting event like football, tennis or a professional golf tournament and if it was his wish to be involved in anything equine then horse racing would have been the more responsible avenue to go down. Charles found the accusation of wasting company time and money a bit rich for his taste, but kept his counsel. There was though one extremely bright point on the horizon; all the added publicity and word of mouth had increased lately beyond all his wildest dreams. In the weeks leading up to the big day, the public demand for information had brought out a local radio and television stations to cover the event. The two days would now be aired on the Sunday just prior to that days obstacle run being shown live, bringing that much needed publicity to Global.

He now seated himself a few rows in front of team Flugal in one of the corporate boxes Global had provided for business associates, customers and friends, and he watched with added interest as Flugal seemingly surveyed the beginning of the course, allowing his charges valuable time to readjust themselves to their surroundings; he found it easy to associate with the trepidation the contestants felt before each run. Like the dressage it had been decided to only give the contestants the information regarding the marathon that morning so that nobody had the upper hand, and as they were all experienced in the event, in one way or another, it was not regarded as to much of a hardship, but here was a local man trying his best to better himself against more hardened competitors and the interest that had garnered was becoming a public relations dream.

Lucy arrived and seated herself at a respectful distance from him, he turned to acknowledge her presence, then quietly gesticulated for her to sit closer to him on his right hand side; she was uncomfortable with the attention he was paying her, people would start to talk and the last thing she wanted or needed was to be the topic of office gossip. It had increased imperceptibly over the past few weeks, and she had noticed that he was not open to ostentatious displays of affection, but rather more reserved in his advancements. Her heart started to race, the degree and frequency of palpitations increased the closer she moved towards him.

'This is the local team and it seems to be very popular!' he said.

She searched through some of the paperwork she had handy. 'His name is Flugal; he's a farmer I think.'

'I thought Williams was the local favourite?'

'Favourite to win!'

Charles nodded, but offered no reply.

'The show seems to be a great success Mr Nostromo.' she added.

'Call me Charles. I want to to call me Charles.' This time it was Lucy who nodded without offering any response. 'I hope so. There's a lot riding on it!....If you pardon the pun.'

They smiled at each other, it was a good moment and both prayed a good omen.

Several Global customers now returned to their seats, after retiring to one of the many hospitality tents around the arena during lunch.

Espying team Flugal preparing to start their run they shared, vociferously, all and any opinions on their chances of improving their overall standing from the morning's dressage; the consensus of opinion though was still that team Flugal was a no hoper, but that on a given day may just have a slim chance of pushing the favourites, if they for whatever reason failed to improve to any significant extent.

'This team are no slow coaches.' blurted out Lucy, who then hung her head the very second she finished speaking.

'Really.' said one.

'Interesting.' said another.

Charles started to feel resentment to the tone used by these valued customers to this woman he now had feelings for, but limited his response to a simple sideways glance, and a half smile; it was all but useless, save the fact it didn't go unnoticed by Lucy. Their eyes met and Charles rather than avert his gaze, as he had done in the past, fixed his sight upon her until any further would have brought embarrassment upon her. He wanted her to be in no doubt as to his true feelings.

Team Flugal pointed out to one another the subtle changes that would he expected throughout the marathon run, unfortunately for them this was the discipline for which they had the least practice, and it had been decided during Chance's injury layoff to only have a light practice at the changes from a trot to a walk that would be expected over the fifteen kilometre, three phase course. They would also be expected to navigate themselves along public roads and through man-made and natural obstacles, these obstacles would all have a time constraint. The time for each obstacle was to be recorded via a timer aboard a tripod at the beginning and end of the obstacle. These it had been decided, as they would not be aware of their true nature, were best dealt with as they came to them; they would have a two minute window to play within each section and as long as they didn't waste too much time in any one particular obstacle then they should be okay. Any inclines and water were just regarded as par for the course and not given any undue concern. Each horse knew his place and what was now expected of them.

Again the clock would start when their noses first crossed the start line, and as before they hit it at pace befitting the space available. This was going to be spectacular run, on that there was no doubt in either of their minds and this was the foundation on which all had based an undoubted will to succeed.

The first phase, phase A could be driven at any pace and the "Boys" kept it at a fast trot, and any tight turns quickly disappeared from view without any trouble, this only added to bolster their confidence. The lads were talking, encouraging constantly; Flugal had not said a word and held his whip purely for effect again, although he knew he would be marked on its effectiveness, but if it didn't needed to be used then why do it, believing it was duly required under the regulations, and then two more sharp turns left and right vanished from memory as soon as they disappeared behind the carriage. Now they could put the pedal to the metal so to speak and make good their forward progress along a section of roadway; it brought gasps from the crowd who witnesses them; this was one of the fastest phases they had seen to date.

Rachelle had studiously researched her new position and shouted encouragement to the "Boys" and Flugal, whilst all the time keeping one eye on the time lest they should fall outside their two minute window, but there were times when she could not contain herself and jumped out of her seat. Her reaction was infectious as her grandmother, Dave and Mrs Flugal and half the witnessing crowd all followed suit, shouting encouragement at the top of their voices whilst still in ear shot. Such was her total involvement in the race that she drew gasps from the crowd as she helped bounce the carriage around the man-made and natural hazards, whether they be fence posts, trees or inclines with what seemed like effortless ease, but throughout it all she paid special attention to stay on board and use her weight to keep them upright.

Charles and Lucy showed their support to all contestants by clapping; Charles thought it prudent to maintain decorum and had instilled in all board members wishing to attend to do the same, although the urge to follow suit with the more popular drivers was insatiable.

No posts were touched as they left the roadway behind them and screamed down to two more turns and down a sharp incline, the rear of the carriage slid dangerously wide on a right hander, but Pogo and Troy, sensing the skid before it took root, had already corrected it and adding all the relevant braking.

Flugal and Rachelle roared their approval; they were now a racing machine, both were having a mighty adrenaline rush along with his lads. Next came the water.

The hazard loomed large on their horizon, but thankfully there was a straight leading up to it with a sharp turn to the left leading to an incline after, they all instinctively knew that this was going to be a seminal part on the run.

Chance called back to Pogo and Troy, who reassured him they were okay with the carriage on the uphill section, as all the weight would again be there's until any slack could be taken up forward of the pole. Biff held the inside track for the turn and led them beautifully into the water without breaking stride, the cooling water was a relief and all the horses grunted under the strain. Troy and Pogo yanked the carriage up to the plateau, taking as much of the strain as possible, leaving the front two free to steer left. The plateau proved to be of little rest-bite and they knew two more right-handers awaited them. It was now that Rachelle quickly checked their time against one of the kilometre marker posts; yes they hadn't wasted anytime on the hazard, but now the added problem was that they were too fast and outside the optimum time for the run. They needed to slow down or incur penalty points.

Flugal called for them to slow, but the initial reaction was to remain on station, so he called again. Still there was no reaction, the lads were so caught up in the moment that they failed to heed his warning. He shouted a third call to slow and this time there was a sharp reduction in forward speed.

Nugget, Nigel, Jed, Ralph and the gang, who had re-positioned themselves to get a better view, cheered themselves hoarse, and they met their team with a cacophony of noise; what a run they were putting together, a miraculous run and laying down a challenge to the others.

The speed of the run to date had bought audible gasps from all; their speed was reckless at best and Flugal pictured catastrophe at every hazard, but was unable until now to call a halt to the run. Pogo and Troy had dug their hoofs in to slow down on hearing Flugal shout, Chance and Biff followed suit and the carriage was brought under control as it swung around the fast, sweeping, right hand turn towards the next obstacle, which was an old oak tree and a brightly coloured fence post. Then it happened. Biff was the first to notice, Troy and Pogo realised a definite alteration in the carriage's make up, Flugal knew instinctively and his heart sank; Chance had injured himself again, but he never showed it! The slower pace remained, the crowd cheered, roaring them on totally unaware of the catastrophe and their need to remain on time. The end of this phase was now less than a kilometre away and two more hazard remained to be negotiated.

Flugal and the boys asked Chance how he was, Rachelle remained mute fighting back the tears whilst all the time keeping track of the time and balancing the carriage as best she could. Chance nodded and reassured them he was okay, and he trotted unhindered up to the hazard. They never touched it and the crowd were none the wiser, only the faces of the team gave anything away.

Five hundred metres was all that remained between them and Chance having a rest; the second phase was a kilometre walk followed by a ten minute rest and cooling down period. The hazard was eventually left, untouched behind them and they entered the walking kilometre with them all clearly worried about Chance and searching to find out how bad he actually was and could he possibly continue. He re-assured them all that he was fit to continue and confident in the fact that any soreness would abate long enough for them to finish. In reality he was in some distress, but he was not under any circumstances going to let on his true physical condition lest they should withdraw, which Flugal clearly would, instead he re-iterated to them all to concentrate hard on the third and final phase.

Rachelle and Flugal kept the walk sedate and tried as best they could to ascertain the extent of his injury. 'He's walking okay Mr Flugal.' Rachelle said, 'but I'm not convinced.'

'No, neither am I, but I know he'd hate it if we withdraw over him, so all we can do is trust in him and his ability, and just continue for as long as he can physically take it!'

They now had another potential problem to overcome; during the ten minute cooling down period the horses were to be examined by as vet to see if they were fit enough to continue. Chance reassured the lads once again, repeating that he was okay to carry on and it was only a minor pull caused by the abrupt reduction in speed putting too much strain on his leg and that once this final phase was past them, a night and a morning's rest was all that was needed. Flugal was not so optimistic, the tone of Chance's voice told him otherwise and the body language of the other three only supported what he feared the most.

The vet duly arrived as the team came to a halt in the designated area to cool down; luck was on their side for the vet hadn't noticed anything untoward in the team completing the kilometre walk, Chance had hidden his injury well. It wasn't the first time he'd run not feeling a hundred percent, and the vet duly cleared them to enter the final phase when ready. Flugal took a huge sigh of relief.

'I knew he'd get us to the end!' Rachelle said leaning over Flugal's shoulder.

'Let's hope he know's what he's doing.'

'I work on the assumption,' started Rachelle, 'that he knows his own body better than we do!'

'Ditto!' replied Flugal and the two of them watered the horses.

Nigel and Nugget during this time, having followed the team around the course, caught them up and re-positioned themselves to get a good view of the final phase, the rest of team Flugal in the stand had the advantage of a large television monitor that picked up the teams at various parts of the course, it was one of the advantages of having the television station cover the event.

Nugget's and Nigel's elation gave way to fear and panic. 'Poor old Chance has hurt himself' Nugget said.

'You sure?' Nigel was desperate for his friend to be wrong.

'I'm afraid so.'

'Can he continue?'

'The vet's not pulled them out so he either doesn't realise Chance is crocked or thinks he can finish.' Nugget went on.

'Chance hid it from him!'

They both nodded.

The time was now upon them to start the last phase of around seven kilometres; this could be done at a walk or a trot with still the time window to play with, but they could not fall behind or be outside the optimum time window, plus there were eight obstacles in this phase.

The team moved off as gingerly as possible without giving the game away and at a walking pace they passed the first couple of hazards without stopping or picking up any penalties. Rachelle throughout kept an eye on the clock as they passed the kilometre marker boards, but it was quite noticeable to the crowd, and the spectators watching the monitor, that team Flugal was markedly slower and all those in the know knew the real reason.

'We got to speed up, they'll suspect something's up!' called out Chance and he quickened his pace.

The crowd once again became vociferous as they anticipated another fast phase by he fastest team in the competition. Slowly, but surely they became quicker and quicker and Flugal and Rachelle roared them all on. Hazard after hazard passed them by and suddenly they found that they were all beginning to enjoy this final phase, even Chance forgot all about the pain in his leg and concentrated on the run, admiring the brightly coloured obstacles that they raced around. The inclines were taken by the wheelers at the rear so to lessen the load on Chance, and Biff led the way through the obstacles. All Chance had to do was offer advice and get round the course. The final two hazards were in sight at five-hundred and three-hundred metres from the finish and here Chance felt the first real stinging pain, but ignored it all and pushed on; mentally he locked it all out and thought only of the hazards, counting down the strides to and from it, then all that was left was the finish and the roar of the spectators spurned them on. He knew they had run well and would be in a good position for tomorrow, but the sharp pain on crossing the line and slowing down wracked his leg, and it took all his self control to maintain his composure until they made their enclosure. All the time the lads consoled and encouraged him.

Flugal was astonished at the pace set and consistency through the hazards, but wasted no time in un-harnessing the team and making sure Chance was okay, the others understood and stood patiently waiting their turn to board the horse-box for the journey home. Dave took the opportunity to commandeer some ice from one of the vendors, and this was placed into a towel and wrapped around his leg to help reduce any swelling.

Once he was made as comfortable as possible, with Biff, Troy, Pogo and Nigel joining him aboard, everything was expeditiously packed away then Flugal made sure it was okay to leave; the organisers wanted to know the reason for the early departure, he told them his wife was feeling poorly, and he confirmed the times for tomorrow's obstacle run, which were thankfully later than today as there was now only one section to go. And with that they left with Nugget riding with Mrs Flugal, Dave and Rachelle's grandmother.

Rachelle begged her grandmother and Mr Flugal to ride in the box with Chance and the lads, but they said no for her own safety, so she had to make do with peering through a spy hole a keep guard on them, all the while talking to the "Boys" for re-assurance.

Each took it in turns to support poor old Chance, who was mortified that his injury had reoccurred and should result in their downfall. Nigel told him not to be so stupid.

'Rubbish!' said Biff angrily. 'This could have happened to any one of us.'

'It was a good run, such a good run!' Chance dropped his head.

'We don't know the full extent yet Chance, so hoofs crossed you'll be fine.'

'These things take time Pogo.'

'Hell Chance, a good night's rest and you never know, you'll feel as good as knew.' Troy tried to sound as encouraging as possible hoping it might hide the inner fear.

Flugal drove as slowly as he dare bearing in mind he wanted to get Chance the proper health care as quickly as possible. Dave had overtaken him earlier and he knew his wife would rustle up some of her miraculous home grown medicine; as good as anything Flugal had purchased from any vet; his wife he recognised as a pure genius in the field and she swore wholeheartedly by using natural home grown ingredients and plant extracts. Any ailment she would say, the good lord had created a remedy for, the secret was to know which ingredients, their quantity and it what order they needed to be applied.

Rachelle could not stop peering back and talking to the lads during the whole drive; Flugal calculated she looked forward all of six minutes over the entire hour it took them to get home.

As they approached the open gate to the farm, Nugget was already waiting, tail wagging, barking something completely incomprehensible. 'Mistress has the potion already ready. Don't ask me how, she must have photographic memory or something, it took her all of fifteen minutes to rustle up!'

Flugal pulled up outside the stables, Dave exited them and helped unlatch the rear door. 'Everything's ready.'

'Excellent.' replied Flugal.

The door now laying safely on the ground, the two men led the other three into the awaiting stables; they were reluctant to leave their friend, but after a little persuasion by them both that young Rachelle was taking care of Chance they allowed themselves to be steered out of the box.

Rachelle hurried in as soon as the last had left and felt Chance's leg. He flinched, but it wasn't as swollen as they all feared it would be. 'It's going to be okay Chance.'

'I hope so.'

'I'm going to stay all night, and care for you better than ever.' And she gingerly walked him down the ramp, across the yard and into the stables. They all watched him very closely to gauge the severity of his injury; to their relief it didn't seem to bother him much bar a minor limp and some minor swelling. Mrs Flugal duly arrived with her "medicine", mixed it into Chance's feed and everybody set to work.

A few of the private owners each arrived by car and offered help.

Chance gave himself up totally to their care once again, in particular obeying Rachelle's every word to the letter, which humoured all concerned and added some much needed relief.

Nigel was viewing the healthcare of his old friend when one of his starling buddies flew past with some hot news. Nigel could not wait to tell all once his feathered friend had departed. 'This is guaranteed to cheer you up.' he said taking a few steps into the stables.

'What is it?' Troy was the first to answer.

'Williams only came second!'

'Excellent news.' laughed Pogo.

'Who beat him?' asked Biff.

'We did!' Nigel beamed a huge smile, the first since Chance's accident. 'We garnered the lowest amount of penalty points' There were muted congratulations; this news, fantastic as it was, only added to the general misery of the situation; they had proved beyond any question they were more than capable of matching and beating any team pitched against them. As the news filtered invariably around the yard, all the livery horses added their congratulations and tried their very best to boost morale.

'That's great news Nigel, thanks.'

'That's okay Chance. We'll beat him again tomorrow.' Nigel had tried to raise spirits, and it was after all excellent news.

The whole episode had been understood by Mrs Flugal; she comprehended the strong bond and affection that had grown substantially between them all on Flugal Farm.

That night Rachelle was allowed by her grandmother and the Flugals to spend the night in the stables. In fact all the team were guests, all except Dave, who chose to go home citing important business regarding seeing a man about a dog. Nugget was curious to know who this strange dog was. Dave being Dave was not particularly forthcoming.

Rachelle made her bed as comfortable as possible and then nestled down for the night, but not before she did one final round of the lads and the livery horses, and setting her alarm for eight thirty. Flugal had made sure that everybody was aware that they needed to be at the course for eleven o'clock.

The final day was to be the obstacle course; each team would complete two laps of the new figure of eight circuit through and around more man-made hazards, bordered by cones and over a bridge at the cross section. On top of each cone stood a ball and if the ball is dislodged each driver would incur a penalty, each cone at the hazard would only be twenty-two centimetres wider than the carriage, plus they had placed cones around the outer perimeter of the course to penalise any teams losing control and running to wide. It is the ultimate test of skill and nerve in manoeuvring a carriage around tight spaces against oneself, one's opponents and the clock. The advantage for team Flugal was it would be a later start, bearing in mind they now sat top of the leader board after the first day, and thus giving Chance's leg a little more time to recover.

Their exploits on day one had not gone unnoticed or without its merits; more and more past students were wanting to return to the stables and resume lessons, along with a whole lot of new prospective students wishing to ride the four hero's of team Flugal, so a good showing now became a must. There were to be lots of other events taking place on the second day; a gymkhana, the events that had begun on the Saturday, a vintage car rally, a steam engine rally and local farmers displaying their prize bulls, pigs, etc.

Once the lights had dimmed for the night the horses were left to their own thoughts. Rachelle was fast asleep.

'Sorry guys!' lamented Chance.

'Look Chance.' started Troy looking around at the others in case they wanted to intervene. 'Nobody, nobody is blaming you for anything. We wouldn't be here if it wasn't for you!' Pogo and Biff grunted approval. 'You advised us, helped train us, and gave us the benefit of your experience.'

'Look at it this way.' butted in Biff. 'If it hadn't been for your original injury we would never have got to know you or each other as well as we have or been able to compete in this race, so the injury has been our friend, I know that sounds stupid, but I don't know any other way to explain it.'

'We're a team.' said Pogo 'and as a team we'll win or lose.'

'I'll run tomorrow, of that you can be sure.' Chance's voice exuded optimism and the lads rested easier because of it.

22

Williams was not in the mood to be charitable to his team or anybody; he imparted a large piece of his mind on one of the marshals before he departed for his estate. Arriving back at the enclosure he fully expected to be announced as the fastest team on the day, his disappointment, after the briefest of pauses, to interpret the significance of his position, was followed by a whirlwind of abuse aimed initially at his workforce and that poor unfortunate marshal.

His drive back to the estate, in his state of the art horse-box, was conducted in eerie silence; it had effect of disconcerting his driver, who knew his master well enough to expect a maelstrom to erupt at a moments notice. If Williams had paid any attention to his drivers navigating skills he would have had cause for concern, but his mind was cemented firmly trying to comprehend a situation for which he had never thought possible. Not only second, but second to none other than Flugal!

How he detested that man; how dare he stand between him and his dream. Who was he: a farmer, no worse than a farmer, a riding instructor, and a small time one at that; if anybody wanted to see a proper riding stables then they had to look no further than his.

'What time is it?' Williams finally deigned to converse with his driver; he caught the poor man so unawares that a momentary loss of concentration resulted in a minor swerve quickly corrected.

'Nearly six, Mr Williams.' came back the timid reply.

'Damn!' Williams had wanted to take his team out for a run, but by the time they got back to the estate, and with other business pending, there would be little time to indulge himself.

'Thank God for that.' thought Lightning; he hated the late day runs, he was always in relaxing mode at this particular time and anyhow they had run well, albeit slower than Flugal. The root cause of their second place lay in having taken slightly longer than allowed to negotiate a few of the hazards and incurred some unwanted penalties. Williams never once bothered himself learning how or what his horses thought at any time, to him they were like all other employees who worked under him: Subordinates, and should be treated the same. If he had taken the time he would easily have abandoned the idea.

'Let's be grateful for small mercies!' Storm muttered quietly so they could all hear, then panicked when he saw Williams turn back to face them, but it was only to collect a drinks bottle from a bag hanging behind him.

* * * * *

Charles Nostromo gritted his teeth; certain members of the board had not stopped ridiculing his idea from the outset and now the voices of dissension had crossed that line, he had decided to end it here and now. Lucy helped clear up the corporate tents; from the mess she conjectured the valued customers had clearly enjoyed themselves. If they were not really into anything of an equestrian nature then the hospitality alone was worth making an appearance.

Charles approached one of the main dissenters; his countenance exuded an arrogance he found repulsive, and in that second he resolved to remove him from a position of harm.

'Charles.' said the man.

He checked, for now, any outward sign of animosity.

'It was okay, all things considered.' The man had chosen his words purely to get a rise out of him and they both knew it.

'Well,' started Charles, 'our guests definitely enjoyed it, even if certain senior employees didn't!' He emphasised the word employees; this man was to know his place.

Lucy passed by within close proximity. Charles felt a sudden desire to display his authority in an ostentatious display of machismo; that would surely impress her; he hated, feared that she would consider him weak if he failed to control those who dared to question his authority, but at the critical juncture he paused and settled on a moment of re-evaluation.

The fates were on his side though; the object of his animosity read intentions far more sinister and immediately placated Charles with a few well chosen verses used to, in past, negotiations, manoeuvre himself out of many a tight political scrape.

Charles recognised the obsequious concession and played the game. When it was all said and done, the man removed himself and Charles instantly sought the one person who really mattered to him at this precise point in time. He was not to be disappointed; the look of admiration she conveyed told him more than a thousand words could ever do.

* * * * *

In the morning Rachelle was the first to rise, eager to see any improvements in Chance's leg; what swelling there was had reduced noticeably and he looked much more at ease with himself. Mrs Flugal's wonder potions of natural remedies and plant extracts had once again worked miracles.

Flugal arrived shortly after and he too inspected his team leader's leg, and yes he confirmed it. It looked much better and not so puffy, but could he run on it!

Rachelle buzzed around the stables checking on Biff, Troy and Pogo, and those livery horses not yet under the care of their owners, making sure they had plenty of feed and water. It was going to be a long day.

Nigel had spent the night lolling in his mud bath; he wasn't going today so he thought what the hell, nobody is going care much what I smell or look like, and therefore indulged himself totally.

Nugget slept in the house, and like a genie out of a bottle he miraculously materialised before the lads very eyes examining the offending leg in minute detail. 'Hey dude? It looks good. Mrs Flugal's magic medicine has done it again!' Nugget looked up and smiled at Chance with that cheeky grin he was almost famous for.

'I wish I'd had it all those years ago.' he said, as he took the first tentative steps out of the stables with aid of Flugal.

Troy, Biff and Pogo followed closely behind with Rachelle, Nugget and Nigel bringing up the rear.

'Hey Nugget?' said Nigel.

'Yeah?'

'You going to the race yeah?'

'I wanted to talk to you about that?'

'You did?'

'I was thinking...maybe I'll stay back here with you and then when everybody's gone we could surreptitiously enjoy proceedings via alternative arrangements.'

'You mean we'll sneak in through the back door, keep out of sight and watch the lads win!'

'That's about the gist of it.'

'Sounds like a master plan to me.' and then he added after a short pause. 'It's a long way Nugget!'

'We'll hitch!'

'Hitch!

'It's part of the master plan!'

'Are you kidding! Who's going to pick up a stray dog and a pig and give them a lift to a race they may or may not be going to?'

The affairs of Chance though diverted their attention until they had more time to discuss their rather dubious travel arrangements.

Chance walked a couple of slow laps of the yard; Flugal led the first, then he got Rachelle to do two more so he could assess Chance's leg from a distance. Nobody spoke. Flugal asked Rachelle to jog two more laps once that Chance's leg was now properly warmed up.

He trotted easily enough, thought Flugal, and he was satisfied that Chance was as good as anybody could have reasonably expected. Rachelle walked him back to the waiting lads standing patiently by the box.

'How d'ya feel?' The tension in Troy's voice shocked even him.

'Okay.'

'Only okay?' Troy's voice relaxed a little.

'Don't you guy's worry about a thing, we're running today even if it kills me.' He was for once glad Rachelle didn't fully understand him, she would have had a fit hearing that last statement. 'So let's get ourselves shipshape.'

Biff and Pogo let out a hoop of joy that sent Troy into raptures; it was all for Chance's benefit; they realised and greatly appreciated the gamble he was taking, and knew if canvassed on the subject of whether to run or not would unanimously have chosen the latter in order to protect their friend from further punishment. Thankfully for them Flugal and Rachelle were blissfully unaware.

Dave turned up shortly after and everybody set to the task of readying for the days racing ahead.

The efficient way the team hit the road in less than an hour with them all seated in the horse box now driven by Dave, so they could all stay in the one place together this time, was a thing of beauty. Nugget and Nigel eagerly waved them off impatient to hit the road themselves.

Flugal and his wife were more than a little perplexed by Nugget's refusal to travel, knowing how much he was cherishing the moment. The lads knew rightly and made no fuss, Rachelle suspected something, but didn't say. At some point on their journey the penny dropped for Flugal and he chuckled quietly to himself.

So Nugget and Nigel were left behind. As soon as everyone was out of sight Nigel left no time in carrying on the conversation where he'd left off.

'Hitch, are you mad!'

'It's a piece of cake.'

'A piece of you cake, to you perhaps. Who do you know around here gives lifts to stray dogs, unless of course you intend to go to the pound, and wandering pigs?' Nugget had to give this some serious thought for a second.

'That's looking at all the negatives.'

'And the positives are?'

'You're letting all that negative energy cloud your judgement.'

'The only thing clouded here is your unflinching optimism hidden behind a veil of incredulity!'

'I don't know what that means Nigel, but it sure sounded good. Right now follow me.'

Nigel obliged and the two friends made their way to the races. The track was approximately twenty miles away and the associated traffic made the drive time little under an hour. Nugget guessed that even if they walked, and he wasn't going to let Nigel know that, it would take them up to four hours; yes they would miss the first half of the day, but not the all second when they would start the obstacle section. Tiredness, he thought, is relative, and if the end goal raised an emotive issue, fatigue could and should not take a foot hold. Ultimately Nugget was a friend to everyone and he didn't want Nigel to feel left out or to miss such a momentous occasion, even if it cost a little inconvenience along the way.

They cut across a field directly opposite the entrance to the farm and by the time they reached the hedge on the far side, Nigel was exhausted; the trip to Ralph's had been negotiated at a gentle pace, this was more like a sprint.

Nugget was first through the hedge and just missed flagging down a passing car. Nigel scrambled, panting to where Nugget was now standing, and fell headlong into him sending the poor dog sprawling head first into the grass verge.

'I can't go on!' gasped Nigel.

'That was only a field.' said Nugget extricating himself.

'I don't care I can't go on! And at such a death defying pace.'

Nugget was interrupted during his reply by the imminent arrival of a second car. He waved a paw and tried his best to look desperate. The driver never gave them a second look and passed on by.

'That went well.' said Nigel sarcastically.

'He never saw us.'

'You don't say.'

'We need to be more conspicuous.' he said turning to face the exhausted Nigel. 'When the next car comes by I'll jump up and down, and you wave a hoof to show them we need to hitch a lift.'

'Whatever.' The resignation in his voice was all too apparent, this was going to be an utter disaster and he started to pine for his luscious mud bath back at the farm. It wasn't long before a third car made its appearance.

'You ready?'

'My hoof is poised to hitch.'

The car approached at a faster pace than the previous two; Nugget jumped up and down furiously, as high as his old legs would let him, and Nigel waved a hoof in that well worn hitchhiking manner.

The driver was so shocked at seeing a half demented dog bouncing up and down by the side of the road, accompanied by a pig with a nasty twitch, that he failed to see the bend in the road until it was too late; he swerved desperately in a vain attempt to negotiate it, but it was all to no avail. The last Nugget and Nigel saw of the car was its rear bumper disappear through a thicket and into a ditch.

'Nigel?' Nugget received no reply. 'Nigel?' Nugget looked over to the spot where Nigel had been "Hitching". It was empty. Nigel's shape could be seen high tailing it up the road. Nugget raced off in hot pursuit.

Team Flugal arrived in good time and set up their camp on the exact same spot as yesterday, only this time Dave was allowed entry, and as before on leaving the farm, they displayed great teamwork and understanding to what was required at the correct time. In no time they were all geared up for their obstacle run later that day, and as before they received all the relevant information regarding the final section there and then. It was now only left to placing some protective strapping on Chance's leg, and make the most of some precious time to relax and once again familiarise themselves.

The lads were given warm up walks at regular intervals; Chance's leg was closely monitored, he still showed no ill effects, but they didn't want him stiffening up. The carriage was prepared, Flugal again confirmed the time of his run; he was last to go as he was atop the leader board. All was so far going as well as he could have wished, except for that deep seated worry again rearing its ugly head on the sagacity of such a venture, and the after effects of failure this would have on any members of his family. Nugget and Nigel being absent were never to far from his thoughts.

'At least we're going the right way!' Nugget panted once he'd caught up. 'I think there's another coming, get your hoof ready!'

Nigel spun round and waved like a maniac, Nugget did his trampoline style act and sure enough the second car left the road.

'I can't be bothered to run again.' Nigel said, trudging forward and Nugget agreed.

The two of them chatted away, each enjoying each other's company so much, that they ate up the miles, blissfully unaware that with every passing minute they were getting ever closer to their goal.

Suddenly the high pitch screech of brakes on tarmac alerted them to the presence of a truck who had spotted the two would be hitchhikers.

'Nugget!' shouted the friendly voice. It was their neighbour Mr Dougherty and his wife. 'What are you and Nigel doing by the side of the road at this time of day and on a Sunday? Silly me you're going to the races aren't you?'

Nugget wagged his tail enthusiastically. 'Sure are, any chance of a lift?'

'Where's Flugal, don't tell me he forgot you both!'

'Er...not exactly.'

'It's unlike him to be that careless. Never mind I'm going that way, you just hop on board and we'll be there in a jiffy, it's only a couple of miles up the road.'

'Only a couple of miles! How long have we been walking!' shouted Nigel.

'See I told you it would work.' Nugget jumped up onto the back of the truck, Nigel followed suit and they were soon on their way to the races.

Flugal made detailed notes of the obstacle course, in the short time he had available to see where all the turns were, where any cones might be a problem, and generally get a feel for Sunday's layout; they were using the arena that had held the dressage yesterday, albeit a larger section of it.

'We're all gonna do whatever we can to alleviate the strain on your leg old friend.' said Troy. 'But if it ever gets to point where you can't go on, you've got to let us know and we'll stop and call it a day.'

'We all agreed last night Chance.' added Pogo.

'It's okay. Thank you all for your concern, but I'm okay honestly. Let us concentrate on this run; we've got to get into the top three, if we do that I reckon this event is ours! We've seen the opposition and the standard required and we can do it.'

'It's between us, Williams, Fulton and Lyndsey.' Dave said eying the filling spectator stands. 'But first we got to keep Chance right!' he added at the end as a caveat and then looked nervously over his shoulder.

Flugal's heart was racing; this was do or die for them all. Failure here would mean total ruin for his wife, his family and him; she loved the farm and it would break her heart to part with it, especially as her spirits had been raised by yesterday's performance and Chance's near miraculous recovery, although he had yet to run he informed her. His children's inheritance would be wiped out; he and his wife had deliberately kept them in the dark, the last thing they wanted was to burden them with their worries. Neither may never have shown any inclination to farming, but any proceeds from its sale would have been theirs, and throughout all of this Flugal kept his outward appearance of a calm, confident man, assured in his own ability to cope and conquer whatever trial and tribulation should be thrown or placed in his way.

One of the advantages of the obstacle phase was the opportunity for the drivers to walk the course, and he now gratefully made the most of this time, conversing with Rachelle, whilst they studied the course in greater detail; it had fourteen obstacles on a tight figure of eight course that needed to be negotiated over two laps. Dave had disappeared again on some "Personal Business", and the ladies were seated in their enclosure enjoying the day.

'It looks easy when your walking it, doesn't it Mr Flugal?'

'It sure does.'

Of the fourteen obstacles, not all of them were coned off for there was included a wooden bridge at the crossover point, which they needed to go up and over, plus the inevitable sharp and fast sweeping turns. The run would be against the clock and any misdemeanour would be costly to the tune of three penalty points.

Whilst everybody was pre-occupied preparing, resting or just counting down the minutes until they could let loose all that pent up emotion and start their run, things were afoot; Nugget would have been the first to notice anything untoward going on, but as he was still in transit so nobody spotted the dark, odious shadow disappearing behind the Flugal enclosure and slipping unnoticed under their carriage.

Williams was now at his most pernicious and wasted no time in getting down to work, he had to win and if the means satisfied the ends then so be it, and with spanner in hand he set about sabotaging the Flugal carriage.

Once Flugal and Rachelle were happy with the layout, and knew where any pitfalls lay in wait, they made their way back to their enclosure for some much needed sustenance and a rest before the excitement really began. On the way back Williams blocked their path.

'Flugal!'

The urge to just keep walking was immense, but good manners prevailed and they kept themselves in check.

'Mr Williams.' Flugal politely replied.

'I just wanted to say good luck this afternoon, and may the best team win.'

'Thank you, and the same to you.'

'I know we got off on the wrong foot and I hope you'll forgive me our little episode in the lane.'

'Forgotten already.'

'That's great. Well got to go and try and attempt to catch you Flugal, all the best.' Williams smiled as he parted.

The afternoon's events soon got underway and the rising decibels from the expectant crowd only added to the excitement; most was dying to see the local man win, even Bennett joined forces with the rising masses, and wished Flugal good luck when he passed by, finding within himself that he was struggling to contain his enthusiasm. Unbeknown to him Williams, who was watching from the enclosure, scowled at the support Flugal now received.

Flugal found himself for once not thinking about Chance's leg, the run was what was really important now, and he knew he had to have faith in his old friend and trust his judgement.

23

The Dougherty's stopped at the entrance to the event and spoke to one of the many marshals checking tickets and allocating parking spaces, and who missed seeing Nugget and Nigel jump off the back of the truck and vanish into the nearest hedgerow.

After the briefest of discussions, when they finally realised their two passengers had hightailed it, they both decided, in the interest of their friend and neighbour Flugal, to see the event for themselves and add any moral support they could. So they paid the entrance fee, parked the car and went in search of wherever their curiosity could cater for them.

Nugget being naturally the quickest led the way, and after a well educated guess that they would be camped in exactly the same spot as the day before, arrived at team Flugal temporary headquarters. Nigel, knowing his presence today would create unwanted attention, kept a low profile and stayed out of sight. They were both mentally preparing themselves for what they fully expected to find: Everybody working furiously on Chance, but instead found everybody trying desperately hard to chill out, relax and wile away the time before their fate was decided one way or another. Williams on the other hand was behaving like a cat sitting on a bed of nails, he didn't know what to be at or who to look for, and then, to top it all, the Flugal's kids, Tom and June, made an unexpected appearance; Mrs Flugal lost herself for a moment and hugged and kissed them both, Mr Flugal was more reserved; he shook his son by the hand and made small talk with him, then kissed his daughter on the cheek as all dad's do. This now partly explained Dave's disappearing act.

The time was getting close for the start of the four-in-hand obstacle phase, and the banter and sledging that accompanied the dressage and marathon sections started in earnest. Flugal knew he had to test Chance's leg and give him the opportunity to stretch it to gauge its usefulness, but at the same time he did not want to draw attention to themselves. There was always the chance the vet would refuse them their run if they knew the truth.

Chance and the lads were all led out by Flugal and Rachelle into the open area, that separated both sides of the enclosure, and walked a couple of lengths then trotted a couple. Flugal could tell right off that he wasn't right. His heart sank.

'It's no good ol fella! You can't run with that leg.'

'Oh yes I can and I will!' replied Chance indignantly.

Flugal realised what he had said and stroked him on the side of the neck. 'It's no good.'

Rachelle came alongside with Troy, Biff and Pogo. 'Please tell me he's okay.'

The look on his face said it all.

'I will run and that's an end to it! I am a professional athlete, and as such I accept the fact that I will not always be one hundred percent when I compete, it goes with the territory. It is a risk, my risk and I take it willingly to protect my loved ones and my friends!'

The lads said nothing out of sheer respect for their elder companion.

'We will run!'

'He wants to run Mr Flugal!'

'I know he does Rachelle, I know he does.'

'We can't withdraw Mr Flugal. We've come this far and achieved so much, the least we can do is to let them all run.'

Flugal desisted with the idea of withdrawing, partly due to his son joining the chorus in convincing him that if Chance could run, even with the slightest chance, and the horse wanted to then he should be allowed to try and make it round the obstacle course.

'You sure about this Chance?' said Troy.

Chance nodded.

'We'll take all the weight.' added Pogo.

Chance nodded again.

'I'll get us round as smoothly as possible Chance.' Biff said lastly.

Chance found himself choking back tears.

The colossal roar that surrounded the first runs set the tone for the days events; Fulton and Lyndsey had run a great phase and scored lightly on penalties, which Fulton shaved by less than a point; it made the hairs on the back of their necks stand up and stirred up the competitive juices in them all, not least Chance. The way he figured it and explained it to the crew, Flugal and Rachelle listened in and understood fully, that as this would be his last ever race he was going to give it everything, even if it meant being in plaster for a while and not be able to give any lessons, it would be worth it to save the farm, his friends and loved ones, faithful master and mistress, and to do it with the best friends anyone could ever wish for made it all the more special. And the icing on the cake was to beat Williams to boot. It was everything they needed and wanted to hear and team Flugal approached the ring, just over an hour and a half later, raring to go and to stick one over on old Williams and his "Quartet of Cruel".

Williams had gained a march on them with his run, it was the run of the day do far, and he now led. He brought his carriage and team to a halt just short of the arena, only to dish out some verbal abuse to Flugal as he neared. Flugal could read his intentions a mile off. 'Get ready boys.' he said.

'Hey you guys.' Storm instantly kicked it all off. 'See the back of our carriage, you better get used to it, it's all you're going to see today come prize giving!'

'Go easy on them Storm.' Lightning said laughing. 'There a lame duck!'

'I'm sure it's a charity day somewhere,' chimed in Tank, 'so we'll have to honour that.'

Thunder refrained from making any remark, he just looked down his long nose at team Flugal with utter disdain and contempt; they were not worthy to be in the same arena as him or his team.

Williams mirrored Thunder in his attitude towards Flugal; not only was the man blocking his proposed seat as the lord of the manor, but he had the temerity to challenge him here. 'This is the time Flugal, the time when see you could never be as good as me or be regarded as being on the same level as me. Look at you, a makeshift team of has-beens and wannabees, who had one lucky run and now think their champions in a second hand rig with a lame former loser as a pathetic excuse for a team leader.' Thunder laughed. 'We've put you firmly in your place with that run and then I'm going to enjoy trashing that farm that was formerly yours.'

Rachelle was seething whilst Pogo, Biff and Troy twitched nervously awaiting their turn to respond in kind, but Chance blocked them and reminded them all, himself just as much, to channel all that dislike, hatred towards Williams and his team into positive energy. His leg be damned, they were going to run them to the wire. Flugal said nothing.

Hearing his horses converse immediately after Williams rhetoric told him all he needed to know in order to ram Williams words down his throat.

The announcer introduced Flugal for the final run of the phase.

As he walked them slowly around the arena, in order to allow them as much time as possible to acclimatise, Flugal and Rachelle both felt comfortable with the layout, and knew it offered them no disadvantage.

The atmosphere was electric. He looked around the speculating crowd and immediately found his wife, kids, Dave and Mrs Perkins, who all waved. Flugal and Rachelle retained decorum and simply smiled.

Sitting to the right of team Flugal was Mr Bennett. He found himself on tender hooks; he was shocked once again as to the level of animosity that arose in him at the sight of Williams; he had figured out his master plan and secretly vowed to guarantee its failure, where legally possible, at every possible juncture, but here he still was on the verge of winning that which he had so odiously pursued, and against the man he so violently detested, whose only crime was to be the rightful, lawful owner. He constantly had to remind himself of his position in society and the future business he may have to conduct with him; it had the desired effect of tempering his anger, but not his will.

The team Flugal entourage looked over at Bennett and out of courtesy acknowledged his presence. Mrs Flugal smiled politely; any thoughts she had she kept them to herself. Bennett turned to her and said openly and sincerely that he wished her husband would beat Williams into the ground. She smiled again and said she hoped so too, and then regretted any bad thoughts she might have had earlier. Bennett pulled a betting slip from his trouser pocket, once he was facing the arena, he studied it for a few seconds, examining every detail, and then carefully returned it to its secure resting place.

Williams, now the keen spectator, never let Flugal out of his sight; this was not a race against the other team, but the clock and he knew Flugal had the team to do just that. He calmed his rising nerves with the thought that they would never make the finish.

Chance was the only one talking in the team; the eagerness to beat Williams raised everyone's desire to win, and they all kept a respectable silence as he spoke, absorbing all the advice Chance imbued into the situation.

The marshal called Flugal forward, never at any time did he come to a complete stop. Then raising his hand gave the signal to move off when ready.

Flugal made that "clicky" sound to signal that the run could start at any time, and the lads responded and sprung into action without a moment's hesitation. The clock began as their noses passed the start line. Flugal may have had a lame horse, but he hadn't figured on the old professional's winning desire for he showed no signs of slowing. Williams cursed. Flugal was suddenly confident that the course would cause no undue hindrance.

The first two of the fourteen obstacles flashed past and the crowd roared their approval, not only was this local man going for glory, but he was going to do it in style.

Flugal's pace remained as high as he approached two left-hand turns that formed the initial segment of the figure of eight styled course and led neatly onto two more tight obstacles The first left turn was tighter than the second and it showed Flugal his worst fears with painfully slow speed; Chance was trying his best to keep pace with the rest, but they had to slow to keep the turn tight and speed was sacrificed.

Williams laughed gleefully.

The second proved less troublesome, and Chance put in a spurt and they managed to keep up a reasonable pace.

Williams glee was short-lived; this infuriated him and he stamped his feet in frustration.

Pogo, Biff and Troy praised Chance and held up their percentage of effort. With obstacles three and four now behind them, there was now a short straight before a bridge that marked the crossover point in the figure eight, Flugal was again confident of maintaining his speed over the bridge. By now both Williams and Flugal had forgotten about the clock; this had become personal, with each living and breathing every single moment in their own little world. Williams though quietly goaded Chance and the "Boys", knowing that failure was inevitable despite their every effort.

Chance called them for more, he needn't have bothered as they delivered right on cue; Team Flugal now expertly accelerated over the bridge, the change of footing causing no discerner-able alteration in the handling of the carriage.

Williams ground his teeth, seething with anger; despite his best efforts Team Flugal had so far run a near perfect phase.

There now presented itself, after the straight, two more tight obstacles followed by two elongated right hand turns.

Williams now the openly chastised Team Flugal, he cared not who heard him, the only thing that mattered was his enemy's total destruction.

During the previous left-hand turns Flugal had allowed the team free reign to be aggressive; Biff had led them in, he had taken it that Chance was going to race flat out for as long as possible, bad leg an all, so he never let up. He could feel the force behind him that Pogo and Troy exerted. For once nothing was said. Flugal took this as a sign that they were all in agreement. Now with two obstacles and right-handlers he did the same. Rachelle had remained mute until now and called for an almighty effort before they re-entered the straight and the bridge for a second time; she instinctively knew that time would be lost in the turns and the straight could be used for a breather, as their forward speed was impressive.

The crowd sensed that Flugal had the competition won if he managed to feel up this pace, and the decibels rose another notch. Flugal had tried in vain to keep Chance's injury quiet, but he knew it would prove quite impossible, so by now everybody probably knew their predicament and this just stoked the flames of passion and emotion for the underdogs to prevail.

Williams was conscious of the support his bitter rival had garnered, and it only added to the contempt he held, and the enjoyment he would gain from victory.

Rachelle could barely control herself, and jumped up and down on the spot, the carriage rocked from side to side, Dave chewed his nails down to the quick; a habit he had never before indulged in, Mrs Flugal and Perkins, June and Tom and Bennett screamed their lungs out once again, oblivious to any spectacle they were providing. Charles Nostromos was ecstatic that the final race was all he could have wished for; a genuine race, clearly against the clock, and supported by such an enthusiastic crowd, and to top it all Lucy was having the time of her life. If there ever was a day to ask her for a date then this was it. Even the Dougherty's were caught up in the moment and cheered on their friend and neighbour.

Nugget, Nigel, Ralph, Jed and the gang chose, for this final round of entertainment, the border by the second sweeping right hand turn before the straight. A cacophony of high pitch squeals and squeaks greeted Flugal as he led the team on the fast gentle right hander, the obstacles and turns had proved blissfully uneventful. Flugal and the lads found themselves chuckling at the sharp change in pitch level; one moment they were being cheered by the deep toned chorus of adult voices, next the high pitch squeals and squeaks interrupted by growls and snorts of their two best friends.

Williams was drooling at the bit with the sheer thought of his victory, but why hadn't it happened yet? He knew Chance would have to slow being one of the leaders, his leg must surely hurt, but so far everything that had been asked of him he had delivered, and if he did not slow before the last fast straight then there was every possibility of Flugal being able to hold him off and win. His team were going to receive the brunt of his frustrations for that.

Flugal steered the team up and over the bridge a second time and to the right to get a better run at the obstacles and turns for the beginning of their second lap. Suddenly the whole carriage shook and started to vibrate, this sudden movement disrupted the horses stride pattern; Pogo and Troy shortened theirs to avoid stumbling, Chance being on the outside pulled up sharply then went again; he felt that sharp, stinging pain shoot up his leg, Biff on the inside stumbled badly; his right foreleg slipped, the left could not keep him upright and his nose hit the dirt; if he could not regain his balance the carriage would swing too wide and more valuable seconds would be lost and penalty points conceded for hitting the cones. Flugal panicking looked over his right shoulder expecting to see a shattered wheel or some such disaster, but there was nothing untoward visible. Instead he was met by a howling Williams, whose voice was clearly discernible over the crowds. This raised his suspicions and a further quick, deep look back told him all he needed to know: His right rear wheel was coming loose. He knew that to stop would knock him out of the race, so all that was left for them was to continue on for as long as the wheel held out, but their pace would have to suffer as a consequence.

Flugal's attention now concentrated on his "Boys"; Chance had leant all his weight to the right in order to haul Biff up out of the dirt, Pogo and Troy pulled their heads up to add as much rearward weight as possible. Biff felt the panic rise within, he had to regain his balance or everything would be lost and he would be to blame. None of the horses had any idea what had caused the carriage to jerk so violently off line; they could only imagine it was something they had done.

Biff could not get any purchase, however hard he tried, on his forelegs. He grunted, part in frustration, part in exertion and dug his hoofs into the dirt in one last great effort, and bent his shoulder, along with the team, to take the strain. At last he felt some force pull against him, Troy and Pogo now bore the full weight of the carriage, and he resolved to exhaust any and all reserves of energy to right the carriage, dug his hooves in and rose slowly, majestically like Lazarus before the great feast, but it was too late for the first obstacle and they sent the right hand cone flying.

They now had the carriage under control. Flugal knew the major portion of the disaster had been averted for now and instinctively looked for the second obstacle. They passed through it without touching either cone.

The right hand turns now provided a welcome breather, so they could settle themselves before the straight and the two obstacles. Here he shouted even greater encouragement to the lads to keep the run going. Rachelle called out to them all that the wheel was coming loose; she didn't want them to think that they were to blame for their demise.

The adrenaline now pulsed through all their veins; the pain in Chance's leg was now nothing more than a minor irritation to him, he absorbed the pain, he welcomed it, he willingly accepted that the harder his exertion the sharper the rise would be in his discomfort.

Williams, confident of victory at last, foolishly began to taunt Flugal. The root cause to Flugal's misery was plain for all to see.

Now the lads were chatting furiously again; the tone of Chance's voice signified he was in great discomfort, but they were getting faster. Pogo and Troy kept the pace high; they gasped desperately for breath, their lungs burning under the strain. Biff helped keep the line tight through the obstacles and over the bridge, and now running at full speed he too displayed a slight limp in the foreleg, due to his stumble. Ahead came the two sweeping right hand turns, after the obstacles.

Flugal felt the carriage slow, as they negotiated the obstacles without collecting any further penalties, and they swung right, but time would now be their enemy, and he found himself shouting support, advice to his boys, with every step they took. His own entourage had shouted derision at Williams for tormenting Flugal, now cheered their team on with all their might.

The "Boys" aware that they were not the authors of their new found difficulties slowed to a pace that allowed them to take stock of the carriage's worth.

'How bad?' called back Biff.

Tory looked over his right shoulder while they negotiated the right turns. 'It's still there. That's all I can say right now!'

'Do you think it will hold?' asked Chance.

'I'm afraid we're caught between a rock and a hard place here boys,' added Pogo, 'we just got to keep going for as long as it holds out and then hope we can drag what's left over the finish!'

'Yep, there's nothing more we can do!' said Chance.

'Okay, then let's go.'

No sooner had Biff spoke than the carriage started to accelerate once again around the second right hander. They still had only dislodged one single cone.

Rachelle and Flugal cautiously called on them to take it easy, but they had made up their minds that it was now all or nothing and the speed in the turn towards the bridge for a fourth time only re-iterated the team's desire to go out fighting.

The noise level from the crowd rose with every step and Williams stood in awe at Flugal's speed towards the bridge; he had to admire their spirit, but sadly compassion was not part of his make-up and he resumed his desire to see their ruin.

Flugal glanced down at the offending rear wheel, the carriage still shook and vibrated, but no more than before, they may still get away with this. Unbeknown to him everybody witnessing this last lap of the final phase was aware of the condition of the right rear wheel and the judges called for his lap to be halted. Flugal failed to see them gesticulating wildly for him to stop and ploughed on towards the bridge and the finish line.

Rachelle now joined Flugal in calling for the "Boys" to rein it in slightly, but as they had no idea how much they would be penalised for losing time and hitting a cone, their forward speed remained high and seemed impressive to them. The vibration, they conjectured, could easily hide their mounting losses.

Mrs Flugal, Rachelle's grandmother, Dave, Bennett and the Flugal's children held their breath and secretly prayed for the carriage to remain intact. The victory was now secondary to their well being.

The vibration from the wheel suddenly caused carriage to swing violently right, and they could not help but hit the right hand cone, marking the boundary of the track, sending the little white ball hurtling towards the fence that surrounded the arena. Williams laughed his head off. The crowd sighed in disappointment then wasted no time in picking up where they left off cheering them home.

The "Boys" all cursed their luck, but they had no time to lose, the bridge and end of the lap were in sight. All that was left now between them and a possible victory was the straight and the bridge for a fourth and final time.

Williams could feel the panic begin to take him over; the carriage was still intact and their two little mistakes had not signalled imminent disaster.

'Damn!' he shouted, which caused several onlookers to shake their heads and "Tut" loudly. He couldn't have cared less and even contemplated finding out where they banked so he could go out of his way to make difficult for them, but they were just small fry and not worth the effort or the time it would sacrifice taking his eye off the big picture. Then it happened.

The rear wheel finally gave out as it left the bridge the final time. Rachelle nearly fell overboard and only saved herself by taking a firm hold of her seat. The wheel snapped   on leaving the axle causing the back end of the carriage to dig in to the ground. The team felt the enormous strain on their shoulders.

'We can make it!' shouted Chance.

They all grunted under the strain; the effective weight of the carriage had almost doubled and the two lead horses felt the pain of their injuries increase tenfold. Chance stumbled. Biff tried to get purchase with his damaged leg and the only outcome was the carriage almost came to a grinding to a halt. The crowd stood, cheering them on to even greater effort.

'We have to finish!' Biff groaned.

The two wheelers took up the slack and dragged the stricken carriage towards the finish, the axle leaving a trench winding its way to the finish line.

Rachelle was in tears cheering them for one last effort, but she knew the race was lost. Flugal sung their praises all the way home and they staggered over the line to the cheers of the crowd ringing in their ears.

Williams loved every final second of Flugal's final lap and finally shouted 'Yes!' as the line inched past. Flugal had lost, he had won.

The crowd fell silent; the team's loss had dealt a fatal blow to the general joviality. Rachelle continued sobbing, Nugget whimpered, Nigel remained silent, the gang didn't wave any betting slips this time; their personal privations were almost tangible.

Flugal pulled up slowly and as carefully as possible; protection was his main concern now for his "Boys". Williams whooped it up with delight: Victory was his.

Flugal had the team at a standstill just inside the arena and dismounted. By the time he had reached Chance and Biff, Rachelle was there inspecting them both, Dave, his son and daughter were running around the perimeter, he could see them making their way over.

On their arrival nobody spoke a word for a few seconds. The look on Flugal's face spelt utter dejection and failure.

'Sorry dad!' his son said, his daughter put a protective arm around him. Dave knelt down and examined Chance and then Biff, both needed urgent medical attention. Chance the more so.

'Sorry lads.' Chance said dejectedly, choking back the tears.

'We gave it our best shot.' Biff said in an attempt to placate everyone.

'We're still a team.' Troy added.

'We're always a team.' Pogo finished with.

'You two were great!' Chance and Biff added. 'We wouldn't have made it otherwise.'

Williams appeared and offered his condolences, smiling all the while.

The announcer reinforced his joy by informing all that Williams had in fact won with Fulton second, Lyndsey third and Flugal relegated to fourth. There was not enough prize money in the lower places to solve Flugal's financial problems.

Flugal, Dave and Rachelle walked the lads back to the box, unbridled them and made them as comfortable as possible, then began the painful job of preparing for the long, gloomy journey home. His kids searched for the vet that was always on call during such occasions for Chance and Biff; they had personally offered to cover any vets bills. Mrs Flugal and Mrs Perkins arrived and although very solemn, did their best to console their husband and granddaughter respectively.

Williams whistled joyously as he and his workers prepared to leave; he had won the race, but the result was of secondary importance to him: Fugal had lost. He couldn't have cared less about what anybody thought of him. The farm was his at last.

The vet's prognosis was not good and it shocked all; Chance was in a lot of pain, and Flugal needed to seriously consider the horse's well being; he may have to put down if his condition deteriorated any further, his leg was that bad, as bad as any break; it was one of the worst he had seen, and the cost of the veterinary bills to Flugal would break him, plus to prolong the animal's suffering had to be taken into consideration and didn't warrant such medical treatment in his opinion. Biff on the other hand would need some convalescence, but would make a full recovery.

Rachelle was crying uncontrollably and hugging Chance around the neck, refusing to let go. 'It's alright Rachelle, I knew the score.' Chance said. Rachelle looked him in the eye, relaxed her grip and stroked him on the end of his nose, he loved that.

Flugal asked if there was any hope, there was always hope, but the vet said he would have to consider the horse and the pain he would endure. Flugal would never contemplate losing Chance or any of his horses. 'We owe it to Chance, I owe it to Chance. Any prize money will go towards their care.' and turning towards the vet. 'I appreciate all you've done and said, but they're all family!' The vet fully understood, but he reaffirmed his caveat for the horse's welfare, and then gave them both a painkilling injection to get them home comfortably and agreed to meet them back at the farm. The son and daughter reasserted their desire to meet all vets bills, and it was settled that all that could be done to care for Chance would be, but at the first sign of his suffering increasing then the merciful option would take precedence.

Nugget and Nigel said their goodbyes to Ralph, Jed and the gang; some were deliriously happy, others in the doldrums, gambling had definitely not paid off for most, and then they all commenced their long journey home.

In no time everything was packed up and ready to go, they all wanted away from there as quickly as possible. It was agreed to send on any prize money and all understood, considering the state of the horses, to get them home as soon as possible. The journey back to the farm for team Flugal was a lonely, quiet one. The early evening clouds drifted across the sky, filling the twilight hour with light of a blue, greyish hue. It did nothing to improve the mood.

At the farm they stabled the horses, taking great care with them all. The vet duly arrived and set about making them both comfortable for the night. When he had concluded he arranged with Flugal a time to be there first thing in the morning. The horses should be fine until then.

The ladies went inside to prepare supper; Mrs Flugal was prepping herself that this would be one of the last meals she would make in her kitchen.

Before long a few passersby popped in and congratulated Flugal and his horses on a sterling effort, a great days entertainment and enquired when they'd be ready to resume riding lessons again. They all wanted back. He tried to keep up appearances, but it was hard.

Now the "Boys" were settled for the night, Rachelle volunteered to spend it with them again after supper; she wanted, needed to spend as much time as possible with her friends. It was then that Flugal realised his trusty Nugget was Nigel were missing; could the day get any worse. They all ate supper with heavy hearts.

24

Our two friends meandered home at their own pace through the fading light, each caught up in their own thoughts. What were they going to do now? Where would they all end up? Would they ever all see each other again? Occasionally each would sneak a peek at the other which only added to the general feeling of doom and gloom.

The fading light eventually gave way to night and the two friends found the darkness a great ally; they were able to cut across fields, taking huge short cuts and made excellent time, and before long they espied the lights of Flugal farm beckoning them home.

'There she blows!' beamed Nugget.

Nigel slowed to a walk from the trot they had been sustaining over the last mile or so. 'Better make the most of it!' Nigel said in a matter of fact way that disturbed Nugget.

'There is always something that can be done.' Nugget said trying to inject some cheer into his pal.

'Like what?' replied Nigel without looking at his travelling companion.

'There's always something.'

'You're referring to the treasure aren't you?'

Nugget smiled; it was the lead in he had been trying to manoeuvre. He always found it hard, mildly embarrassing to open up conversations on topics that can easily be ridiculed, and which he truly believed in. 'Yeah that treasure.'

'Nobody's found it, it doesn't exist!'

'I found it!' Nugget fired back eagerly, and waited for Nigel's reaction.

'Really!' His reaction left a lot to be desired.

'Really I found it. I tried to show Dave.'

'You went treasure hunting with Dave!'

'Yep, I couldn't show him, he didn't understand.'

'He won't. He's a nice man, but he will never truly understand.'

'I tried-'

'-where was it again?' Nigel butted in.

'The field with the poor irrigation, down by a line of trees. Marked with a big "X"!'

'A big "X"! That simple eh?'

'And I can show you tomorrow if you like, you and me we can dig it up and save the farm.'

'That simple?'

'That simple!'

'Nugget?'

'Yeah.'

'I don't want to get my hopes up and neither should you. We need to keep this quiet. It would kill me to hurt them some more.'

'I know. You're right, but I'm right, it is there.'

The two prospective treasure hunters entered the farm; Nugget turned left towards the farmhouse, Nigel right to the stables, both agreed to see each other later if on if they could.

Flugal's mood lifted at the sound of Nugget pawing at the back door and the sight of his furry friend, tail wagging, brought a huge smile to his face.

Everybody was still at the farm, accepting the Flugals invitation to stay, including Dave, and enjoying the hospitality.

Nugget was overwhelmed with the affection from everyone who witnessed his arrival; all asked where he had been to be out so late. He kept his counsel.

Nigel walked solemnly into the stables and his eyes were drawn automatically to Chance, standing head bowed asleep. Biff had joined him in the land on nod. Only Pogo and Troy were awake to see his arrival, chatting quietly amongst themselves.

'Hi guys.' Nigel whispered.

'Where you been?' asked Troy.

'Saw you race. Me and Nugget sneaked in.'

'You know the bad news then?' Pogo whispered back. Nigel nodded, and as much as he would have loved to prolong the conversation, he just couldn't, so went to his part of the stables to lay down for the night.

The day broke to find Williams with a spring in his step. He had his favourite scrambled egg and bacon with coffee for breakfast, and enjoyed every succulent morsel, even the coffee was at the correct temperature. This felt like his birthday, everything bode well for the day ahead when he would take the first significant step to finally acquiring Flugal Farm and realising his ambition. He knew Flugal could no longer rely on any more resources to save himself and this thought cheered him on as he drove to the bank to have an unscheduled meeting with Bennett, and Bennett better not think him clear of any danger once this business deal was finalised, he was not going to find himself manager for very much longer. He would see to that.

* * * * *

Mrs Flugal prepared breakfast for all her guests with a tear not very far away. Nugget woke up Nigel early once he had got out of the house, Rachelle and the lads were still asleep. Nigel was very appreciative for the wakeup call and let Nugget know; it took him a few minutes to gather his senses and get his bearings. Nugget made whatever arrangements were needed and waited patiently for the infamous early riser to appear in the yard. Nigel, bleary eyed, finally made his entrance and followed, dopey like, a step or two behind Nugget down to the field. Nobody saw them leave.

Dave, the Flugals, their kids and Mrs Perkins ate breakfast in silence. The vet was due soon and Flugal wanted to have everything ready, Rachelle ate hers with the horses, she had kept a good eye on them all since being up, and informed him they slept soundly with no interruptions. She was oblivious to the absence of the two treasure hunters.

Dave departed shortly after the vet arrived, promising to be back in less than an hour.

The vet started Chance's and Biff's medical treatment and arrangements were put in place to ensure both had adequate accommodation to complete the course of treatment; this was yet another nail in Flugal's heart. He also couldn't find Nugget or Nigel again and he wore the worry clearly for all to see.

It was one of those days that just seemed to fly by and left its participants wondering how a day can evaporate so quickly.

Dave returned, as promised within an hour, looking extremely pleased with himself; he was dying to talk to Flugal who was preoccupied with the lads.

Williams, at this point, made an uninvited visit on its way to the bank; his only aim was to rub salt into Flugal's wound, and he knew it wouldn't take much. He stood, hands on hips, and scanned the surrounding buildings and land. 'It's a lovely place Flugal!' he shouted across the yard to the stables, where he knew Flugal was residing.

Flugal refused to rise to the bait and kept on with his dealings with Chance, Biff and the vet.

'This here land of mine,' he went on again, 'is going to give me great pleasure in the years to come, once I've flattened this monstrosity of a farmhouse!'

Luckily for all concerned Mrs Flugal, Tom and June failed to hear Williams derogatory comments and threats.

'Well must go Flugal, I'm a very busy man and I've just got to see a man about a farm.' A laughing Williams turned on his heel and walked out of the farm to his waiting car, parked conveniently in the lane.

The vet finished up for the day, pronounced that he was pleased with Biff, but still had reservations about Chance and only time would tell on such an old horse. He promised to call round at the same time tomorrow and gave Flugal strict instructions and the required medical supplies to ensure his good work could not be undone.

Nigel and Nugget slipped and slid their way precariously down to the lower part of the field; Nigel complained constantly what a nice warm bed he had given up for this lost cause, this muddy adventure. Nugget knew he didn't mean it. It was just Nigel's way. 'Just think about the treasure.' he said.

'If it's there!'

'It's there, have faith.'

'The only guarantee this morning is that my nice warm bed back at the stables is tragically going to waste, as I speak.'

'There's the trees!' Nugget called out.

Nigel looked ahead, slid because he was not looking for sound footing, did the splits and ended up belly down in the mud. Now he could take a good look at the trees. 'Which tree is it?'

'It's not around a tree!'

'No?'

'It's by the rocks.' Nugget pointed to the boulders half submerged in the field.

'Those rocks? Which rock is it under?' asked Nigel.

'It's not.'

'No?'

'It's by the side of the large one like a told you!'

'Where?'

'By the side.'

'And how are we going to know.' Nigel was quickly losing all faith in this expedition.

'The shadows, you know the shadows that make the "X"!'

'The shadows!' repeated Nigel disbelievingly.

'Caused by the branches of the trees like I explained. It's that simple.'

'That simple. You're kidding me.' Nigel scrambled eventually to his feet and the two slipped through the mud down to the waiting boulders. 'So now we have to wait for the sun to shine yeah.'

'Yep!'

'Better pray it doesn't rain then Nugget.'

The thought of rain had not come into Nugget's equation. 'Yeah, better pray.'

Dave intercepted Flugal prior to him entering the house; he could see he was disturbed and had to be delicate in his dealings with his friend. 'I need to have a talk.'

'Maybe later Dave.' said Flugal stopping a few paces short of the house. 'I need to make arrangements for the "Boys". The wife and I need to come to some very painful decisions, like where are we going to live. The bank will be here pretty soon. I've been putting that off too. I've got no choice now.' Flugal entered the house. Dave stayed in the drive.

Nigel stood on the large boulder and studied the field with an ever so vacant expression; he had no idea what he was looking for, he knew it was branch shadows, but there were so many. There was nothing in the field to announce to anybody, let alone somebody who knew what they were looking for, that there was buried treasure here.

Nugget meanwhile ran around like a demented fool, jabbering away, marking out the shadows that could make the "X" signifying the buried treasure he had so set his heart on finding and saving the farm.

The hours drifted by and morning merged into afternoon and still Nigel sat on the boulder, still shadows flittered across the muddy field, still Nugget failed to standstill on the same spot for more than a couple of seconds, and still he was unable to identify the "X".

'I'm hungry Nugget! How about you?'

'Now's not the time to be thinking of your stomach.'

'My stomach governs most of what I do!' insisted Nigel and he found himself again studying the branch shadows drifting inexplicably across the field. 'I would strongly recommend it as a life philosophy.'

Nugget failed to appreciate Nigel's pearls of wisdom, he needed to find that "X".

Dave found himself wondering aimlessly around the yard, but always ending up outside the house. He thought again about pursuing his friend, but chose to go and talk to the lads and Rachelle instead.

He found Rachelle taking a break, seated in her favourite position outside Chance's stable. Biff, Troy and Pogo were playing a board game, he thought about asking where they got it, but decided it was better not to ask. Pogo was winning.

After watching the three younger team members play for a few minutes; their competitive spirits, borne out of the race, fuelled by this friendly game, he made a gentle enquiry 'How's your patients?' he asked Rachelle.

'Doing fine.'

'How's you?'

'Oh, okay. I worry about them. Where will they go? What will become of them?' Rachelle fought back any emotion fearing embarrassment; it was becoming an hourly habit with her. She had taken the decision not to display any emotion in front of Chance or the lads. 'I hope they find good homes.'

'Flugal's already had some offers.' The lads stopped playing their game. 'Williams is one.'

'I hope not!' Rachelle echoed everybody's thoughts.

'There's a stables down on the south coast that makes two. He'll try and find good homes, but the end of the day he can only make a choice out of what's available.

'If I could buy you Chance.' Rachelle said now standing, stroking his forehead and carefully hugging him tightly, all the while choking back the tears. 'I would and we could live together forever and go for rides every morning, afternoon, and evening.'

'Sounds like paradise Rachelle.' Chance said.

'That's you sorted Chance old boy.' said Troy. Neither of them ever got jealous of the others; each only wanted what was best for their friends and teammates.

'Best not think about it!' Dave's words rang true.

'I'm going to take Dave's advice and take my go.' Pogo kicked the dice and pulled off the score he needed. 'Yes! Beat that you guys!' Biff and Troy struggled to raise any enthusiasm, but played manfully on, primarily to keep a sense of togetherness and their minds off their impending doom.

Nugget for the first time that day stopped barging around in circles and focused all his attention on the shadows creeping across the field towards the boulder. He asked Nigel not to move and watch the branches inching their way slowly in his direction.

About this time Flugal exited the house and was confronted by Dave, who saw at last the opportunity to open discussion on his all too important topic.

Flugal had managed to avoid him earlier; he knew Dave's intentions, he knew he owed his friend money and he intended to pay it all back, but the subject of remuneration between friends, when one had none, had destroyed many a friendship and he loathed to open such discourse in case it should jeopardise their relationship. He was now seriously cornered.

'Hey mate, I really need to talk to you. It's urgent.'

'Look can we discuss this later.'

'No!' Dave was adamant and it struck fear into Flugal. This was bad; surely he knew his financial position.

'Oh!'

'This is urgent!'

Okay.' Flugal submitted; he knew he could not get out of it this time, he inwardly grit his teeth and awaited the news guaranteed to signal the end of their long friendship.

Dave pulled a piece of paper from his trouser pocket and unfolded it. Flugal saw it contained a long list of numbers which he clearly saw were the hours Dave had spent doing valuable work around the farm. 'I need you to look at this.'

'Do I have to? I know what it says.'

'You do?' the surprise in Dave's voice shocked Flugal and planted the first seed of doubt in his mind. He now wanted to double check those numbers scrawled across the slip of paper.

Nugget by now had identified what he thought were the two branches he had been searching for, and instantly pointed them out to Nigel. Nigel was to observe them closely in case he was wrong. No, he thought, those two are the right ones that he and Dave saw last week before the race.

At this late afternoon hour, the branches crossed forming a perfect "X" and he called to Nigel to aid him in his digging, as he pounced on that particular spot of muddy field. Nigel for the first time that day felt that Nugget may be on to something; there was a perfectly formed "X". Both started digging furiously to discover what lay beneath. Nugget figured they had only a short amount of daylight left and they both dug like mad dogs and pigs.

Dave handed Flugal the list of numbers. Flugal was now sweating profusely, his heart hammered against the inside of his chest. He composed himself and focused on the list. It was Dave's betting schedule.

'What's this?' Flugal said frowning.

'Bets I made.'

'I can see that.' Flugal's eyes went to the bottom of the page: £15,105.00. 'You won all of that!'

'Sure did, thanks to you and the "Boys".'

'Well congratulations.' Flugal's heart rate calmed down and the sweat on his hands dried up. 'Don't forget I still owe you for all the work you've done around the farm.' Dave's winnings made mentioning his debt to his friend a whole lot easier.

'No you don't. I won't hear a word about it, that was a favour.'

'I can't-.'

'-you can and will.' Dave said purposefully 'And you can take that too!'

Flugal was speechless. Mrs Flugal came out to find out what all the raised voices were about.

'I can't-.' Flugal tried to reiterate.

'-you can and you will.' Dave stressed a second time.

'What's going on?' Mrs Flugal said, now followed by Mrs Perkins, Tom and June.

'I'm giving you both my winnings.'

'What winnings?' she said and her husband handed her the slip of paper.

As soon as she saw the amount she declined as Flugal had done 'I'm sorry Dave.'

'I only won that money because you raced, I only bet because you raced, and I bet fair and square with a reputable bookmaker, so it's all above board and legal.' Flugal tried to speak, but Dave had the floor. 'I value our friendship far more than fifteen thousand pounds; you two are the only people who always accepted me just the way I am, and I shall always be eternally grateful for you letting me into your home and to be your friend.' It was Dave's turn to stop himself choking up. 'And anyhow what am I going to do with it? I've got everything I ever wanted.'

Nigel and Nugget were now covered head to hoof and paw in mud, dirt and grass; they had dug and dug and dug and nothing had happened.

'It's not here Nugget.'

'A little further.'

'It's not here.' Nigel stopped digging. 'It's not here, give it up, we gave it our best shot and came up short, it was a good try!'

'No, it's here, I know it is!' pleaded Nugget.

'Okay, okay, two more minutes, but only because you're my friend, and then we're going to investigate all that shouting.'

Nigel dug his hoofs in, and buried his snout into the soft dirt to push it rearward between his front legs and nearly knocked himself out.

'You found it!' shouted Nugget.

'I found it alright.' said Nigel, keeling over.

Nugget dived in on hearing the thud of Nigel's nose on the hard, foreign object. He brushed away the earth to reveal a small, brown wooden box with metal reinforced corners. 'The treasure Nigel, the treasure!'

Nigel forgot about the pain in his head and nose and helped pull it clear of the hole; it was heavy for a small box. How were they going to open it? Nugget tried to bite it open with little success. Nigel asked Nugget to kindly step aside and he gave the box an almighty whack with his hoof; the lid was no match to Nigel's brute strength and it flew into the air and landed on top of the boulder he had frequented earlier.

Two sets of eyes peered into the dark interior of the box and there to their astonishment lay a crumpled brown piece of parchment. 'It's a map!' exclaimed Nigel.

'Wow!' replied Nugget.

Nigel removed the parchment, unfolded it with great care and attempted to read the old writing, discoloured with age. 'I don't understand a word of it.' he said. 'I forgot I can't read human!'

'Here let me.' Nugget studied the jumble of words. 'I don't understand it either.' Nugget scratched his head. 'I thought I could read human, but none of those words make any sense; they don't rhyme or anything, it's like, it's a riddle.'

The two treasure hunters formed the same idea at exactly the same time, and looking each other straight in the eye shouted 'It's a riddle!'

Nigel ran around in circles, behaving more like Nugget. Then they both ran as fast as their legs could carry them up the field, through the gate, and along the path back to the farm, to deposit the riddle into the hands of someone who could decipher it. Along the way the two of them came to the conclusion that Mrs Flugal was the one above them all who had the best chance, as Nugget had witnessed her often do crosswords puzzles in her spare time.

As they approached the farm they noticed a different air about the place, a more cheerful countenance, even the livery horses were laughing. Pogo and Troy were in the yard positively dancing, everybody else hugged one another. They couldn't possibly have known what they were up to, each asked each other. They had both kept their little adventure quiet.

Rachelle danced in the doorway to the stables, keeping one eye on the festivities and the other on Chance and Biff, and to cap it all that man Bennett was there laughing his head off too and actually hugging Flugal of all things! Mrs Flugal and Mrs Perkins were both crying, Dave, Tom and June all laughed and clapped simultaneously.

'How did they know?' asked Nugget.

'I'm as baffled as you are.' came Nigel's reply. 'They must have seen us leave and kept out of sight all this time.'

Flugal saw Nugget and Nigel arrive and rushed over to give them both huge hugs, not giving a damn about the muddy state of his clothes. Nugget wagged his tail at seeing his master so joyful, Nigel wasn't used to such outward shows of emotion from Flugal and just nodded, but he was as equally as happy.

Flugal noticed Nugget was carrying something.

'What's this?' Nugget released the paper over to Flugal's grasp. Flugal inspected it, opened it up and examined the faded writing. 'Why Nugget you have a riddle for me.' he then turned to everyone in the yard. 'Nugget and Nigel have brought us a riddle. Will this day get any stranger!'

'We know it's a riddle.' snorted Nigel 'We just can't decipher it!'

Everybody came over to examine the brown parchment. The two treasure hunters kept an eye on Mrs Flugal, expecting her answer imminently, but it was Bennett who sussed out its meaning first, if not what it meant. 'Maybe it's to do with the Dougherty legend. I hear tell nobody's yet found the treasure she allegedly buried!'

'Allegedly!' barked Nugget. 'Me and Nigel have found it.'

'Where did you get it?' Mrs Flugal asked.

'In the field!' replied Nigel, Nugget ran toward the field barking, wagging his tail, and then back to the group; he did this a number of times.

'Not that field. We were right!' Dave exclaimed. 'Nugget and I went down to the field with the irrigation problem to look for the treasure. We figured that that would be the most logical place to look.' Everybody expressed astonishment and wonderment that Dave took a dog on a treasure hunt. Dave countered by showing them the riddle.

When all the excitement had died down some, Nigel and Nugget asked Pogo why everybody was so happy. Pogo looked them straight in the eye, so they would know he wasn't making this all up, and told them the farm had been saved by Dave, and more surprisingly Bennett's winnings over the carriage race. Pogo could see they were confused. So he went on; Dave and Bennett had placed sizeable bets, not on Flugal, but on Williams! They had figured out, quite wisely, that Flugal had the faster team, and would win in a fair race, but Williams would not let Flugal win no matter what, that Williams would cheat his way into guaranteeing Flugal's failure and victory for himself with Flugal coming nowhere. Both men then bet on Fulton finishing second, who they both agreed had a faster team than Lyndsey and Michaels, and then spread bet to ensure they had covered which other team out of Michaels and Lyndsey would come in third. Bingo they won big; a very smart bet!

The farm was now saved.

In the end Chance and Biff stayed put for their treatment and both eventually made full recoveries, Troy and Pogo promised to become the finest teaching horses ever seen, Mrs Flugal cried tears of joy for days, Tom and June promised to return more frequently, Bennett became one of the most popular and fairest bank managers around and took great pleasure in advising Williams that Flugal Farm was no longer available, Dave spent a lot more of his time doing odd jobs for people, Flugal pledged Chance to Rachelle; to ride for as long as they both could, Nigel jumped and rolled his heart out in his newly filled mud bath and Nugget said they could now concentrate on digging up the treasure, once the true answer to the riddle was known, and pay all their friends back and still have money to spend. Did they? Well that's another story.

Lightning Source UK Ltd.
Milton Keynes UK
UKOW01f1950081017

310633UK00001BA/38/P